THE SONG OF GAIA

ZOË TAVARES BENNETT

Book Cover by Zoë Tavares Bennett.

First edition 2024

THE SONG OF GAIA

ZOË TAVARES BENNETT

MEDITERRA
PRESS

To Helen of Troy,
the face that launched a thousand ships
and a thousand stories.

And in memory of Sister Stella,
principal of St. Paul the Apostle School.

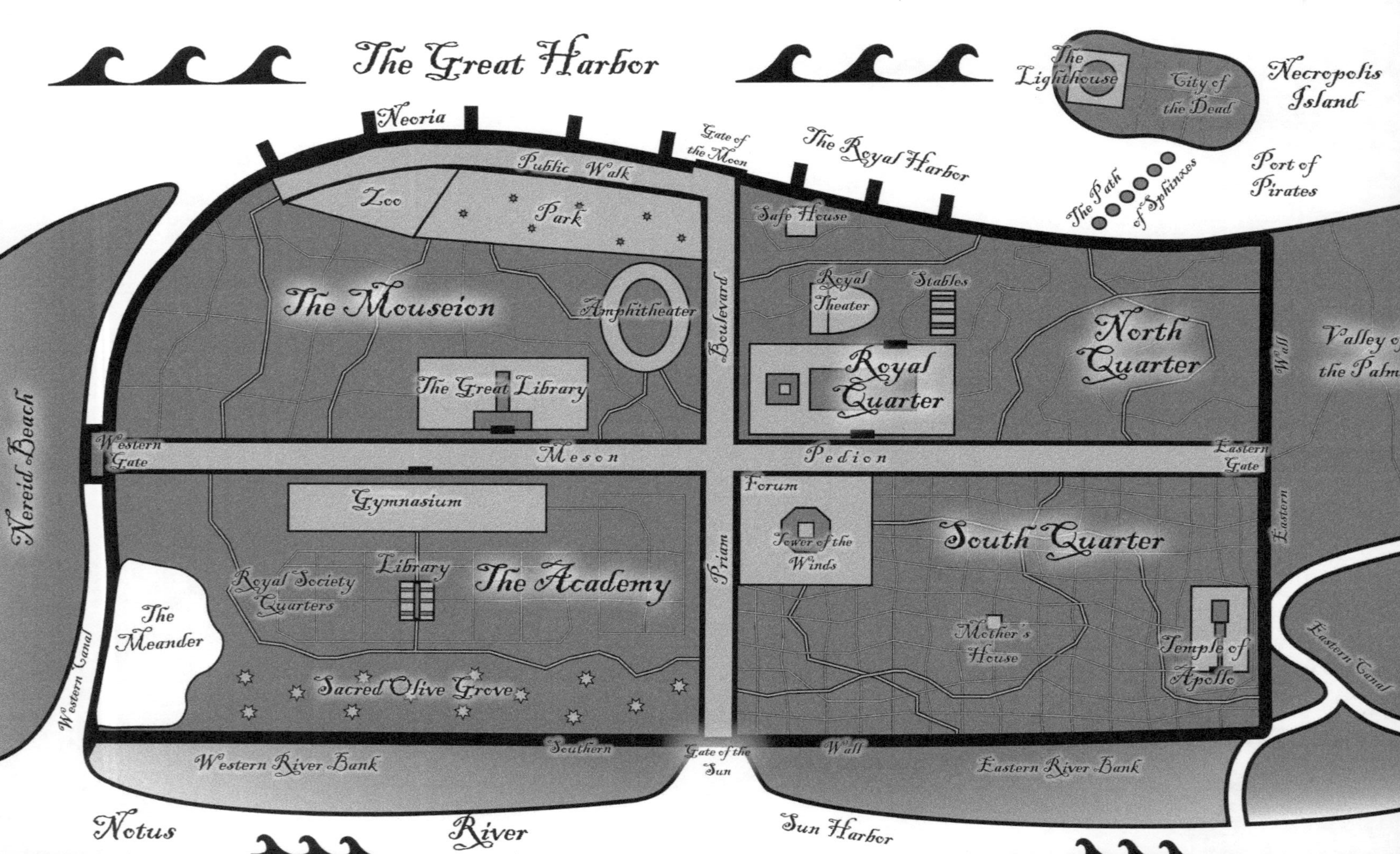
The Great Harbor
Neoria
Gate of the Moon
The Royal Harbor
The Lighthouse
City of the Dead
Necropolis Island
The Path of Sphinxes
Port of Pirates
Public Walk
Zoo
Park
Safe House
Royal Theater
Stables
The Mouseion
Amphitheater
Boulevard
North Quarter
Royal Quarter
Wall
Valley of the Palms
The Great Library
Nereid Beach
Western Gate
Meson
Pedion
Eastern Gate
Forum
Gymnasium
Tower of the Winds
South Quarter
Eastern
Library
The Academy
Priam
Royal Society Quarters
The Meander
Mother's House
Temple of Apollo
Eastern Canal
Western Canal
Sacred Olive Grove
Southern
Gate of the Sun
Wall
Western River Bank
Eastern River Bank
Notus
River
Sun Harbor

ὕμνον ἄειδέ μοι, μοῦσα, λόγοισι μελίφροσιν ἀλλά
ἡδυτερεῖ φωνῆ κλέπτην διὰ νυκτὸς ἄειδε
ἐρχομενῳ πρὸς δ' ἄντρα νεηνίῃ ἀνδρὶ ἐοικώς
ἔνθα πολύτροπος αὔτης ναὸν ἴεν πόδας ὠκύς
ὥς ἄδυτου φύλαξ ἒν χειμῶνι ἀπεβήσετο νόσφι·
κλέπτης εὗρεν χάσμα βάθη πέτρας πολύκαπνον·
ἔβλεψε φέγγος ἒν δὲ φάραγγ' ὅτε πρὸς τὸν ὄψ εἶπε
τὸν κλέπτην χαίρειν· τί σύ μου δόμον εἰλήλουθας;
ὥς ἔφατ' ἡ θεὰ· τῇ καὶ φωνήσας προσέφη φώρ·
τὸν λίθον ἁγνή πότνια· χεῖρ' ὀρέγων ῥόον εἶπε·
καὶ τότε γῆς ἄπο θερμὸν χλῶρὸν τὸν δ' ἕλε λᾶα
τὸν δ' ἀπαμειβόμενος προσέφη κεχολωμένα θυμῷ
οἶδας ἔχειν δύναμίν; σοι λεξω· κεῖνος λίθος εἶχε
τὸν κόσμου μυστήριον· ὥς ἔφατ' ἡ θεὰ τῆς γῆς·
κλέπτης παύσας ἔτρεψ' ἰδεῖν καπνὸν καταπίνειν
βωμὸν· καὶ τότε μορφὴν ὄρφνης ἐξαναδῦσαι
οὐδε γε γυναικὸς ἀλλὰ δράκοντος ἔθει δ' ὃ συνῆκε
ἡ θεὰ τὸν εἶπον· μή δῶρον θεῖον ἀφῇς μου.

Ξ

Tis true without lying, certain and most true. That which is below is like that which is above and that which is above is like that which is below to do the miracle of one only thing. And as all things have been and arose from one by the mediation of one: so all things have their birth from this one thing by adaptation. The Sun is its father, the moon its mother, the wind hath carried it in its belly, the earth is its nurse.

—From the *Emerald Tablet,* translation by Isaac Newton of the Latin (Nuremberg, 1541)

The Daughter of Zeus

Some say a cavalry corps,
some infantry, some, again,
will maintain that the swift oars

of our fleet are the finest
sight on dark earth; but I say
that whatever one loves, is.

This is easily proved: did
not Helen—she who had scanned
the flower of the world's manhood—

choose as first among men one
who laid Troy's honor in ruin?
warped to his will, forgetting

love due her own blood, her own
child, she wandered far with him.

—Sappho, fragment 16, translation by
Mary Barnard

I

THE MONTGOMERY ESTATE TOWERED above her like an ancient grave.

Alex lingered on the porch with her suitcase at her feet and looked up at the house her father had recently inherited, rescuing it from neglect and ruin. Then she tried to envision the house abandoned for centuries, the walls crumbling into the earth until only the rotting shingled roof would be visible like the tip of a pyramid with its vast body sunken beneath golden sands.

The house had always intimidated Alex as a girl. The massive stone walls were veined with ivy and jagged cracks. The grand staircases and ornate ceilings had always made her feel small and cold. And her grandmother—an imposing woman who had overseen the affairs of the house with a strict religiosity—had terrified a young Alex with her upright posture and icy blue glare.

Her father, Malcolm Montgomery IV, had grown up in this house, and his father before him. So when Alex's grandmother passed away a few years after her grandfather, her father became the sole inheritor of his childhood home, though with little else in regard to his inheritance.

In the hopes of cutting down his monthly costs, Malcolm decided to move the family from the suburbs of New York back to Greenwich and restore the old mansion to its former glory. Now Alex found herself packing up her life in her sophomore year of college and moving into her recently deceased grandmother's house in the middle of the woods.

Her father was already inside, surveying the living room. Alex dragged her suitcase into the foyer, a duffel bag slung under her other arm. The house looked as if no one had stepped foot inside for years, a thin layer of dust coating the furniture and flying motes dancing in beams of sunlight from a sliver of open window.

"Cleaners should be coming in the afternoon," her father said, glancing down the dark hallway as if he saw something there that Alex did not.

Her father had always loved this house. She knew to him it represented the Montgomery family, the long line of men bearing his name like a badge of honor. Alex had distinct memories of wandering the halls alone—for she, too, was an only child—and stumbling across disused offices and strange rooms filled with curious, foreign-looking objects.

She only had foggy memories of her grandfather, Malcolm Montgomery III, who she would later learn was no better than a failed lawyer and an alcoholic. He would rage against his wife, against his son, and against the world for no apparent reason save his own inadequacy, to the point that one day his heart simply stopped. But Alex knew her father had loved him despite his flaws. When they would visit her grandmother she would find her father lounging on the back patio, a cigar in one hand and a Scotch in the other, just like his father had before him, proudly surveying the grounds of his estate.

Alex's new bedroom was on the second floor, down the hall from the master bedroom, and a spare room that would be converted into the bedroom of her half-brother, Malcolm V, or baby Malcolm as she liked to call him. Her stepmother, Simona, would arrive with baby Malcolm tomorrow after the cleaners finished their work.

She looked out the window of her bedroom. The back patio extended to a pool and fire pit, with a wide green lawn beyond it which was in dire need of mowing. All around them rolled the gently sloping hills and dells of Greenwich, still covered in patches of snow from a rough winter storm at the end of February, the branches of the trees swaying bare and brown in the wind.

After unpacking her room, she found her father on the phone in the living room, giving terse instructions before hanging up. His sharp blue eyes found hers and he frowned.

"Is there a problem?" she asked.

"Simona is not going to like the furniture. Those couches must be at least fifty years old." He motioned to the leather couches that her grandfather had insisted on keeping and that his wife never had the chance to change before she died. "And the kitchen needs a remodel. Half the stuff in this place is outdated."

"I think I like it that way," Alex mused, half-joking, her eyes wandering over the faded floral wallpaper and crystal chandelier hanging over them. "It adds character."

Her father raised a brow. "You're like your mother, then. She always preferred old things." He paused thoughtfully. "She loved this house. Especially the library. She used to read these cheesy romance novels she liked in there."

Alex didn't answer. Her father hardly ever mentioned her mother, and Alex disliked being reminded of her. A sudden vision of her mother sitting in an armchair in the library, a book loosely held in one hand as she gazed into the fireplace, passed before Alex's eyes, but whether it was a real memory or simply her imagination she did not know.

Malcolm took a deep breath in and forced a grin. "When is Warren arriving?"

"Tomorrow."

Her boyfriend, Warren, had Crew training somewhere in Florida during the last week and a half of Spring Break. He would arrive in Boston tomorrow morning and drive here to see her before spending a few days in New York City. Her father had always loved Warren and liked to joke that he was the first-born son he never had.

"I was thinking we could roast marshmallows in the fire pit once everyone is here."

"Do we have marshmallows?" Alex asked doubtfully.

"No," Malcolm said. "But you can go buy some. It's not like you have anything better to do."

"I'll have you know I still need to finish an Econ paper due the first week we get back to school," Alex called after her father, who was already disappearing down the hall towards the kitchen with a laugh.

She rolled her eyes and grabbed her car keys.

2

ALEX HAD ALWAYS LOVED to drive.

At sixteen her father had bought her a white Audi that she nicknamed *Lady Montgomery* due in part to her elegance but also because the creamy white color reminded Alex of her grandmother's white fur shawl that she wore almost every day of her life.

She slid into the tan-leather driver's seat and fired up the engine. Music blasted from the radio and she rolled down the windows despite the evening chill in the air. The paved driveway gave way to a winding, asphalt road under her tires as she drove through the woods and valleys to the nearest supermarket.

The road sped under her effortlessly. She never liked the suburban streets and their gridded, stop-sign-riddled mazes. Her long drives to Harvard were her favorite drives because she cut through swathes of green country, the two-lane highway snaking a never-ending path. On those drives, she got the same overwhelming sense of possibility as she did when gazing across the ocean's distant horizon, where sky and water met, promising a life different than the one she was living.

Of course, it wasn't as if Alex *didn't* like her life. In almost every way she was perfectly content. Since sophomore year of high school, she had been dating the same boy, who she knew wanted to marry her one day. She played soccer growing up, had good grades, and got accepted into Harvard, her father's alma mater. In school, she studied Economics and planned to go to law school. Once she and Warren married, they would probably have children, and eventually they would retire, perhaps in this very house if baby Malcolm didn't inherit it.

Her whole life was planned out and each year she checked off another stepping stone on the path before her. But all that fell away while she was driving, where nothing mattered but the road ahead and the wheel smooth and steady beneath her hands.

It took her only thirty minutes to drive to the supermarket, buy a pack of marshmallows and a few other grocery items, and return home. She regretted the short drive but soon forgot about it when she saw a familiar car parked in the driveway.

She heard his voice as she entered the house.

"...practice matches before the season starts."

Warren stood beside her father, a Harvard Crew backpack still on his shoulders and a duffel bag at his feet. He was wearing a soft gray sweater and his skin was a golden tan from hours rowing under the Florida sun. His hair had grown out over break into loose blond strands, and he sifted his fingers through the fringe when he saw Alex, a smile on his face.

"You're back early," Alex said, dropping her grocery bags at the door before Warren hugged her.

He kissed her briefly, always embarrassed to display affection in front of her father. "I asked to leave training a day early to see you."

"Really?"

"No, I just got the date wrong," Warren said with a wry grin. "Thought I'd surprise you."

Alex felt a twinge of annoyance, but she wrote it off as a delayed response to her car ride ending. "You definitely surprised me."

"I was just about to give Warren the grand tour," her father said, patting Warren on the back. "But maybe you should get settled first."

Alex gratefully showed Warren to her room.

"This used to be my grandparents' house," Alex said, opening the door to her new bedroom. "My dad always loved it here."

Warren entered the room and set his backpack on the edge of the bed. He glanced at Alex curiously. "Do you like it?"

Alex nodded, looking around with a sigh. "Well, it's a beautiful house."

"Come on," Warren said, taking her hand and reeling her close. "I can tell something's up. From the moment I saw you I knew you were upset."

"I'm not upset," Alex said in surprise. She wondered if Warren had read the annoyance in her and felt a slight guilt at his misplaced concern. "The house is strange, that's all. As a kid, I thought it was haunted. It seemed so big and scary when I was smaller."

"Haunted?" Warren teased.

"Hey! I had to play alone. And my grandmother was a terrifying woman."

"But seriously, Alex, you'd tell me if something was bothering you, right?"

Alex squeezed his hand, forcing a smile. "Of course. Now let me give you the grand tour."

She led him from the room and back downstairs. The first few rooms they tried to open were spare rooms used mainly for storage or guests, or else her grandfather's antique collections. One room was locked, another a small broom closet. They tried the last door down the hall and suddenly entered the library.

It had to be the oldest room in the house, built before cars and electricity so that several obsolete gas lamps still lined the room. The windows were shut up with thick, velvet curtains that blocked out all light. Several chairs and desks were draped with a thick canvas cloth for preservation. The heavy air inside had a musty smell that had scared Alex as a child more than it had intrigued her.

On the far wall was a great old-fashioned fireplace, and beside it was the soft leather chair Alex had envisioned her mother spending hours curled up in, now worn from generations of use. As if seeing the chair triggered her memory, Alex recalled a time when she had sat on her mother's lap while she read, her hands stroking Alex's hair silently until she fell asleep and was carried off to bed.

"My mother used to read in here," Alex said, though she didn't know why she said it. She had never really spoken about her mother to Warren before.

Warren tore his gaze away from the shelves and shelves of books kept safe behind an iron grate. "Your mother?"

"Yes. She loved this library."

He frowned. "Is that why you're upset?"

"I'm not upset," Alex said more tersely than she expected. "And if I was, it would have *nothing* to do with my mother."

"That doesn't sound like nothing to me." He shook his head. "I'll never understand why you insist on forgetting someone that was a part of you. You've never even told me anything about her."

"That's because there's nothing to tell."

"She's your mother," Warren said, as if that decided everything.

"Not anymore," Alex countered, before leading them out of the library and shutting the door behind them.

After all, who was Warren to criticize Alex about her own mother? Warren could never understand. He had perfect parents who loved each other, a perfect family, with no unanswered questions about the past, no blemishes on an otherwise normal life. Alex, on the other hand, constantly harbored the shameful secret of a mother who had left her family, who had abandoned her only child, without a single explanation or even a goodbye.

They walked out to the back patio in silence. Warren snuck glances at her as they passed the pool and strolled towards the edge of the property. Alex had spent many summers frolicking all across the backyard, playing soccer with her father on the grass, and building hidden fairy homes in the trees. While the inside of the house had haunted her with its loud groans and dark hallways, the rambling woods stretching beyond it were like an enchanted forest.

They stared at the softly rolling hills, the piles of brown leaves and muddy snow. In a few months, the trees would be filled with green leaves and flower buds, and the grass a plush carpet on the earth. Then the rains would come, endless rains, filling up the creeks and rivers, nourishing the ground so that the grass would shoot up in thick, untamable stalks. Then the heat would bake the flowers until they wilted, browned, and fell, and winter would rush in with one big exhale of snow and sleet, burying the house in several feet of white, until they were back where they started one year ago.

Alex felt the months rolling off her back like rain, like a song that kept repeating itself, faster and faster each time it went round. The years were piling up fast, she felt. It was only yesterday she was exploring every hole in the bark, every path in the valley, when the groans of the house were ghosts instead of just the wind.

Now she was nineteen years old—the last of her teenage years—and in only two more she would graduate from college and become an adult. Everyone said they were the best years of her life, but Alex had the keen sense that those years had already passed her long ago, or else they did not exist.

"What are you thinking about?" Warren asked.

Alex started. She had almost forgotten he was there, so accustomed to visiting the house without him. "Nothing. Just that spring is almost here."

Warren looked at her, then nodded absently. "It was already summer in Florida."

"Oh, I forgot to ask! How did training go?"

Warren dutifully recounted the grueling hours on the water and practice matches against other teams as they walked back inside the house. Her father was going to start barbecuing and asked Warren if he would like to help, so the two of them brought glasses of cold beer out to the patio and spoke about Crew and Harvard while tending to the steaks.

Alex was about to go up to her room when she glanced down the hall. The door to the library was opened a sliver, even though she was almost certain she had closed it.

A shiver crept up her spine. She took the stairs two at a time and did not come down until dinner.

3

THE FOLLOWING DAY WAS warm enough for them to put on swimsuits and pretend it was summer instead of mid-March in Connecticut.

Alex shifted on her pool chair, the Montgomery estate basking in the noonday sun behind her. She was too lazy to get into the sparkling blue pool which would surely be deceptively freezing. After all, only a few weeks ago this house was layered in snow, though March had ushered in a spell of heat right in the nick of time.

Her hand searched the ground for her margarita. The glass was ice-cold, rimmed with salt, and she lifted it to take a sip, wincing at the heavy-handed pour. Warren had insisted on making the drinks himself and had gleefully spent up her father's expensive tequila.

She glanced at Warren lying on the pool chair beside her. He was already looking at her.

"What?"

"Nothing," Warren said, shaking his head fondly. He passed a hand down his abdomen, which was much paler than his arms and legs. "I need to tan."

"It looks like you got some sun in Florida," Alex said, nodding at his legs. "You're almost as dark as me."

It was a joke, of course, because Alex was several shades darker than him. Though the winter had paled her skin, a few days in the sun would bring back her natural bronze.

Warren gave her a half-hearted glare in response.

"At least you don't burn," she added.

He glanced at his tan legs, dusted in fine golden hair, sculpted lean and muscular from his many years playing sports. His legs were secretly one of Alex's favorite things about him. They had always looked like that, since high school. Warren had already been so mature and respectful, as if his brain had kept up with his body when so many of the boys remained immature.

She remembered how jealous all the girls were when she started dating the captain of the Crew team, the smart and perfect Warren van der Linde. They started dating in their sophomore year of high school and then attended Harvard together. All their friends expected them to get married. Even her father approved, especially since Warren planned to go into consulting as he had.

Warren smiled at her. "We should make this a tradition."

Alex almost winced. She hated that word, tradition. She tried not to think about the future in general, but then Warren looked at her like this, as if he had everything he could ever want. A part of her resented him for it.

"Are you okay?" he asked, more in accusation than concern.

Alex tried not to roll her eyes. Warren knew she hated talking like this, but he did it anyway, as if to test her or poke at an old wound. She didn't answer right away, perhaps to annoy him.

"Alex?"

"I'm just thinking."

He looked at her expectantly. She sighed and took his hand, watching their fingers thread automatically, his palm a familiar texture against hers. This wasn't the first time they had this conversation, after all, the kind where she felt that Warren could never understand her.

"We're almost halfway through college," she said finally, allowing herself to be serious, though she hated it. She rarely liked to take things that mattered seriously. "It's all happening so fast, that's all."

Warren frowned, staring at their hands clasped between them. "College...or us?"

She looked up at his smooth, symmetrical face in surprise, studying the steady blue eyes framed in blond hair cropped elegantly around his head. He was the spitting image of his father, an attractive, six-foot-five Dutch lawyer and former Olympic rower, but his smaller features were like his mother's, a blond bombshell born and bred in the upper echelons of New York City, so that his angular cheekbones and delicate lashes appeared feminine. During the day, with the sun shining overhead, the strands looked almost golden.

"We only have two more years," she said, turning away, already tired of the conversation. Sometimes being with Warren was like staring straight into the sun when all she wanted to do was look at the stars. "I wish we had more time."

"Aren't you excited, though? To get out into the real world?"

"What does that even mean, *the real world?*"

"You know, life." As if it was as simple as that. Maybe for Warren, it was.

Alex shrugged. "Having a job, then. Living on your own. Responsibility."

"How about adulthood!" Warren said, almost passionately. "Taking on the family business. Getting married. Having kids. There's so much to look forward to, right?"

The last word felt like a challenge. They locked eyes, and Alex tried to hide the resistance she felt. Perhaps Warren could read her better than she gave him credit for.

It might surprise anyone else that someone as handsome as Warren wanted to settle down so young, but it made perfect sense to Alex. He came from a traditional family much like hers, where their lives were planned out before they were born, and shouldering the family's share of responsibilities became second nature. It just so happened that Warren found comfort in this stability, while Alex felt restless just thinking about it.

"Don't you worry, though?" she asked, hoping she would see her own doubts reflected in those clear blue eyes, though she knew she wouldn't.

"Worry about what?" His face was troubled, a crease forming between his brows, but she only saw his earnest love for her and the life they could build together. A small bit of herself suffocated under that look. She was right. He could never understand her.

"Nothing," she said, kissing his knuckles. "Really, it's nothing."

He didn't look like he believed her. She had never been very good at lying anyway.

The glass doors of the patio swung open. Her father stepped onto the patio and walked over to the other set of pool chairs. Following close behind him were Simona and baby Malcolm, who was fitted in tiny swim trunks and floaties.

Alex caught Warren glancing at baby Malcolm with a half-lidded gaze. She took another sip of her drink as Warren's eyes landed on her. They seemed to say, *See? That is what the future can hold.*

"I love you," she said, wishing she had never brought it up, pleading with her eyes to change the subject.

Warren relented, tightening his hold on her hand. "I love you too."

And for right now, that was enough.

4

"WARREN," HER FATHER SAID without preamble, setting down a box of tools beside the cold fire pit with a grunt. "Help me with the fire, son."

They were all sitting down around the fire pit, huddling under blankets. Even though it had been a hot spring day, the nights still reminisced of winter's chill.

Simona sat beside Alex on the curved, stone bench circling the pit, her light brown hair in a high messy bun. Baby Malcolm began to fuss on her lap, bundled up in a puffer jacket. Simona gave him a marshmallow and he quickly calmed down. She ruffled his fine golden curls, sharing a smile with Alex at her trick.

Malcolm had met Simona through a friend three years ago and had gotten married a year later. She was a model from Romania, though she hadn't worked since they married. Alex got along well with Simona, who was only eight years older. Two years ago they had baby Malcolm, who had the temperament of an angel as long as he was eating anything sweet. Alex always felt more like a babysitter than a sister to him.

Soon the fire was sputtering to life, red-orange sparks floating into the black night sky. Warren sat down beside her again, slinging an arm around her shoulders. Each of them took a metal skewer, capped with a puffy marshmallow, and lowered them into the fire.

"So, Warren," her father began, and Alex internally groaned. "How are those internships coming along?"

"I have applied to several, sir. Still waiting to hear back from them."

This launched a tedious conversation about job prospects to which Alex felt no need to contribute. She turned to Simona, who was trying to clear the marshmallow that baby Malcolm had managed to smear all over his cheeks.

"He's getting so big," Alex said, only because it was the right thing to say. She had never really enjoyed children, though she could not say why.

Simona laughed. "Too big. Soon he can't sit on my lap."

Baby Malcolm made a face as if he understood.

"Oh, he didn't like that."

"You can't sit on mommy's lap forever, my love. Oh, how would you live without me?" Simona cooed, pressing him close to her chest.

Despite her slight irritation around children, Alex's heart ached watching them, the way Simona beamed at her son with a look of pure love, a love which demanded nothing in return, a love that gave unconditionally.

Alex tried to recall whether her own mother had ever looked at her like that, but it was almost impossible. Her mother had left them when Alex was almost ten years old—the night before her birthday—and never came back. There was no note, no explanation. Her father had kept a stony silence on the subject, but Alex had picked up on the side glances and low whispers from family and friends. Her mother must have had an affair with someone else and left, too ashamed or too indifferent to keep in touch. It wouldn't be the first time something like that happened, and besides, her father never denied those rumors.

But from the little Alex did remember of her mother, she had been very elegant. Perhaps all mothers seemed elegant to their children. She glided in her memory, wandering from room to room in their house, so wise and serene, a creased book always in hand and a small smile that made it clear she found something amusing that had nothing to do with the present and everything to do with the words on a page. But the moment Alex tried to hone into the details, her eyes, her voice, or even the feeling of her mother's arms around her, the memory faded away, like trying to hold the wind in her hands.

It didn't matter anymore. She wanted to tell Simona that in answer to her question, but the words repeated themselves in her mind instead as the fire dwindled to embers.

Alex had long learned how to live without her mother.

Once Simona left to put baby Malcolm to sleep, the night's festivities came to an end. Alex and Warren both had to get up early tomorrow. Warren was driving to New York City to visit some friends, while Alex would drive back to her apartment in Harvard to get situated before the last two months of school and final exams.

"Alex, could you clean and put these away?" Malcolm asked, handing her the metal skewers. "They go down in the garage."

She brought them to the kitchen sink, scrubbing until the burnt marshmallow washed down the drain. Warren stayed behind to help her father with the fire pit. Alex knew he liked to hear her father call him *son*.

Alex made her way down to the garage, turning on the light. Compared to the rest of the house which was now spotless and tidied up by the cleaners, the garage still housed multiple storage boxes piled on top of each other, spilling with pool equipment and various tools, as well as winter gear like skis, snowboards, and old, forgotten coats.

She scooted around the mess, wondering where she should put the skewers. Near the far corner was a box which had been pushed aside earlier, a hand print in the dust coating it.

As Alex gently placed the skewers against the wall, a small cardboard box hidden among the clutter caught her eye. Large, black letters on the side spelled out a name she would recognize in a heartbeat.

Elena de la Fuente.

Her mother.

5

It was her mother's maiden name.

Elena de la Fuente.

The letters were faded. A fine layer of dust clung to the box after years of abandonment. She knelt on the floor and dragged the box closer, her heart beating loudly in her chest. It couldn't be larger than a shoe box. The cardboard opened stiffly under her prying grip.

Inside there were several confusing objects. Alex could see an ornately carved case the size of a book and made entirely of gold. Beside that rested a slim dagger, barely larger than a letter opener. The handle sat smoothly in her hand when she picked it up, like it was just polished, shining silver with a green emerald inset on the hilt. The edge looked sharp enough to cut skin. She carefully placed it on the floor.

Alex turned back towards the golden case. The lid opened easily. Inside was a book, much smaller in size, with a worn brown cover and no title. She gingerly opened the book to the first page. The paper was so thin and delicate to be almost translucent. Carefully handwritten text began immediately on the next page, and it took her a moment to realize the small, narrow words were written in a different language.

Alex read the first line, concentrating on making out the cramped letters.

μῆνιν ἄειδε θεὰ Πηληϊάδεω Ἀχιλῆος

Most of the letters were completely baffling to her, but she recognized the letters theta and pi as Greek, though she could not be certain.

Alex wondered why her mother had this and why it was kept in the golden case. She shifted the golden case and worn book to the side. Underneath was another larger book that had been hidden from view, bound in black leather. She opened the cover and saw her mother's name written in the upper right-hand corner in loopy, girlish handwriting.

On the first page, her mother had scribbled the date September 13th, followed by a long paragraph.

Today was a lovely day, much warmer than it has been all week. I didn't do much work, but can you blame me? The garden looked so lovely, and I always spend my time in the library these days. I am sure Sister Stella will reprimand me when she learns of my late assignments, but it can't be helped...

It must be her mother's diary during school. But when? There was no year marked, though she had to have been around Alex's age or younger if she was still in school. She flipped through more pages, skimming the paragraphs, stopping when she saw a familiar name in a very short entry on November 22nd.

I cannot stop smiling. Today Alexandros took me to the Academy and we walked all across the city. I am going back tomorrow.

She moved on to the next page, puzzled. Her father's name was Malcolm, not Alexandros. She couldn't recall that name ever being mentioned. Alexandros must have been a schoolboy crush. Her stomach twisted uneasily. Her own name, Alex, was short for Alexandria, a nickname her father had given her a long time ago.

She flipped through the diary again and found no year written for any of the entries. Her mother had written all the way to the end of the book.

Alex glanced at the last page and went very still.

Scrawled on the bottom margin, written in thick black ink and a sturdier hand—so very different from the light, graceful script of the rest of the diary—was the last entry, as if years later her mother had opened her old diary on a whim and crammed in one last sentence.

July 19th.

Her heart pounded. It was the day before her birthday, the same day her mother had left ten years ago. Alex could hardly focus on the words, her head spinning.

I must follow the sad nightingale.

Before she could figure out what the words meant, footsteps near the garage door snapped her back to the present, and she shut the book and dropped it in the box.

Alex remained still, breathing hard. Then the footsteps receded, the sound of wood creaking and suddenly ceasing, as if it had been a ghost. *Or the wind,* she reminded herself, but she had trouble catching her breath.

Once it was silent once more, she snatched the box and hurried upstairs.

6

THE HOUSE HAD NEVER felt so haunted before.

Even with Simona and baby Malcolm somewhere inside, his shrieks growing louder as the night cast them in a gloomy darkness, Alex could barely walk the polished hall floors without her mother's absence gnawing at her.

Once she left the garage, Alex had snuck into the library where she had hidden her mother's box under the armchair. She figured it was the only place in the house where no one would come snooping on her. After Warren had fallen asleep, she had tiptoed downstairs to the library.

Now she sat by the fireplace, its ashes cold, her mother's box in front of her. A small old-fashioned lamp on the table beside her chair shined a dim light on the objects. She held the golden case and silver dagger in her hands, rotating them in the light as if they might contain a clue, then set them back in the box.

Her eyes strayed to the diary. Alex opened up the slim black volume again, her fingers caressing the pages, white and crisp, with now familiar fading words written on them. The first thing she did when she had sat down was read the entire diary front to back. Then she had read it again.

Her mother had loved school, that much was apparent. In the beginning, her daily entries were filled with ramblings about disciplining nuns and witty gossip about Jeanine who snuck over to the boys' dormitories at night and came back with tangled hair, found sound asleep after the second bell had rung.

Later, the stories were shortened, sometimes to only one sentence, musings and phrases about gods, myths, and philosophies that probably wouldn't make sense to anyone but Elena. She also wrote less often, with two given dates as far as six months apart. These entries described a more sophisticated education, as well as personal, with some days only talking about a particular project she was working on and others her secret longings and hopes, many involving Alexandros.

Apparently, she studied Classics. It was clear she loved mythology, and Alex quickly deduced that the book in the golden case must be an old copy of a Greek text. The last part of the diary especially mentioned the library, and how she would spend hours there at a time, picking apart different hymns and myths, like she was researching something.

It might be impossible to know when she was writing this for certain, but she referenced her fourteenth birthday near the beginning of the diary on December 5th, with the date being repeated only three more times. Since she left such long gaps later on, however, it would be hard to say how old she was by the end. But if Alex calculated the dates correctly, Elena was either eighteen or nineteen before the final entry. The same age as Alex now.

The second to last entry was as mysterious as her age.

April 23rd. I am to leave the school. Final exams considered unnecessary.

No explanation, no reaction. Was she happy? Was she heartbroken? Why the statement, so final and bare? And why pick up the diary again, so clearly discarded for at least another decade, just to write *I must follow the sad nightingale?*

The diary provided no more answers. Alex carefully placed all of the items back into the box, then returned to her room, hiding the box under her bed and slipping inside the covers. She lay in the darkness for a moment, staring up at the ceiling, and tried to picture her mother as a girl like herself, gossiping with her friends, studying Classics, and staying up after hours in the library.

The mother she remembered lacked some of that vibrancy, the youth so apparent in her eager scrawl. There was a calmness, a stillness to her memory like a faded photograph, a moment forever caught in time.

But Alex had been too young when she left, and these memories of her mother were merely a childish longing for an answer to the question she had been silently asking herself all these years.

Why did she leave?

7

Warren left early in the morning before anyone had woken up, kissing Alex on the forehead while she was still asleep and quietly sneaking out the door. The moment he was gone, Alex woke up and began to pack.

She stowed her mother's box carefully in her suitcase, covered by her clothes just in case. The last thing she wanted was for her father to see her bringing a box with her mother's name on it.

As they ate breakfast, she secretly studied her father's face, the familiar, pale complexion, blue eyes, and graying hair that had once curled reddish blond, so different to her own tan skin and dark brown hair cut straight and sharp across the shoulders. Even her eyes—one green and one brown—marked her as different. She wondered if he knew about the box, if he had seen it earlier when rummaging around in the garage. A part of Alex knew for certain that he had not known it was there, or else he would have thrown it away or hidden it better.

Her mother's name echoed in her mind. *Elena de la Fuente.* Why not Elena Montgomery, her father's name? Did she keep her maiden name? Or was this box from a time before she met Malcolm Montgomery, in a place where she spent her time in libraries and wrote about life in a diary?

And why had she written her diary in English, not Spanish? She knew her mother's first language was Spanish. Alex used to speak it as fluently as English, but even when she was young Alex had picked up on the quiet disdain for her mother's language, a flicker of critical eyes from others, even a distant memory of a stranger asking her mother if she was her nanny as they played at a nearby park.

A certain shame had grown in her heart, and she had seldom spoken Spanish even when her mother still lived with them. And when she left, Alex never spoke Spanish again.

Alex was slowly realizing that she never knew her mother, not really. Ever since Elena had left them, her father had barely pretended she existed. Though Alex could have searched for answers herself, a part of her hadn't wanted to know, and had always felt angry and betrayed. What if she really did have an affair? What if she hated Alex and never wanted anything to do with her? Or, worst of all, what if she was already remarried and had another daughter to replace her?

The only time her father had ever mentioned her mother was a week after she had left. Alex still had not understood what had happened or where her mother had gone. She had left no note and no means of contacting her. The house was always quiet as an only child, but it was quieter then without her mother's soft footsteps down the hall.

Alex remembered tiptoeing into her father's office that morning, though she had strict rules not to disturb him while he was working.

The door was already unlocked, a sliver of her father's office visible. She gingerly pushed it open, then poked her head inside. Her father was sitting at his desk, his face covered by his hands and a half-empty glass of amber liquor at his elbow.

She must have made a noise because he had bolted to his feet. When he saw it was her, he had sighed and dropped back into his chair.

"Dad?"

He took a sip of his drink before answering, not looking at her. "Yes?"

"Where did mom go? Is she coming back?"

Alex would never forget his smile. It was the bitterest thing she had ever seen. Then he had spoken in a peculiar voice she would later understand as sarcasm. "She disappeared into thin air. Go to bed, Alex."

She never asked about her mother again, but the words had stuck with her. *Good riddance,* she would tell herself as she got older. Who wanted a mother that would leave her only child?

But that last sentence written in her diary opened all of the doubts and questions she had kept locked up in her heart since that very day.

I must follow the sad nightingale.

Alex knew her mother must have written that sentence on the day she left, ten years ago on the night before her tenth birthday. It was the only explanation worth her time, and Alex didn't want to contemplate the other possibility. The possibility that this entry was a complete coincidence, that her mother had left simply because she wanted to and not because she was forced to.

Her father gave her a worried look as they finished breakfast. She had been silent all morning. "You and Warren aren't fighting, are you?"

"Of course not," she said flippantly.

But she actually wasn't so sure. Warren never went long without texting her, even in their previous fights, but now she hadn't heard a thing from him since he left this morning. He had surely arrived in New York City by now, but he hadn't texted her to confirm that he had arrived safely.

She knew he was hurt by her doubts about the future. But before this the stakes were low, they were too young, and nothing they did ever had a consequence. Those days were over now. An engagement was no longer a distant future.

Alex didn't know what she wanted anymore. Warren should be the perfect boyfriend. He *was* the perfect boyfriend. He had always been respectful, kind, and attentive. She never had to beg for love. She never had to do much at all. They got along well, rarely fought, and understood what each other's lives were supposed to be. So why was she getting cold feet now?

But that wasn't true. She had been doubting her love for Warren ever since she had turned nineteen and realized that this was her last year as a teenager before life took hold of her in its unflinching grip. Now it was as if opening the wound her mother had left behind had forced Alex to question everything about her life, not just Warren.

Once Alex finished packing up her car, she found her dad in his new office upstairs. She knocked on the door, and suddenly she was ten years old again and everything she thought she knew was gone.

"Come in."

Alex tiptoed inside the office, just as she had all those years ago. As a child she had always liked walking into her father's office, his desk a mountain of private information and valuable paperwork, a mystery to her childish ignorance. Since she was young, Alex would envision herself older, working as a lawyer for some flashy company and carrying on the Montgomery legacy, when she could have an office desk with important papers on it just like her father. When had she traded that dream for another? Did she even know what dream she held now?

"Alex," he said, surprised, typing something on his laptop. He looked up when he finished and eyed her suspiciously. "Do you need something? I thought you were leaving."

She tried to act casual. "I just had a question."

"About what?"

Alex hadn't thought this far ahead. Somehow, in her imagination, the conversation would just happen. She asked the first question that came to mind. "How did you and mom meet?"

Her father raised a brow. "Where is this coming from?"

"I just realized that I didn't know."

He sighed, rubbing at his eyes and closing his laptop, as if sensing a longer conversation. "We met at school, close to where your mother grew up. The New Academy, it was called, in a small town in California, close to the border of Mexico. I forget the name but it had something to do with the sun. In Spanish, of course."

"You met at school?" Alex asked, bewildered.

She had always assumed they met in New York City or someplace nearby. They had never told her and she had never thought to ask until it was a forbidden subject. Now she had the sudden panic that everything she knew was merely her own mind filling in the gaps.

Her father shrugged. "I was technically not a student, just conducting research with a renowned mathematics professor there for my graduate thesis. They had a very famous archive collection which I was using for my project."

He paused. "Elena was in her last year there when she got pregnant with you. We decided to elope. Got married right there at some church called the Lighthouse. The rest is history."

Alex was stunned. "You eloped?"

"It had to be done. Her family was very religious. After that, she moved back East with me to New York where you were born a few months later."

It hit her very suddenly and she almost flinched from the realization.

April 23rd. I am to leave the school. Final exams considered unnecessary.

Her mother had left school because of *her*.

"I see," she said, her voice weak.

Her father gave the barest of smiles. "Your mother was the most beautiful woman on earth."

"Was?"

He grimaced. "I don't know where she is now. I tried to look for her when she left, but there was nothing. For all I know..."

"Wait," she said, not letting him finish that thought. "Her parents? Are they still alive?"

"No. They passed away a few years after she left us."

"Why didn't we ever visit them?" Alex asked angrily. She had never wanted to know anything about her mother's family, shame always choking her throat before the words would come, but now she wanted to know everything.

"Elena never wanted to. She always said this was her new life now. Besides, she didn't exactly leave on good terms."

The anger left her as quickly as it had come. Her mother hadn't wanted to go back and visit her parents? Had she hated where she grew up that much? Alex didn't get it. It seemed like she had loved school intensely. The desert mountains and palm trees were her home.

"You have to understand," her father said wearily, "your mother came from a very destitute place. She might not have had a nice welcome back there. Of course, my parents did not exactly approve of our marriage either, but they respected my decision and treated her as a part of the family."

Alex knew about this already. Her grandparents had kept an even icier silence about her mother than her father. She remembered overhearing her grandmother arguing with him shortly after her mother had left.

She never belonged here, and she knew that, her grandmother had whispered. Her father had said nothing in response.

But the words had stayed with Alex and made her mother out to be a dreamlike figure in her memory, always too far away to touch, like she only existed in some other realm.

"You said that you tried to look for her...?"

Alex didn't know how she wanted to phrase the rest of that question. Her throat closed up, refusing to admit how much she cared about the answer.

Her father looked at her, and his eyes held a terrible sadness she had never seen before. "Eventually they told me to stop looking, that she didn't want to be found. I haven't heard anything from her since. I never told you because I thought—"

"You thought I couldn't handle the truth," Alex interrupted bitterly, feeling her world tilt upside down. "You thought it would make me feel better to think she had abandoned me than to think she was dead."

"She loved you." He sounded tired. "She loved you very much."

But sometimes love was not enough.

8

It was bitterly cold, as if winter had begun retreating only to change its mind and clutch the world in one last gasping chill.

For the first time in her life, Alex was dreading the drive back to school. Thoughts of her mother kept spiraling inside her mind. Her life felt like complete chaos, even though nothing had changed. How could she pretend to be interested in economics when her mother could be out there now, waiting for someone to find her?

She could not even face the alternative, arguing that she would know if that were the case. But would she know?

These doubts haunted her drive back to Harvard as the afternoon turned wet and rainy. Her father looked relieved as they said their goodbyes, one arm waving as she sped down the driveway, the other around Simona's shoulders. He had avoided being alone with her since their conversation, perhaps scared she might ask more questions.

Rain pelted her windshield all the way through Connecticut. The golden case and the dagger rested on the passenger seat beside her. She felt possessive over them, as if they belonged to her instead of her mother.

The drive was usually only three hours long, but she made it nearly four with several long stops on the way to eat and stretch her legs, as though she were playing for time. Alex also wanted to look through her mother's things again, to hold the dagger loosely in her hand and skim through the smooth pages of her diary, just to make sure she did not dream it all up. It wouldn't be the first time she made things up about her mother.

She stopped in Worcester for a snack, grabbed a sandwich to-go at the first commercial supermarket she saw, and sat idle in the half-empty parking lot. After taking a few large bites, she set her sandwich down and opened the golden case again, carefully holding the worn, brown book and turning to the first page. As before, at first glance, the words seemed incomprehensible as she honed into the foreign alphabet. Then the thick, curved letters shifted into focus and she traced her finger over the strange words, half-imagining she knew what they meant.

After a few minutes, she put the book back into the case and continued eating, looking out across the parking lot at the crisp blue sky riddled with wispy clouds. The sun was quickly sinking towards the horizon. A strong wind whistled against the car, and she shivered on instinct. Up this north, spring took much longer to shrug off winter's chill. Her gaze clouded as she wondered whether her mother had left for warmer weather, then almost smiled at the thought.

A bird cawed loudly nearby, and she shivered again, this time to shake herself from her reverie. She needed to get going or she'd be driving in the dark.

Traffic built up as she neared Boston, but soon she was rolling into Cambridge, where flowers had already begun to grow since she had left two weeks ago. She parked her car and hauled her bags up three flights of stairs to her apartment that she shared with her closest friend, Chloe. Their other close friend, Owen, had already parked his sleek gray Porsche in the driveway.

Alex was the last to arrive from break. Chloe had visited family in China and Owen had wasted his time in New York City, where he had probably seen Warren, Alex realized belatedly. They had both been on the Crew team freshman year before Owen quit and had spent a few weeks during the summer sailing together, so they were good friends.

Chloe and Owen were already arguing about what they should order for dinner. When she entered the living room, they stopped, Owen smirking and Chloe scowling.

"Finally!" Chloe stalked towards her. "You can be the deciding vote."

"I want Indian food," Owen said, following close behind. "And Chloe—"

"And I think we should get pizza. I haven't had good pizza for weeks!"

"Two weeks at most," Owen muttered. "I've had nothing but pizza since I came to this godforsaken country."

Chloe rolled her eyes. "Spare me, Owen. You were in Mexico for the entire winter break."

Alex nearly sighed. They always bickered like this. After a short-lived relationship in freshman year, they had been on and off, always fighting each other over everything. Owen found Chloe attractive but annoying, while Chloe hated that Owen found men—and really, anyone besides her—attractive too. It was a wonder how they stayed friends.

She had met Chloe first when she sat next to her in a core Statistics course. They had gotten to talking and had a lot in common. Alex's mother had left. Chloe's father had left. They both had houses in the suburbs of New York City and Greenwich, so they saw each other a lot last summer. Both of them liked to run by the river and they would meet up weekly to run together and gossip in a café afterwards.

They met Owen through Warren in the early weeks of freshman year, and a natural trio emerged once Chloe and Owen started dating. Owen was from South Africa but grew up half the year in London. He was from a wealthy aristocratic family and spoke in a posh accent that Alex and Chloe constantly teased. He had a haughty, refined air about him which Alex thought came either from an unlimited credit card or being ridiculously attractive with brown skin and green eyes.

"I agree with Chloe on this," Alex said. She didn't care what they ate for dinner, but between pissing off Chloe or Owen, she would always choose the latter. "My vote is pizza."

"Thank. You." Chloe threw an arm around Alex's shoulders, then stepped away quickly and asked in a flippant tone, "So, how was your break?"

She hesitated. All that Alex could remember was finding the box of her mother's things and the strange new tension between her and Warren, neither of which she wanted to talk about now.

"It was good," she said. They both looked at her expectantly. "What?"

"Nothing," Owen said with a smirk, "except that it sounded miserable.

Didn't Warren visit you?"

Chloe narrowed her eyes, sensing her reluctance. "A little trouble in paradise?"

Chloe always teased her for what she called Alex's too-perfect relationship with Warren. She, on the other hand, had stopped believing in love when her father had left at an early age and, like her mother, thought the next best thing was to have as many noncommittal flings as possible. So Alex's nearly four-year relationship with an expected engagement after graduation was practically sinful, though Alex thought she was more jealous than anything.

Warren, Chloe had said one day in an airy tone, *is just familiarity, not love.*

Alex had never taken her seriously before.

"He visited some friends in New York," she said, willing herself to sound more reassured than she felt. "You saw him, right?"

Owen shrugged. "I might have. Don't remember much if I'm being quite honest."

"Why am I not surprised," Chloe muttered sarcastically. Then she looked at Alex with an exaggerated air of seriousness. "You can always change your mind about him, no matter what people expect of you—no matter what *he* expects of you."

"What does that mean?" Alex asked, dreading where this conversation was going.

"Babe, don't you think it's time to move on? Are you really going to marry Prince Charming?"

That was Chloe's usual nickname for Warren. Even though she knew where this was coming from, Alex could not just stand there and take it. For Warren's sake, if not for herself.

"Maybe I *want* to marry Prince Charming. Maybe I *want* a happy ending," Alex replied, perhaps a little too viciously.

Chloe flushed but hid it with a shrug. Her eyes flickered over to Owen for only a second, but he was not looking at her. "Do what you want, but when you're walking down the aisle and it's too late, don't say I didn't warn you."

"I love him."

The words sounded small and pathetic when she said them aloud.

Chloe raised a sharply drawn brow. "Are you sure that's enough?"

Later in the night after an argument-filled dinner and exciting stories from Spring break, Alex pleaded exhaustion and shut herself up in her room. She slowly unpacked, taking her time to fold her clothes nicely and put them away. Her heart quickened its beat once everything was put back in its proper place, her mother's box safely stored under her bed.

Alex pulled out her computer as she had been itching to do all night.

It didn't take long to find the town where her parents had met. A quick search told her that the school must have been in Tierra del Sol, California and the church was indeed called the Lighthouse Church.

It was a popular place for off-roading, being quite deserted. Other than that, the area boasted of nothing more than dust, trees, and rock. She could find nothing about the New Academy or college, just a phone number listed under the church. Alex wondered if the Academy had closed, or had even existed at all.

She closed the computer. Nothing online would answer the questions in the deepest part of her heart, the secret questions she had not realized had been there all along.

Alex checked her phone. No texts from Warren yet. He would be arriving tomorrow. She wondered what she would say to him, and how she could return to the way things used to be. But in the face of her mother and the sudden mystery of her disappearance, Alex knew that she could never return to how things used to be.

Everything had already changed.

9

THEY WERE JUST STARTING to dig into their Indian food when someone knocked on the door.

Chloe and Owen were now arguing over the movie they should watch tonight as it was the Sunday before classes started, so Alex took the opportunity to sneak away from their petty argument and open the door.

Warren stood on the other side of the threshold, a large bouquet of roses in one hand.

She could only stare.

He had combed his hair and was dressed in a white shirt and crisp navy blue boat shorts. Alex always used to like how those shorts cut right above the sharp indent of his quad, chiseled from years of rowing. His eyes shined with so much hope and love that she could not ignore, and her own eyes filled with tears despite herself. She threw her arms around him, embracing the familiarity, the grounding effect that Warren had always had in her life.

"You didn't text me," Alex said when she stepped away, taking the flowers carefully.

"I needed to see you, and apologize."

"Apologize for what?" she asked.

"For being too focused on our future together and letting you slip away from me in the present." It sounded rehearsed, and Warren patted his hands against his shorts nervously. "We've been together for so long that sometimes I forget it's not inevitable that we will end up together, that I still need to fight for us, to show how much I love you."

He looked so sincere that Alex could not help kissing him. It was like second nature to her, the shape of his lips achingly familiar against her own. His hand gently caressed her back.

"You don't need to fight for us." She pulled him closer. "I'm already yours."

Alex allowed her old love for Warren to well up inside, warm and safe like the rising sun. Chloe was wrong. She did love Warren, and that was enough.

"Who is that?" Chloe called from inside.

Alex rolled her eyes, then grabbed Warren's hand and led him to the kitchen.

Owen acknowledged Warren with a head nod, which Warren reciprocated with a knowing grin, most likely remembering their escapades in New York City. Chloe looked surprised and slightly irritated when she saw Warren, but she still gave him her signature glossy smile and offered him their Indian food, which was Owen's choice for takeout tonight.

"Would you like a plate?" Owen offered.

"No thanks," Warren said, glancing at Alex. "I was just stopping by."

Alex looked at him. "You don't want to stay the night?"

He brightened, then replied softly, "I want whatever you want."

"How sweet," Chloe said, not even trying to smile. Her eyes lingered on the bouquet with unveiled disgust, like he had brought a dead animal into the house and not flowers.

Warren's brows furrowed at her reaction, and Alex almost laughed.

"Let's go to my room," she said, dragging Warren away from them.

"Not too loud, please!" Owen called after them, earning a stinging slap on the arm from Chloe. "Hey!"

"You're an ass, you know that, right?"

"I thought you loved my—"

"Don't finish that sentence, Johannes Owen Godfrey the Third."

Alex closed the door on their endless arguments which were just flirting in disguise.

Warren sat on her bed, and she immediately climbed on top of his lap, pulling him in for a deep kiss before he could say another word. His hands settled hesitantly around her waist, then he wrapped his arms around her tightly.

He broke away, laughing. “What’s that for?”

“I missed you,” she said, but it wasn’t true. She felt uneasy, almost guilty, and wanted to make up for it. Somehow she knew this was all her fault. Warren smiled, unaware.

“Me too,” he said in that slow, honest voice that Alex had first fallen in love with. “I don’t know what I would do without you.”

Alex kissed him, just so she didn’t have to speak. She ignored the tightening in her chest, a signal that she couldn’t breathe, that she was suffocating. Warren was here, and that was enough. Right now, that would hold her steady.

Warren pulled away, quiet, looking at her. She had never initiated so much. “I love you.”

She could not say it back, even though she had said it countless times before, any words dying in the back of her throat. Instead, she tugged at the hem of his shirt, loving the way his eyes glinted, like sunlight on metal, and her body flared to life. It had been so long since she had felt truly present, her nerves in tune with the physical world around her.

Suddenly they heard a crash of dishes and clear voices from the kitchen.

Warren blushed, placing a hand on her arm. “Let’s wait.”

He had always disliked how thin the walls were in her apartment and preferred when Alex spent the night at his place where he lived alone. When they had first started dating, Alex had been surprised that Warren was so reserved, and they never touched each other if one of their parents was home.

She nodded, wanting him not to care, not about this or anything, before she reluctantly pushed off him, standing up straight and breathing in deeply.

Warren looked at her again, and she saw in that glance that he didn’t recognize her anymore, but they both ignored it. They had come to a sort of truce. For now, they were satisfied with pretending that nothing had changed.

“How was New York?” Alex asked, painfully attempting a smile.

Warren automatically recounted his time visiting old acquaintances and partying with Owen, his chest still rising and falling heavily. She sat listening and nodding her head as he talked about restaurants and museums and walks in Central Park, when her attention was pulled to a small bird sitting on the windowsill inside her room, staring at her. It had brown feathers streaked with white and looked for all the world as if it was meant to be there.

Alex could not look away, her heartbeat quickening. How had it gotten inside? The window was closed. Had it been there the whole time?

The bird kept staring at her keenly, as if it saw her and knew her, and perhaps it was her mother's diary and the resurrection of an unreal past, but Alex's breath caught in her throat as she watched its little head cock and its beady black eyes gleam almost human.

I must follow the sad nightingale.

"Are you listening?"

Alex almost gasped, thinking for a moment that the bird had spoken those words to her, but it was Warren, just Warren, and in the time that she glanced at him and back to the window the bird was gone, as if it had disappeared into thin air.

10

Alex pretended for the next few weeks.

She laughed and kissed Warren and went on walks holding his hand. He didn't suspect anything, and remained cheerful, though not entirely pacified. They both knew something pivotal had changed, as if the foundation of their relationship had been thrown up in the air and they had no idea what it would look like when the dust settled.

They talked a lot, more than they did anything else together. She used to prize that about Warren, that he enjoyed talking with her, just talking. But now Alex was left wondering what they used to talk about, and why she ever found it interesting. She always felt like they had important conversations, but now they bored her. Their talk was just chatter, about old school friends and old memories and trivial news and half-formed plans. It all meant nothing compared to her mother, the mystery she was still trying to untangle.

Today Alex had a meeting with the head chair of the Classics department. She had gone to the library with her mother's book and asked around about the language it was written in. After a few librarians squinted at the cramped handwriting—sharing dubious glances when Alex said she had found it among her mother's belongings—they advised her to email Professor Ezra. *He would know what to do,* they had said, as though there was something that must be *done* about the strange book.

Professor Ezra's office was on the south side of campus, in an unassuming red brick building faced with white-trimmed windows. She had never known the Classics department had offices anywhere on campus, or that it was even a major, but she found his office easily on the first floor, third door to the right.

Alex knocked hesitantly.

"Come in," came the distracted response.

She opened the door and stepped inside. And stared.

Professor Ezra sat in front of his desk typing at his computer, an iced latte and a half-eaten bagel beside it. But that was not what shocked her.

He was young, hardly older than forty, with round black glasses, curling brown hair, and a friendly smile. She had expected an ancient, hunched scholar with a long white beard and a staff, not a baby-faced caramel latte drinker with a sleek Macbook.

"Are you Professor Ezra?" she asked, unsuccessfully hiding her doubt.

Professor Ezra nodded knowingly. "Alex, right?"

"Thank you for meeting with me, Professor."

"Please, please, take a seat."

He motioned towards the plush leather chair in front of his desk and Alex sat down carefully, the book resting on her knees. She had decided to ditch the golden case unless it seemed like she had stolen it from a museum.

"So I believe you have a book that you would like me to take a look at?" Professor Ezra asked without preamble.

"Yes." She handed the book over and he took it gingerly, his brows hitching up. "I found it over break. It was my mother's."

"Was?"

"She...she left," Alex said uncomfortably. "A long time ago. But this book was in a box of her things. I wanted to know what language it was written in."

Professor Ezra already had the book open to the first page. His fingertips brushed the cramped script, his eyes scanning the lines. A smile curved on his face. "Huh."

Alex leaned forward. "It's in Greek, right?"

He shook his head with another huff of laughter. "Fascinating." His eyes flickered to her like he was about to divulge a secret. "It's in *Ancient* Greek, for starters. The *Iliad,* no less."

"Interesting." She flushed at how little she knew of the *Iliad,* let alone Ancient Greek. Her ninth-grade English class had only read the *Odyssey* in translation.

Professor Ezra seemed to sense her confusion and waved his hand in the air. "But that's not as interesting as the fact that it is entirely handwritten from start to finish." He peered at the letters from an angle, frowning. "Earlier than the fountain pen, I would guess."

"You mean it's old?"

He glanced at her sharply, and for the first time, Alex felt a slight sting of judgment. "Perhaps. It's hard to tell sometimes. You'd need an expert to accurately date the book, especially without any publishing information."

"Do you think my mother could have written it? She used to study Classics."

Professor Ezra laughed as if she had told a very funny joke. "I highly doubt it."

He didn't elaborate, and Alex had the violent urge to leave before she punched that smile off his face. It didn't take a Classics major to know that it was a mocking smile.

She stood up. "I'm sorry, Professor, but I actually have another appointment soon..."

"This book should be given to Special Collections," he said pointedly. "Much more information can be gleaned from a closer inspection. They can also preserve it better with the right tools."

"No thank you," Alex said quickly. "It's my mother's. One of the last things I have of her."

Professor Ezra studied her for a moment too long, and she tried not to fidget. "May I ask you a personal question, Alex?"

Dread washed over her. The last thing she needed was a reason to report a professor for inappropriate behavior. "Sure."

"How long ago did your mother...leave?"

"Oh." She shrugged, hiding her relief. "She left when I was ten years old."

He nodded slowly, his eyes clouding with a passing thought before he smiled and held out the book. "It was nice to meet you, Alexandria."

She took the book, nearly fumbling it at hearing her full name. "Th-thank you."

He must have seen her full name on her email, or he looked her up before their meeting. Alex felt his eyes on her as she left the office and walked all the way back to her apartment without stopping, her mother's book clutched to her chest.

Once she was in her room, the book safely stored in the box and hidden, Alex collapsed on her bed. All she wanted to do was sleep. Sleep and sleep until her life passed her by like a dream and her mother was whoever she wanted her to be.

Then she heard her phone *ping* beside her. She looked at the screen. Warren had texted her to have dinner.

Alex buried her face into her pillow and screamed.

II

THREE DAYS AFTER SHE met with Professor Ezra, Alex walked to the closest bookstore and bought a copy of the *Iliad*.

It took her a good two weeks to read it on top of school work and friends and the difficulty of avoiding Warren. When she finished, though, her heart sank. There was nothing. No answer to her mother's disappearance, just the story. Alex did find eerie parallels, but they only left her with more questions.

Helen of Troy and her mother, Elena, shared the same root name, and they both left their husband and daughter. Even Paris, also known as Alexandros, shared the name of the boy in her mother's diary. Not to mention her own name, Alexandria.

Her mind ran ahead of her with a possible explanation. Perhaps her mother had really been in love with Alexandros all this time and had left behind her family for him.

So she left for love.

But did she? Then why write *I must follow the sad nightingale* the day before she left?

Alex was behind in two of her classes and final exams were quickly approaching. She spent all night in the library, alternating between studying and rereading her mother's diary.

Classes trudged on through April with more intensity than ever, as professors stressed that finals were right around the corner while simultaneously adding more coursework. Alex struggled to find the motivation to study when she felt so close and yet so far from discovering what happened to her mother.

Soon even the diary began to tire her. The words started to mean less and less the more she reread them. She could barely read a single entry without wondering if her mother was out there somewhere, or...

She pushed the thought away, then criticized herself for it.

Why should she avoid it? If her mother was dead, then she could stop obsessing over her stupid diary, or her useless copy of the *Iliad* and her strange silver dagger. Alex could hide it all in a box somewhere in the house where no one would find it for years except the dust motes and mice.

But something deep inside her resisted letting go.

Her mind drowned with words, words from her mother's diary, brief lines from the *Iliad,* a bird sitting on her windowsill looking at her sharply, asking, *Are you listening?*

Listening for what?

Alex yearned for something, but she could not name it. Maybe her mother, though it felt false to call it that. Maybe an answer to a question. Maybe she was merely clinging to a past that no longer existed.

Final exams were scheduled in two weeks and yet she could not bring herself to care that she would need to ace half of them if she wanted to keep her current GPA. It all seemed so insignificant compared to her mother, to the life she had left behind on the other side of the country, the possibility that she was dead and Alex had never known it.

She imagined her mother, so elegant, so serene, wafting from room to room in her memory. And she tried to imagine that mother, *her* mother, the gravity of her earth and the hurricane that stormed through her life when she left, and tried to imagine her instead as a girl, just shy of twenty, the same age as Alex herself, finding her hopes and dreams squashed under the footstep of a man she might not even have loved.

Alex could just see it then, her mother twisting in her seat as the car drove away from the school, where she had reluctantly abandoned all those books, all that passion, seeing the rambling stucco walls of the church shrinking on the horizon. And those words and phrases that flew out of her like rain, like birds uprooted from trees, she had to harbor in her mind, locked in a chest of everything she held close to her heart, the classmates and desert mountains and rows and rows of dusty, old books in that damp library no one had ever loved as much as her.

No wonder she had nothing to say upon leaving. No wonder her second to last entry was so bare and brutal. *Final exams considered unnecessary.* Of course they were unnecessary, as a wife to a husband whose wealth could buy that small, secluded school a thousand times over. But no amount of money could buy what that school had meant to her. No amount of money could chain her restless spirit forever. At some point, the flight must have mattered more. Some exact moment the scales had tipped, the sun had shone just right through the windowpane as it had in the library's stained glass windows at dusk.

A moment of pause, when the past slipped in unwittingly, a bird darting through a window halfway to shutting closed that settled on the windowsill and asked, *Are you listening?* A sweet siren song, seducing her with visions of the past, of the school, of her friends, of a different time when she had sat under a shadeless tree with a book written by a man dead for centuries, when she had never thought twice about the color of the new furniture or which China set to serve the society ladies tea.

Perhaps it was at that exact moment she wrote *I must follow the sad nightingale*, even more as a pretty turn of phrase than anything else, before she disappeared into the bright sunlight forever, leaving a house, a husband, and a child behind.

A life for another life. Would the gods call it justice? Would Alex? Did anybody truly have the right, except her?

Yet these musings were nothing more than mere half-imagined dreams she kept grasping at, if only to convince herself that all of it, the diary, the *Iliad,* and the dagger, meant something, that they were pieces to a larger story instead of forgotten belongings of a woman who had ultimately left them behind.

From the few scraps of memory she still had, Alex knew her mother had been sad, that she had not been happy in her new life. She knew that when she contemplated her mother's death, it was not an accidental one that was most realistic. It was more likely that one day her mother had decided to take her own life, and had done so in a way that left no traces behind.

The thought always left Alex lightheaded. She didn't like to dwell on subjects like that very often, and in fact, she was constantly terrified of death. So the possibility that her mother had willingly taken her own life was almost incomprehensible.

But it was the only option that explained the strange nature of the events, the disappearance, the futility of trying to find her.

With these dreary thoughts, the days dragged on, and Alex noticed that she spent more time in her room, and more time in the library, desiring to be alone and in silence. Warren's texts dwindled, and they saw less of each other. Alex wondered idly if they would break up, though she knew he would never be the one to do it.

But no matter how many times she read the diary, no matter how many hours she spent in the library puzzling over the *Iliad,* rereading the lines mechanically, no matter how many times she dreamed of discovering one final clue to her disappearance, Alex always ended up at the same inescapable conclusion.

Her mother did not want to be found.

12

"You've been keeping to yourself lately," Chloe said, sipping her iced coffee.

Chloe's eyes lingered around the café, probably looking for a new potential fling, then settled on Alex accusingly, as if she were the reason there were only elderly couples here.

They had just finished their usual morning run and had stopped for a coffee, despite Alex's reluctance to do anything anymore, thinking that perhaps she would be less suspicious if she agreed to some activities now and then.

"I've been...studying."

Chloe looked surprised, then jealous. She knew Alex never studied more than she had to, which Chloe had always envied, being naturally competitive. "For finals?"

"Not exactly." Then catching the other girl's look, she added, "Law school. The test score is everything."

Somehow she was lying easily, but it was the wrong thing to say. Chloe also planned to go to law school.

"Already?" Chloe's voice hid a slight waver, both worried and critical.

"It's never too early to start preparing."

Chloe raised her brows, dubious. "Right."

They both sipped their coffees at the same time, then Chloe cleared her throat, shifting in her seat. She looked around before leaning forward and lowering her Prada sunglasses. Alex was surprised to see a flicker of concern in her dark brown eyes.

"I'm worried about you," Chloe said, though she sounded like she hated saying it. "Warren has been telling Owen things."

Alex tried to hide the shock she felt. "What things?"

"How you never text him anymore or listen to him when he's talking," she said, flipping her long black hair over her shoulder in an attempt at lightness. "Silly things. He's probably just scared you might finally be moving on from him."

She could not answer right away.

Warren had been talking about her to *Owen?* He never shared personal things like that with anyone, not even Alex sometimes. Owen must have shared them with Chloe or perhaps had been encouraged to, so that Warren's concerns be indirectly mentioned to Alex. It left her with a sick feeling in her stomach.

"So you guys have all been talking about me when I'm not there?" Alex asked, her voice lifting in betrayal.

Chloe's eyes widened. "No, it's not like that at all. We just feel that you've been a little MIA." She narrowed her eyes. "You haven't found someone new, have you?"

"No!" Then Alex blushed at how scandalized she sounded.

"Okay, okay, no need to get all flustered. I was joking." But Chloe looked slightly disappointed. "Well, whatever it is, you can talk to me about it."

Alex considered telling Chloe about her mother, the box she found, the diary, the golden case and silver dagger. She desperately wanted to voice her thoughts out loud, to have someone tell her she was not spiraling into madness. Besides, if there was anyone who would understand, it would be Chloe.

Instead, Alex asked, "Do you ever talk with your dad?"

Chloe blinked at her, then shrugged, averting her eyes. "Not really. He moved back to China, so I can only see him when I visit."

"Did you see him over break?"

"Briefly." It was clear she did not want to talk about it. Chloe forced a smile. "He's really busy with work."

Suddenly Alex felt a hot flame of jealousy flare inside of her. She would give anything to see her mother, no matter how brief. Then the feeling subsided, and she just felt hollow.

"Over break, I asked my dad about my mom," Alex said, quietly. She did not know why she was telling Chloe and not Warren. Except that she knew exactly why. Chloe would never pity her. "And he said he didn't know where she was. That she could be dead for all he knew."

Chloe looked at her for a long time, then grasped her hand. She was rarely physically affectionate, only in short bursts, but Alex knew their worth.

A fierceness took hold of Chloe's dark eyes, as if she already knew about her mother's diary and the pain she had been in. "Be careful, Alex. Only search for answers if you are willing to find them."

She looked like she knew this from experience.

Alex swallowed uneasily. "I will."

"Good." The look fell away from Chloe's face, and she sighed, releasing Alex's hand. "Now, what are you going to do about Warren?"

Alex groaned.

13

It was the last day of classes before finals week.

Alex barely managed to wake up early enough to make it to her nine o'clock class. The professor had brought cookies to celebrate the end of the semester. While a few of the students lingered to chat with the professor and socialize, Alex slipped out as soon as she could. She spent most of the day hiding in the library and only leaving for her next class as early afternoon faded into evening.

After a quick dinner alone, she met Chloe and Owen back at the apartment. It was Friday, so Chloe already had her sharp winged eyeliner drawn and pink gloss on her lips. Owen sat on a stool in Chloe's room while she lined his eyes with a black pencil.

"Oh, splendid, Alex," Owen said upon her arrival. "Is she making me look like a raccoon?"

Alex laughed. "Don't worry. You'd make a hot raccoon."

"Stop complaining or I won't spend my expensive glitter highlight on you," Chloe snapped, pinning Owen's jaw in place and lining the underside of his right eye. "And stop blinking."

"I can't prevent my blinking," Owen muttered.

Alex took a deep breath. "I think I'll stay in tonight."

Chloe whirled on her. "No. Not again."

"You've been bailing on us ever since you got back from break," Owen said, crossing his arms. "You and Warren should just fuck and make up already."

"This isn't about Warren," Alex said irritably.

Owen rolled his eyes. "Warren has a game tomorrow so he won't be going out. You don't have a choice this time, love. You're coming with us tonight."

"It'd do you some good," Chloe retorted, returning to Owen's makeup. She uncapped a small tub and started dabbing glitter highlight on his cheekbones. "All you've been doing is moping around when you should be enjoying your time in college."

"Besides," Owen added, "we'll be going to a gay bar tonight. No creepy frat boys to fend off."

Alex hesitated. She had planned to go over her mother's diary again, but even the prospect of rereading it yet one more time made her slightly nauseous. Perhaps they were right. A proper break might do her good.

"Fine. I'll go."

Owen grinned. "We love you, Alex."

Chloe frowned, looking Alex up and down. "I'll do your makeup." That was as close to *I love you* as Chloe got.

By the time Chloe finished Alex's makeup, Owen had already mixed some Rum and Cokes. He had changed into his signature baggy jeans and white tank, his curls falling over his forehead and the sides of his head freshly shaved.

"How do I look?" Owen asked, giving them a spin.

"Like a slut," Chloe said without hesitation.

Owen grinned. "Perfect."

"We all look great," Alex said, hoping they could keep the peace until they got to the bar.

Once they were sufficiently tipsy they ordered a ride to the bar. Inside was lit in dim red lighting. The dance floor was not crowded this early in the night, but all the booths and tables were taken. They found empty seats at the far end of the bar and ordered drinks.

Owen immediately began flirting with the tatted bartender, while Chloe surveyed the room with her catlike glare.

"Do you think he's gay?" Chloe whispered, pointing at a tall, muscular man with a shaved head and tight pants.

"Yes."

"What about him?"

"Yes, Chloe. This is a *gay* bar."

"Are you sure? What about that nerdy-looking one in the jeans?"

Alex glanced at the man leaning against the far side of the wall and nearly spat out her drink. It was Professor Ezra.

"I know him," Alex said. She quickly turned around so that her back faced him. "I met with him last week. He's a professor at Harvard."

"Ooh, introduce me," Chloe purred. "He's cute, Alex. Always liked an older man."

"For the thousandth time, Chloe, these men are all gay," Alex snapped.

Owen popped up beside Alex. "Not all of them. Some could be bisexual." He winked at Chloe, who rolled her eyes. "Who are you talking about anyway? Maybe I can chat him up and see."

"No, Owen, absolutely—"

"He's gone." Chloe was looking at the far wall, a strange look on her face.

"What?" Alex swiveled around in her seat. Sure enough, the spot on the wall where Professor Ezra had been was empty. "How? Weren't you watching him?"

"Weird," Chloe said. "It was like he just...disappeared."

Alex's stomach turned. *She disappeared into thin air.* She felt a rush of sorrow choke her throat, and she wondered in horror if she would cry, her eyes stinging. She must be drunk.

Chloe turned around, sighing. Then she glanced at Alex. "How do you know him, anyway? What does he teach?"

"Classics," Alex whispered, her hand tightening around her glass.

Owen and Chloe shared a confused glance, but Alex was too dazed to care.

"Come on," Owen said, holding out both of his hands. "Let's go dance."

Alex and Chloe both reluctantly took his hand and let him drag them to the floor. Owen brought Chloe close to him and then twirled her, before reeling Alex in for a spin.

The music pulsed beneath the floor like a heartbeat, and Alex closed her eyes, the world falling away as she sang along to the songs and danced close to her best friends. She found herself between them, Owen's hands at her hips and Chloe's hands linked with hers, following the rhythm together.

People crowded around them, pushing them closer together. Owen's chest moved against her back, damp with sweat. Chloe's hair brushed her cheek, sweet like coconut. A wave of heat rolled through her, heat and then a gripping panic. She needed to get out. She needed to leave.

"Air," she muttered to Chloe, hardly more than a gasp, before she pushed her way through the tight crowds that had migrated to the center of the dance floor.

There was a dull buzzing in her head. She beelined it to the door, shouldering her way to open air, wondering if she was about to vomit. She staggered against the wall once she was outside. The horizon tilted before her, and Alex realized she was way more drunk than she thought.

"Alex?"

Suddenly Professor Ezra stood before her. She straightened up, then swayed, and had to keep a hand against the wall to keep herself steady.

"Are you okay?"

Alex nodded, unable to speak. She would have thought professors would avoid encountering students out at night, especially at a gay bar. But Professor Ezra looked as he did when they met, in fitted jeans and a black sweater. The letter E was stitched on the front in red.

"I've been thinking about our meeting," he continued, his eyes lighting up as if he found this particular moment amusing.

"Oh?"

"Have you ever considered taking a Classics course?"

Alex stared. "No."

"You can take Ancient Greek over the summer and join the intermediate class in the fall," Professor Ezra said. "If you are anything like your mother, you might find it interesting."

"I am nothing like my mother," Alex answered coldly. There was a strange glint in his eyes that she did not like. Almost a fascination, as if she were another dead language he could decipher. "Goodnight, Professor."

She walked back to the door and opened it, then hesitated. Perhaps she had been too rude, but the alcohol had stripped her of all caution. Alex turned as if to apologize, but when she looked at the spot he had been standing at, she saw that he was gone.

With a fumbling step, she went back inside, her hands shaking until she downed another drink.

14

Sunday night rolled around and Warren asked Alex if she wanted to watch a movie at his apartment. She begged Owen and Chloe to pretend they already had movie plans just so she wouldn't be alone with him.

"You should break up with him already, babe," Chloe had drawled.

"I just need space," Alex had protested.

So she invited Warren to join their movie night. They decided to watch *The Lord of the Rings,* which Chloe had never watched to the absolute horror of Owen and Alex. Besides, they had wanted to binge the series this year anyway and these next two weeks were their last chance.

She sat in between Chloe and Warren, while Owen took the armchair. Warren held her hand, his thumb skimming the back of her knuckles lightly. Chloe and Owen quietly bickered over who was more attractive, Aragorn or Legolas.

Alex had to side with Owen this time. She loved the dark locks and rugged look of the Ranger. Warren had always seemed offended by this, perhaps because he was blond, and joined Chloe on team Legolas.

"He's just so beautiful," Chloe sighed. "Like an angel."

"He's an elf," Owen deadpanned. "Aragorn is sexy. He's a ranger. You can't deny that."

"They're both hot," Alex said dismissively, trying to ease the tension before it boiled over into something else. "Can we just watch the movie?"

They hardly made it halfway through the extended version. If Alex wasn't so tired, she would have insisted on finishing it, but she wanted an excuse to remove her hand from Warren's. They lingered in the kitchen cleaning the dirty dishes in the sink before filing off to bed. Warren's fingertips skirted her waist after they changed into pajamas. Her heart leaped and settled in her chest. A part of her still responded to his touch, but the rest of her shrunk away, her chest tightening as she ignored his searching gaze, walking to the bed and pulling down the covers.

"I think I'm just gonna go to sleep," Alex said, looking away.

Warren stood still, as if battling his annoyance, then moved towards the other side of the bed. When he was under the covers, he looked at her like he wanted confirmation of his suspicions, but Alex refused to speak when she still didn't have the words.

"Did I do something wrong?"

She hated him, truly despised him, at that moment. Then the moment passed and she shook her head. After all, it wasn't about him. Not really.

"It's nothing that you did, exactly. I just...realized some things."

"What things?" he asked sharply.

Something in his tone sparked a flame in Alex's heart. "I don't know. Us. Our relationship, I guess. Who I am and what I want to do with my life."

"You mean that you don't know if you want *me* to be a part of your life," Warren said, his expression grave.

Alex just looked at him, the truth in his words hitting home like the straight shot of an arrow.

Warren sighed. "I'm tired. We can talk about this later."

He rolled onto his side, facing away from her. Alex blinked away unbidden tears, then slid into bed, careful not to touch him. It felt strange to be so close to him and yet not know him at all.

Soon Warren's breaths became shallow and regular, and he flipped over in his sleep, his brows furrowed and his mouth frowning. Alex stared at his face, following the familiar slope of his nose, the light pink lips, the golden hair curling over his forehead. Her heart ached deeply, but she was not sure it was love anymore. Perhaps it was only pity.

She crept out of the covers, quietly pulling out her mother's box from underneath her bed. Warren stirred but did not wake up. She took out the diary as she had wanted to do all night. The supple leather had become a comfort to her when she could not sleep. She ran her fingertips along the spine, across the cover, then skimmed through the pages.

Suddenly her thumb caught against the inside of the cover where the endpaper had begun peeling. She had never noticed it before. Her finger ran underneath the edge that used to be glued to the cover and to her surprise felt a slight ridge, as if another smaller paper had been squeezed underneath.

Now Alex was fully awake. She opened the diary wider and peeled back the curling corner of the endpaper. There was indeed a small slip of paper wedged underneath, and Alex could now see where someone had glued the endpaper back down. Her heart began beating so loudly she feared it might wake Warren up.

She carefully used the silver dagger to unglue the rest of the endpaper from the cover until she could slide the piece of paper out. Then she held the paper under the light from her window, where the nearly full moon shone brightly in a cloudless night sky. The paper had been torn from some kind of old parchment, with a few lines of carefully handwritten Greek on it, just like the *Iliad*. They read:

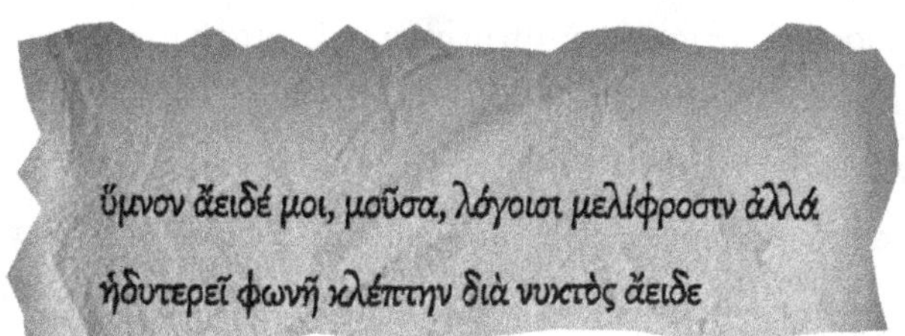

Her mother must have hidden it. But why?

Alex moved, the paper coming up to the light so that it became half-translucent, revealing scribbled writing on the back. She flipped over the piece of paper, and sure enough, there was her mother's all too familiar handwriting.

The Prince of Thieves.

That was all she had written, underlined urgently.

The phrase nagged at the edges of her memory. *The Prince of Thieves.* Where had she heard that before?

She couldn't remember.

Without making too much noise, she opened her laptop and turned the brightness down. She searched up the name but to no avail. Nothing relevant came up. She tried *thief Ancient Greek* and *lord of thieves* but still nothing.

Then it came to her.

The diary, one of the later entries, the ones she had mostly skimmed for being too poetic and abstract to mean much at all. She flipped through the diary, trying to recall the date. It took her a long time to find it.

September 9th. The Prince of Thieves. He said he was many things but I think he is just a god with too much time on his hands.

A god? Alex reread the stanza, then tried searching for *the Prince of Thieves god.* Still nothing, but she did not lose hope this time. This was not an insignificant discovery. Finally, she tried *the god of thieves.*

Hermes.

The name resounded in her chest like a bell struck loud and clear.

Hermes, the god of shopkeepers and merchants, travelers and transporters of goods, and thieves and tricksters, but also a herald of the gods and a messenger between worlds. Why did it sound like her mother had spoken with him? She softly turned the pages of the diary, rereading entries that she had brushed off as merely mystical or fanciful.

October 26th. I am being watched. I feel their eyes on me, the eyes of eternity, the gaze of gods.

November 19th. The city is not a place, he says, but a road. One for mortals, one for the gods.

January 7th. He surprised me today. Walking home, there he was in the shape of a bird, singing a mournful tune, looking at me. He never helps, just talks. The bird is only a messenger after all.

The bird. She recalled the bird that had sat on her very windowsill, looking at her, when she almost thought it had spoken to her. *Are you listening?*

Perhaps the bird had really asked her that, but Alex immediately shook the thought away. What did she think, that the bird was a god? And that god was Hermes? She was losing her mind, her very sanity. She was so terrified that her mother had died that she would rather believe a bird was actually a god than accept that she was gone forever.

Alex could hear Chloe's warning in her mind. *Only search for answers if you are willing to find them.*

She continued to reread through the diary, finding little phrases that spoke of divinities, of cities that were eternal, of roads for mortals and gods. It felt as though her mother had been writing in code and it was up to her to read between the lines. But it was agonizing the more she read, as everything connected and yet nothing connected, like puzzle pieces that looked like a perfect fit but when seen up close clearly did not, no matter how much they were forced together.

Her mother's words seemed to stitch together another world full of gods and goddesses, a world that could only exist in dreams. But somehow, for Elena, they were real. Even if it only existed in her mind. Perhaps this was the world her mother had longed for. Perhaps this was why she had left Alex all those years ago, either for another life or for death.

The moonlight shined on the windowsill where the bird had sat all those weeks ago. She had been a different person then. So much had changed, and too little.

Maybe her mother had died somewhere. Maybe it had even been her choice.

No. Alex refused to believe it.

These words could not amount to such an end. Her mother had loved life too much. She had loved some other life, so much that she left her only child for it.

Then had it all meant nothing? Had leaving her only daughter cost her nothing? Or had the choice been made almost unwillingly, torn in two directions with one pull just a little stronger?

She thought of Warren, the life they had planned together, the routine of their love, the small gaps in the larger picture, the emptiness that overcame her like a faintness of breath when she held his hand and imagined their children prancing across some manicured lawn, just as she had once.

Some days this all meant nothing. Some nights she closed her eyes and thought of her life and knew that it all meant nothing, nothing, *nothing.* She wanted to be uprooted, she wanted to be shaken. She wanted to gaze upon mountains and deserts and a faded school filled with dusty, ancient books, to lock a phrase up in her heart forever before the car rolled away and life folded up into marriage and children and planning event after event until all was spent and dried up and the only thing she could do was unlock that phrase and clutch at the memory of a memory.

Sometimes Alex wondered if she had a choice, if the scales of her life were waiting to tip in one direction over another. Sometimes she looked at the stars and this civilization rose and fell in her absence, in her flight there and back again.

Are you listening?

Then she heard it, a low, mournful tune, a birdsong drifting on the breeze, or something else, something more.

I must follow the sad nightingale.

It was then that Alex realized it with a sudden glaring certainty. She must leave, she must leave to find her mother, she must discover the truth once and for all, whatever the consequences.

She must leave school, exams considered unnecessary.

15

Alex packed a suitcase and her backpack on Tuesday morning and drove. Her Statistics exam was in an hour, but she did not plan on attending.

She filled up on gas and cashed some money from her savings so her father wouldn't be able to track her card. Like her mother, she wished not to be followed. She also stocked up on snacks, water, and other essentials.

By the time she got on the road, Chloe had already reached out to her asking if she wanted to run again on Thursday. Alex ignored the message and continued driving.

After an hour on the road, she realized as if coming up for air that she did not know where she was going. She knew Tierra del Sol was in California, but how should she get there? Her body had gone on autopilot when she left, and once she had gotten in the car she had started on the same route back to the house in Greenwich.

But she didn't want to go back to Greenwich.

Checking the freeway signs, Alex saw an exit up ahead for Albany, NY and took it impulsively. But now she was nervous. She hadn't thought anything through, simply up and leaving, disappearing into thin air just like her mother. It had momentarily relieved her feeling of suffocation, of purposelessness, like cutting off something that had tethered her to one spot. But now that she was free, the world unraveled around her like uncharted waters.

Her car jetted down the two-lane highway due west, and the moment she saw a shoulder on the road up ahead, she pulled into it. Her head fell into her hands and she almost screamed. What was she doing? This was insanity. She should turn back and forget this ever happened. No one would ever need to know.

Alex grabbed the steering wheel to take the ramp off the freeway when there was a clear tap on her windshield. She looked up.

A bird was perched on the hood of her car, the same one she had seen on her windowsill. It knocked its beak on the window, making the tapping noise again.

Alex didn't move, watching it with her heart beating loudly, the impossibility of it rendering her immobile. Its eyes were beady black, but she swore there was a knowing gleam in them. The bird hopped and turned, looking up with a cocking twist of its neck.

Instinctively, she looked up—and saw the highway sign. *Buffalo 446 mi.*

When she looked back down, the bird was gone. A frustrated shout was torn from her throat. Her eyes burned. She wished someone would tell her what to do. Then she remembered her mother's diary.

The bird is only a messenger after all.

Was the bird a god? Was that what her mother had truly thought? At this point, Alex would believe anything if it would bring her closer to finding her.

She imagined her mother wandering the empty halls of that big house, hiding in the library if only to save herself from the glaring scrutiny of her husband's family. Had she asked the empty air for direction? Had a bird appeared and pointed to the blue sky, telling her *go, go, go?*

Perhaps Elena had listened, and when the bird had disappeared into thin air, she had disappeared too.

Alex didn't know, but it didn't matter anymore. She had chosen to follow the trail of memories her mother had left behind. Maybe she had made that choice the moment she had seen her mother's name on that box.

The car rumbled to a start and shot down the highway again. Rolling green hills streaked past her windows and the sun arced across the sky. Alex's eyelids grew heavy as the day went on, and once she entered Buffalo, she took the next exit, stopping at a dingy motel on the outskirts of the city right next to the highway. She had driven for nearly seven hours straight.

Once she sank onto the springy mattress, the day's events seemed to pile up on her, weighing on her eyelids so that all she could do was close them.

She fell into a fitful sleep, dreaming of a bird with the shadow of a boy who was not a boy but a thief in the night, with black, beady eyes staring straight at her.

16

Alex woke up and for a moment forgot where she was.

Streetlights shone a faint glow through the flimsy curtains, illuminating the small motel room and her suitcase thrown on the ground at the foot of the bed. Alex grabbed her phone. It was nearing seven o'clock at night, the sun having set while she was asleep.

She had received another message from Chloe, consisting of three question marks. Warren had also texted her, reluctantly asking if she was okay, since she hadn't answered his texts from yesterday or earlier in the morning. Their fight on Sunday night had created a cold tension between them Monday, which she had avoided by sneaking off to the library after breakfast.

Sighing, she ignored the messages and shut down her phone, not wishing to be tracked or feel that growing guilt inside her. Then she quickly changed into fresher clothes, her mind restless and her stomach growling.

At the front desk of the motel she found glossy maps of Buffalo and fliers of restaurant ads. She took one of each, then unfolded the map, mostly out of curiosity. One side had the entire city of Buffalo displayed with colored icons indicating famous landmarks and popular restaurants. The other side was filled with different ads for various attractions in Buffalo. One caught her eye.

Cave of the Winds — tickets on sale! Discovered in 1834, it was originally called Aeolus' Cave, after the Greek god of winds...

She quickly read the rest of the description and learned that the tour led straight under Niagara Falls, where a piece of rock had once jutted out and formed a hollow cave under the waterfall before it broke off. Supposedly the wind became very loud as it echoed in the cave.

Alex couldn't resist something so apparently tied to Greek myth. Besides, she had never visited Niagara Falls before and might never again.

She drove her car across town, picked up dinner on the way, and bought a ticket right as the last tour was beginning. Her tour guide was a typical old New Englander, with glasses, white tufts of hair, and a patterned sweater vest covered in a large dark coat. He suited up in the same clear poncho and special footwear that was given to her at the front desk.

He motioned for the cluster of tourists to come closer. Alex hung back at the edge of the group, huddling in her coat. Although spring was well underway, the water in the Falls was still ice cold, and the wind whipping off the currents slipped past all of her warm clothes.

"Welcome, everyone. My name is George and I will be your guide. Today we will be touring the Cave of the Winds!" he exclaimed, motioning around with stiff arms. A few tourists halfheartedly clapped. "In 1834, a cave was discovered under the waterfall. It was formed from a rock that stuck out under the water creating a dry hollow that allowed people to experience Niagara Falls up close. The cave was given the name Aeolus' Cave, after the Greek god of winds. Since then the rock has fallen, but the name still stands. To get there, we will take an elevator down one hundred and seventy feet! Then we will follow the wooden walkways to what is called the 'Hurricane Deck.' There you will be a mere twenty feet in front of the Bridal Veil Falls. But be warned, folks, you will get wet, so please wear your ponchos. Walk carefully and follow me!"

Alex was the last inside the elevator, which heaved and hummed deep into the Niagara Gorge. She wondered if the flimsy plastic she had put over herself would keep her dry, and when she heard the thundering water like a stampede of elephants overhead she seriously doubted it.

The elevator came to a groaning stop and the group poured out onto the wooden walkway. Mist from the waterfalls obstructed her vision, and despite being well-lit, she still squinted to find George.

He was waddling away with surprising agility, beckoning them and moving his mouth. She realized he must have been shouting, but all she could hear was the deafening roar of the water.

With difficulty, the group moved on, trudging across the slippery wooden planks. Water sprayed from all directions, and Alex didn't dare look up to try and find the waterfalls. Cold sank into her skin, chilling her to the bone. Her teeth chattered, and she wondered why she had thought this was a good idea.

George shouted over the noise. "Careful…find the railing…"

Alex followed the rest of the group to a small deck with a railing that looked alarmingly flimsy. The other tourists broke off into the smaller groups and pairs that they had come with as everyone migrated to the railings. Once she reached the railing and placed her hands on the ice-cold metal, Alex allowed herself to look up.

She sucked in a breath, her hands gripping the railing with all her might.

Water gushed over the craggy cliff-side, pouring into the river below and rushing right underneath the wooden walkway she was on, which seemed to sway with the mere momentum of the waterfall. Her heart hammered as the waterfall continually doused her in sprays of icy water.

Suddenly the waterfall lit up with rainbow lights beneath the water, a brilliant array of colors streaking through the flying droplets. After a few long seconds, or perhaps minutes—her perception of time lost in the unending collision of water and light—she distantly heard George say something, perhaps beckoning them away.

It was at this exact moment she heard a voice, as clear as if someone had spoken in her ear, and yet distant like a shout on the wind at the same time. She stood riveted to the spot, staring at the Falls.

The wind whipped past her face like a cold breath against her cheeks. The voice was swift and airy, but unmistakable, echoing deep in the hollow of rock and lashing back out across the river, speaking in a language she did not know.

Then Alex realized the voice was not one voice but many, and there were other voices, deep and rumbling ones, and they sounded at once like a song but also like water and wind clashing in battle, a clamor of screams and shouts.

It was the most beautiful and terrifying thing she had ever heard.

A hand on her arm woke her and the voices disappeared. She turned and George was by her side, motioning to continue down the walkway. Alex took one last look, straining her ears for the melodies, the distinct voices, but all she could hear now was a dull drumming of water.

"We must go," George said in her ear, and she noticed his voice sounded different than before. Smoother, almost younger. Her ears were still ringing from the waterfall. She let him lead her away in a daze.

Later at night, she lay down with her eyes open, staring at the ceiling. She tried to recall the voices she had heard at the waterfall, but all she could remember was a white noise.

She fell into a deep sleep, where she stood in front of a cave with water gurgling in its depths so that it sounded like a song and a hand touched her arm but instead of an old man it was a bird and it perched on her shoulder, beckoning, *go, go, go,* until the song became so loud it sounded like a scream.

17

Alex left early the next day, not wishing to stick around too long. Her skin prickled every time she thought of the waterfall. Besides, there were still many miles to cover, and the more she lingered along the way, the likelier her father or one of her friends would find her before she got there.

Her next stop was St. Louis, Missouri, nearly eleven hours away. The drive took her on a scenic route along Lake Erie. Then at Cleveland she merged onto the I-71 towards Columbus, Ohio, where she stopped for lunch.

It was a little past seven in the evening when Alex rolled into St. Louis, endless green plains dotted with quaint suburbia gradually crowding until she was downtown, looking around for a place to stay the night.

The next day she drove seven hours to Oklahoma City. Even though she planned to drive all the way to Albuquerque, New Mexico, her body ached by the fifth hour, and she couldn't imagine driving ten more of them. Her eyes could barely stay open, and she gratefully fell into her cheap motel bed. By morning, she felt bruised and sore, but much more rested.

It was a beautiful day, with blue skies and not a wisp of a cloud in sight. She had the continental breakfast provided and realized that her hotel sat right along the Oklahoma River. The water glittered a deep muddy blue under the morning sun, with lush green trees hugging its banks. She walked the trail along the river, relishing the warmth of the sun at this time of year.

Reluctantly, her thoughts strayed to Warren. He would have loved this river. She hadn't turned her phone back on, relying on maps at hotels and freeway signs to guide her across the country, at least until she was closer to Tierra del Sol.

Was Warren worried? Had Chloe told him she was not at home? Had he notified her father, telling him she was missing, her car gone? Or perhaps Harvard had noticed that she wasn't attending her exams, her friends too busy cramming last minute to realize it themselves. Either way, someone would find out eventually.

A part of her felt guilty for disappearing like that, for leaving her boyfriend and her friends without a warning. But most importantly, for completely neglecting her final exams and risking her entire college career on a whim.

She wondered what her mother would think, if she would consider her daughter ungrateful of the privileged life she had secured for her.

Clearly her mother had grown up poor. She had not suffered or starved, she was just poor. Elena's parents had led a simple life, where money put food on the table and a child was entertained by the sands and rocks of a never-ending desert. Her mother had been poor in things, but rich in a lust for life. Alex read it in her diary, the dreams she had, all those stories that filled the world with a certain kind of magic.

Alex could not help but feel inadequate now, caught chasing the shadow of this woman. While she was her mother's daughter—there was no denying that—she was also her father's first child, his only daughter, and she carried his legacy of East Coast education and business, of wealth and influence, a legacy generations in the making; in short, a legacy she could not leave behind as easily as her mother had.

While she half-resented the stuffiness of it all, she also found herself proud of her father and the life he had built for them, and his father before him, and his father before. These men had cultivated and toiled for their name, so her father could stand on his balcony with a Scotch at his elbow and survey the sum total of his legacy and nod and pass it on to better hands.

Alex was those hands, and they were the hands of a woman.

And yet, despite it all, she was still her mother's daughter, who was destined to leave this legacy for words on a page, for a bird caught in the wind. She held her father's legacy like two hands on the wheel and yet all she could think about was how she could just drive away.

And what was she leaving for? A glimpse of a woman she never really knew? A whisper from a mother who reserved words as thread for creating worlds that didn't exist?

But perhaps she was leaving for another reason entirely. Perhaps she wished to escape long-made legacies and marriage proposals and the steady march of adulthood. Perhaps she wished to understand her mother, who was once just a girl before she was a wife and a mother.

Or perhaps, like Elena, and like Helen of Troy before her, she was simply leaving for herself.

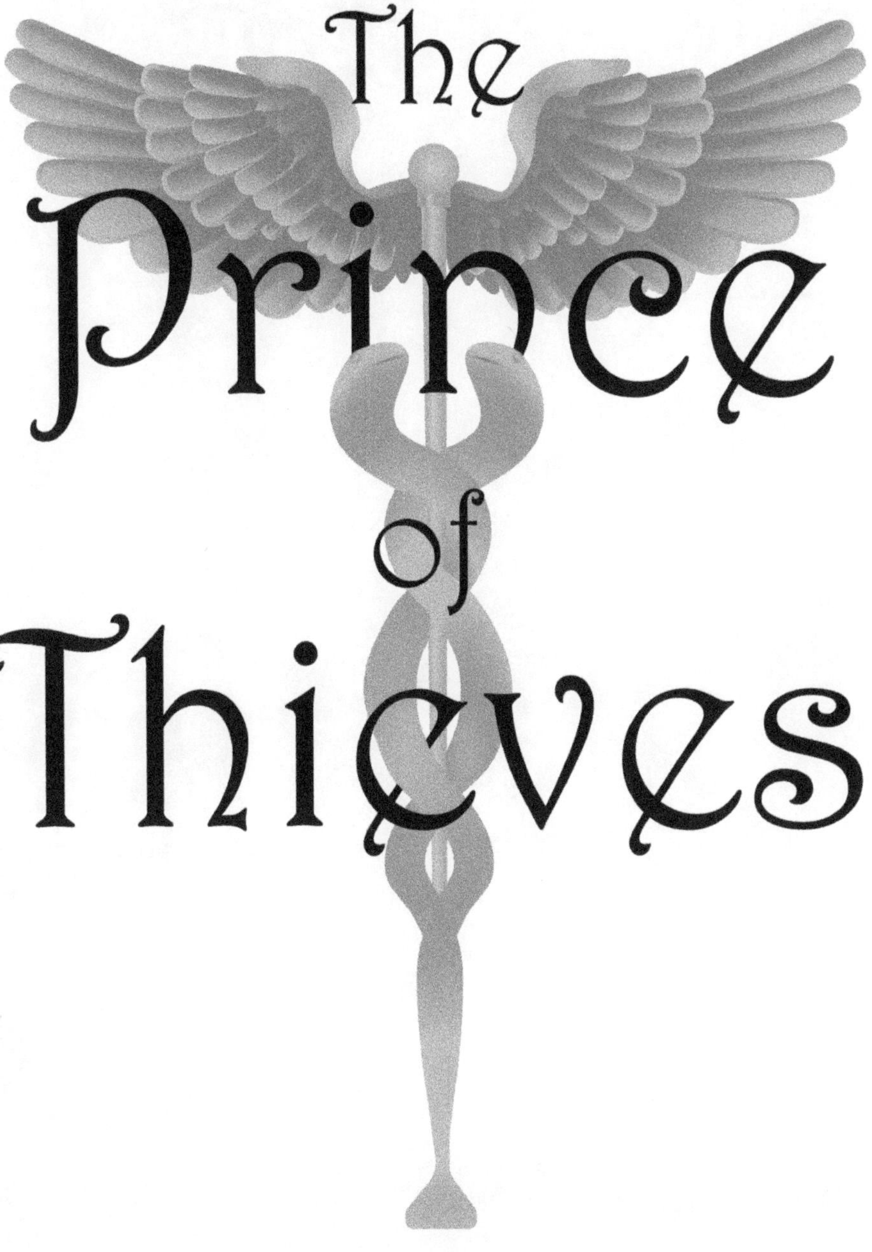

The Prince of Thieves

For then she bare a son, of many shifts, blandly cunning, a robber, a cattle driver, a bringer of dreams, a watcher by night, a thief at the gates, one who was soon to show forth wonderful deeds among the deathless gods. Born with the dawning, at mid-day he played on the lyre, and in the evening he stole the cattle of far-shooting Apollo on the fourth day of the month; for on that day queenly Maia bare him. So soon as he had leaped from his mother's heavenly womb, he lay not long waiting in his holy cradle, but he sprang up and sought the oxen of Apollo. But as he stepped over the threshold of the high-roofed cave, he found a tortoise there and gained endless delight. For it was Hermes who first made the tortoise a singer.

...

He cut stalks of reed to measure and fixed them, fastening their ends across the back and through the shell of the tortoise, and then stretched ox hide all over it by his skill. Also he put in the horns and fitted a cross-piece upon the two of them, and stretched seven strings of sheep-gut. But when he had made it he proved each string in turn with the key, as he held the lovely thing. At the touch of his hand it sounded marvelously; and, as he tried it, the god sang sweet random snatches, even as youths bandy taunts at festivals.

—*Hymn to Hermes,* 13-25;47-56, translation by Hugh G. Evelyn-White

18

From Oklahoma City, she planned to drive over nine hours to Albuquerque, New Mexico. Alex had begun to feel the effects of driving many hours in a row over several days, but she grabbed a coffee and left her hotel early anyway.

With the radio turned on to a station playing old folk music, Alex passed the time easily. The fields and hilly plains of Oklahoma faded and soon the red rock of New Mexico jutted from the earth.

As she neared the city, mountains loomed over the horizon, the sun setting red hot between their flat crests. Perhaps due to exhaustion or sheer recklessness, Alex impulsively changed highways, driving away from the city and north towards the mountains. The highway eventually led to Santa Fe in the northeast, but her headlights flashed on a small sign pointing left to a historic site up in the mountains.

Without thinking, she followed the sign and drove. She drove until she made it to the foot of the mountains, and then she kept driving, up and up steep inclines and around sharp curves until she saw signs of a campground that guided her to a clearing with parked RVs.

The sun had long set, Alex's headlights the only lights flashing in the deep darkness of the mountains. She spotted an information cabin and pulled up beside it, then paid for a parking spot for the night. The park ranger showed her to her spot, a square slice of land nearly on the edge of a deep ravine.

As she prepared for bed, she began to seriously regret her decision. She had no sleeping bag, hardly more food than some bags of chips and granola bars, and with only her small, cheap flashlight she could not find the signs pointing to any public restrooms. Fearing wild animals or worse, she squatted in the trees to pee and hurriedly got in the backseat of her car.

Among the other large RVs and campers, she felt unsafe and unprepared in her small, expensive Audi. But it was nearing midnight and Alex wanted to get an early start tomorrow. So she huddled under another layer of sweats and a sweater, relocking the car doors and taking a deep breath to calm herself.

Then she looked up. Through the sunroof Alex could glimpse a sky full of stars, more than she had ever seen back home, swirling and flashing with different colors. She wondered if this was the kind of sky her mother had grown up under, if she had come to the endless stretches of suburbia and felt cut off, so suffocated under the smog.

Suddenly she saw a shooting star, slicing the sky open in white light. Alex felt large, watchful figures, like gods or mountains, on the borders of her dreams.

The bright, morning sun woke her up in the same position. Her heart began racing before her thoughts caught up to her emotions.

Today she would drive to Tierra del Sol, the last and final destination on her cross-country trip, where she hoped to solve the mystery of her mother's disappearance. She found the public restrooms which smelled faintly of mold and urine, then quickly left the campground before any others woke up.

Alex was grateful to be returning to civilization and grabbed breakfast on the way at a local café. The air was hot and dry as the sun climbed higher in the sky. She filled up on gas, then reluctantly turned on her phone, since she'd need it from this point on.

As she had expected, there were multiple missed calls and texts from different people asking where she had gone. She bit her lip, feeling the guilt rise up in her chest. Her eyes pricked with tears at what they were going through because of her.

Warren's last few texts had been frantic, pleading with her to return, to be okay, to be alive. Her father had texted multiple times and threatened to get the police involved. Chloe, Owen, and Simona had all reached out, as well as a few other people she had hardly considered friends, sending words of encouragement.

She realized with a belated shock that they probably thought she was dead.

Of course they would think that. They had no idea about anything, about her mother or the box of her things. Not even Chloe had known, though it had felt like it. Alex was completely alone.

She hesitated, then decided it was safest to text Chloe. *I needed to find out the truth about my mother. I'll explain everything when I get back. Tell the others not to worry.*

Then she shut off her phone, not wanting to see her reply. She was afraid that if she did, she would lose all resolve and drive straight back. *No.* She needed to do this. She needed to know once and for all.

Instead of using an online navigation tool as she had planned, Alex bought road maps between there and California. She traced her finger along the highways. She had to take the I-40 towards Phoenix, then I-10 West toward Los Angeles, and exit on the AZ-85 before merging onto the I-8 toward Yuma and San Diego. That would bring her alongside the border of Mexico until she arrived at Tierra del Sol.

Even after driving nearly eight hours to Phoenix, Arizona, Alex didn't want to waste any more time. She filled up her tank again and bought a few energy drinks. Then she kept driving.

Alex laid the map on top of the golden case and silver dagger that she had pulled out of her suitcase and kept on the passenger seat beside her. The mountains were red and rocky, a vast desert stretching ahead and behind her.

She felt very small, like an ant crawling in the dirt, but she cherished how different it was to the New England hills, the dense woodlands and mossy creeks. There was something alien about the desert, almost like another planet, created in its shimmery horizon miles and miles out of reach, the blue sky curving like the reflection in a spoon overhead.

Soon she exited the I-8 onto CA-94 W, where she took a left onto the main street of Tierra del Sol. As she had expected, the street ran through a very small, desolate town, surrounded by mountains, rock, and dirt.

Alex had to drive through the entire town before looping back around in search of a motel. She found one in the busier part of town, right across the street from a church, which she guessed to be the Lighthouse Church. It was nearing ten o'clock at night, but they had plenty of rooms open and she booked one for three nights.

There had been no Academy or school in sight. She wondered if she had driven all the way here for nothing, if her father had mistaken the town, or if the New Academy no longer existed. Even though she was exhausted, she dropped off her suitcase in her room and gathered her strength to explore.

She crossed the street to the Lighthouse Church. It was built like a Spanish mission as her mother had described, with stucco walls and red tiling on the roof. A bell tower rose up in front, over large, wooden doors.

Alex walked up the steps, then pushed on the heavy oak doors. Surprisingly, they opened.

The church was empty. It was eerily quiet, each of her footsteps echoing in the small space. Ornately fashioned lamps were lit around the perimeters, but otherwise she walked in a hazy gloom, and her heart beat faster at each flickering shadow.

Behind the altar loomed the familiar icon of Jesus on the Cross, the blood on his wounds a bright ruby red. Alex was not religious, but her father had been raised Christian, and she knew the story well enough.

She walked down the main aisle, past the wooden pews, then exited one of the doors that flanked both sides of the altar. It led to a courtyard dotted with fruit trees, just as her mother had described in her diary. Alex looked around, breathless.

If that was the back of the church and this was the courtyard, that meant the two-story buildings on the left and right wings were the dormitories. Then that also meant her mother's coveted library stood across from the church.

It was a squat, older building compared with the rest. Alex wondered if she was trespassing on private property at this point, but she didn't really care, not after she came all this way. So without thinking more about it, she crossed the courtyard and quietly entered the library.

The doors opened without a noise. Inside was dim and dusty.

When the door shut behind her, Alex felt the close walls trapping the heat in, as well as the musty smell of old books. She tiptoed almost reverently past tall shelves that touched the ceiling, and large wooden desks presumably for studying.

Her fingers brushed the flaking spines of books as she turned down a random aisle. Alex could almost picture it then, her mother lingering here at night, patiently reading the titles, carefully selecting the right book that would lead her down a spiraling search.

"The library is closed, you know."

Alex jumped and turned around, swearing under her breath. She realized that the voice had come from a man stretched out on a wooden desk pushed into the corner, half-hidden in shadow. He held a book loosely in one hand and a bottle of wine in the other.

He smiled wryly. "Don't worry. I don't work here. Well, technically, I do. But I'm not the librarian, so I won't tell." He held a finger to his lips, an amused glitter in his eyes.

Alex stared, still in shock at the intrusion.

The man was younger than she had initially thought, perhaps a few years older than her, with black curling hair and light brown skin. He was quite handsome in a rugged kind of way. *Like Aragorn,* she thought randomly, with a shade of stubble on his jaw. He was also very drunk.

"I'm sorry. I'll go," she said, turning to leave.

"No, please," he said, sitting up and then bracing himself against the edge of the table when he began to tilt. "It's my fault. I scared you."

"I'm not supposed to be here anyway," Alex said hurriedly, wishing she had never entered the library.

He raised his dark brows. "You aren't a student here, then?"

"A student?"

He smiled again and stretched his arms wide. "Welcome to the New Academy."

Alex forgot to breathe. So her father was right. This was the school her mother had attended before she eloped. This was where her mother had spent hours and hours reading.

This was her home.

"My mother was a student here. A long time ago." She felt the need to say it out loud, even to a complete stranger.

"Oh?"

"She studied Classics." It was all she knew, in the end.

The man didn't seem surprised. "And you?"

"Economics." He looked slightly disappointed. "I go to Harvard."

He took a long swig of his wine, but not before she saw the distaste on his face. Alex watched him drain the bottle, his throat working, then set it aside. He ran a hand through his hair, but it only made the thick strands more unruly.

"You're not from here, are you?" he asked, though it wasn't really a question.

She bristled at his tone but shook her head. "New York."

"I see." And he did seem to see straight through her, though what he saw Alex could only guess. "What's your name?"

"Alex."

"Alex," he repeated. "Is that short for something?"

No one had asked her that in a long time. She wondered if that mattered. It felt like it did. "Yes. Alexandria."

At last, he smiled once more. "Alexandria." The name rolled smoothly off his tongue, as though in a different language. "My name is Ari."

"Nice to meet you," Alex said automatically.

He stared at her. "Are your eyes different colors?"

Alex nodded in surprise. Few people noticed it that quickly. "Yes."

"Well, it was nice to meet you, Alexandria."

Then without another word, Ari hopped off the table. After finding his balance, he grabbed the bottle of wine and disappeared around the corner. She heard the library doors open and shut softly. After a few moments suspended, Alex returned to the courtyard, her thoughts jumbled. Ari was nowhere to be found. She looked around as if in a dream.

If this was indeed the New Academy, then where were all the students?

She realized it was late and also a Sunday. She must have missed the evening service, unless there were only enough inhabitants for a morning Mass, which wouldn't have surprised her. Perhaps most of the students went to bed early.

Tomorrow was Monday. She decided to come in the morning and find someone she could speak with. *Someone else,* she corrected herself.

But she could hardly count Ari as someone affiliated with the New Academy. And besides, he had been...inebriated. He could have been saying anything.

When Alex returned to her motel room, she sat on the mattress, her mother's diary in front of her, the golden case and silver dagger beside it. This was the place, the source of her mother's memories. She felt so close to the answer she could almost taste it, like nearing the beach and tasting salt in the air.

She remembered Chloe's warning, which felt like so long ago. *Only search for answers if you are willing to find them.*

But unlike before, Alex felt like she was finally onto something.

19

Alex awoke early the next morning with an unfamiliar burst of energy. Outside the streets were still quiet, but now and then she heard a car rumbling somewhere nearby. There was also this subtle murmuring, a buzzing in the air, that she had not noticed yesterday. With a laugh, she realized it was the cicadas in the trees.

She crossed the street, adjusting her sweater. It was hotter than she had expected, especially for early May. Alex held her breath as she opened the doors of the church.

People. That was her first thought.

Not many, but several were scattered around the pews, kneeling in prayer. Most of them were elderly, probably locals. There was no Mass, thankfully, but this was still a change from yesterday.

Alex walked quietly around the back of the pews, not wishing to disturb anyone or draw attention to herself.

"Excuse me, ma'am. Are you in need of assistance?"

She whirled around just as she reached one of the exit doors in the front of the church, cringing at how quickly someone spotted her as an outsider. The question had come from an old woman sitting in the first pew, her small, wrinkled hands folded on her lap. The words were spoken with the faintest accent Alex could not place.

"I'm sorry," Alex said, embarrassed. She hadn't thought anyone would notice her this soon. Somehow, she had thought herself nearly invisible, like a ghost. But if she were a ghost, this woman had no problem seeing her. "I was just looking around."

The old woman stood up slowly, holding the back of the pew for support. She had curly white hair cut in a bob and gentle eyes, dressed in a long black skirt and a pale blue sweater, a large silver cross dangling over her chest. Alex realized belatedly that she was a nun.

"No worries, child. I only wish to help. Is there something I may assist you with?"

After a beat, Alex nodded. "I would like to speak with someone about the New Academy."

"You are in luck! I am the principal of the New Academy." The nun smiled, then took a few steps forward, stretching out one of her wrinkled hands. Alex wondered how old she must be. "You may call me Sister Stella," the nun said. Alex froze at the name but managed to shake her hand. "What is your name, dear?"

She cleared her throat, remembering Ari, the way she felt like a different person when he had said her full name. "Alexandria."

Her white eyebrows hitched up slightly at her name before she smiled. "Follow me, Alexandria."

Sister Stella led her slowly across the front of the church and behind the altar. They walked up a flight of ancient-looking stone steps and found themselves in a narrow hallway that ended in a cramped office space. Sister Stella took a seat behind a small wooden desk and motioned for Alex to have a seat in front of it.

"Alexandria," she said. "What brings you to the New Academy?"

"Well," Alex began, then stopped. Sister Stella continued smiling encouragingly. She had no idea how to phrase it and wished she had practiced before rushing over here. "I'm looking for my mother."

Sister Stella raised a brow, but she looked much less surprised than Alex had expected. "And who is your mother, may I ask?"

Now Alex had to explain this without sounding like a complete lunatic, lest even this gentle nun escorted her off the premises. "Elena de la Fuente. She used to go here, then left when she married my dad. But...she's been gone for ten years. I have no idea where she is, but I was hoping to find out." Alex paused.

This was the first time she had told anyone the truth, so she might as well tell the whole truth. "My mother wrote about you in her diary."

Sister Stella nodded slowly. "Yes, I knew your mother."

Alex stared. "You did?"

"Oh yes. She was one of the most gifted students I ever had the pleasure of teaching."

She felt a rush of pride for her mother. "She studied Classics."

"Yes, that is our specialty." Sister Stella looked out the window, pondering. "If you would like, I believe one of our Ancient Greek courses must be finishing up soon. I could introduce you to the professor, an alumnus who recently graduated, Mr. Melamed. He would love to give you a tour of the New Academy. Perhaps you would be interested in a summer intensive course? Professor Melamed would also be teaching the course."

"Oh no," Alex said quickly, her cheeks heating. "I don't study Classics."

Sister Stella gave her the same look Ari had given her when she had said she studied economics. "Very well. Would you still wish to meet Professor Melamed? No one besides myself knows as much about this place as he does, and I unfortunately must attend to a few things in the meantime. Perhaps we could speak more at lunch. You will dine with us in the Main Hall, won't you?"

"I—yes, thank you," Alex stuttered, not wishing to be rude and decline the generous offer. She rose to her feet with Sister Stella and followed her out of the church.

They strolled across the courtyard, then walked under one of the many adobe archways that lined the garden, leading to a shaded colonnade that wrapped around the entire courtyard and connected the dormitories with the library. Sister Stella slowed down around a corner, where a group of students milled about, notebooks and pens in hand. Alex quickly realized that this was the Greek class they were meant to observe.

She searched for the professor and saw him at the front of the group, reading from a book in his hand, which was the exact same book she had seen him holding the day before when he was drunkenly lying down on a table in the library.

Ari.

He hadn't seen her yet, his eyes trained on the book, his mouth moving rhythmically, forming words that Alex had not yet attempted to understand in her shock at seeing him.

She strained her ears and realized he was not speaking English.

"...τίνος νόμου δὴ ταῦτα πρὸς χάριν λέγω; *In favor of what principle do I say these things?* That's the question, isn't it." A few laughs. "Now listen to this: πόσις μὲν ἄν μοι κατθανόντος ἄλλος ἦν, καὶ παῖς ἀπ' ἄλλου φωτός, εἰ τοῦδ' ἤμπλακον, μητρὸς δ' ἐν Ἅιδου καὶ πατρὸς κεκευθότοιν οὐκ ἔστ' ἀδελφὸς ὅστις ἂν βλάστοι ποτέ. *If my spouse were dead there could be another, and there could be children from another man, if I came short of them: but since my mother and father lie buried in Hades there is no brother who can ever be born again.*" He looked up, glancing around the class, which had become hushed, pens hovering in the air, all the students mesmerized by his words. Then his gaze landed on Alex and he froze, then forced a smile. "We'll end there. Lot's to think about. Please read the next one hundred lines for Wednesday."

The students gladly dispersed, chattering amongst themselves. A few who noticed Sister Stella greeted her or waved with a smile. She knew all their names.

Sister Stella stepped forward, and Alex forgot all about the students, her heart dropping into her stomach. Ari was looking straight at her, his hand still holding his book open.

"Good morning, Professor Melamed," Sister Stella said. "I hope you had a good class."

"I did, thank you," he said, without looking away from Alex, who tried not to fidget under his gaze.

"I was hoping to introduce you to—"

"Alexandria," he said, slowly, as if each syllable had to be pronounced. To her horror, she blushed.

Sister Stella looked at her in surprise. "Are you already acquainted?"

When Alex said nothing, Ari snapped his book closed, smiling easily. "Yes. We met at Harvard."

"Ah, I see. In that case, I will save my introductions. Alexandria here was hoping for a tour of the New Academy. Her mother had once been a student here. I thought perhaps you would be willing to show her around as our most knowledgeable student and now, beloved professor."

Ari checked his watch, running a hand haphazardly through his hair which was much more tame today, combed and styled into curls that fell around the nape of his neck. Somehow, though, he managed to look as roughly hewn as yesterday, even in his pressed button-down.

"It's fine," Alex said sharply, wishing she hadn't agreed to anything. "A tour isn't necessary."

"Of course it is," Ari said, barely glancing at Alex. "Follow me, please. Thank you, Sister."

"Thank you, Ari," Sister Stella said with an intimate smile. They have clearly known each other for some time. "I will see both of you at lunch."

Alex watched her walk slowly back towards the church, her heart sinking with dread. She turned towards Ari, who was standing a few feet away and looking at her with a peculiar expression. It irritated her.

"You go to Harvard?" Alex asked doubtfully.

Ari nodded, then started walking along the corridor which wrapped around the courtyard. He was taller than Alex, though not as tall as Warren, and walked with strong, slow strides.

She fell into step beside him. "Why didn't you tell me?"

"Yesterday?" He shrugged. "Because I dropped out a year ago."

"So you don't go to Harvard?" she asked exasperatedly.

"Not anymore. I was doing my PhD there, but decided to quit." He gave her a quick look as they circled the courtyard. "Please keep this between us. I would lose my job here if Sister found out. She only thinks I'm taking a year off."

"Why did you drop out?"

He frowned. "Because I wanted to."

Alex crossed her arms but asked no more questions. Why was he so rude?

She studied the scene through the archways they slowly passed by. Students milled about the fruit trees, some stretched out on the grass studying, some were in groups, talking and laughing freely. There were other classes of students with professors leading them at a leisurely pace around the corridor and across the courtyard, lecturing on different subjects.

"The New Academy considers the open air its classroom. That's how the Ancient Greeks did it anyway." Ari added that last statement with a tinge of sarcasm.

Alex wondered why he sounded critical since he had chosen to study that culture so specifically. *Not anymore,* she reminded herself.

She pointed to the two twin buildings flanking the courtyard. "Those must be the dormitories."

He raised a brow. "Maybe a tour isn't necessary." But he pointed to the building on the right wing. "That's the girls' dormitory. This is the boys' dormitory. Before the New Academy was a school, these dormitories were for the sisters and brothers who were a part of the church. Soon they began instruction for boys interested in joining the clergy, and then girls a few years later who wished to join the sisterhood. For a time students had the choice at graduation to join the church or use the education to pursue further studies either at the New Academy or elsewhere." He looked at Alex curiously. "Your mother probably attended the school when it was still common to join the church after high school. The New Academy only became an official college very recently."

Alex wondered if her mother had planned to become a sister, but the thought was ridiculous. Her mother was a true student of Classics. No matter the convention of the time or her family, she would have pursued an education over everything.

Everything except her, Alex corrected regretfully.

"So when you attended was it not a college yet?" Alex asked as they walked around the colonnade towards the church.

Ari avoided her searching look, walking slightly ahead of her. "I was one of the last class years that they admitted to the upper school, as we called it before it became a college. Basically, I took ninth to twelfth grade here, plus two years of upper school which would complete a program equivalent to a college degree in Classics. College courses in Classical studies technically began in eleventh grade and counted towards your degree. I graduated and was accepted into the Classics graduate program at Harvard. Then you know the rest."

"You were teaching Greek today, right?" she asked, remembering the way he had recited the text, his heavy-lidded eyes focused on the book, his voice almost unfamiliar around the strange syllables. "Whatever you were reading sounded dark. Something about everyone being dead."

"Yes. *Antigone.*"

"What is it about?"

"Exactly what you said." He looked amused. "Everyone being dead."

"And what is it really about?"

Ari spoke with a slight edge. "A spoiled rich girl who doesn't get her way so she throws a fit and rebels against her uncle and when there are actual consequences for her actions she kills herself."

Alex rolled her eyes, but she felt the sting of an insult in his words. "It doesn't seem like you enjoy Classics that much. Why do you teach it?"

His face shuttered and Alex knew she had hit the mark. She felt vindicated, as if finding his vulnerability made up for how he had exposed hers.

"You said your mother grew up here, right?" he asked, his voice tense.

"Yes?"

"Well, I did too. And if there's one thing I've learned is that it's impossible to leave."

"My mother left," Alex protested, but she recalled her mother's second to last entry. *I am to leave the school. Final exams considered unnecessary.*

"If she left, then why are you here?"

Alex said nothing, her throat tightening at how little she knew.

"You are very strange, Alexandria." He stared at her in unveiled disturbance. "Who are you?"

"I already told you, I'm—"

"No." He took a small step closer, questioning. "Who is your mother?"

Alex stood rooted to the spot, terrified of his sharp, searching gaze and what his words implied. But the answer came easily to her lips. She had asked herself that same question again and again for her whole life.

"I don't know."

20

Ari ended the tour shortly afterward, claiming he had to finish grading some papers before lunch, which would begin soon. Alex had the sense that he didn't like her very much.

"Besides," Ari had added before walking away. "You've already seen the library."

She watched him walk into the boys' dormitory, disappearing up the stairs. With nothing else to do before lunch, Alex wandered back across the courtyard. She glanced at the opening doors of the library as a student walked out carrying a stack of books in his arms. Perhaps a second look around couldn't hurt.

Alex pushed open the heavy doors and walked inside.

Unlike the last time she had been in here, the sun shone through the stained glass, lighting the floors in a colorful glow. Dust motes floated in between bookcases, where students crouched over the desks in concentration or browsed the shelves for books.

Alex glanced at random titles as she strolled down the rows. *Myths and Gods. Ancient Greek Sculpture. Reading the Odyssey. An Introduction to Latin Epigraphy.*

She paused, catching the title of a small book hidden at the end of the row.

Helen of Troy.

The book was hardly worn, the red cover illuminated with gold. She gingerly opened the book, which crackled as the spine creased, and read the title page.

Helen of Troy, or *The Face that Launched a Thousand Ships.*

The first page was a drawing of ships at sea, the waves cresting against the hulls. Alex tried to imagine a thousand ships sailing to war for a woman who had left her family for another man. Then she remembered what her father had said. *Your mother was the most beautiful woman on earth.*

Then why had he stopped looking? Why had he answered her leaving with a half-hearted search, accepting her disappearance or death as if they were even close to being the same thing? *Eventually they told me to stop looking, that she didn't want to be found.*

But her mother had eloped because she was pregnant, not necessarily because she loved him. Could it truly be that her father was the man she had left with and not the man she left *for?* Was it really some boy named Alexandros that she had truly loved, before life forced her to make the first impossible decision?

Helen never asked for a thousand ships to save her. Maybe, like her mother, she had not wanted to be found. Maybe she simply wished to disappear from a life she never wanted, and here was Alex, trying to save her. For what? To bring her back?

For the first time, Alex doubted whether she should even try.

"Alexandria."

She looked up, nearly dropping the book.

Ari watched her from the aisle, leaning against the bookcase. "Thought you might be here. It's time for lunch."

Alex hurriedly placed the book back on the shelf. She felt guilty, as though she were spying instead of merely browsing the shelves. She followed Ari in silence across the courtyard, cutting through the grass instead of taking the long way around.

Breakfast, lunch, and dinner at the New Academy were served in the basement of the Lighthouse Church, a surprisingly spacious room with several long dining halls running its length, with the kitchens next door. The room was crammed with students, their boisterous conversations echoing against the wall and their lunch plates piled with food from the buffet next door.

She ignored the many curious eyes turned her way as Ari led them in between rows to a table squashed in the middle of the room, balancing their heavily laden plates above the students' heads. Sister Stella sat there with several other faculty members, smiling and gesturing to an open space in front of her, barely wide enough for two people.

Alex ignored how her arm pressed up against Ari's as they sat down, their legs brushing. She tried to inch away without touching the person next to her, but failed. Ari hardly noticed her struggle, greeting Sister Stella as if he did this every day, which Alex realized he did.

"Professor Melamed," Sister Stella said in her delicate voice. Alex wondered again where her lilting accent was from and thought it to be Irish. "I trust the tour went well?"

"Yes," Ari said, more pleasantly than he had said anything to Alex. "Though I suppose Alexandria should answer that."

Sister Stella turned her gaze to Alex, who forced a smile. "I loved it."

"Oh good! You know, you are so much like your mother," Sister Stella said, before her smile faltered, glancing at Ari. "But perhaps we should speak about that when we are in private."

"No, please," Alex said quickly, not wishing to miss anything Sister Stella might remember about her mother just because they were with company. "I don't mind talking about it."

"Very well," she said, inclining her head. "Might you explain to me what happened to her? You say she left when you were ten years old and you do not know where she went?"

Alex felt Ari's keen eyes on her and her ears burned. It sounded stupid when Sister Stella put it that way. "Yes. She just...disappeared."

"Strange," Sister Stella said, shaking her head, her blue eyes bright with sadness. "Very strange."

"How is that possible?" Ari asked in barely hidden disbelief. "People don't just disappear."

She felt a stab of guilt at these words. Less than a week ago Alex had left her entire life behind without a warning, disappearing like her mother, and giving her family and friends no means of contacting her. Ari stared at her curiously like he could read the guilt on her face.

"My mother...she loved her life here. I thought she might have come back here actually. She talked so much about it in her diary. About this place, the school, and her life before she had to leave."

Sister Stella glanced at her sharply. "Before she *had* to leave?"

Alex nearly winced. She was sure her mother had never mentioned her untimely pregnancy, nor that she had eloped. But it was much too late to keep that a secret any longer. "She was pregnant with me, so she and my father eloped. My father...They must have decided that her education was no longer necessary, given the circumstances."

"I see," Sister Stella said slowly, her hands folded in front of her. "I had always assumed she no longer wished to study Classics. It was a dying field even then. Your mother...she was talented, unlike any pupil I had ever met, perhaps save Mr. Melamed here. She had a gift, a passion that could bring worlds to life. I sincerely wish you had more time with her."

"Then you have not heard from her since she left the New Academy?"

Sister Stella sighed. "Unfortunately, the day she told me she was leaving was the last day I saw her. I had hoped she would find happiness in her new life."

She always said this was her new life now.

For a moment, they were all silent.

At last, Sister Stella asked warily, "I suppose you still wish to discover where your mother is?"

Alex nodded. "I thought she would come back to the New Academy. That's why I left. I mean, that's why I came here."

"Alexandria, my dear," Sister Stella said hesitantly. "Ten years is a very long time. There is a chance..."

"With all due respect, Sister," Alex interrupted, "I need to know what happened to her. No matter what."

There was a flicker of surprise in Sister Stella's eyes before she inclined her head. "Then I pray you shall find the answers you seek."

21

After lunch, Ari excused himself, as he had to prepare for his next class. But before he left Alex in the courtyard, he took a step closer to her, and Alex ignored the sudden racing of her heart.

"Meet me in front of the library at nine o'clock tonight. I have something I want to show you." He almost stepped away, then added, "Make sure no one sees you."

Alex was confused as she watched him walk away. She did not know how she would pass the time until then, and wandered about the courtyard, ignoring the critical gazes from nearby students. She almost decided to sit down when Sister Stella approached her and asked if she would like to take a look at her mother's old files.

She accepted, and together they walked back into her office, where a small stack of old manila folders was already placed on her desk. Sister Stella handed her the first file wordlessly, slipping on a thin wiry pair of glasses to flip through the next file.

Alex opened the folder. The first paper contained a short list of personal information—name, birth date, birth city, guardians—typed beside a small old-fashioned photograph of a beautiful young girl who could be no older than sixteen.

"She was so young," Alex whispered, brushing a fingertip along the unfamiliar features, the long brown hair, the dark round eyes, the small, unconscious smile. So this was the girl writing all those words in that diary. It was hard to imagine the youthful face in the photo could be her mother, the same woman who left her only daughter without an explanation, never to be heard from or seen since.

"Ah yes, she never did retake her school photo," Sister Stella said. "We didn't have enough money to print yearbooks, so we usually only updated profiles every few years or so."

"Did you ever meet her parents?" Alex asked, closing the file which had no more information save the classes she had enrolled in and the overall grade for each year, all of which were A's.

Sister Stella handed her another file. "Yes, they always attended Mass every Sunday until they died." She paused. "They wished Elena would become a sister. That is why they enrolled her in the school. I daresay they were...disappointed when Elena chose a different path. But they were very devastated when she left."

"I see." She opened the next file and stared at what she saw written there. At the center of the blank page was typed *Senior Thesis: The Prince of Thieves*. "This was her thesis?"

"Yes," Sister Stella said with a sigh. "Or the rough draft, at least. It was the final dissertation required of all students in their last year of upper school here. She never finished it, but I kept it all the same. Her work was, after all, very inspired."

"Can I keep this?" she asked, clutching the folder.

"Of course," Sister Stella said. "That is why I am showing it to you. I have already made copies of all this for my records." She handed over the last folder, which was almost twice the size of the other two folders combined. "And this was some of her other classwork. Essays, quizzes, exams, and the like. I thought you might wish to look through it."

Alex grabbed the folder. She flipped at random through the pages and glimpsed a quiz on Ancient Greek grammar that looked very complicated and a short answer exam about Roman history, before carefully closing the file. Sister Stella was looking at her with a sad smile.

"I must say, I was surprised to hear that you had not pursued Classics," Sister Stella said wistfully. "I suppose a part of me was hoping I could recruit you to the New Academy."

"I wish I had too," Alex said, blinking furiously. She did not want to cry.

"Well, if you ever change your mind, we always conduct a summer intensive in Ancient Greek, taught, of course, by our very own Mr. Melamed."

Alex recalled Ari's soft-spoken words to her after lunch and nearly blushed. "Thank you."

Sister Stella led her out to the church, where Alex said goodbye and headed back to her motel room. She needed to look over the files in private.

Once she was situated on her bed with the folders in front of her, Alex began reading her mother's thesis. She couldn't believe the title was the same one scribbled on the back of that scrap of paper and hoped to find another clue as to who exactly was the Prince of Thieves. But after reading the first few pages, Alex was quickly disappointed.

It turned out that the Prince of Thieves was, indeed, Hermes, but her thesis was merely on the Homeric Hymn to Hermes, which she closely analyzed with respect to its mythological references. For instance, she was very concerned with the symbolic importance of the tortoiseshell he used to make a seven-stringed lyre. She argued that the middle string of the lyre, represented by the muse Mese, linked the god Hermes to song and the oracular significance of Delphi, where she was worshiped alongside Apollo.

Elena had also found the connection between travelers, messengers, and thieves and the middle string of the lyre to be that they all involved a kind of transition, a theoretical bridge, one concerning place, the other song. She related it to Hermes' ability to cross into Hades, as he did when returning Demeter's daughter, Persephone, from the Underworld back to her mother. Therefore, Hermes and his seven-stringed lyre symbolized the transitory power of song, which, she claimed, could metaphorically—or even physically—transport the singer or poet to a divine state where he could access the power of the gods themselves, so potent it could even hold back the gates of Death.

When she finished reading, Alex understood why Sister Stella had called it *inspired*. There was something about the way Elena wrote, the way she argued, as if it were not her opinion but reality, and she was merely revealing the truth.

The last file was the least interesting since the papers were mainly quizzes on grammar and vocabulary, exams on 'sight passages' of Latin and Ancient Greek, and shorter essays on specific works, history, or research topics. Her grades were all very high and exemplary, and it was clear the professors admired her work. Alex wondered if given the choice, her mother would have gone on to take her PhD, perhaps even at Harvard. Would she have done so if she hadn't gotten pregnant with Alex?

Soon the sun began to set and Alex returned to the church. Sister Stella had invited her to dinner as well, which she was grateful for because her funds were already very depleted from the hotels and gas on the trip. Ari wasn't there, however, and she instead spoke to the other professors, who were all older than Ari but not old enough to remember her mother.

Once dinner finished, Alex said her goodbyes and promised to visit tomorrow, if only to explore the grounds of the school beyond the buildings. It was clear Sister Stella wished to convince her to join the New Academy, but the thought of giving up Harvard and law school afterward was ridiculous. Even though she skipped her exams, she was sure her father could make a call or two and have her enrolled again. She could make up for the exams with a summer course or repeated semester, and her life would be placed on the right track again and chug along without looking back.

The thought sat in her stomach uneasily as she returned to her motel to wait for nine o'clock to come around. She reread her mother's diary just to give herself something to do, but her mind kept drifting to Ari and the secrecy of their meeting. What was he going to show her? She half-wondered if he was going to make a move on her and almost laughed aloud, though her heart beat clumsily at the thought. Ari's dislike for her was clear, and she had the feeling whatever he was going to show her tonight had more to do with her mother than with herself.

At last, the motel clock ticked to fifteen minutes till nine. She figured it would be better to give herself plenty of time to watch her back and enter the New Academy without catching anyone's attention.

The streets were quiet and dark, save for one large street lamp at the corner of the church. Some faint music could be heard from down one of the streets, and happy shouts of people. Alex walked around the church and found the side gate into the courtyard that she had glimpsed earlier.

As she approached, she saw a small silver lock below the handle. The gate was locked. She would have to try to sneak through the church. Alex grasped the lock in frustration and was about to try and shake the gate open when the door swung inside. The lock had only been hooked to the gate as a precaution. She shook her head ruefully before walking into the courtyard.

Alex glanced around in case teachers were patrolling at night, but the colonnade was empty. She tiptoed down the hall, hoping the roof and Roman-style columns would provide cover from any wandering eyes in the windows above.

Finally, she approached the library door. This time the heavy wooden door was certainly locked, the gold metal of the lock gleaming in the weak moonlight. She heard footsteps and whirled around, her heart in her throat, but it was just Ari stepping out of the shadows in the corner.

"How long have you been there?" Alex whispered.

Ari quelled her with a look. "Long enough."

He slipped a small key out of his pocket and expertly unlocked the door with nimble fingers as if he did this all the time. Alex recalled the first time they had met and supposed he did. Ari led them down the main aisle, passing the rows and rows of books.

"Where are we going, by the way?" Alex asked. They had continued walking down the main aisle and were nearing the end of the building, where the bookcases crowded into the last available space.

Ari raised a brow. "To the library."

"Is this not the library?"

He smirked, and she fought against a wave of annoyance at his aloofness. "This is the *new* library that was built fifty years ago. Not many know this, but it was actually built on top of the old library, which was moved to a floor below."

As he said it, they stopped in front of an old, wooden door that had several cracks running through it. At first glance, she had thought it was a broom closet. Then Ari procured a thick iron key and fitted it into the lock on the handle. The door gave way and they walked down a musty staircase.

"Wait," Alex said, pausing at the first step. "Why are you showing me this?"

Ari glanced back at her in surprise and shrugged. "I thought you would like to see it, considering your mother went here." Then he continued down the stairs. Alex hesitated, before following after him. The staircase led them to a dark hall with a low ceiling. Ari shined a small flashlight, walking carefully down the hall until they entered a spacious room with books lining the entire perimeter from floor to ceiling. Alex looked around in awe.

"Is this the archive collection?" Alex asked, almost whispering.

Ari smirked again, but this time Alex could not look away. "Follow me."

He walked to a small door on the left and pushed it open. On the other side was a smaller room, with piles and piles of old scrolls lining the walls, and a wooden pedestal encased with glass in the center. They stood in front of the pedestal. She peered inside, but it was empty.

"They never put anything in there," Ari said, his voice still quiet. It was clear despite his carelessness that he had a deep reverence for this place. "Look at this."

He showed her a small statue set inside one of the bookshelves. It looked like a youthful monk sitting cross-legged on the floor, a book opened in front of him. Alex noticed the letter E carved into the front of the cassock and wondered where she had seen it before.

"It's called the Squatting Scribe. It's as old as this library."

The name instantly rang a bell. Alex remembered having read it in her mother's diary. *The Squatting Scribe.* But what had her mother written about it? She could not remember, but it could not be a coincidence. "Do you think my mother might have had access to this part of the library?"

Ari shook his head. "No. Only the brothers and sisters have the key. They guard this library religiously."

"Then why do you have one?"

"I don't."

"What?"

He grinned. "I've been sneaking into this library since I was twelve. I made this key myself."

Alex did not understand, but before she could reply, they heard voices coming from down the hall. For the first time, Ari looked alarmed, turning off his light and putting a finger up to his lips. Her heart beat fast in her chest. They scooted behind the door, which was still wide open. She hoped whoever they were would not enter the room, otherwise they would surely get caught.

The voices grew louder. They were nearing the door. Alex realized one of them was Sister Stella. "...her daughter, Alexandria. Elena was to take my place. She married before graduating."

"Regardless, you must keep an eye on her," said another voice, male, raspy and ancient.

Ari's eyes flicked over to Alex, who flushed but did not move a muscle. The footsteps came closer until they must have been hovering on the other side of the wall. She saw a faint gleam of light from under the door.

"Very well," Sister Stella said. "Only, I would hope, being her daughter and all..."

"She is not Elena."

Sister Stella sighed. "No, I suppose not. Oh! This door should be closed. I am certain I closed it earlier."

Alex held her breath, keeping her eyes trained on the door. Suddenly an unfamiliar, gnarled hand grabbed the edge of the door and pulled with surprising strength, shutting them inside with a bang, dust lifting from the rattled bookshelves.

"Thank you, Brother," Sister Stella said primly. "And while you are here, may I show you something which I think might interest you? It is derived from the Orphic Mysteries, but quite novel in idea."

The Brother seemed to hesitate, then relented. "I suppose I can be gone a little while longer. Please, Sister, lead the way."

Their footsteps receded down the hall in the opposite direction they came, and their murmuring voices faded. Alex let out a long sigh of relief, though she was still shocked by what they had just overheard.

"Quick," Ari said. He opened the door and without lingering, they retraced their steps back upstairs to the new library.

22

"Where are you going?" Alex asked in a whisper, as they were still in the library. Ari looked back at her but said nothing. She thought he almost looked concerned.

Ari only stopped walking when they exited the library. He gave her that look again, which was not concern, she realized with annoyance, but puzzlement.

"What?" she asked.

He looked away. "Nothing."

"Just say it." They had passed the time for pleasantries a long time ago. When he said nothing and looked out at the courtyard pensively, she spoke again. "You're thinking about what they said. About my mother. And me."

Ari reluctantly turned to her, his gaze hard. "Yes, I am."

"And?"

"I don't understand. That's all." He began to walk away, and Alex called after him, wondering how he could possibly abandon her now. He stopped and raised a brow. "Don't you want to find out?"

Alex merely stared at him, then hurried to catch up as he headed inside the church and down the hall to Sister Stella's office. There were no lights turned on, and it appeared everyone had gone to sleep for the night.

"This is a bad idea," Alex whispered, glancing around nervously.

"Relax," Ari muttered, opening the door to Sister Stella's office gently. "She's still in the old library."

"Sister Stella already gave me all of my mother's files."

Ari gave her a strange look. "Do you really believe that?"

Alex was silent. She had been so sure she could trust the gentle-eyed Sister Stella, but now she didn't know what to believe. *Regardless, you must keep an eye on her.*

"You said your mother grew up here, right?" Ari asked. Alex nodded. "When did she begin studying here?"

"According to Sister Stella, since she was fourteen."

Ari was rifling through the drawers at the desk, then opened the file cabinets one by one. "Well, she certainly kept an eye on it. Here. Elena de la Fuente." He slid out the files and flipped through them, before pausing at the last and glancing up at her critically. "Did you know she conducted independent research in her last year under the supervision of Sister Stella?"

"No," Alex said, her heart thundering. "I didn't see that file."

He flipped through the pages with a frown. "Interesting. This is some obscure stuff she was studying. Not found in your everyday library or taught in the main curriculum. Your mother seems to have had access to the old library for her research." Then he looked at her keenly. "Your mother was no ordinary student if she had access to the old library."

"Even if that were true," Alex said, "it doesn't explain why Sister Stella and that man were talking about me."

"No, it doesn't," Ari murmured. He handed her the file and she took it shakily. "Unless, of course, it does."

"What do you mean?"

"I told you they guard the old library religiously. If your mother had the key, maybe they are worried you have it too." He paused. "Remember what Sister Stella said? *Elena was to take my place.* I thought your mother was in school to study Classics, not to be a sister."

"She was. that her parents were disappointed she didn't go into the church."

Alex glanced down at the file and flipped through the pages. She realized they were lesson plans on certain subjects and reports written by her mother, all researched in the archive collections on arcane topics that had no meaning to Alex. Perhaps all those ramblings in her diary about her projects were about this independent research. But that still didn't explain why Sister Stella was told to keep an eye on her.

"I just don't understand," Alex whispered. "What could be so special about the old library that they would have to guard me from it? And what does it have to do with my mother?"

Ari shook his head, taking the file back from her and sliding it inside the cabinet. "I don't know. But I do know there's more to this than some independent research project. Sister Stella is hiding something, and we have to figure out what."

"We?"

For the first time, Ari looked embarrassed, but he shrugged it off. "Only if you want my help."

Alex felt annoyed and said nothing. She only wanted him to help if *he* wanted to help, not the other way around. But she also knew he would be the only one who could help her.

"You would need to go back to the old library," Ari said, reluctantly, as if admitting he were interested in helping was painful. "That's where you'll find your answers."

"That's impossible," Alex said sharply. "If Sister Stella was told to keep an eye on me, how on earth would I be able to hang around the New Academy without making her suspicious? Unless I was a student, which I'm not..."

She trailed off when a ghost of a smile hovered over Ari's mouth. "Eureka."

23

Breakfast was served continental-style, with pastries, toast, bagels, and cereal. The basement of the church was not as crowded as lunch or dinner, with very few students milling about alone and in pairs, eating quickly or even taking their breakfast to go.

"Classes start in an hour," Ari explained as they took a seat at the faculty table.

Sister Stella only appeared fifteen minutes later, as Alex was still eating her croissant, which she had smothered with the packaged butter and jam. Ari had a finished cup of black coffee in front of him and said he had already eaten earlier.

"Then what are you doing here?" Alex asked in a whisper as Sister Stella approached their chair.

"You'll see," Ari said under his breath, just before smiling and greeting Sister Stella good morning. "How are you today, Sister?"

"I am well, thank you, Professor Melamed." Her gaze fell on Alex. "Have you had any progress in your search, my dear?"

Alex shook her head, unable to speak.

"Ah, well, if nothing else I am glad we were able to meet, however brief. Though I had hoped, as Elena had, that you would have taken to the Classics..."

Before Alex could answer, Ari leaned forward with a half-smile. "But she has."

She could hardly believe what she was hearing. "What? No—"

"She's just being modest," Ari said smoothly, and Alex stopped protesting when she felt Ari's leg press firmly against hers. "She has studied Latin and some Greek before college. Her father insisted on Economics as a major, so she doesn't consider herself a Classics student anymore."

It was the perfect thing to say. Sister Stella lit up in triumph. "Oh, why didn't you say so before? I knew you were like Elena. I could sense it the moment I saw you!"

"Maybe she could take my Greek summer course here," Ari suggested casually, finally glancing at Alex, a knowing look teeming in his dark eyes, and she glowed hot inside like a match lit in the dark. "Just to brush up on grammar and vocabulary."

Sister Stella turned to her fiercely, and Alex nearly shivered under those blue eyes, remembering the conversation they had overheard.

"...her daughter, Alexandria. Elena was to take my place. She married before graduating."

"Regardless, you must keep an eye on her."

"Yes, you must, Alexandria!" Sister Stella said energetically, though the reason for this enthusiasm was dubious to Alex. As if sensing her hesitancy, Sister Stella recovered herself and added, "Just for the summer, of course. I could hardly expect you to neglect your studies at Harvard."

Alex smiled forcibly, while the guilt of doing exactly that welled inside of her like a bucket collecting rain, each drop bringing her closer to overflowing. But she had questions that needed answering, a destiny to discover, and that was her mother's.

"It would only be six weeks and only two other students would be taking it," Ari added, and Alex heard the silent suggestion. He was thinking about her mother. This was the only way she could stay at the New Academy without suspicion and have access to the old library.

It was the perfect plan. Too perfect. But what other option did she have?

"I would love to," Alex said.

Sister Stella clapped her hands together. "Then you must move into the dorms immediately."

After breakfast, Alex returned to the motel to pack up her things. Ari had told her before that the summer course was only held as a practicality for those who lived in the area but preferred to remain at the New Academy instead of living at home. Given how few actually did so, there was no cost for either the course or lodging, just a small participatory fee that would cover the books. It would start officially next Monday, but Ari met with the students often when not teaching his classes, and he wanted to introduce her to them tomorrow.

Alex knew that he only wanted to look through her mother's belongings as soon as possible, which she had mentioned to him after breakfast. A part of her resented the interest Ari had in her mother, as if Alex was only interesting to him insofar as she was the keeper of her mother's memories. Then she remembered that molten look he gave her at dinner and pushed those thoughts away.

She sat on her bed, holding her mother's diary in her hands. She carefully turned the pages, if only to find some calm and remember what she was doing this all for. Suddenly she remembered the Squatting Scribe in the old library, the way the name had struck her as familiar. Where had her mother written about that? She flipped through the pages, skimming the words.

Eventually, she found it near the end of the diary, a sentence that had been entirely meaningless to her—until now. Alex stared at the words, written a day before the entry about the Prince of Thieves. Her heart beat fast as the fragments of her mother's life seemed to be slowly woven together by an invisible thread, the thread of Fate.

September 8th. The Squatting Scribe is a door.

24

Sister Stella showed Alex to her dorm once she returned. She parked her car in the dirt lot beside the church, knowing she would probably have no need of it for some time.

Her room was situated on the second floor of the girls' dormitory, with a small barred window that overlooked the courtyard. Alex thought she could just make out Ari's dark curls disappearing past an archway.

"I hope you will find your accommodations suitable," Sister Stella said, and Alex looked up, ignoring her knowing smile.

"Oh yes, thank you," she said, looking around the small dorm room. "It's perfect."

It was perfect. Though the room was smaller even than her motel room, the glossy wood floors, white walls, small desk, clean bed sheets, and a large dresser for clothes all touched her as charming. Her mother must have grown up in a similar room.

"Then I shall leave you to make yourself at home," Sister Stella said, but she lingered. "If you need anything, please do not hesitate to find me. I am always willing to help."

Alex nodded, and Sister Stella left quietly, letting her unpack in peace.

Not a minute of silence passed before she heard a knock on the still-open door and looked up. A girl dressed in the forest green and khaki uniform of the New Academy stood in the doorframe, half obscured in the darkness of the hallway, a fist poised to knock. She smiled pleasantly.

"Hello," the girl said, in a voice deep and rich in tone for her short stature. "I noticed you were moving in. Are you here for the summer course?"

"Yes," Alex said, her stomach twisting uncomfortably. It was not the first student she had seen in the dormitories, but most were packing up to leave, and this girl was the only one who had approached her. "With Ar—Professor Melamed."

The girl brightened, a laugh playing on her lips. "Ari, yes. Ancient Greek. I thought it was only gonna be me and Zeb, so this is great news."

"I signed up last minute. I don't go here."

Surprise etched on her face, then melted away. "Oh! Where do you go?"

Alex hesitated. "Harvard."

"Wow, why are you here then? Harvard has one of the best Classics programs in the world!"

She shrugged, wanting to change the subject. "I'm Alexandria, by the way."

"Penélope," the girl said, slightly confused at the evasion but taking it in stride. She stepped inside with her hand stretched forward, and Alex shook it.

Now that Penélope stood in the light of her room, Alexandria could see that she was even shorter than she had thought, with long dark hair down to her waist, tan skin, and brown eyes. Alex thought distantly that she looked like her mother had in that photo, but slightly older. Penélope held herself upright with an ease and confidence that intimidated Alex as much as it intrigued her.

"So, have you ever been to the New Academy before?" Penélope asked.

"No," Alex said, then catching Penélope's warm gaze, "but my mother went here. She grew up in Tierra del Sol."

When Alex did not provide more of an explanation, Penélope nodded, though she had the same slightly curious look that Ari had when she had told him the same thing. "Me too. And you...?"

"New York. Actually, Connecticut now."

A slow comprehension passed over her face before Penélope smiled brilliantly. "Well, if you ever want a tour of Tierra del Sol, I would be happy to be your guide, though I can't promise it will be anything as interesting as New York. My room is across the hall, five doors down."

"Thank you," she tried to say warmly, but failed, her father's curtness escaping her tongue.

Penélope sensed her reserve and looked behind at the door, as if contemplating whether to leave or not. She looked at Alex, still holding the handle of her suitcase. “I’ll let you unpack, but maybe we could go together to see Ari in an hour? Zeb and I like to annoy him when he’s grading papers. It’s really fun.”

Alex could not resist a smile at that amusing image. “I’d like that.”

25

Penélope returned to her room an hour later. Alex had unpacked, folding her clothes and gently placing them in the dresser. She could barely believe she was here, that this dorm room was hers, that she was enrolled in a summer course in a language she did not know.

But her mother had lived here and studied that language, and that was all that mattered.

Penélope led her across the courtyard to the library, where Ari was indeed bent over his desk, a red pen hovering over a stack of papers. A hooded blond boy was sitting up on the ledge of a stained-glass window beside Ari, his shoes on the desk. He was clearly teasing Ari, jostling his shoulder with his foot, but he stopped when he saw Penélope and Alex walking towards them.

Ari smirked when he saw Alex walking alongside Penélope. "Well look what we have here."

The other boy frowned, looking at Alex in irritation, as if she had interrupted an important conversation. He had cold blue eyes, a paler blue than Warren's, with ghostly white skin and sharp features, his cheekbones, jaw, and pale brows drawn harshly on his face.

"Hey guys," Penélope said. She gestured to the blond boy. "That's Zeb. This is Alexandria. She's taking the summer course with us."

Zeb eyed her skeptically. "Really?"

"Yes. She goes to Harvard but her mom grew up here," Penélope explained as she pulled up two nearby stools, gesturing for Alexandria to sit. She did, ignoring Zeb's icy, judging gaze on her.

"Harvard," Zeb repeated, with barely hidden scorn. "And you study

Classics?"

"Yes," Alex said defiantly. She saw Ari glance at her in surprise, then amusement, which he quickly hid, lowering his eyes to the papers on his desk. "Well, I used to. A little. My mom studied Classics. I'm majoring in Economics."

"Right," Zeb said, his voice flat. His attention returned to Ari, and Alex felt slighted. What was his problem? "Are you done grading those yet? I need help studying for my final. It's in two days."

Ari continued grading, his pen flicking checks down the page in front of him. "That's a lie," he drawled without looking up. "You don't want my help, you want the answers."

"He's our professor this year for Greek," Penélope told Alex, and Zeb cut Penélope a sharp glance which she did not notice or pretended not to. "We have our final soon and he refuses to give us the answers. Isn't that so rude?"

But her look was fond as she settled it on Ari. He set down his pen as if sensing her eyes on him, before he leaned back and stretched his arms with a yawn mid-smile, his shirt tightening around his biceps. Alex caught Zeb staring under lidded eyes, before looking away, frowning.

"It's fair, that's what that is," Ari said, settling once more in his chair. "And I can't risk losing my job, especially not for you two."

"You've become such a downer ever since you became a professor," Penélope complained.

"You knew him before this?" Alex asked, then remembered that they had all probably grown up together in this town. She felt like an intruder, and not just because of Zeb's attitude. But Penélope's face lit up.

"Oh yes," she said, smirking. "I'm a senior, so I knew him when he was still a student here. And I've known Zeb since we were babies, isn't that right?"

"Unfortunately," Zeb muttered, but he gave her a half-smirk. *"Es una niña rica, ¿no?"*

Alex was momentarily confused, until Penélope shot him a dark glance, and replied, *"Pórtate bien."*

"Enough," Ari said, rolling his eyes. He clearly understood them. Alex felt her cheeks grow hot from the exchange which was obviously about her. They thought she did not understand them, but instead of feeling defensive, she only felt ashamed, because Zeb was right. She didn't belong here. "I am going to give Alexandria her placement test to see where she's at and she doesn't need you two distracting her. Don't you guys have to study for that exam anyway?"

Penélope glared at Zeb, who shrugged, having probably been on the receiving end of many such looks. "Yes, unfortunately. Meet me in the courtyard, *Pepa*."

Without looking at any of them, he hopped off the table and left, slinging his backpack carelessly over his shoulder.

"Zeb is just moody," Penélope said once he was out of sight.

While that might be true, Alex doubted that was the only reason for his coldness towards her. But Penélope did not voice it, so Alex would not bring it up.

"Do you want to go to lunch in an hour or so after your test?" Penélope asked brightly. She seemed determined to keep the atmosphere light and warm, for which Alex was grateful. Other than Sister Stella, who had her own dubious reasons, Penélope was the only person who had truly attempted to make her feel at home.

"Yes, that would be great," Alex said with a genuine warmth of affection. Then Penélope said goodbye, following Zeb out of the library, leaving Alex alone with Ari.

"So...about that placement test," Alex began.

Ari grinned. "Doesn't exist. Besides, we both know how you would score."

"Hey! I might know more than you think."

"Oh yeah? What are the first declension endings?"

"The first *what* endings?"

"See?"

Alex was silent, a small smile on her face which she forced away. She knew they were flirting. As soon as she admitted it, the guilt welled up in her throat, and she crossed her arms as if that would fend her off from the fact that she liked it.

Ari sensed her retreat and changed the subject. "So, what do you think?"

"What?"

"About Penélope and Zeb."

"Penélope is very nice," Alex said, then stopped. Ari laughed, so she continued. "And Zeb is...interesting."

"Zeb's a good kid. He only acts rudely to scare people."

"Well, it's working," Alex joked. "How old is he?"

"Nineteen, I think." Ari scratched at the stubble on his jaw, making him seem older just then. "He's a sophomore in college."

"Same as me," Alex said, almost like a challenge.

Ari studied her and then nodded. "He'll grow on you," he said and left it at that.

A silence ensued, which Alex wondered how to breach. Should she bring up her mother? The Prince of Thieves? That was what she was there for, after all—not to study Ancient Greek. A part of her did not want to share those objects, feeling oddly possessive over them, but she knew it was the only way to find her mother.

"I have my mother's things," Alex said hesitantly. She had brought them in her backpack, hoping to have some alone time with Ari to show them to him.

Ari lifted a brow and said nothing, but he leaned forward just an inch more, an intent look on his face that Alex shied away from. She took out her mother's things one by one—the diary, the Greek copy of the *Iliad,* and the silver dagger, and laid them out on the table. Then she told Ari everything she knew besides the strange incidents with the bird.

During her explanation of how she found them, the research involved, and the meeting with Professor Ezra—whom Ari said must have been a new hire as he had never met him before—Ari had stood up and began pacing the small space between shelves. Now he sat on top of the desk, fingers drumming against the edge.

Alex sat nervously waiting for his reply, glancing repeatedly at Ari's pensive frown.

Ari picked up the *Iliad.* The diary and the dagger lay on the desk beside him. He turned over the book in his hands, leafing delicately through the pages, his eyes lowered as he read lines at random. She could not help but notice how pretty his hands were, with long, deft fingers and well-kept, oval nails. "Strange. It's handwritten."

"Professor Ezra said the same thing."

"Well, it's not as strange as this," he said, picking up the slip of paper Alex had shown him, her mother's scrawled *The Prince of Thieves* filtering through the handwritten Greek lines. He paused, rereading the stanza. *"The Prince of Thieves.* I have never read this poem in my life, and trust me, I've read them all. If your mother was taught Classics here, she would have known that too."

"So she found one that was lost. It doesn't mean anything." But even as she said it, she knew it was not true. She knew her mother would not have kept that poem hidden in her diary if it meant nothing.

Ari shook her head. "No, it doesn't work like that. Maybe she wrote it herself. Or someone else did." But he didn't sound very confident anymore. He brushed the scrawled writing with his fingertip. "Very strange. It's almost like she was searching for something."

"I found something else," Alex added reluctantly.

His eyes snapped up. "What did you find?"

"In my mother's diary. On September 8th, she wrote that the Squatting Scribe is a door. I think she was talking about the Squatting Scribe in the old library."

"The Squatting Scribe?" Ari repeated. "Are you sure?"

"Yes."

"That's impossible."

Alex just shrugged. "That's what my mom wrote. I don't know what it means, but taking it literally..."

"How could it be a door?" Ari asked, almost demanding. "A door to what? Another library?"

"I don't know." She paused. "But don't you want to find out?"

It was what he had said yesterday. Ari looked at her sharply. "We would have to be more careful. We almost got caught last time, and now..."

Regardless, you must keep an eye on her.

Alex was a liability. She felt suddenly hostile towards him. “You don’t have to do it if you don’t want to.”

A flame of defiance leaped into Ari’s eyes. “I’ll meet you outside the girls’ dormitory at eleven tonight.”

26

Alex and Penélope walked over to the dining hall. There were more students than at breakfast, but for the first time, Alex felt comfortable squeezing past the tables, and no one gave her a second glance walking beside Penélope. She dutifully followed the other girl down the buffet line and to one of the tables near the entrance.

"I'm so happy you're here for the summer," Penélope said immediately upon sitting down. "I need a girl around here, you know? And I have four older brothers at home, so you can imagine."

"Wow, that's a lot of brothers. I have a half-brother, but he's only two years old. My dad remarried," Alex said. She rarely liked to share things about her personal life with people she hardly knew, but Penélope was open and without affectation, so Alex trusted her. Besides, she would be leaving this place by the end of the summer.

"You said your mom grew up here, right?"

"Yes, she did. And she attended the New Academy. It was only after she got pregnant with me that she and my dad eloped."

"That sounds like a real love story," Penélope said, her voice taking on an almost dreamy tone. Alex did not want to contradict her, so she withheld her doubts. "My parents wouldn't stop having kids. Our house is a mess, and it's so crowded. That's why I stay here over the summer. To find peace."

"It must be fun to have siblings, though. I always hated being an only child."

"I love my brothers, but they can be so annoying," Penélope said. "I would love to have a baby sister."

"Babies can be annoying too, trust me," Alex said wryly, thinking back to baby Malcolm's many fits and tantrums hardly soothed with a pacifier or sweets.

Penélope laughed. "I'm sure. But they are cuter."

"That's true," Alex relented. She caught herself smiling and wondered how Penélope could make her feel so relaxed and familiar, as if they had known each other for years. It was never that way with Chloe, whose deeply hidden insecurities always managed to rise between them like phantoms of the past, hindering too free-flowing of conversations.

"We're going to have so much fun this summer," Penélope said, returning her smile easily, a hint of a laugh already hovering in her eyes. "Promise?"

"Promise."

After lunch Penélope met up with Zeb to study for their final exam, so Alex returned to her dorm room. She felt antsy, like the night could not come quick enough. But she also felt another feeling, and it took her a long time to realize it was dread. All this searching and finally she had a solid lead she could hold onto. But what if it amounted to nothing? What if she was chasing shadows, phrases in a diary that were only written in metaphor?

There was the other possibility, too, which caused Alex's stomach to turn. She could find her mother on the other side of this so-called door, this last piece of the puzzle, and then she would learn once and for all what happened to her mother. But what if she didn't like what she found?

Only search for answers if you are willing to find them.

The hours slipped past swiftly. Soon dinner rolled around, and with trembling hands, Alex headed to the dining hall. She expected it to be full, but there were hardly any students there. She was about to join Ari and Sister Stella at the faculty table when Penélope called her over to a table in the far corner where she sat with a scowling Zeb.

She picked at her plate as Penélope explained that almost all the students had finished their exams and left. Zeb was in the same prickly mood as earlier and barely spoke to Alex, allowing Penélope to explain how the summer course usually went, the various activities to do around Tierra del Sol, and some harmless gossip about the faculty and students. Alex tried to pay attention, but her gaze kept sliding back to Ari, who never looked over at their table once and left very soon after he finished eating.

Alex allowed the dinner to drag on even though it pained her, if only to keep herself distracted from the fact that in less than four hours she would be sneaking back into the old library.

Penélope hardly noticed her distress, and with her usual bright smile said goodbye to Alex as they left the dining hall at nine o'clock and dragged a mute Zeb with her to the library to study.

She spent the rest of the time reading the diary and trying to look for any hints of what she might find, but her mother never explicitly said what the door of the Squatting Scribe might lead to if it was, in fact, really a door. Before she knew it the clock nearly struck eleven, and she only had enough time to shrug on a sweatshirt and slide into her shoes before tiptoeing out of her dorm room.

The dark hallway was empty and silent, most students having gone to sleep or keeping to themselves quietly. She crept across the hardwood floors, wincing at every creak and loud footstep that echoed in the air. At any second Alex expected to encounter another student or even Sister Stella herself, but she descended the last step and opened the door to the outside corridor without incident.

Ari stood leaning against the wall. She noticed he had just showered, his dark curls damp against the nape of his neck, and he was wearing a sweatshirt and casual shorts so that anyone might mistake him for a college student.

When he saw her, he put a finger up to his lips, then motioned for her to follow. They kept close to the walls in shadow, hoping no curious night owl decided to look out of their window tonight.

They approached the doors to the library. Ari produced the key and unlocked the door as he had done before. Inside, the library was dark and chilled, not a single light turned on, the only visibility from the moonlight filtering weakly through the windows.

Alex kept right behind Ari, her heartbeat in her throat. She swallowed, but her mouth was dry. They reached the door at the back of the library. Ari opened the lock as easily as the first time, and without a word, they slipped inside and down the steps.

She could barely make out the steps in front of her, but Ari did not turn on a flashlight. Instead, she felt a hand grasp hers, and Alex realized he was going to lead them in the dark by memory.

When they landed on level ground, Alex let out a breath, but Ari's hand remained firmly holding hers, so that her heart refused to beat calmly again. He pulled her forward into the darkness, slowly, one step at a time. She heard a hand latch onto metal, then the low groan of a wooden door swinging wide.

They walked inside the room, and when the door was shut behind them, his hand released hers and a light flashed in front of her. Ari's face glowed above his flashlight, shadows flickering where the light failed to touch. With a slight jerk of his head, he motioned to his right, then shined his light in that direction.

Immediately the Squatting Scribe fell under the soft yellow beam of light, the carved stone statue as still and squat as ever. They approached it carefully and crouched down to examine it better. Ari reached out a hand and touched the top of the Scribe's balding head. Then he pushed.

Nothing happened. Ari prodded and pulled the statue everywhere, around the cassock, the book he was holding in his lap, the sandals, and the engraved slab he sat on. The Squatting Scribe remained as impassive as before, the blank eyes staring off into space.

Beside her, Ari stood up with a frustrated sigh. "Your mother was wrong."

Alex did not reply, still looking at the Squatting Scribe, wishing the hard stone would reveal the answer, not just to this mystery but to all of them, every question and doubt that her mother had ever given her. Alex's finger lightly traced the E carved into the cassock. What did it stand for? She wished the Scribe would speak, that anyone would in this dark, entombed library.

Suddenly there was a loud *crack* and light danced across the ceiling. Alex jumped and Ari cursed. She placed a hand on her pounding chest. The flashlight had clattered to the floor. Ari muttered an apology as it rolled over to her feet. She picked it up and stood.

The light flashed quickly around the small room. It looked exactly as she had seen it the other night, with scrolls crammed in the shelves floor to ceiling and the empty podium erected in the middle of the room. The light caught the edge of the podium and Alex noticed something etched into the wood that she had not seen last time. She walked over to it and shined the light directly over the carvings.

They were words, but not in English. Ari joined her, passing a fingertip over the carvings, reading silently with furrowed brows.

"Greek," he whispered, surprised. "τὰ χρήματα Μεγάλου Ἀλεξάνδρου. *The belongings of Alexander the Great.* I can't believe I never noticed that before."

How had Ari never noticed it before? She shivered, wondering if someone had answered her plea for help. She was acutely aware that she shared her name with Alexander.

"What does that mean? *The belongings of Alexander the Great?*" she asked.

To her surprise, Ari half-smiled. "I don't know. But he was known for always sleeping with a copy of the *Iliad* and a dagger under his pillow."

For a moment, neither of them spoke, but then realization dawned on Alex like a rushing tide and she turned to Ari with her breath caught in her throat, who was already looking at her in shock.

"Your mother—" he began, but before he could continue, they heard a noise from outside and quick footsteps.

They shared a wild look, and in her panic Alex switched off the flashlight, descending them in an even deeper darkness. She heard the footsteps growing louder, more purposeful, and she gasped involuntarily, turning around without knowing which way was the door to hide themselves better.

A hand grabbed her arm and together they strode forward in the darkness. Many things happened at once. Alex reached out just in time for her hands to find a bookshelf, she felt her knee graze something rough and bumpy—the Squatting Scribe, she realized in a jumble of panic—and then the wall gave way under her weight, the bookshelf moving forward smoothly, revealing a gaping hole and stone steps lit by sconces.

Alex did not think twice. She surged towards the opening in the floor and down the stairs. Behind her Ari followed without a word, closing the door behind them.

For her mother was right, the Squatting Scribe was a door.

She could barely smile in triumph, her body still humming from the narrow escape, and her legs speeding down the stairs automatically. Neither of them dared to speak, in case their pursuer realized they had come this way and decided to follow.

Their flashlight illuminated the stairs in a faint white haze. Alex noticed the walls were streaked with char, the plaster having burnt off in larger slashes the lower they descended.

It felt like hours before they reached the end of the stairs, finding themselves in another sort of library more cavernous in height, with high, arching ceilings made of pale gray stone. At second glance, it seemed as if they had entered a wide hallway, both directions fading into the distance.

Much of the walls had similar charring as the staircase, but as if it had happened long ago and no one had bothered to fix it. There were no shelves as in the old library. Instead, niches were carved into the stone, each filled with scrolls and anciently bound books stacked up high on the ledges, many of whose binding had been burnt to black. She realized there must have been a fire at some point. Then why had it not reached the Old Library upstairs?

Alex looked at Ari, who stepped out and quickly scanned left and right, before muttering, "Come on."

He started walking across the marble floor, down the hall.

"How do you know where we're going?" she asked.

"I don't," was all he replied, and continued at his quick pace.

Alex grabbed his sleeve and yanked, forcing him to come to an abrupt stop. "Listen to me. We have no idea where we are."

"We're in the library," Ari said, puzzled, rubbing his arm. "Another level of it."

But Alex had been the one to read her mother's diary, not Ari. "We should be careful—"

They heard footsteps again, and Alex's lungs constricted, her fingers fumbling to turn off their flashlight. There were two pairs of footsteps, she realized, as the sounds echoed louder on the marble floor.

"Here," Ari whispered and pointed to a large column beside the wall. They stood behind it, hoping that whoever was walking past would not look too closely at the darker shadows on the floor.

Voices quickly followed the footsteps. Alex held her breath. The ridges of the column dug into her back, and she felt Ari's chest brush against hers as he leaned closer to the column so as not to be seen, his face a few inches above hers.

"...the decrees have become absurd. The King must watch himself, lest the people revolt."

"The people cannot revolt if all of them are abandoning the city."

Alex snuck a glance at the two figures once they passed by their pillar. They were short and frail, hunched in white robes as they hobbled down the hall. She could not see their faces behind dark veils, but Alex thought they sounded like old women. Like Sister Stella, she realized.

She felt a pressure on her arm and looked at Ari. He indicated with his eyes that they should follow. Alex shook her head urgently.

"It's our only chance," Ari whispered, and he looked so certain, so adamant, that she relented, nodding her head. He was probably right. They had barely found the door without getting caught; next time they might not be so lucky.

"Quietly," she warned.

They crept silently down the hall close to the wall bordered by columns in case they must hide, following the two women a good distance away. Suddenly the women disappeared up ahead, and Alex saw as they approached that they had turned the corner.

They had gained ground despite their old age, and Alex and Ari had to quicken their pace if they wanted to keep them in their sight. She hardly had the time to look around and appreciate the vastness of the hallway, the endless niches filled with scrolls and books. Where were they? Could this really be just another level of the library, somehow older than the old library?

The two women had mentioned a king and a city, both very foreign to the

New Academy or Tierra del Sol. Could this be the place her mother had written about in her diary?

November 19th. The city is not a place, he says, but a road. One for mortals, one for the gods.

Alex felt herself hoping she was wrong, remembering what else her mother had written, a twisting feeling inside warning her that someone, somehow, was watching her.

October 26th. I am being watched. I feel their eyes on me, the eyes of eternity, the gaze of gods.

She shivered, and Ari cut her a glance, but they continued walking in silence. At last, they turned down yet another hallway and found themselves on a balcony flanked by two ornate marble staircases, watching the two white veiled women descending the right side of the staircase and exiting through two large, wooden doors that engulfed them in size.

Once the doors closed behind them with a loud bang, Alex and Ari carefully walked down the stairs after them. Together they pushed open the doors, which swung outward with surprising lightness. The moment they stepped out of the doors, however, Alex wished they had remained inside.

They stood on the porch of a large building with elegant white columns half-painted in red spaced evenly in front, partially obscuring their surroundings. But even through the gaps, Alex could see that the building faced a wide street crowded with people, the night sky looming above a foreign, dusky purple and dazzling with more constellations than she had seen that night in New Mexico.

Alex felt dizzy as she watched carts in the street pushed by donkeys, carriages wheeling past, and the people walking by, dressed in colorful tunics, dark reds and vibrant blues and rich greens, many threaded with ornate gold and silver designs, their shoulders draped with equally colorful cloaks. Everything about them was strange, but Alex could only look at the women; their hair was braided and pinned in strange styles, their thick, dark curls brushed cheeks and necks of all shades, and flashing jewelry hung from their ears and neck. Soldiers wove through the crowds, unsuccessfully containing the crowds that flowed up and down the street as they conversed and shouted animatedly. She doubted they were speaking English.

"Where are we, Alexandria?" Ari asked beside her, his voice faint amidst the clatter and chaos below.

"I don't know, but we should start walking," she said, this time taking his hand and moving them into the surging crowds. People had begun staring at them, two obvious foreigners standing at the steps of a building and gaping at their surroundings.

She knew instinctively that they could not draw attention to themselves, and not just from the side glances they received, which were unapologetically scathing and critical. They had to blend in. Then she looked down at their clothes and almost laughed. Everything about them was a glaring sign that they did not belong here, from their clothes to their hair to the way Alex was holding Ari's hand. She dropped it quickly as if it were scalding.

Ari's lips were white and pressed together. "I don't understand," he kept whispering to himself.

She wished he had listened to her, that they had never followed those old women in the library. Was that even the library? If they had descended the stairs from the old library, how could they exit on the top floor?

Nothing made sense. It was as if they had left the New Academy and the time and place they knew and found themselves in an altogether foreign city that was living in a completely different century. And yet, while a part of her panicked at the unfamiliar street and sky, another part of Alex was awed. This was what her mother had written about in her diary. This was why she had loved the library.

If her mother had found this city by accident, just as they had, then why leave it? Even if she were pregnant, why the urgency? Alex could never imagine her mother giving this up, the impossibility of this place, a doorway into another world entirely.

Suddenly Ari stopped, pointing silently at something across the street. She looked and saw black, iron-wrought gates with a large sign above, a single word painted in gold on it in a now familiar alphabet.

ἡ Ἀκαδήμεια

"The Academy," Ari whispered roughly. He started towards it and Alex was forced to follow after him. He reached the gates and touched one of the glossy rods. The gate was locked. He turned to Alex slowly. "How can this be the Academy?"

Alex was reminded of an entry in her mother's diary, one of the first she had read and which she would never forget.

November 22nd. I cannot stop smiling. Today Alexandros took me to the Academy and we walked all across the city. I am going back tomorrow.

Later, she would connect the Academy she was talking about with the school in Tierra del Sol, assuming Alexandros was a classmate and he had shown her around in a nearby city. But she was wrong. When her mother wrote about the Academy, she was not talking about the *New* Academy. That meant Alexandros was not a classmate, but a citizen of this strange city. Her mother had fallen in love with someone *here*.

Before she could reply, Alex heard a roar of cheers very close by, only a few yards down the street. She craned her neck and saw a large crowd standing in a circle. They were mainly young men and they were all wearing the same clothes, deep blue tunics, like a uniform, though many of them had shrugged it off their shoulders, leaving their torsos glistening under the moonlight. In the middle of the circle were two of them, their naked chests gleaming with sweat, stalking each other with their hands raised in front of them.

Someone shouted something and all of them laughed, the two boys pausing in their fight. Ari stiffened beside her. Alex realized one of them had broken off—a tall, gangly brunette with sharp brows and a wide grin that did not speak a kind welcome—and he was staring straight at them. He said something else, nodding his head at her and looking down slyly at her legs, bare in jean shorts. Alex could not understand him, as he had spoken in another language.

But Ari had understood. He answered with surprising steadiness, his mouth working laboriously through those strange syllables. She knew he was speaking Ancient Greek, and also how odd it must be for him to speak it with someone instead of reading it from a page. The brunette laughed in response, abruptly and with abandon, then spat something back that sounded vulgar even to Alex's uncomprehending ears.

But Ari did not look embarrassed, only angered, his face darkening.

"What is he saying?" Alex asked worriedly.

Ari did not look away from the brunette, his eyes narrowing. "He thinks you are very attractive. He also says your clothes are indecent for a woman to wear."

Alex rolled her eyes, but her stomach flipped uneasily. "Typical."

"And he also wants to fight for you."

"What?"

Finally, Ari looked at her, his face grim. "He thinks that you are...available. And he wants to fight for a night with you. Actually, he wants to fight *me* for a night with you."

"That's ridiculous."

They were all laughing now, probably at her reaction as Ari translated. Another boy called out to them, then another, until the crowd worked themselves up into a frenzy. Many of the nearby pedestrians were casting them suspicious looks, some even pointing at them, and Alex felt very exposed. They had to get out of this situation before a soldier noticed them.

"We should leave," Alex said urgently. "This is dangerous."

But Ari was no longer looking at her, his jaw clenched and his hands in fists at his side, staring down the group of Academy students. He rolled his shoulders back and began walking towards them. Alex just managed to pull him back.

"What on earth are you doing?"

He looked at her fiercely, then glanced back at the rambunctious group, which had cheered viciously when Ari had started in their direction. "Teaching a lesson."

Then he shook her off and strode over to the group purposefully. Alex trailed after him as he approached the brunette, who looked fairly surprised that Ari had taken the bait. He purred something in Greek, clearly meant to goad, but Ari only nodded brusquely and broke through the crowd to the empty space in the center.

"Ari!" she called out to him, but her voice was drowned out by the cheers. She could not believe this was happening.

A wiry grip took hold of her wrist and then the brunette was pulling her through the crowd after Ari, where several hands tried to brush her body as she passed. She yanked her arm back, glaring at him, and stepped closer to Ari. The brunette only smiled at her as if he had already won.

"We need to leave," Alex said to Ari. "Now. People were already staring at us." For now, they were hidden by the crowd, but how long would that last?

Ari ignored her protests, taking off his sweatshirt and shirt underneath as if in reply, his eyes focused solely on the brunette. "Step back."

Alex rolled her eyes and reluctantly took a step away, but not close enough for the other boys to touch her. "Fine, just don't complain to me when I'm cleaning your bloody face."

She watched Ari roll his neck, then bounce on the balls of his feet, shaking his wrists out. The brunette did none of this, only prowling slowly, his lanky limbs hanging loosely at his sides. He looked so thin and wiry next to Ari's fuller chest and muscular arms, a boy next to a man. At that moment, the absolute absurdity of her situation dawned on her, and she had the urge to laugh, and then probably cry.

The brunette said something again, softly, but loud enough for Ari to pale, eyes flickering over to her, before settling on his opponent again with a hard glare. Ari lifted his fists and the brunette laughed his high-pitched howl, which the crowd echoed. He shook his head as he sauntered up to Ari, lazily, like he might be taking a nice stroll in a garden.

When he was almost a foot away, Ari swung, his arm shooting out lightning fast, so fast Alex could hardly see it. But it swiped air, Alex realized in her confusion when no grunt of pain followed, and she saw that the brunette had slid away like an eel, darting behind Ari and tackling him from behind.

They flew to the ground, rolling on top of each other. She cried out while the crowd around her roared, the sound so deafening that she could not hear the fighters wrestling each other, only foreign phrases and shouts of encouragement spat behind her. She clasped her hands together, biting her lip hard to prevent herself from running over and trying to help him, knowing it would only make things worse.

Ari was struggling to gain ground, the brunette's lanky limbs like snakes, twisting and turning with surprising strength and agility. He had Ari nearly pinned, his knees firm on Ari's legs. Then she saw it. An opportunity. The brunette had glanced over at her, to make sure she was still there or that she was watching, Alex did not know, but it was enough. Ari swung again with his free arm, his fist connecting with the brunette's jaw in a sickening crunch.

Then Ari leaped to his feet, the brunette sinking to the ground, clutching his face, pain bright in his wide eyes, looking suddenly like a teenage boy, lost and confused. Alex almost smiled at the victory, but then Ari buried another punch into the brunette's eye, blood instantly gushing from his nose, then another into his gut, and another, until the brunette lolled helplessly to the side, nearly flat on the ground, muttering incoherently.

Alex did not try to stop him, watching almost hypnotized, and to her surprise, neither did the crowd. Only their cheers lessened with every smack that resounded from Ari's knuckles connecting with the brunette's body until there was scarcely a murmur, the brunette splayed out on the ground, still breathing and conscious but moaning from the pain.

Finally, Ari stood up, wiping the sweat from his brow with his forearm. He said something low in Greek, to which the brunette blinked, then to Alex's complete surprise the boy smiled a very bloody smile. He muttered something back in a reedy voice.

The crowd was dead silent until the brunette finished speaking, then they surged forward in cries of triumph, passing Alex to embrace Ari as if he were their new champion. She lost sight of him in the crowd which had engulfed him in their praises until he emerged sitting upon their shoulders, a wild grin on his face that Alex had never seen before. She realized that the Academy was for boys younger than Ari and that he was probably stronger than everyone there, but just then, his naked torso glistening with sweat, he seemed like one of them.

A rough voice called to her, and she realized the brunette was still on the floor, left behind bruised and bleeding by the crowd which had taken Ari a few paces away, speaking excitedly with him. The brunette said something to her that she could not understand, almost gently, his eyes no longer sneering. She wished she could understand.

"I'm sorry," she stammered. "I don't..."

"He's asking where you are from," said a smooth voice from behind her, and she swiveled around, but there was no one there, just the Academy gates and the busy street gurgling past like a loud brook.

She turned back to the brunette, who looked at her in concern. Had he not heard the voice too?

"I'm from up there," she said anyway, only half-joking, and gestured upwards, for that was all she knew about how she had arrived in this strange place.

But it was the wrong thing to say.

The brunette's eyes widened and he whispered in a hoarse voice filled with fear, "Δαῖμον."

This time Alex understood him well enough, the word passing through her like a cold wind, chilling her to the bone.

Demon.

27

When Alex told him afterward, Ari laughed, delighted.

"Hey, it's not funny! He called me a demon," Alex protested.

But Ari only laughed again. She had never seen him like this, as if he were lit up from the inside, his tan skin glowing. It was different from Warren's brightness, his optimism and good humor. Ari was shining like the moon, a silver glitter in his eyes, a light that only shined because of the shadows surrounding it.

They had managed to escape the rowdy group of Academy students, which was what they were, Ari confirmed after speaking with them. Ari had been celebrated as a champion, and they asked where he had come from and if he would like to join the Academy. He had given excuses, claiming only to be visiting, a tourist. It turned out that the brunette had gracefully accepted defeat when Ari had claimed victory. He would not, however, share any of the words that the brunette and he had exchanged during the fight.

After they left the group, Alex had quickly led them down the street, past the library, and turned left into the first deserted alley she could find to regroup without drawing even more attention than they already had. Now she and Ari were leaning against the wall, recounting the fight so that they would not have to think about what they were going to do next.

"He didn't call you a demon," Ari said with a shake of his head. "A *δαίμων* is just a divine being. He was calling you a goddess."

"I guess I did tell him I'm from the sky."

Ari looked at her quizzically. "How did you know what he was saying?"

Then Alex remembered the voice that had spoken, so strangely familiar, the memory of it tugging on another memory long forgotten. She almost shouted in frustration as she tried to recall it. A voice...Could it be the voice of a god? Where had she heard that voice before? So smooth, so young and supple, but young and supple like trees were when only a hundred years old, youthful in age yet ancient in their youth.

"Alexandria?"

She remembered. Niagara Falls. Not only the haunting voices from the water but her tour guide, the way his voice had sounded different when had he called her away, almost younger, smooth like aged wine. But it was impossible. Either way, she would not tell Ari now that she was hearing voices, not when he was glowing like this, as if he had come alive and there was nothing that could bring him down.

"I guessed," she said, shrugging. But she could not quite meet his eyes. The glow in Ari's face dimmed ever so slightly. "We should figure out what to do next."

"We should figure out where the hell we are first," Ari said, something cutting in his tone. "Unless you've already guessed that too?"

Alex remained silent. She owed him nothing, not when she had warned him against this, not when this meant more to her than it could ever mean to him.

But Ari was looking at her seriously, all lightness and mockery bled from his eyes. "Do you think you know where we are?"

"Yes," Alex said softly. "I think my mother is here."

"How?"

"I think she came back. I think she left us to come here. She loved this city." *She loved someone in this city,* she did not say.

"But where are we?"

Alex did not know, but her mother did. "She called it a road, not a place. I think it might be some kind of...in between."

"In between what?"

She fell silent, her cheeks growing hot as if embarrassed by what she thought, even though they had encountered so many strange and impossible things today. Ari raised a dark brow and she saw that blood matted the fine hairs. Perhaps she owed him more than she thought.

"Gods and mortals," she said, reluctantly. "I think this is a road between the realm of the gods and the realm of mortals."

Instead of disbelief or laughter, Ari stared at her intently, as though her words had sunk him deep in thought. He looked away abruptly, then up at the sky, which had never deepened to a night sky black, an otherworldly gleam keeping the purple dusky, as if it were the dawn of night instead of day approaching.

Then he dropped his gaze down to her, a curious expression on his face which she could not quite name. "You are very strange, Alexandria."

He had said that to her before. Instead of scaring her or irritating her, this time the words sent a thrill in her, like a rough wind ripping the leaves off branches in a winter storm.

"My mother is here, I know it," she said firmly. "And I'm going to find her."

They decided to walk down the alley, as it was the most deserted part of the city they had seen. Alex could not shake the voice from her head, the creeping sensation that someone was watching her, following her down the shadowed alleyway.

Ari had subdued some since the fight, but his eyes still wandered around with a faint gleam, like an animal looking out across the plains after killing their prey, satisfied but still humming with adrenaline.

After a half-mile, the alley dropped them off at the shore of a harbor lined with shipyards. The harbor was beautiful under this sky, a wine-dark sea, the stars reflected above and below. Ships and small boats were constantly anchoring and setting off, white sails dotting the horizon and shouting shipmates swarming on the briny decks.

There was a long stretch of boardwalk that hugged the shipyards, where many couples and families walked along in richly woven fabrics, large ornate street lamps lighting the way. Ari and Alex kept close to the edges of the boardwalk covered in shadow, not wishing to be looked at too closely. They found a leisurely pace, watching cargo unload from a large ship, an intricately carved siren at its bow.

Alex understood, now, why her mother had wanted to come back. This was the kind of place where one fell in love easily. She eyed Ari discreetly, the dark brows, the surprisingly full mouth, warm brown skin that glowed bronze under this sky. He had broad shoulders, broader than any of those boys at the Academy, and he had a solidness to his posture that was different from Warren's stiff, lanky demeanor. What had Alexandros looked like? Why had her mother chosen her father instead of Alexandros and a life in this city?

Was it only about the money and religion, or something else, something Alex could no longer see twenty years too late?

The boardwalk soon approached a large cross street running straight to the edge of the shipyards, where a fence that separated the boardwalk and the shipyards rose into a tall gate looming over the harbor. Alex paused when they passed before it, mesmerized by its size and command over the street.

A low thrumming noise echoed behind them. Alex looked around for the source of the noise but saw nothing except the bustling of the shipyards and the quiet strolling of those on the boardwalk.

"Look," Ari said quietly, staring at the mountains in the distance that had seemed mere dark shadows until now. "The sun."

The sun was indeed peeking over the mountains, a hot red glow like the end of a cigarette, hovering in the dip between mountainpeaks where a valley of desert suddenly lit up in a dusty gold. Alex squinted her eyes, thinking she could make out palm trees dotting the desert, and even a thin path snaking its way through the sand. Then that thrumming noise grew louder, more distinct, so that Alex recognized it as drums and footsteps marching together.

She turned and saw a large squadron of soldiers in glinting bronze armor crawling toward them on the boardwalk. There was a leader on horseback, trotting in front, bellowing orders to those on foot. He gave a sweeping survey of the scene, and Alex shrank back into the shadows of a nearby building. She recalled what they had overheard in the library from those old women.

"...the decrees have become absurd. The King must watch himself, lest the people revolt."

"The people cannot revolt if all of them are abandoning the city."

Dawn. The city was awakening. What they had witnessed thus far was the nightlife, the vibrant, resisting festivities of a city ruled under a harsh king, perhaps even a tyrant. But if that were the case, then this city had just become that much more dangerous. Already Alex felt the hostility of the city rise up against her, the glare from the horseman's helmet seeming to land directly on her.

"We can't stay here," Ari murmured, as if reading her thoughts.

"I know. The soldiers—"

"No," he said with a shake of his head. "The sun. It's morning. We have to go back."

Alex realized he was talking about the New Academy. If they did not go back soon, everyone would find out that they had disappeared, including Sister Stella. Then they would not be able to return quietly.

"It might not be morning there. I don't know if time works differently here," she said. "Besides, what is there back at the New Academy?"

Ari studied her carefully. He always seemed to read her like a book. "You want to stay."

"I want to find my mother."

"She could be anywhere," Ari said softly. He put a hand on Alex's arm when she began to protest, and she nearly flinched at the touch. "I will help you find her, but we can't keep searching the city blind. The New Academy and the library will be invaluable to us. There are answers there, I know it. Besides, we'll get caught if we stay here dressed like this."

Alex looked into Ari's dark, heavy eyes as if his soul were sitting within the irises. She knew he was right. They had to return to the New Academy. It was the only way.

He took a small step closer. "Your mother will lead us to her, but you have to trust her."

She nodded. "Let's go back."

28

THEY WALKED AWAY FROM the gate and hurried down the cross street which was now illuminated by the sun hanging in the sky.

During the night, the streets had been overrun by people dressed luxuriously, gliding from one place to another, caravans and wagons filled with goods and people. But in the daylight, the streets were crowded by haggard workmen carrying equipment to different shops from the shipyards, merchants and Academy students dutifully walking to their final destination, and soldiers routinely surveying the area. There were scarcely any women on the main streets, only the occasional veiled figure walking alongside a well-dressed man. They shied away from anyone's wandering gaze, keeping their heads down and hoping not to be noticed by one of the soldiers.

As they continued from the shipyards down the cross street, Alex noticed that they passed an unfamiliar part of the city. To their left were large, ornate homes with colorful gardens and painted walls, the most polished buildings she had seen here besides the Academy or the library, which she had hardly been able to make out at night. To their right was a park and a wide, oval structure decorated with gold and marble and topped by a canvas cloth, which Ari told her was an amphitheater.

Finally, they reached a familiar intersection, and Alex saw the library and the Academy to the east, the other end of the street stretching into the west towards the desert. They turned the corner and quickly strode towards the library. Ari glanced across the street at the Academy, the wrought iron gates, and the low, white buildings behind them, trimmed with dark blue tile. There was no crowd outside anymore, only an occasional student passing in and out of the front gates.

The library loomed before them, imposing with its columns and grand wooden doors. With one last glance at the city, Alex and Ari ascended the steps and opened the doors, stepping inside quietly. There was no one, no old women, no soldiers, that stopped them. The wide marble staircase was empty, sparkling under the weak light that fell from windows high up on the walls.

Alex led them up the staircase and back the way they came. They walked in silence, knowing that anyone could be close by and hear them. As they walked down the familiar hallway, Alex noticed small dark openings between the tall niches, which she had not seen before in their rush to follow the old women. She wondered where those tunnels led—to rooms filled with more scrolls or another endless hallway like this one?

"This is it," Ari murmured beside her, pointing at a wooden door streaked with soot. They pushed it, the door swinging open without a sound, and together they walked up the stairs to the old library.

Despite what they knew, Alex imagined the door opening and finding themselves in another level of the library with the same halls, the same niches, and they would be stuck in this city forever. She was surprised to find that she was not afraid of the thought. Instead, Ari eased the door open carefully, revealing the same scroll-filled room back at the New Academy, and the same empty wooden podium in the middle.

She let out a sigh. Ari closed the bookshelf behind them, the Squatting Scribe as immovable and silent as they left him. They did not linger, in case Sister Stella or someone else happened to be in the library.

After listening for footsteps or voices, they opened the door and ascended the steps to the new library above. They walked quietly passed the familiar shelves of books, holding their breath.

Just as they passed the desk where Alex had first met Ari, an unmistakable voice spoke. "Who's there?"

It was the old man they had heard talking with Sister Stella. His voice was raspy and low, but it seemed to echo all around them in the stagnant air of the library. Alex and Ari froze.

"You can't hide from me," he sneered, followed by a soft clicking noise and footsteps coming from the front of the library, shrouded in darkness. He must have been keeping watch in one of the rows.

Alex could hardly breathe. She looked at Ari, who shared her alarmed face. There was no way past the Brother without risking getting caught.

"Students are not allowed to be in the library past curfew," the voice wheezed, taunting, and Alex thought he must be closer, perhaps a few rows away. It was too late to make a run for it.

They backed away from the main aisle toward the dark corner of the row by the stained glass window, same as the one where only yesterday Zeb had been teasing Ari, sitting up on the windowsill and prodding his shoulder. Alex's back hit the wall and she gasped.

Footsteps quickened. They would be found any moment. Ari glanced behind him, then pulled his hood up, moving toward her.

"Kiss me," he said.

She looked at him, startled. "What?"

"I said—"

But she had understood, her stomach dropping in anticipation, and she reached out and grabbed the front of his sweatshirt. Then from one moment to the next Ari pressed up close and kissed her. His mouth was warm, gentle, and almost familiar in the way dreams could be when someone real became a phantom of the night. She felt an arm snake around her waist, the other gently cupping the side of her face.

"There you are! Hey!"

But Ari only held her tighter, his body flush against hers. She could hardly think as his fingers brushed the sensitive nape of her neck.

"Be gone! I will have none of this perversity in my library!"

Suddenly they felt someone roughly grab their shoulders and yank them away from the wall. Ari grabbed her hand.

"Run," he whispered.

She did not hesitate, tearing herself from the old man's iron grip and shooting past the cloaked figure without a second glance, sprinting out of the library behind Ari.

They heard the old man cry after them, nearly growling. "Corrupted children!"

Once they were outside, Ari pointed towards the girls' dormitory and Alex ran for the door without saying goodbye, climbing the steps two at a time and only stopping to breathe when she was in her room, the door locked and her hands trembling at her sides. Then she rushed to her window, looking out through the crack in the blinds. Ari was gone. He had probably gone back to his room. She pressed her fingertips to her lips.

A cloaked figure stepped out of the library, looking around the courtyard and up at the dormitories. Alex stepped away from the window with a gasp, her heart hammering in her chest. Who was that man? She had never seen him around the New Academy before. But he knew Alex, and her mother. He was the one who had told Sister Stella to keep an eye on her. Was he connected to the city in some way? And perhaps her mother as well? He was yet another mystery to add to the long list that her mother had started.

They should have stayed in the city. No matter how dangerous it could be, that was where her mother was, Alex could feel it. Now they would have to sneak around the library, searching the endless rows of books for some clue, some hint of the city and what this all meant. It would be nearly impossible to sneak past both Sister Stella and the mysterious Brother now.

But even as she felt the hopelessness of the situation, Alex fell asleep with a small smile on her face.

29

Alex slept until noon. She woke up from a hazy, nightmarish dream where she was being chased down unfamiliar, dark streets. Her skin was burning hot as if she had a fever and her head was pounding.

As memories of the city rushed through her head, Alex knew she had to see Ari as soon as possible to discuss what they had seen and what they were going to do next. He was probably in the library grading papers. The library. Then she remembered the library last night, his arm around her waist, his lips soft on hers...

She shook her head. It had happened out of desperation, to escape getting caught. Any two students could have snuck into the library at night to mess around.

But did that make it right? If she had a boyfriend back home, did that make it right? And if maybe, just maybe, she wanted to kiss him again, did that still make it right?

Alex knew the answer, but a part of her did not care, the part that had come alive the moment she stepped on the gas and drove away from everything she had always known. The other part stayed silent.

She took a quick shower down the hall and then made her way to the library. As she had expected, Ari was there grading papers. But he was not alone. Penélope and Zeb were seated around his table, clearly there to bother him.

"Good morning," Penélope said in her low, welcoming voice when she saw Alex. "Slept in?"

"Yes. I went to bed late," Alex replied, sitting down on a stool beside Penélope and ignoring Ari's gaze which had landed on her the moment she arrived and had not gone away. Zeb noticed and scowled.

"That makes two of you," Penélope said with a smirk, glancing at Ari.

Now Alex was forced to look at him. Penélope was right. He would have looked hungover if Alex did not know better. She glimpsed small red scratches on his cheek and a faint bruise only just visible on his brow.

"Did you even comb your hair?" Penélope teased.

"I went to bed late," Ari muttered, self-consciously running a hand through his hair. He caught Alex's eye and she realized he was blushing. She looked away quickly.

"Fun night?" Zeb asked Ari challengingly.

Ari raised a brow. "If you mean grading papers, then yes, my night was very fun indeed."

Alex scoffed, unable to help herself. She saw Zeb and Penélope exchange a startled glance. She turned to Ari coolly. "Grading papers? Is that the best you can do?"

Zeb stared at her in surprise, but Penélope only smiled in delight.

"What do you mean?" Ari asked, his eyes narrowed.

"Oh nothing," Alex said sweetly. "But we all know what *grading papers* means. A professor and his student...it's a tale as old as time."

Penélope's mouth fell open in shock, then she laughed. Even Zeb cracked a smile.

"That's a good one, Alexandria," Ari said, and his eyes were dark and glittering, as though something cold and bright lay hidden deep within the shadows. "But I promise, if I had, I would not be afraid to say it."

Alex shrugged, but her pulse stuttered under that look. It was the same look he had given to the brunette Academy boy in the city last night before the fight. Out of the corner of her eyes, she saw Penélope watch Ari curiously.

"But tell me, Alexandria, what were *you* doing last night?" Ari asked, almost taunting.

She smiled slowly. "Wouldn't you like to know, *professor*."

Ari's lips parted, shocked, then he smiled unwillingly. He began to speak, then stopped, shaking his head in exasperation, the smile returning to his face again.

"Oh she's good," Penélope said, eyeing Alex in wonder. "I think you might be blushing, Ari. Or should I say, *professor.*"

"Not bad," Zeb said to Alex, though rather reluctantly. "You've officially been accepted into our secret society."

"Oh? May I ask what this secret society entails?" Alex could barely hold back a smirk.

"We torture Ari," Zeb said in a flat voice that only made it all the more ridiculous.

"Daily," Penélope added.

"I see," Alex said in mock seriousness. "And if I joined such a society, would I be obligated to make Ari as annoyed as possible?"

"Absolutely," Zeb replied.

"Naturally," Penélope said with a grin. "Isn't that right, *professor?*"

Ari groaned, covering his face with his hands. "I give up."

Suddenly Penélope gasped, looking at her watch. "It's already one o'clock!" She glanced at Zeb pointedly. "We should study. Our final is tomorrow morning. Let's go to the garden so that we can focus for a few hours."

Zeb hopped down from his usual spot on the ledge, a bare nod the only acknowledgment before he followed Penélope down the main aisle toward the door.

After they had left the library, Ari let out a laugh. "You are something else."

"I thought we had already established that," Alex retorted easily. Too easily.

"We should talk about that by the way."

"About what?" Alex asked with a smirk. "How we found a door that led us to an entirely different time and place or how you actually do have a professor-student kink?"

It was a bold thing to say. Ari went very still, his dark eyes on her. She did not move under that look, holding his gaze and letting the thrill rush over her like the black of a night sky unfurling across her skin.

"The first one," Ari said, finally. "For now."

Alex nodded, ignoring the heat burning on her cheeks. "The Squatting

Scribe is a door."

"That's one way to put it," Ari said wryly. "But a door to what? A city?"

"A road," Alex offered.

"Or an illusion," Ari countered. "We can't be sure."

"Either way, my mother's there, and we're the only ones who can find her." She knew she sounded severe, but the situation warranted some gravity. Her mother could be in trouble. Anything could have happened to her in that city.

"Your mother was searching for something," Ari said slowly. "Isn't that what you said your mother's diary felt like?"

"Yes. And I think it has something to do with the Prince of Thieves."

Ari nodded. "I agree. There's only one problem."

"Which is?"

"Your mother only kept a fragment of the original hymn. We need the rest to know exactly what she was searching for. It could explain what your mother was doing in the archive collection."

"Let me guess," Alex said. "That's what the library is for?"

Ari smirked. "We'll start searching tomorrow."

30

A LIGHT KNOCK SOUNDED in her dorm, startling Alex from a much-needed nap. She got up from her bed, raking a hand through her hair and straightening out her clothes. The little hours of sleep last night combined with the high spikes of adrenaline had wiped her out for a few hours.

"Who is it?" she called out.

"Sister Stella, dear."

"Shit," she whispered, then replied loudly, "I'll be out in a second."

After grabbing her shoes and hiding her mother's things in the desk drawer, Alex opened the door. Sister Stella stood on the other side, hands folded in front of her and a kind smile on her face.

"Good afternoon, Alexandria," she said. "I thought I might invite you for a walk around the school grounds. I am not sure if Professor Melamed has taken you already."

"No, he hasn't." She made a mental note to annoy Ari about that later.

"Then I will show you. The New Academy was built in a small but beautiful valley that is worth a tour if one has the time to spare. Follow me, Alexandria."

They walked out of the girls' dormitory and across the courtyard. Alex saw Penélope and Zeb lounging under a lemon tree, flipping through a book and arguing animatedly. At least, Penélope did the talking, while Zeb sat back and either rolled his eyes or scoffed.

"You know, your mother particularly enjoyed this courtyard," Sister Stella said, eyeing Penélope and Zeb as if she saw more than what was there. "She would have spent all day out here if I had not required her attendance in class."

"Yes, she wrote about that too."

Sister Stella looked at her curiously as they passed through the corridor and down a shaded hall that led them to the same gate she had snuck into last night. "This diary that your mother kept...did she write about all of her days at the New Academy?"

Alex could sense the probing in that question. But more than one could play that game. "Yes, up until she left."

"Ah. And did she ever mention her studies?"

"All the time. That's how I knew she studied Classics. She was very passionate about it."

"Yes, yes, Elena was a very passionate student," Sister Stella said, glancing at Alex shrewdly. "I see that same passion in you, my dear."

"Really?" Alex hated how hopeful she sounded.

"You are still trying to find your mother, is that not so?" Sister Stella asked carefully.

Alex nodded wordlessly. They had walked past a small cemetery and were now approaching a large running track with patches of dust and grass in the center of the field. Desert mountains surrounded them, spotted with palm trees and large rocks, the unfamiliar dry heat shimmering on the horizon so that Alex thought she glimpsed the stone wall of a city and tall, gleaming gates before she blinked and the vision disappeared.

"I was really hoping that she came back here," Alex said, half-truthfully. "From the way she spoke about this place in her diary..."

"Your mother came to me one day. Before she left. I have never forgotten her words." Sister Stella paused, looking out across the vast desert as if the past resided there. "I meant to tell you before, but I did not wish to upset you."

"What did she say?" Alex asked nervously.

"She said that her life had been taken from her and that one day her daughter would pay the price."

She always said this was her new life now.

"What does that mean?"

Sister Stella sighed. "I do not know. Perhaps she knew that her new life would become unbearable. It is hard to say now. I tried to convince her to remain at the New Academy, that she always had a place here. But she refused."

"She should've stayed here," Alex said harshly, blinking her eyes and realizing they were filled with tears. "At least then I would still have a mother."

She felt Sister Stella's hand on her arm, and she saw that same bright excitement in her eyes, an inner intensity that overflowed her quiet, unassuming exterior. For a moment, Alex could see Sister Stella as a young girl too, just beginning her studies, a willful but wise soul. Had she found the city too, like her mother had, and decided to never leave?

"I believe your mother would never have left you if she had a choice."

"You always have a choice," Alex whispered.

"Not always. Love is not a choice, and neither is death."

"So you think she's dead then?" The embarrassment from her tears gave her some boldness to say the words.

Sister Stella was silent for a few moments. "I think you will not know peace until you find out the truth."

As they walked back from the track, Alex thought she heard the mournful song of a nightingale far, far away.

31

"ARE YOU OKAY?" ARI asked with a sigh, closing his book loudly.

Alex looked up from the book she was skimming through. Ari was stretched out on the desk in the library, a book balancing between his chest and his hand. He was looking down at her where she sat on the ground, leaning back against the bookshelf.

They had been searching for any mention of the city or the lost hymn all morning but had found nothing for the last two hours. Penélope and Zeb were almost done with their exam and soon they would be forced to stop.

"Yes. Why?"

Ari shrugged. "You seem...distracted."

"I'm fine."

He did not speak. She looked at him lying back on the desk like the first time she had seen him, his dark hair splayed out on the wood, fine fingers flipping lazily through a book.

"Why did you kiss me?"

"Is that what this is about?" Ari asked, surprised.

"No." She sighed. "I have a boyfriend, that's all."

"Back home?"

"Yes. Warren."

"Warren," Ari repeated, as if that explained a lot. Maybe it did. "How long have you been dating?"

"Almost four years."

"Damn." He ran a hand through his hair. "That's a long time."

"It is," Alex said. "We started dating in high school. He was captain of the

Crew team and goes to Harvard too. We were probably going to get engaged after graduating."

"*Were?* What changed?"

"Everything. My mom. This place." She glanced down. "You."

Silence. She ran a finger down the spine of her book, listening to their quiet breaths, the creak of wood from somewhere inside the library.

Finally, Ari spoke. "There usually isn't anyone guarding the library at night. I thought that was the best way to avoid getting caught. It didn't mean anything."

Alex nodded, trying not to show the inexplicable disappointment she felt on her face.

"Do you regret coming here?" Ari asked carefully.

"No," she said, then sighed. "But I left a lot behind."

"Warren." He sounded mocking.

"And my friends," Alex added pointedly. "And my dad. Simona and baby Malcolm, my half-brother. Harvard. My life."

He gestured to the library around them. "But aren't you finding out the truth about your life?"

"Sometimes I can't tell if I'm searching for the truth or just running away from it."

"Poetic," Ari said sarcastically, sitting up and setting the book down beside him. She glared at him half-heartedly. "What? You're being dramatic. From what you've told me, your mother disappeared. We're trying to find her. It's as simple as that."

"But what if it's not," Alex insisted. "What if there's more to it?"

"More what?"

She paused. "I talked with Sister Stella yesterday. My mother had gone to her before she left with my dad. She told Sister Stella that her life had been taken from her and that one day her daughter would pay the price."

"So she knew she was going to leave you ten years later?" Ari asked doubtfully.

"I don't know," Alex said miserably. "That's what it sounds like. Maybe this was all a mistake. Maybe she did want to abandon her family and I'm risking all I've worked so hard to achieve trying to find someone that doesn't want to be found."

"That's what this is about, isn't it?"

"What?"

Ari shook her head, and for the first time, he looked truly angry. "You have a chance to find your mother and you're worried about what? A stupid Harvard degree? A boring boyfriend who will never make you truly satisfied? What about the truth? What about your mother? What are you so afraid of?"

"That she's dead!" Alex exclaimed in frustration, pent up from days of accumulating stress and doubt. "What if I would rather not know? What if I should have stayed home? What if I am throwing away my life for a ghost?"

"You're scared," Ari said in disbelief. "You've lived your whole life spoon-fed that now you can't stand not knowing what comes next."

"You know nothing about my life," she said scathingly.

"No, I don't. But I know that if there was even the slightest chance that my mother wasn't dead, I would take it. As it is, both my parents are dead and I've been stuck living here in this place since I was twelve. I would take your life and all its problems in a heartbeat."

"You were at Harvard, just like me," Alex said accusingly. "Why did you drop out?"

Ari stared at her in silence, his mouth set in a grim line. When he did not answer, Alex huffed a laugh. Before she could come up with another scathing remark, she realized that Penélope and Zeb had carefully approached their desk. Ari quickly set down the book beside him and stood up. Her ears burned as she wondered how long they had been listening to their argument.

"Um...are we interrupting something?" Penélope asked, glancing between Alex and Ari. When neither of them answered, she held out a stack of papers. "My exam. We finished."

Ari cleared his throat, taking the papers distractedly. "Thank you. I-I'll look them over right now."

Zeb handed him his exam too, his expression unreadable.

"So," Penélope began cautiously, "are we still going out tonight?"

"Out?" Alex asked, raising a brow.

"Ari didn't tell you?" Penélope asked with a smile. Alex refused to look at Ari. "We're celebrating tonight!"

"Celebrating what?"

"Finishing our exams, of course," Zeb answered coolly. He glanced at Ari. "Unless you're not feeling up for it, Ari."

Ari had been staring at the exams in his hand, apparently lost in thought. He looked up at his name. "No, I am. I'll see you guys later."

Then he left, his hands gripping the papers tightly. They all watched him leave in slight bafflement before Penélope dragged her wide eyes back to Alex, while Zeb looked at her accusingly.

"Phew, what were you two arguing about?" she asked.

"Nothing," Alex said quickly. Too quickly.

Penélope raised a brow but didn't press it. "Well, what about you? Are you going to come out with us?"

Alex hesitated.

"Se siente mucho," Zeb said half-sarcastically. It was a colloquial phrase but Alex understood well enough. *She's too good for us.*

"Actually," Alex said sharply, "I'd love to."

Zeb raised his brows in faint surprise. Penélope grinned. "Great. We'll meet outside the church at nine."

"Where exactly are we going?" Alex asked meekly.

This time Zeb smiled. "You'll see."

So Alex found herself getting ready in her dorm room with Penélope, painfully reminding her of all those nights getting ready with Chloe and Owen. She gave a sideways glance at the silk skirt, black corset, and high heels Penélope had on and felt under-dressed in her jeans. Penélope had swept her long hair into a slick high ponytail and was applying bright red lipstick in the mirror.

"You look so hot," Alex said without thinking. It was something she would have told Chloe.

Penélope looked startled, then flashed her an embarrassed smile. "Oh, thank you. You too."

"Where are we going by the way?" Alex asked quickly to change the subject. Tierra del Sol was a very small town after all.

"It's just a local bar, but the drinks are cheap."

"So it's just going to be me, you, and Zeb?"

"And Ari," Penélope reminded her.

Alex nodded. "Oh, right."

But she read the reluctance in her. "Did something happen with Ari?"

"No," Alex said quickly. "We just had...a disagreement. It's hard to explain. But I get the sense he doesn't like me very much."

Penélope shook her head ruefully. "You never knew Ari before, but I did. I was a freshman when he was a senior. He was...wonderful." She smiled sadly. "He was the prize jewel of the program. His passion for Classics, for the language, the culture, everything, it was mesmerizing. He was obsessed. He could practically converse in Ancient Greek. Ari was a genius. Then he went to Harvard." Her eyes darted to Alex and then away. "Something changed. He stopped caring. It was like he didn't believe it mattered anymore. He came back that first summer a different person. The next year he would visit for weeks at a time, doing nothing except drinking at the bar or hanging around the track. I don't know how he kept up with school."

Alex did not tell her that Ari had dropped out after his first year. "Why are you telling me this?"

"I don't really know if I'm being honest," Penélope said with a sigh. "I've just never seen him this animated before. Not since he's gone to Harvard. I can't explain it, but ever since you came, it's like *he's* back too. Like he's himself again."

She recalled the glowing look he had in the city, then pushed the image away. Penélope didn't know the real reason for his newly lit passion, and it had nothing to do with her. But Alex remained silent.

Soon after they were done getting ready it was nearing nine, so they headed out together. Alex could not quite believe that she was going to a bar in the middle of nowhere with near strangers, but she supposed more impossible things had happened in the last few days.

They met Zeb and Ari in front of the church where they were already waiting. Ari avoided looking at her directly, so Alex walked alongside Penélope while the boys followed behind them, Zeb attempting to find out his grade on the final.

"I haven't finished grading them yet," she heard Ari say exasperatedly.

Suddenly Penélope linked her arm with Alex's. "So, tell me. Are you dating anyone?"

"Yes," Alex said, half-surprised. She had been so accustomed to Chloe's revulsion around the topic of dating that she forgot most girls talked about it for fun. "Warren. We've been dating for almost four years."

"Ooh! That's lovely!"

"But I'm not sure it's going to work out," Alex said honestly, the truth slipping out easily as it always did around Penélope. "I sort of ditched him to come here."

"Really?" Penélope asked in wonder. "Why?"

This gave her pause. Alex did not know how much she should tell her. She also sensed eyes on her and knew Ari was listening intently now. "I had to get away. I felt...trapped. My entire life was planned. I had no freedom."

Alex knew how she sounded, like a rich kid who was sick of comfort and safety, looking for a little thrill in the real world. And in some ways, she was that girl. But she could not tell the whole truth and risk her position at the New Academy. For now, she would have to play her part.

But Penélope only sighed in agreement. "I totally get you. My parents expect me either to go to law school or medical school. But I just want to study Classics. It doesn't really pay, though, so I'll probably become a lawyer and live a miserable but comfortable life."

"That does sound miserable," Alex said in surprise. Penélope laughed. "Sorry, it's just that you're so happy and confident. I thought you had your life all figured out."

"I guess I could say the same for you," Penélope replied with a smile, nudging Alex with their linked arms. "Oh! We're here."

Alex had not noticed the walk from the New Academy down the road, but they had already passed the motel she had stayed at and were now standing in front of a small bar with a neon sign that read *El Sol.*

"Welcome to the best bar in town!" Penélope exclaimed. "Come on, I'll introduce you to everyone."

Alex walked nervously beside Penélope. They entered the bar, and to her surprise, the entire room was filled with old couples drinking, smoking, and playing cards. Everyone turned to them when they walked in, then cheered seeing who it was.

"Penélope, Zeb, Ari, *¡llegaron!"* someone said, coming towards them.

Penélope circled Alex's shoulders. *"Hola, Eduardo. Esta es Alexandria, mi nueva amiga."*

Eduardo, a middle-aged man with black curly hair and a blue baseball cap, approached them with a grin. He shook Alex's hand warmly. *"Mucho gusto, Alejandría."*

She nodded helplessly and smiled.

"Let's get a seat at the bar," Penélope said, leading Alex away.

They sat on the barstools in front of a high, wooden bar, where a beautiful woman with dyed blonde hair and a long black dress was deftly preparing a cocktail shaker on the other side. Alex felt Ari sit down on the stool beside her, and she fought the urge to jump when his arm brushed hers.

The bartender swept her glance over them, her eyes lingering on Ari, which Alex could not help but notice with a sinking feeling. *"¿Cómo están, chavos?"*

"Sería genial si pudiera tener un shot," Zeb said sweetly. He turned to the rest of them. "Tequila, anyone?"

They ordered shots of tequila. Alex ignored the occasional glance from Ari as the night wore on, talking to either Penélope or Zeb, though they sat right next to each other. Music came from a live band in the corner of the room. There were two guitarists with different kinds of guitars, a bassist, and a woman singing in a low, smooth voice.

"We should dance," Penélope suggested, her eyes sparkling. "Come, Zeb."

Instead of refusing, as Alex expected, Zeb took her hand with a small smile and walked to an open space among the tables. Alex watched him in fascination. Zeb placed his hands on her hips and she circled hers around his neck. Then they began to dance. It was like nothing Alex had ever seen at any party back East. Penélope moved her hips rhythmically along with Zeb as their feet stepped forward and backward in unison.

Everyone in the bar clapped along, whistling loudly when Zeb flung Penélope out at arm's length and coiled her back into a shallow dip.

Alex felt a hand on her arm before she heard his voice, soft but clear amidst the song and noise. "Do you want to dance?"

"I don't know how," she said quietly, looking at him. Ari held her gaze as his hand slid down her arm until he loosely held her hand. Then he stood up, Alex standing with him automatically, their hands locked.

"I'll show you," Ari said, pulling her towards Penélope and Zeb. "Come, the main steps are simple."

She ignored the amused looks her way, as well as Zeb's slight sneer, instead focusing on Ari's dark eyes which she had avoided all night, his unruly curls falling over his forehead and his muscular arms bare in a crisp white shirt. He guided her hands up around his neck, her fingers brushing the delicate hair at the nape. Then his hands settled on her waist, the thumbs skirting her hips. She held her breath.

"Watch my feet. We move together, back and forth. Right foot forward, left foot forward, then right foot back, and left foot back. See? Again. Right, left, right, left, good. Again. Yes, exactly. Next come the hips, they move with the beat. *Sígueme.*"

Alex's face burned as her feet struggled to follow the steps, the entire bar appearing to watch her with barely concealed amusement. But soon she matched Ari's pace, the light step back and forth, and all she could think about were Ari's hands on her waist, guiding her hips, rolling them, *one, two, three, four, one, two, three, four...*

"Look at me," Ari whispered.

She looked up. Her body seemed to move of its own accord, stepping in time to the beat of the music, his hands at her hips tightening. She could now hear the woman singing, but it was a faraway sound, separate from this moment.

Ari did not look away as his hands slowly brought her closer to him, so close their hips were almost brushing, only their breaths left between them.

His mouth lowered to her ear. "Now you're dancing, Alexandria."

32

A POUNDING HEADACHE TORE her from a restless sleep, her hair stuck to her forehead with sweat. Alex groaned as she rolled out of bed and checked the small alarm clock on her bedside table. It was not even nine in the morning yet. She passed a weary hand across her forehead, closing her eyes against the pulse between her temples.

There was a sudden knock on the door and her heart skipped a beat. Was it Sister Stella again?

"Who is it?" She cringed at how hoarse her voice sounded.

"Penélope!" was the eager response.

Alex nearly groaned. "I'm—I need to shower."

"Come meet us out in the courtyard! And wear a bathing suit!"

"What?"

But there was no response. Alex shook her head as she got ready for a shower, then found Penélope and Zeb in the courtyard stretched out on towels in their bathing suits. When they saw her, Penélope sat up with a grin.

"It's over eighty degrees today," Penélope explained. "We thought it would be fun to kick off the summer properly. Here." She held out a hard seltzer. "For the headache."

Alex took the cold can and looked around. "Where's Ari?"

Zeb cut her a glance.

Penélope shrugged, handing Alex a spare towel. "Hopefully grading our exams. I want to know my grade."

"Wait...if you want to sunbathe, why not go to the beach?" Alex asked. "We can't be that far away."

The two of them shared a glance, then looked back at Alex blankly. Finally, Penélope said with an embarrassed air, "We don't have a car."

Alex smirked. "Well, I do."

Thirty minutes later Alex had her beloved Lady Montgomery flying down the highway, Penélope singing along with the music, an arm waving out the window. Zeb sat in the back seat with his hood up, appearing nonchalant save for his eyes which avidly took in the scenes outside the window.

Alex didn't bother speaking. Instead, she turned up the radio and followed the freeway signs to Chula Vista, which she had seen on her physical maps had the closest beach. The route took them up and over the mountains, the road's twists and turns slowing them down. It took an hour and a half to reach Chula Vista, a wide stretch of modest Californian suburbia, where she followed tourist signs pointing to the Silver Strand State Beach, a strip of sand built across the bay.

They parked the car and got out. The beach was packed for the first wave of summer heat. Penélope and Zeb were quiet as they headed out and grabbed an empty spot on the sand. They stretched out in their bathing suits, soaking up the blazing heat of May in Southern California. Alex had to close her eyes not to feel the rush of panic overtake her as it always did when she had a moment to think.

It looks like you got some sun in Florida. You're almost as dark as me.

Warren would have loved this beach. He always talked about visiting California with her. Then she thought of her mother, who had probably never driven out to the beach, who had probably never owned a car until she married her father. Maybe that was why she left with him. She had gotten in his car and for the first time, she was free to go wherever she wanted, regardless of money, regardless of the consequences. But then Alex remembered the city, the donkeys straining against the weight of those carts laden with goods, the carriages filled with veiled faces and colorful tunics. It was impossible to know what her mother would have chosen, which life she had truly wanted.

As the sun began to sink toward the horizon, Penélope sat up and looked at Alex with a frown. "We should help pay for the gas."

Alex felt suddenly embarrassed, and she gazed out at the ocean, shading her eyes. On the one hand, she knew it was ridiculous to demand gas money. But on the other, she didn't want to insult them by denying it either. "Don't worry about it. It's my thank you for being so welcoming."

But Penélope only shook her head. "That's very nice of you, but we have to pay you back somehow." She thought for a moment before her eyes brightened. "Would you want to meet my family?"

She looked at Penélope. "When?"

"Today. For dinner. I always go back home for dinner on Saturdays," Penélope said. Alex imagined four older brothers and the chaos of the dinner table. She felt herself shrinking from having no experience with siblings besides a spoiled toddler. "You don't have to if you don't want to."

"I do!" Alex said quickly. "But I don't want to give your parents more work. You have four brothers as it is!"

Penélope laughed. "Well, two of them won't be home this summer, if that makes you feel better. Don't worry, everyone is going to love you."

After they put on their clothes, Alex drove them straight to her house, as dinner would already be well underway by the time they arrived back. It turned out that her parents lived several miles down the road from the Lighthouse Church and Penélope usually biked home.

"It's just around this bend," Penélope said after a few minutes on the road.

When she turned the corner onto a dirt driveway, Alex saw a small, one-story house made of stucco with a well-groomed garden in front.

Penélope led them inside with a key. They entered a small living area with couches and a TV. On the other side of the partition wall was the kitchen and round dining table. Alex could see Penélope's mom flipping tortillas on the stove while her dad arranged the table with hot food.

"Hey, Mom, Dad, this is my friend, Alexandria," Penélope said.

They both looked up with identical surprised but pleased expressions. Then her mother came over to them, hugging Penélope and then Alexandria. When she released Alexandria, she frowned at her daughter.

"*Pepa, cariño,* why didn't you tell me? I would have made more food."

Penélope rolled her eyes fondly. “Don’t worry. I’m sure there’s enough food.”

The dinner was almost ready, so they sat down at the table as the rest of the food was placed in front of them. Penélope’s mother called her brothers to the table, and a moment later two male versions of Penélope ambled from the hall, introducing themselves to Alexandria in English and sitting down without another glance, as if it were perfectly normal that she was there.

Alex’s heart filled with a stinging jealousy despite herself. She felt the wholeness of the family around her, the bantering across the table, hands reaching out to serve each other food, an elderly golden retriever trotting around the table having appeared from somewhere in the house.

They spoke in a natural mix of Spanish and English, with Penélope or one of her brothers translating easily for Alex though she did not need it, asking her what she thought about the town, the New Academy, and her life in New York. The older brother of the two went to school in Boston, and they shared similar stories traversing the city and enduring the harsh winters.

Her old life on the other side of the country, as she saw it, seemed pale in comparison to this vibrant family, even the food an array of colors, the switching back and forth from Spanish to English like a melody in the background as they ate. Zeb appeared at ease among the banter and the boys, throwing in his own biting comment now and then that always threw the family into hysterics.

All too soon they were driving back to the New Academy, the sun having set long ago. Stars winked high above and Alex swore she saw a shooting star. She felt full on food, intoxicated with love for this place, the possibility in every constellation, in every mournful song of a nightingale.

“I’m sorry they were so loud,” Penélope said once they were back in the girls’ dormitories, Zeb having slunk away across the courtyard upon arrival with his usual curt goodbye.

“What? I love your family. Can I come every Saturday?” Alex asked. She led them to her room and they sat on her bed as if they were in middle school and having a sleepover.

Penélope laughed. "Of course! They loved you too. I've only ever brought Zeb and Ari over, so you can imagine how happy they were to talk to a girl for once."

"I can't imagine Zeb liking such a happy place. It doesn't match his all-black aesthetic," Alex joked.

"Actually, before we went to college I used to bring him over for dinner almost every day after school," Penélope said.

"Really?" She could not hide the shock in her voice.

"Yeah, he had a pretty shitty time at home. His dad wasn't always in the picture. I think his mom tried but she was still hung up on his dad. That kind of stuff is hard on a kid." She bit her lip suddenly. "Please keep this between us. He doesn't like people to know that."

"Of course," she said quickly, and didn't say that Zeb would eat her alive if she dared mention it to his face. Suddenly she saw Zeb in a whole new light, a light very similar to the one that cast all her memories of her mother in a dull gray color. She swallowed at the silence that had become palpable, knowing the words that were going to come out of her mouth.

"My mom left when I was ten," Alex added quietly, picking at a thread in the bed sheet. "I never really tell people, because they always think it's so sad. And it is. But I was always angry, never sad, and I just wanted to scream. I wanted to curse my mom out, and my dad for letting her leave, and everyone else just because. So I never told people in case one day I really did scream and everyone thought I was crazy."

She saw Penélope look at her sadly, but it was not pity, but rather a gentle sympathy for which Alex was surprisingly grateful. "Zeb screamed with me once. It's one of my favorite memories of him. One night, we were out somewhere getting drunk together. We must've been seventeen. In high school, we were best friends. We were each other's only friends, really. We were talking and somehow got around to his dad, who had done time and had just been released. And he just screamed. I held his hands and we screamed together. We never talked about that night again."

Alex could not speak. Her throat had closed up and she felt hot tears sliding down her cheeks. Yet her heart glowed for the first time with what could only be called true understanding.

Penélope gently touched her arm. "If you ever need to scream one day, I'm here."

33

THE DINING HALL WAS closed. Alex looked around the courtyard but there was not a soul to be found. Even though it was Sunday morning, she still expected to see students wandering around, the last few stragglers packing up before going home. Where had everyone gone?

Then she heard faint singing and realized it was coming from the church. She almost laughed. It was Sunday! Everyone was probably at Mass in the morning. She wondered if Penélope and Zeb were attending, though they had not struck her as particularly devout. It seemed in her obsession with finding her mother and the discovery of the city she forgot that the New Academy's original purpose was to educate the brothers and sisters of the church.

With nothing else to do, Alex decided to go on a walk. She passed the library without a glance; she spent enough time in there as it was. Instead, she left the courtyard through the side gate she had once snuck through, wanting to see those looming mountains again, and tried to remember the route Sister Stella had taken when giving her a tour of the grounds.

At last, she found a small dirt path that snaked around the cemetery and down into the wide valley where the track stood gleaming in the early light of the morning. She noticed a small figure running at the far end of the loop as she walked down the rather steep decline. As the figure approached, his broad, bronze chest shining with sweat and his loose dark curls bouncing with each step, Alex realized with a start that it was Ari.

Ari seemed to notice her a beat later because he came to a skidding stop a few feet away with wide eyes, his chest rising and falling rapidly as he tried to catch his breath. They were both silent for a long time. Ari squinted at the mountains far away, where the sun shone brightly overhead.

"Have a good Saturday?" Alex asked when he refused to speak.

He shrugged. "Finished grading papers."

Alex struggled not to sweep her gaze over his bare, tanned shoulders, the dark hair peppering his chest and trailing down his abdomen. "Why are you not at Mass?"

"I could ask you the same question."

This time Alex shrugged. "Not religious."

Ari glanced at her sharply. "Why are you here?"

"Don't worry, *professor*, I wasn't stalking you," Alex said irritably. "Everyone was at church and I thought I'd take a walk. I had nothing else to do anyway."

"You could be researching."

Alex rolled her eyes. "I needed a break."

A slight smile tugged at his mouth. "You sound like Zeb."

At this, even Alex could not hold back a reluctant laugh. Ari shook his head in amusement, then wiped his forehead with the back of his hand. A bead of sweat he missed rolled down the side of his temple. Alex swore he was even more tan than before, and she blushed when he shifted on his feet and she briefly saw the sharp indents of his hips.

"You knew that woman, didn't you? At the bar." Alex hadn't planned to confront him, but the words left her mouth before she could stop them. The question had been nagging at her all day yesterday and she was annoyed she didn't have a chance to ask him about it sooner.

But Ari only raised a brow. "I know most people in this town."

"But you *know* her." She sighed when he did not answer. "Fine, you've slept with her."

"I thought I only slept with students," Ari muttered, lightly kicking away a small pebble on the track. "Her name is Rosamaria. She's a friend of mine."

"A good friend?" she pressed. He glanced at her curiously, that look on his face as if he wanted to read her like a book. She began to blush and crossed her arms. "Stop that."

The movement broke his concentration and he looked at her anew. "Stop what?"

"You always give me this look," she said, trying to sound angry. "Like I'm a very interesting artifact."

He grinned. "But you are a very interesting artifact."

"I'm also a human being."

"That's still to be seen."

"Ari, be serious." But she was smiling. "Whatever. I'm sure she's not the only one anyway."

"Who?" he asked, confused. She hated that he had already forgotten while she could never forget that look at the bar, a silent claim that had somehow made her more jealous than at any time in the four years she had dated Warren.

"Rosamaria."

He didn't meet her eyes. "There's been a few. I have never dated anyone as long as you have, though."

"What's that supposed to mean?"

"Nothing," Ari said, turning away. "Everyone has their path in life. It just so happens that mine is quite different from yours."

"Spoken like a true scholar," Alex mocked.

He nodded absently. "That's me."

They both remained silent for a long moment. Alex began walking down the track, if only to avoid looking at his chest any longer. Ari reluctantly fell into step beside her as though it was the only thing to do, and they strolled for a time in silence. Alex could not help remembering their argument on Friday.

She cleared her throat. "I didn't know you've been living here since you were twelve."

Ari grimaced. "Sister Stella took me in."

"Can I ask how your parents died?"

He sighed. "I don't really know. My dad died when I was too young to remember him. My mom raised me in the valley, not far away from here. But we were alone, living in poverty. One day she got sick and had to go to the hospital. She left me here and I never saw her again. Sister Stella has been my guardian ever since."

"What was her name?" Alex asked softly.

"Semele. They were immigrants. I only learned English when I came to the New Academy. And then some Spanish."

"What did you speak before?"

"Greek, actually. Modern Greek." That explained his natural abilities in Ancient Greek.

Alex watched Ari sift a strong hand through his hair, ignoring the panging in her heart that felt both like longing and mourning.

"I wish I spoke Spanish. It was my mother's first language," Alex said, remembering how helpless she felt whenever Zeb and Penélope spoke in Spanish and she could not retort a swift reply, or when Eduardo had greeted her at the bar and all she could do was smile, too ashamed to even say hello.

Ari was silent. The only sound that could be heard was the humming cicadas in the trees and the crunch of dust and sand beneath their feet. He refused to pity her, as always, but for the first time, Alex was intensely grateful for it.

"Do you think we'll find her?" Alex asked, quietly.

He looked at her fiercely. "Yes, I do."

"I think we need to go back to the city. If my mom is still alive, that's where she would be."

Ari raised a brow. "We can't just go back to the city blind. It's too dangerous. Do you remember how lost we were?"

"What do you suggest?"

"We need to know what your mother was searching for." Ari paused. "We need to know the rest of that hymn, and I think I know where we might find a clue."

"When do we start?"

Ari smirked. "We can start right now."

34

Alex found Ari in the back of the library an hour later after showering and changing, hidden behind a stack of books, his hair still wet from his shower.

He saw Alex approaching and raised a brow. “Took you long enough.” As she sat down Ari slid a book across the table. “Here. You should read this.”

She picked up the book. It was a green canvas book with the title *Homeric Hymns* in small gold lettering on the front. “What is it?”

“The *Homeric Hymns*.”

“Well, I got that, thanks.”

“Do you have that poem your mother found? The one where she wrote *The Prince of Thieves?*”

Alex rummaged in her bag and pulled out her mother’s diary, where she kept the slip of paper safely stored in between the pages. She handed the paper to Ari and he laid it on the table between them, the Greek verses face up. After reading them again, he tapped the paper where the lines were carefully written.

“It’s as I thought. The verses are in dactylic hexameter, which is a meter Homer used for the *Odyssey* and *Iliad* but also the *Homeric Hymns*. Each line consists of six feet, and in each foot, syllables are arranged either long-short-short or long-long depending on a bunch of rules I won’t even get into. The first line reads like the first line in an epic or hymn, when the poet calls upon a god or muse to sing. It reads ὕμνον ἄειδέ μοι, μοῦσα, λόγοισι μελίφροσιν ἀλλά.” He spoke with a slight emphasis every third syllable so that it sounded like *hum*-non a-*ei*-de moi, *mou*-sa, lo-*goi*-si me-*li*-phro-sin *al*-la. “So ἄειδέ μοι means *sing me* and ὕμνον means *song*. So *sing me a song*. Μοῦσα is in the vocative case.”

"Vocative case?" Alex asked in slight exasperation.

"These are things you'll learn in my class," Ari said with a wink. "The vocative case means it's an address. So it reads, *Sing me a song, Muse,* addressing the Muse directly. The *Odyssey* starts somewhat similarly with ἄνδρα μοι ἔννεπε, μοῦσα, which translates *tell me about a man, Muse.*"

"Enough with the Greek lesson, Ari. What does the rest of the line say?"

Ari shot her a cool look. "Patience, Miss Alexandria. The entire line translates: *Sing me a song, Muse, with words sweet but...*"

"But what?"

"That's the next line. ἡδυτερεῖ φωνῇ κλέπτην διὰ νυκτὸς ἄειδε. *Sing me a song, Muse, with words sweet but with voice sweeter, sing about a thief in the night.*"

Alex frowned. "So is the thief in the night Hermes too? The Prince of Thieves?"

Ari sat back, crossing his arms. "It sounds like it. That's why I gave you that book. Because Homer already wrote a hymn to Hermes."

She opened the book to the table of contents and scanned the various hymns until she found the one to Hermes. She flipped through the pages and raised a brow. "It's long."

"Well, I doubt your mother's hymn is only two lines. The paper also looks like it's been torn from a full page. We're missing the rest of the poem."

"How is this supposed to help us?"

"Well, for one, if your mother's poem is somehow a lost hymn, which I still think is impossible," Ari said, "then it might have been Homeric. Because your mother's hymn was also written in Homeric Greek, which is a dialect you mostly see in Homer's work. He uses certain verb forms and vocabulary. The second reason is that Homer's *Hymn to Hermes* might provide us with a clue since it's written about the same god. Is that convincing enough for you?"

Alex sighed, opening to the first page of the hymn. Then she began to read. *Muse, sing of Hermes, the son of Zeus and Maia...*

It took her longer than she expected to work through the hymn. Hermes was born to the goddess Maia and Zeus, described as a son of many shifts, blandly cunning, a robber, a cattle driver, a bringer of dreams, a watcher by night, and a thief at the gates. On his first day after being born, he turned a tortoiseshell into a seven-stringed lyre, stole the oxen of Apollo, invented fire, and made it back into his crib before dawn. But his mother was not deceived by his innocent baby act, and soon Apollo himself discovered the theft. Hermes managed to appease Apollo, however, when he played his lyre, which so enchanted the son of Leto that the two made up and became friends as well as half-brothers. It was an amusing and strange story, though it didn't explain her mother's hymn.

"I think we found our Prince of Thieves," Alex said, closing the book. "He's even called a prince of robbers and a thief at the gates." She paused. "Your mother, Semele. Her name was mentioned."

Ari almost smiled. "The mother of Dionysus."

"So if Hermes is the thief in the night," Alex continued slowly, "then the question is..."

"What did he steal?" Ari finished, his eyes flashing dangerously. "That's our next clue."

The Son of Semele

What I remember now
is Dionysus, son of
glorious Semele, how he appeared
by the sand of an empty sea,
how it was far out, on a promontory,
how
he was like a young man,
an adolescent

His dark hair
was beautiful, it
blew all around him, and
over his shoulders, the strong
shoulders, he held a purple cloak.

—Homer, *Hymn to Dionysus,* lines 1-6,
translation by Charles Boer

35

Ari dropped a thick textbook on the desk in front of her, and Alex nearly jumped at the sound. Penélope and Zeb stifled their laughs at her shocked face. The cover of the book was an ugly orange with the title *Greek: An Intensive Course* above an antiquated drawing of a seated student about to write.

"Hansen and Quinn," Ari said. "It's the standard Greek textbook. For the next few weeks that's going to be your bible."

Alex pointed to the drawn student. "Is that supposed to be me?"

Ari raised a brow. "Turn to page one. Let's start with the alphabet." He turned to Penélope and Zeb, whose smirks dropped under his stern gaze. "You two are going to begin reading Book One of Herodotus' *Histories*." He paused. "At sight." Penélope and Zeb groaned.

The rest of the morning passed laboriously, with Penélope and Zeb struggling to translate the Greek on the spot and Alex trying to memorize the letters of the Ancient Greek alphabet, with Ari quizzing her on their names and teaching her to pronounce a few words afterward. It was even more difficult than she had imagined learning Ancient Greek would be.

Lunch came at last, and Penélope and Zeb complained about Ari's choice of Herodotus.

"Why couldn't we read, I don't know, the *Odyssey?* Or Greek lyric?" Penélope asked.

Zeb rolled his eyes. "You just want an excuse to read Sappho. I'd prefer tragedy. Give me some Plato or even Euripides."

"Ugh, Plato is annoying. All he does is answer his own questions. And he still makes no sense!" Penélope sighed. "I want epic love stories like Odysseus and Penelope! Or Achilles and Patroclus!"

"They both die in the end," Zeb said pointedly.

"That's what makes it epic!"

"What about the *Homeric Hymns?*" Alex asked hesitantly. Both Penélope and Zeb looked at her, startled.

"I've only read the *Hymn to Demeter,*" Penélope admitted. "They aren't that exciting. Mainly origin stories about the gods. But they're very important religious texts."

"Are any new texts ever...discovered?"

Zeb nodded. "Yes, though rarely. Papyri are sometimes found buried in Egypt. We have found fragments of Sappho there, for example, but the majority is not important, just letters or everyday transactions."

"Can I ask you a question?" Penélope asked, glancing at Alex carefully, who nodded. "Why are you taking this intensive course? Why learn Ancient Greek?"

Alex struggled to think of a response, but she was saved from answering when Ari's shadow covered their table. He had finished lunch and expected them to get back to work. She followed, relieved, and returned to her Hansen and Quinn textbook without a single complaint. The rest of the day she learned the rules of accents and was just introduced to the five noun cases—Nominative, Genitive, Dative, Accusative, and Vocative—when the class ended.

"No homework for tonight," Ari said. "We'll start slow and ramp up in a few weeks."

"That was slow?" Alex asked in disbelief, her mind reeling with grammar rules that revolved around a different alphabet she had hardly memorized.

"Just wait until you get to the verbs," Zeb said with a smirk, before he left to take a nap, Penélope not far behind. Ari had not gone easy on them, quick to correct any mistake or berate their imprecise translation.

Alex lingered, rifling through the textbook and glancing at the subjects of later chapters. *Present Indicative. Aorist Middle. Participles.* It was all a jumble of nonsense. Her heart sank. There was no way she would be able to keep up or even pretend she had an interest in any of it. While her mother had been a gifted

Classicist, Alex had never enjoyed studying languages, preferring the clean logic of math and the usefulness of economics and statistics. Ancient Greek, on the other hand, was a slippery, complex language, full of contradictions, exceptions to the rule, rules that felt arbitrary, and a strange vocabulary that had nothing to do with their lives now.

Ari raised a brow, the hand putting his Herodotus text in his bag pausing. "Remember, this is all to find your mother."

"Right." But it didn't feel like that anymore. She might be trying to find her mother, but this was her life, and right now it felt like she was throwing away everything she knew to study a dead language on the other side of the country in the middle of a desert.

"What's on your mind?" Ari asked softly.

Alex glanced up at his gentle voice, which she so rarely heard. "I wish I was more like my mother, that's all. Maybe it would be easier to find her if I understood Classics the way she did."

"I think you're more like her than you realize, Alexandria." He continued to pack up his books. "We should continue researching tonight. During the summer the library closes at five. Meet me outside after dinner. Try not—"

"—to be seen," Alex finished, slinging her bag over her shoulder. "I know."

Ari shook her head. "You are something else, Alexandria."

"Ari," she said with a small smile, and he gave her a strange look. *"I know."*

36

THAT NIGHT THEY CONTINUED to read various books that Ari felt could provide them with more clues. She read the rest of the *Homeric Hymns* in translation, then a couple of books written *about* the *Homeric Hymns,* then specifically about the *Hymn to Hermes,* and even books about the archaeological history of fragmentary hymns.

They found nothing important even after hours of reading, and at midnight Alex called it, hopeful that tomorrow they would find something useful.

The next morning she continued the Greek intensive course, doing exercises on the five noun cases until she felt confident in the differences, then moving on to the declensions of nouns. It turned out that the Ancient Greek language not only had different endings, or declensions, for words depending on how they functioned in the sentence, but there were different kinds of nouns, each with their own declension patterns further differentiated between three genders.

Her head felt heavy as she returned to her dorm after class to nap. She almost slept through dinner and grabbed a hasty meal before heading to the library to meet Ari.

The week passed swiftly with all of the work, the days blurring in the monotony of the library and reading day and night. Before she knew it, Friday classes finished, so that in only one week Alex had already learned the five verb forms and was now grappling with the *aspect* of verbs, which felt like yet another useless linguistic distinction, though Ari assured her the differences were very important.

Alex closed the book she was reading, setting it aside with a sigh and rubbing at her eyes. Across from her Ari looked equally exhausted, his eyes half-closed, and the book in his hands nearly slipping from his grasp. But he glanced up questioningly at her sigh.

"It's been almost a week and we haven't found anything," Alex said.

Ari raised a brow. "We've barely touched the library's collections."

"We've read enough to know that the library is not going to help us," Alex countered. She lowered her voice. "We need to go back to the city."

"No."

"Ari, listen to me—"

"No, listen to me." Ari looked around warily. "The city is dangerous. We don't know how it works there. We got lucky last time. No one caught us and no one looked at us too long. We could get trapped there, imprisoned, or even killed for taking one wrong step. It may all just be an illusion, but I felt every one of those punches, and those soldiers had real-enough-looking swords."

Alex rolled her eyes impatiently. "Nothing is going to happen to us." But she felt the truth in his words like a shiver down her spine.

He looked at her sternly. "If we get caught coming back from the city, we'll never be able to return, and you can forget trying to find your mother. We need to do it right this time."

Then he returned to his book. Alex glared at him, but in vain. He did not look up.

"What's going to happen when Penélope and Zeb notice our absences at night?" Alex asked quietly. "What if one of them lets it slip to Sister Stella? Or what about when the summer course comes and goes and I have no reason to stay here? Do you think Sister Stella will let me hang around then?"

Ari closed his eyes and sighed. She sensed his will fighting against hers, but this was *her* mother, not his, and she had the right to find her in whatever way she wished. And she knew like a compass seared on her heart that the answer to her mother's disappearance was in that city.

"We are running out of time, Ari," she continued in an urgent whisper. "Think about it. It'll take the two of us years to read every book in this library, and even then we might not find anything."

His eyes flew open, a slow smile on his face that only spelled danger. "What if it's not just the two of us?"

37

"THIS IS A HORRIBLE idea," Alex said, pacing the small space next to the library desk. Ari was perched on the spot Zeb once sat, his back against the stained-glass window.

"What do you mean?" Ari asked with a grin. "You thought it was a great idea yesterday."

"Because I didn't think about it!"

Ari rolled his eyes. "You're overreacting."

She glared at him. "We're talking about a doorway into a city that doesn't exist. And we have to convince them to help me find my mother who is probably dead! What if they don't understand? Or worse! What if they don't believe me?"

"Just trust me."

"What are you two arguing about this time?"

Alex turned at Zeb's snarky voice, her heart pounding. She saw Penélope and Zeb standing a few feet away.

"Nothing," Ari said dismissively. Alex's stomach turned. "You two are late."

Penélope raised a brow. "You're the one who's usually late." But she took her seat, followed by Zeb. Alex was still standing. She felt too nervous to sit.

"Before we begin, we have something to tell you," Ari said, glancing at her. "But Alexandria should probably be the one to say it."

"Tell us what?" Zeb demanded at the same time as Penélope asked sharply, "What is he talking about?"

"It's nothing serious," Alex said quickly, realizing what they were thinking.

"Well, I wouldn't say that," Ari muttered. She glared at him, and he put up his hands. "Sorry, I'll be quiet."

Alex turned to Penélope and Zeb, but mainly at the former, who looked at her encouragingly. "I didn't want to join the summer intensive to learn Ancient Greek."

"I knew it," Zeb said immediately.

Penélope shoved his shoulder. "No, you didn't. *Cállate por favor.* Let her speak."

"I never studied Classics and don't plan to. I didn't even know what that was before...before I learned that my mother had studied it, here at the New Academy. My mother disappeared when I was ten, the night before my birthday. She never said goodbye or left any means of contacting her."

Zeb looked startled, then frowned, but did not say anything. Everyone was looking at her, including Ari.

"Then over Spring Break, I found a box of her things. There was a copy of the *Iliad* in Ancient Greek, a dagger, and a diary. I learned that my mom and dad had eloped because she was pregnant with me, and she even left the New Academy before graduating. But her last entry in her diary was on the day before my tenth birthday. I always thought she had left us to remarry. But her diary made it seem like she hadn't wanted to leave at all. Then I found something hidden inside the cover of her diary."

She turned to Ari, who wordlessly handed her the black volume on the desk, which he had taken to his room last night to read. Alex opened the front cover and picked up the small piece of paper between her fingers.

"I found this." She handed it to Penélope. "Things began to connect. It seemed my mother was searching for something while she was here, related to someone called the Prince of Thieves. I left school without taking my exams to come here and find out what happened to her."

Zeb finished reading the paper, then looked up. "What does this have to do with us?"

"Zeb!" Penélope exclaimed.

"No, it's okay," Alex said to Penélope. "It's a fair question. In all honesty, I wasn't planning on telling you guys. Ari was sort of an accident. But together we found something that changed everything."

"And what could that be?" Zeb asked sarcastically.

"A door," Alex said simply. She glanced at Ari nervously, who nodded for her to continue. "There's a door in this library that leads to a foreign city, and I think that's where my mom is now."

"A door?" Penélope asked slowly. "To a city?"

"Yes. My mom had written about it in her diary, but I didn't understand it until I came here. The city is a kind of realm, a road between gods and mortals."

"Gods?" Zeb repeated in disbelief. "Do you hear yourself? Who would be stupid enough to believe this?"

"Me," Ari said, and Zeb stared at him in surprise. "I believe her because I saw the city with my own eyes. It's real. Gods or no gods, the city exists when it should not. It's as simple as that."

"You saw this place?" Penélope asked. "When?"

"Last week," Alex said quietly, averting her eyes from Penélope's. "We found it together."

"All this time? And you never said anything?" Penélope demanded, and Alex was surprised to find disappointment in her eyes. Somehow this felt worse than Zeb's disbelief, because she had not expected it when she should have.

"I didn't know if I could trust you," Alex said, then immediately winced at how that sounded. "We overheard Sister Stella being told to keep an eye on me. She taught my mother when she was here, and she made it seem like they had something to hide. We think it's the doorway to the city."

"Take us to this city," Penélope said firmly. "Then we'll understand."

"I-I can't," Alex said, glancing at Ari.

"Why not?" Zeb challenged.

"It's too dangerous," Ari said, and Zeb flushed, sitting back. "We almost got caught three times. The door is hidden below, in the old library that this floor was built on. Sister Stella and others guard it constantly. I had always thought they guarded the archives, but now I realize they are guarding an entrance."

"We know nothing about this place," Alex continued. "And if I want to find my mother, I need a plan."

"If we can't go to the city, what do you need us for?" Penélope asked. "It seems things would be a lot easier if we didn't know anything."

"Well, for the past few days, we've been trying to find the original hymn that my mom kept hidden. We think it might be somewhere in this library, and that it will explain how the New Academy and the city are connected to my mother." She exchanged brief smiles with Ari. "But we haven't been very successful. That's why we need your help. We can't do this alone. If I'm going to find my mother, I have to find out what she was searching for, and that starts with finding the rest of the hymn to the Prince of Thieves."

They were silent, mulling over the words that had been said. Alex and Ari shared an anxious look. Zeb's face was more dark and closed off than usual. Although she had doubted this plan all along, a small part of her had still hoped.

"Look, I know this sounds crazy—" she began.

"The school records," Zeb interrupted, looking up.

"What?"

"The school records. Have you looked through those?" he asked, raising a sharp, condescending brow.

Alex looked at Ari, who shrugged. "I didn't even know we had them, and I thought I had read the entire library."

Zeb gave a fake smile. "Trust me, I wouldn't know about them either if not for an extremely tedious architecture class where I had to look up the exact measurements of the Lighthouse Church. They record everything about the New Academy from its founding until some time in the late eighties. I guess they stopped recording them manually when the Internet came around."

"Where did you say those records were?" Ari asked. "Because class starts now."

Zeb hopped off the ledge. "Follow me, *professor.*"

They disappeared around the corner, leaving Alex and Penélope alone. She was terrified that Penélope would hate her for lying, for pretending when Penélope had only been welcoming and kind.

Penélope stood up and walked over to Alex. She took both Alex's hands in hers. "I don't know what this city is about, but I believe you. We are going to find your mother, no matter what it takes."

"Promise?" Alex asked with a shaky laugh.

"Promise."

38

The school records turned out to be exactly what they sounded like. Each volume—handwritten pages bound by leather—contained meticulously detailed records of the New Academy's founding, construction, and purpose.

"Look out for anything strange," Alex told them. "Any mention of a city, a door, a thief, or another academy. Anything at all."

But her mother had done the work for them.

"I think I found something," Penélope said, one of the records opened on her lap. Her fingers caressed the page. "Someone put this old parchment in here, where it talks about the original library. Look. It's in Ancient Greek and handwritten. The first few lines were torn off."

"I guess we'll be working on some Greek after all," Zeb muttered, closing his own leather-bound record and hovering over Penélope's shoulder.

Alex turned to Ari, holding up the small scrap of paper that her mother had kept. Ari took the paper and aligned it with the bigger parchment. He read over the lines quickly. "Yes, this is it. It fits perfectly."

He paused, reading the rest of the poem to himself. Alex could not help it anymore. She walked over to Ari, peering at the page. The entire hymn was written by hand, in a restrained, practiced script as though it had been written in the Middle Ages. It read:

ὕμνον ἄειδέ μοι, μοῦσα, λόγοισι μελίφροσιν ἀλλά
ἡδυτερεῖ φωνῇ κλέπτην διὰ νυκτὸς ἄειδε
ἐρχομενῳ πρὸς δ᾽ ἄντρα νεηνίῃ ἀνδρὶ ἐοικώς
ἔνθα πολύτροπος αὔτης ναὸν ἴεν πόδας ὠκύς
ὥς ἄδυτου φύλαξ ἒν χειμῶνι ἀπεβήσετο νόσφι·
κλέπτης εὗρεν χάσμα βάθη πέτρας πολύκαπνον·
ἔβλεψε φέγγος ἔν δὲ φάραγγ᾽ ὅτε πρὸς τὸν ὄψ εἶπε
τὸν κλέπτην χαίρειν· τί σύ μου δόμον εἰλήλουθας;
ὥς ἔφατ᾽ ἡ θἐα· τῇ καὶ φωνήσας προσέφη φώρ·
τὸν λίθον ἀγνή πότνια· χεῖρ᾽ ὀρέγων ῥόον εἶπε·
καὶ τότε γῆς ἄπο θερμὸν χλῶρὸν τὸν δ᾽ ἕλε λᾶα
τὸν δ᾽ ἀπαμειβόμενος προσέφη κεχολωμένα θυμῷ
οἶδας ἔχειν δύναμίν; σοι λεξω· κεῖνος λίθος εἶχε
τὸν κόσμου μυστήριον· ὥς ἔφατ᾽ ἡ θὲα τῆς γῆς·
κλέπτης παύσας ἔτρεψ᾽ ἰδεῖν καπνὸν καταπίνειν
βωμὸν· καὶ τότε μορφὴν ὄρφνης ἐξαναδῦσαι
οὐδε γε γυναικὸς ἀλλὰ δράκοντος ἔθει δ᾽ ὅ συνῆκε
ἡ θὲα τὸν εἶπον· μὴ δῶρον θεῖον ἀφῇς μου.

Ɛ

Alex ran her eyes over the words, wishing she could understand. Then her eyes fell to the bottom of the page, where there was a small E written in the corner.

She pointed to the E. "An E was carved on the Squatting Scribe's robe as well. That can't be a coincidence."

"No, it can't," Ari said slowly.

"The Squatting Scribe?" Zeb asked dryly.

"It was the door into the city," Alex explained. "But what does the E stand for?"

"Or who," Penélope suggested.

"Read the rest of the hymn already," Zeb said impatiently.

Ari followed the next line delicately with his finger. "νεηνίῃ ἀνδρὶ ἐοικώς is a typical Homeric construction, literally meaning *looking like a young man.* ἐρχομενῳ πρὸς δ' ἄντρα, *coming into the caves.* So, *looking like a young man, he came to the caves*...ἐρχομενῳ is dative because of ἐοικώς—"

"Enough with the lesson, Professor Melamed, just translate it. We all know you can read Greek on sight," Zeb interrupted, though he was leaning over Ari's desk, listening intently.

Ari rolled his eyes, but he straightened up, a determination hardening his eyes. "Fine. I'll translate it all at once:

"Sing me a song, Muse, with words sweet but
with voice sweeter, sing about a thief in the night.
Looking like a young man, he came to the caves,
where the trickster entered her temple with swift feet,
since the keeper of the sanctuary had gone far away for winter.

The thief found the smoke-filled chasm in the depths of rock.
He saw a glimmer in the ravine when a voice said to him:
Hello, thief. Why have you come to my home?
So spoke the goddess, and the thief replied to her saying: The stone,
Holy Queen, his hand reaching into the stream as he spoke.

He grasped the green stone, hot from the earth,
and she said to him with anger in her heart:
Do you know the power you hold? I will tell you—that stone holds
the secret of the universe. So spoke the goddess of the earth.

The thief, pausing, turned and saw smoke engulf
the altar. A shape emerged from the darkness,
not of a woman but a snake, he realized, and ran.
Then the goddess said to him: Do not waste my precious gift."

No one spoke for a long time, the words seeming to vibrate in the air and then settle like dust on the shelves. Alex's head was spinning. She stepped away from Ari's side and sat down on a chair.

"One thing is pretty obvious, isn't it?" Penélope said. They all turned to her in surprise. "Don't you see?"

"Obviously we don't," Zeb said.

Penélope pointed to the paper. "In the first stanza. *The trickster entered her temple with swift feet, since the keeper of the sanctuary had gone far away for winter.* It's the Temple of Apollo. According to Homer, Apollo killed the serpent Python, a child and protector of Gaia at Delphi, in order to establish his oracle. Later it was a widely accepted belief that Apollo deserted the temple during the winter months. It has to be that."

"Wait," Alex said. "I remember something from the Hymn to Hermes that talked about the serpent Python. I thought it might be a good example of his thievery. Let me find it." She pulled out the book of hymns in her bag, which she had kept in case she needed to refer back to it. It only took her a few minutes to find the passage. *"For I will go to Pytho to break into his great house, and will plunder therefrom splendid tripods, and cauldrons, and gold, and plenty of bright iron, and much apparel; and you shall see it if you will.* Maybe he's talking about the Temple of Apollo."

"So the thief is Hermes and he is stealing something from the Temple of

Apollo?" Zeb summarized doubtfully. "What is he trying to steal?"

"The stone," Ari said. "Apollo is gone for the winter. A boy slips into the temple and tries to steal a green stone. Gaia tells him that it holds the secret of the universe. Then he runs away." He paused, then his eyes widened. "The stone. The stone is green. That's it."

Zeb raised a dubious brow. "A green stone?"

"The Emerald Tablet," Ari said slowly, as if he thought everyone should know it. "It's a Hermetic text associated with the Hermes Trismegistus. It's essentially a text about alchemy and magical properties. That must be the stone they are talking about."

Penélope smiled, the pieces of the puzzle fitting together. "There's only one question left."

"Where is the stone now?" Ari asked. Finally, Ari looked at Alex, as if he had been waiting for this moment all along.

"It's in the city," she said. "I know it."

39

"So, TELL ME AGAIN why your mother was trying to find this Emerald Stone?" Zeb asked. He was lying on the grass, his long, pale legs splayed out carelessly, a forearm shielding his eyes from the sun directly above them.

"Not this again," Penélope muttered, focusing even harder on her book as if that would block out Zeb's voice.

"I'm just asking," Zeb said. "Because she better have a damn good reason after we've spent literal days researching about it."

He was right, despite how much that pained Alex to admit. Ever since they discovered the original hymn that her mother had hidden, Ari had marshaled them to read through hundreds of books over the next three days in search of another text that mentioned the Emerald Stone and its possible connection to the myth. He was certain that was how she found the city, but Alex was not so sure.

Now it was Friday, and they had not found a single mention of the myth, the Emerald Stone, or anything even loosely related. She was constantly on the verge of passing out on her bed from exhaustion or boredom. But Zeb could never know this, so she closed her book and sighed, trying not to roll her eyes when Zeb's head flopped to the side dramatically to look at her.

"The myth says the Emerald Stone holds *the secret of the universe*," Alex said. "Does that not satisfy you?"

"But even if that were true," Zeb persisted, "why did she not choose to live like a normal teenager instead of going on this mythical treasure hunt? Why didn't she just go out to bars? Get drunk?"

"Is that what you think normal teenagers do?" Penélope asked. "No wonder I'm your only friend."

"That's not true," Zeb said, crossing his arms. "Ari's my friend. Speaking of, where is he? Why isn't he here reading like the rest of us?"

This time Alex did roll her eyes. "We've already talked about this. If Ari, who is supposed to be our *professor*, spends all his time around his students, reading a million books a day, someone's bound to notice."

"Of course Ari gets a free pass with you," Zeb muttered. "We all know the truth."

"What's that supposed to mean?" Alex asked sharply, though she knew the answer. "I have—"

"—a boyfriend, I know," Zeb interrupted. "That's never stopped anyone before."

"Don't listen to him," Penélope said, glaring at Zeb. "He's just trying to get a rise out of you because he's bored."

And jealous, Alex did not add. She could not afford to lose his help, if not his friendship. Besides, she wanted to speak with Ari. "I think I'm gonna go. I'll see you guys later?"

Penélope looked at her worriedly. "Sure. Dinner?"

Alex nodded and began walking away.

"Say hi to Ari for me," Zeb sneered once she turned around, triumph flashing in his eyes when Alex glanced back and blushed. For all their differences, they were very similar, which Zeb used to his advantage too often.

She left them bickering in the courtyard, hardly glancing at their books. Even Penélope was exhausted from the reading, rubbing her eyes and yawning. Alex felt guilty that she had roped them both into something which did not concern them. But then she remembered Penélope's face when she told them about the city. *All this time?*

They were in it now, whether she liked it or not.

Alex found Ari in his usual position, lying across a library desk in the most unprofessional manner, his shirt riding up his stomach, revealing the barest sliver of skin. He had not noticed her yet, completely absorbed in his book.

"Ari," she said softly.

He sat up quickly, startled. When he saw it was her, he relaxed. "Alexandria."

She could hear her name said like that a thousand times. "I guess this time I'm scaring you."

Ari frowned. "I never really apologized for that night. I don't usually get that drunk, but you caught me on a bad day."

"I thought you were pretty cool for it," Alex admitted.

He cocked his head. "Did you now?"

"Don't let it get to your head," she said, "but yes."

"And do you still think I'm cool?" Ari asked challengingly. With him, everything was a challenge. Alex smirked, enjoying the competition which was so foreign to her.

"You do look very cool while wrestling, but other than that..." she pretended to think about it. "Yeah, that's it."

"Very funny, Alexandria."

"I have been told I have a sharp wit," she said, watching him hop off the desk and ruffle his hair.

"With my outrageously good looks and your unparalleled witticism, we make the perfect team, don't we?"

Alex forced herself not to smile. "Okay, that's enough. I had something serious I wanted to talk with you about."

"Is my chiseled jawline not serious enough for you?"

"Jesus Christ, Ari, just listen to me."

"Don't say the Lord's name in vain or Sister Stella might expel you for it."

"We already know she believes in very different gods," Alex countered.

"Fair point."

"I wanted to talk with you about the Prince of Thieves."

Ari immediately transformed. He stood up straighter and his eyes gleamed, as if a light shone from within. "What about it?"

"I'm not sure we're going about this the right way, that's all," Alex said casually, but she winced on the inside, knowing Ari would absolutely disagree.

"In what way?"

"I just think we're limiting ourselves if we believe that my mother was only trying to find the Emerald Stone."

This quieted Ari, who walked back over to his desk and hopped up on the edge.

"My mother wasn't just trying to find some stone in a myth," Alex continued. "There has to be more to it."

"This is not just some stone if the myth is true," Ari countered. "The Emerald Stone holds the secret of the universe."

"I know, but you don't understand. You don't know my mother."

"And you do?" he asked, but the moment he said the words, he grimaced. "I'm sorry, but it's true. You may think you know her, and maybe in some ways you do, but there is a lot that you don't know."

Alex's face grew hot. She hated how he made her feel so thrilled one moment and so infuriated the next. "I'm not saying the Stone isn't part of it. But my mother disappeared. She wasn't hunting some mythical object for the fun of it. There is something much bigger going on, something that made her leave, something that we can't see. If we just went back to the city..."

"No."

"Ari, we've been searching for days now and we've found nothing. The people guarding that door would not leave precious information about the city just lying around."

"But your mother did," Ari pointed out.

"And she's not here anymore, is she?" Alex asked, her voice raising. She closed her eyes, refusing to cry in front of him. "We're not going to find any answers here. We have to go back to the city."

"Then go," Ari said harshly. He sighed. The words echoed in her chest painfully.

"I should never have come here," Alex said, wanting to hurt him like he had hurt her. "I should just go back home and forget I ever came here."

He looked up at her fiercely. "Maybe you should."

"Fine."

"Fine."

Alex turned around without another word and left the library, blinking tears away. She went straight back to her dorm room and flung herself on the bed. They were just words, words that meant nothing in the end because she would not go back home, and they both knew it.

She closed her eyes. Ari was right after all. Alex had her mother's diary, but besides that, Elena might as well be a complete stranger. She was someone who left her life a long time ago and never came back. So why was she trying to resurrect old ghosts now?

But Alex knew why.

Her heart longed to return to the city, to walk the streets her mother had walked once, to be a part of a world much greater than hers now. Maybe her mother had tried to find the Emerald Stone, more out of boredom than belief, stuck in this place like Ari had been, and ended up stumbling on something much different, something more.

Maybe Helen of Troy longed for new horizons, to give her something to believe in when her old life had none.

Suddenly she felt it, that feeling she had in the city, like a pair of eyes on her that crept up her spine. Alex sat up on her bed, looking around, her heart pounding. She saw a shadow pass the window, then a sharp tap like a beak on glass, and she gasped.

I am being watched. I feel their eyes on me, the eyes of eternity, the gaze of gods.

There was another tap, louder, coming from the door, and she saw another shadow underneath her door frame before realizing that the tap was a knock on her door.

"Who is it?" she called out, her voice trembling.

"Penélope!"

Alex sank back against the pillows, breathing hard, before laughing quietly to herself. Now she was becoming paranoid. Great.

"Come in!"

The door knob turned, then Penélope's head appeared. "What's up?"

"Not much."

"Is something wrong?" Penélope asked worriedly, hearing the waver in her voice and stepping fully into the room.

"Nothing," Alex said with a sigh. "I just hate boys sometimes."

"Ari pissed you off again?"

"He can never accept that I might be right sometimes." Alex paused. "I told him I wanted to go back to the city, that we would never find anything up here. He disagreed and basically told me that I should never have come here."

Penélope's mouth fell open angrily. "He did not say that."

"I might have suggested it first, but he agreed."

"Well, either way, he's being stupid. I know him. When you're not there you're all he talks about. *Alexandria said this, Alexandria did this, Alexandria saw this...*"

Alex laughed at Penélope's imitation of Ari. "Oh come on, he does not."

"Maybe not like that, but still. He would never want you to leave, not before we find your mother. He may be an idiot sometimes, but he does care about people, and he cares about you." Penélope shook her head. "But enough about Ari. We can deal with him later. What about we go out together, just us two? Zeb has been annoying me all day. We can have a girls' night and get drunk and dance."

Alex grinned, because that was exactly what she needed. *"¡Vámos!"*

40

An hour later they walked up to *El Sol,* dressed in their shortest dresses and already tipsy, having taken shots while putting on each other's makeup.

Alex entered the bar with a new confidence in her step. When someone from a nearby table approached and introduced themselves to her, Alex replied in a simple Spanish phrase, not worried about her accent or rough grammar.

"Come on, let's get a drink," Penélope said, and they walked over to the bar holding hands. Tonight there was another bartender, a handsome man with a mustache and a striped shirt half unbuttoned. The bartender smiled at Penélope and she smiled back, blushing. *"Dos mojitos, por favor."*

Alex raised a brow, and Penélope blushed even more. When they had their drinks, Penélope rushed her to the center of the room where several couples had already begun dancing. With one hand holding their drinks, Penélope drunkenly attempted to twirl Alex around, laughing whenever they spilled some of their drink on the floor.

"No, no, así, señorita."

An old man had stepped in and was trying to teach Alex a new dance, while Penélope and his wife laughed to the side. Despite nearly tripping over herself and not knowing a single person besides Penélope, Alex felt as light as air, as if nothing could touch her.

Penélope had a beautiful smile on her face. The bartender kept sneaking glances at her from the bar, which only added a glow to Penélope's cheeks. Alex mentioned it to Penélope.

"Oh no, they all do that," Penélope said, waving her away. "Besides, he's one of my brother's friends."

Alex left it at that, pulling Penélope back to the center of the room, dancing properly now that they had finished their drinks, twirling and moving their hips as the band and the locals cheered them on.

"Oh god, I haven't had this much fun in so long," Alex said, her chest constricting at the truth of it. They had stopped dancing to go to the restrooms, which were hidden in the back of the building. Someone was in there already taking an annoyingly long time, so they waited in the cramped hallway.

Penélope smiled. "Sometimes you just need a break from the boys. I'm so happy I have someone to do that with now."

The door to the bathroom opened and Ari stepped out. Alex's whole body froze as if she were seeing a ghost. He stopped when he saw the two of them waiting there.

"Ari?" Penélope asked in surprise. "What are you..."

The door opened again, and the other bartender with the dyed blonde hair stepped out. *Rosamaria*. Her eyes glanced over Alex and Penélope before she whispered something to Ari and walked past them.

Alex felt cold all over. She almost shivered when Ari nodded his head silently, then brushed by them without another word. Penélope stared after Ari in disbelief, shaking her head.

"What an idiot," Penélope said softly.

Alex did not know what she meant by that. "I'll wait here. I don't need to go."

Penélope bit her lip, as if she knew Alex was lying, then walked into the restroom. When the door closed, Alex allowed her face to drop into her hands. Why did she care? She had a boyfriend. Warren. But it was Ari's voice who said his name, almost mockingly. *I have never dated anyone as long as you have, though.*

And that was the worst of it all, because it was not even true. Alex had stopped dating Warren for a long time.

41

"CAN I HAVE ANOTHER book?"

Alex looked up, startled at Zeb's question. It had been silent for so long that the sound of another human voice felt like an intrusion in the still, deathly quiet of the library.

Ari wordlessly handed Zeb another leather-bound volume from the stack on his desk. They lapsed into silence again. The turning of a page, a small sigh, and faraway murmurs and footsteps were the only sounds that broke the quiet. It was Monday once more and instead of working on Greek, they decided to search for more evidence about the Emerald Stone.

Time passed slowly. Alex's head pounded. She needed to take medication. Reading for so many hours straight was catching up with her. She had barely exchanged more than a few words with Ari today, though it was not for a lack of trying on his part. Whenever he spoke to her, Alex did not have the heart to reply. She was drained. After seeing Ari with Rosamaria, Alex had thought she would be upset, or even sad. Instead, she only felt resigned. After all, from the moment she arrived until now, nothing had changed, even if at times she thought it had.

It must have been nearing late afternoon, the light from outside dimming as the minutes or hours wore on. Alex had no idea how long they had been sitting here, wasting a beautiful summer day shut up inside the library, reading meaningless texts. Her current book was droning on about the linguistic importance of a certain grammatical structure used in Homer's epics, which she barely understood, hardly knowing any Ancient Greek. She started to skim a little faster.

...by placing the dative...Homer intensifies... the mirroring quality—

"Pardon me."

Alex jumped, closing her book. Sister Stella was standing a foot away from where she sat on the floor, her back against the bookshelves. The others had looked up as well, staring at Sister Stella in mingled surprise and worry. Had she found out what they were up to?

But Sister Stella was only looking at Alex. "May I have a moment outside with you, dear?"

"Of course." She got up shakily. Her worst fears were coming true. Sister Stella had discovered that Alex did not know any Ancient Greek, that she was a liar and a thief, unlocking doors she was not supposed to open.

She glanced one last time behind her, where Penélope looked more terrified than her, Zeb watching her leave with furrowed brows and Ari sitting as still and expressionless as a statue.

When they exited the library, Sister Stella turned to her.

"Now that we are alone, I feel at liberty to explain. There are people here who would like to see you."

"People?" Alex asked, perplexed.

"Yes," Sister Stella said pleasantly. "Right over there. They claim to be your friends. Do they look familiar?"

Alex looked across the courtyard and froze. In the middle of the fruit trees, standing with several suitcases by their sides, were Warren, Chloe, and Owen.

42

She could not believe what she was seeing. Owen was on his phone, Chloe had large black sunglasses on, swatting away at small gnats searching for fruit, and Warren, her Warren, was staring straight at her.

"Shit."

Beside her Sister Stella's brows rose, but Alex did not care. Her heart pounded slowly, like the drum of a death march. They were here, at the New Academy. It was incomprehensible.

Warren began walking towards her, and then Alex's legs moved forward, hesitantly, until he was there, in front of her, and she was engulfed in his arms, in his smell, so nostalgic and familiar, like returning to an old childhood bedroom. His arms were strong wrapped around her. She was reminded of other arms, another strength, but she pushed those thoughts away, focusing on the warmth of Warren's neck beside her cheek.

He pulled away and stepped back, clearing his throat. It looked like he wanted to say something, but before he could, someone had darted forward and barreled into Alex, imprisoning her in a tight, wiry hug. Chloe.

"I can't believe you left me," she said in an odd whisper, and Alex realized she was choking back tears. This more than anything made Alex blink faster.

When she finally released her, Owen came forward. To her surprise, he looked mildly worried. After he hugged her less dramatically than the others, he put a firm hand on her shoulder. "You're here."

Alex nodded, unable to speak. She looked to her right and saw that Sister Stella had left them, perhaps to give them space. But Alex wished she had stayed behind, if only to break the awkward silence that came next.

Warren stared firmly at the ground, while Chloe fiddled with her sunglasses. Only Owen looked her in the eyes. He sighed, realizing that he would have to be the one to break the ice.

"You left without saying anything," Owen said quietly. "We thought maybe you had gone home. But after a few days, we called your father just to make sure, and he said you weren't there. We wanted to look for you right away, but your father didn't let us, making sure we finished our finals first. He considered getting the police involved and had already hired a private investigator. Then you texted Chloe. Warren convinced your father to let us come get you."

"Come get me?" Alex repeated tersely. "What does that mean?"

"Nothing," Owen said quickly. After an angry glance from Warren, he rolled his eyes. "Fine. Then you speak."

Warren straightened up, and Alex was reminded of his height, the leanness of his limbs. "We're just glad that you're alive."

But he said it harshly and without his usual tenderness. Chloe crossed her arms. She had pulled herself together. "Well I, for one, need an explanation. What the hell, Alex?"

For some reason, this relieved Alex, and she shrugged. "I had to leave."

"Without letting us know?" Chloe asked sharply. Alex almost smiled at her tone, the sunglasses, her acrylics long and sharp as she placed her hands on her hips. She had missed Chloe's attitude.

"I thought you might stop me from leaving." She addressed all of them, but her eyes flickered to Warren. He looked at the ground angrily.

"What about school? Your family?" Chloe demanded. "Your *life?*"

"You wouldn't understand—"

"Try me."

Alex was silent. How could she possibly explain everything? How could she explain how a bird on her windowsill had spoken to her, how the sound of a waterfall was like the chaos of gods in battle, how every breath she took at that goddamn school felt like it could be her last?

"She doesn't have to explain," Warren said warily.

"So now I'm the bad guy?" Chloe said, glaring at Warren. "You were the one complaining the whole time coming here. I'm just saying what we are all thinking."

Owen rolled his eyes. "Please, stop. You two have been arguing this whole time."

"And you," Chloe said, turning on Owen, who raised a brow. "Don't act like the peacemaker when you always side with Warren."

"Well, darling, that's because he's usually right," Owen said sweetly. Chloe narrowed her eyes at him, and was about to respond when another voice spoke instead.

"What's going on here, Alexandria?"

They all turned. To Alex's horror, Ari was standing behind them. She tried to signal with her eyes that he should leave, but he either did not notice or ignored her.

"Who are you?" Warren asked Ari sharply. "And how do you know Alex?"

"Yeah, who are *you?*" Owen repeated, but in a tone of approval, looking Ari up and down.

Chloe threw up her hands with a derisive laugh. "Incredible. Ignore him."

"I'm Ari, a professor at the New Academy," Ari said, ignoring all of them except Warren. "I'm guessing you're Warren, Alexandria's boyfriend."

Warren looked at Alex, ignoring Ari. "What's going on here, Alex?"

"There's a lot to explain—"

"Ari, what's taking you guys so long?" Zeb stepped out of the library, Penélope right behind him. When he saw Warren, Chloe, and Owen, he stopped. "Oh."

Alex took a deep breath in. "You guys should probably sit down for this."

43

"I JUST—I KEEP GOING over it, in my head, trying to figure out why," Warren said, almost in a whisper. "But I can't. I don't get it."

They were in a different row in the library, standing in the corner against opposite bookshelves. She could just hear Chloe and Owen asking the others a million questions.

After Zeb and Penélope had shown up, it was too much. Alex led them all into the library and with the help of Ari, they explained everything from finding her mother's box in the Montgomery house to their day in the city to the discovery of the rest of the Prince of Thieves hymn.

Surprisingly, besides a few pointed questions, they had needed less time to believe her than Penélope and Zeb had. Once Alex had finished explaining everything and answering most of their questions, Warren had pulled her aside to talk privately, more concerned with knowing why she left him than anything about her mother or a magical city. She had ignored Ari's gaze lingering on them as they let others put up with Chloe and Owen's constant bickering.

"I couldn't tell you," Alex said. "I couldn't."

"I thought you died."

Alex felt her eyes burn. "I know."

"Then why? Why?"

"I don't know what you want me to say," she said, starting to sound angry despite herself. "I explained everything. You even believed the city and my mom and the Emerald Stone. Everything. Why can't you accept that I had to do what I did?"

"Because those things don't matter to me as much as you do!" Warren groaned in frustration, turning around and resting his forehead against one of the shelves.

Alex stepped towards him because she could not respond, she could not lie any longer. She placed a hand on his back hesitantly. Warren immediately tensed under her touch. She tried to call up those memories, the old attraction, the love, or even the hate, but nothing, nothing rose up inside of her. Her hand dropped, and he turned around.

"We should go back to the others," Warren said. She nodded and began to walk away when Warren's hand shot out and grabbed her wrist. He looked at her, eyes bright with pain. "I do forgive you, if that means anything to you anymore."

Alex wished she felt something, resentment or simple gratitude, but Warren was a part of her past, and looking at him was like watching a fading sunset and wishing for the sunrise.

But he was still a part of her, even if it was her past. "It does."

They walked back to the others together. Ari searched her face when he saw them return, and Alex averted her eyes. Beside her Warren stiffened, noticing the interaction, but said nothing.

"And you've never sailed?" Owen asked Ari, who returned his attention to the conversation again. "Because you definitely have the physique for it."

Ari shook his head. "No. You see, I live in a desert."

Owen nodded his head slowly. "Yeah, that would make things difficult."

Usually Alex found Owen's bold flirting very amusing, but now it irritated her. She glanced around and saw that she was not the only one. Chloe was cutting Owen a scathing look and Zeb's face was growing icier with every word that Owen said.

Penélope looked relieved when Alex sat beside her. If she thought Zeb and Ari were annoying, she had another thing coming.

"Well, well, look who decided to join the party," Owen drawled, smirking at Alex and Warren.

Alex rolled her eyes. "I was hoping you'd be done talking by the time we came back, but I guess that's too much to ask for."

Penélope laughed. Zeb looked at Owen as if he could not decide whether he was charmed or annoyed by him.

Warren seemed to ignore the conversation entirely, only looking at Alex. "So what's next?"

She turned to him, surprised. "What?"

Chloe nodded in agreement. "Yeah, what's next? Are we going to find your mother or what?"

Alex was speechless. She had thought...

"Did you think we'd just leave after everything we learned?" Owen asked, grinning.

"But where are you gonna stay?" Alex asked in disbelief. "The motel?"

This time Ari spoke, smiling faintly. "Alexandria, please welcome our new students of the Ancient Greek summer course."

44

"So let me get this straight," Owen said, crossing his arms and looking at Alex. "You all have been reading *books* in order to find your mother?"

Ari raised a brow, looking mildly offended, but it was Zeb who narrowed his eyes at Owen. It was just the first day of their recently increased Ancient Greek summer intensive but Alex wondered if they would last the first hour together. Everyone seemed to have someone to glare at, even Penélope, who was usually the most willing of them all to assume the best in others.

"It's called research," Zeb said slowly. "Don't you go to Harvard?"

Owen shrugged, unfazed. He probably considered Zeb's taunts as child's play compared to Chloe's blows which always seemed to hit below the belt. "Some days I do. But that seems hardly relevant."

"Please," Ari said with a gesture of his hand and a tight smile, his patience clearly wearing thin. "Elaborate."

"What Owen is trying to say but failing miserably," Chloe drawled, finally taking off her sunglasses that she had not removed since they had settled in the library, "is that books can give you a hint of her mother's situation but not who she was. When the police investigate someone's disappearance they try to understand the motive, the circumstances, the emotions. Those things always tell more about a person than facts ever can."

Ari, Zeb, and Penélope shared disbelieving looks which Alex could not help but smile at, though the smile faded when she caught Warren studying it.

"Like when Alex disappeared," Warren said quietly, and Alex's cheeks grew hot. Was he ever going to stop punishing her for that? "The investigator questioned each of us about Alex, what she was like before the disappearance, and why she might have felt the need to...leave."

Chloe rolled her eyes. "Unnecessary, Warren. But essentially, yes, that is exactly what I mean."

"So what do you suggest we do instead?" Ari asked.

"We have to figure out who Elena was," Chloe said impatiently. She turned to Alex. "What was she like? Tell me the first thing that comes to mind."

"She loved to read," Alex said without thinking twice.

Ari gestured towards her. "See?"

"No," Alex continued, the spirit of her mother's diary filling her voice like air in her lungs. "You don't understand. Yes, she loved to read the myths. But she was almost obsessed, to the point that she felt they were real. She saw them as the truth. As history. And when she found the city, I think she fell in love. Maybe in more ways than one." She paused. "The city was all her myths come to life."

Penélope nodded slowly, realization alight in her eyes. "We've been taking the myths as metaphors, or even riddles, when your mother never saw them like that."

"If these myths were real to her," Zeb said, frowning, "then the Prince of Thieves is real, not just a story. We have to start reading all the myths like she did, like they are real."

"As history," Ari echoed. He looked at Alex, a familiar determination hardening his face. "So instead of reading history to find the myths, we read the myths to find the history."

Chloe's eyes glittered. "Exactly."

Owen clapped his hands together, looking around eagerly with a pearly-white grin. Zeb nearly flinched at the sound, so loud in a usually quiet place. "Where do we start?"

No one spoke. Slowly, one by one, all eyes turned to Alex. She was her mother's daughter after all. She was the only one who knew the answer, and her mother had given it to her at the very beginning.

"We start with what my mother left me," Alex said softly. "The *Iliad*."

Ari locked eyes with her, and she knew from that passionate gleam in his face that he finally understood what she had been trying to tell him this whole time without truly voicing the words.

"Helen."

45

Penélope was stretched out on Alex's bed, flipping through her mother's diary. They had stopped their "class" for lunch and a break before they started up again in the afternoon.

The addition of Warren, Chloe, and Owen was shocking and yet not entirely unwelcome. Before they came, their strategy had been to read every history book in the library to discover anything more about the Emerald Stone and the Prince of Thieves. Now, they had hardly touched another book, discussing her mother's diary, memories Alex had of her, and any connections with the *Iliad.*

Alex had never spoken so much about her mother. She felt exhausted, but also lighter. For so long she had kept her mother's past and disappearance as buried inside her as possible. Once her mother had left, most people in her father's circles simply acted as if she had never existed, an unspoken judgment except in their eyes, which always lingered on her, making Alex's throat close up. Even Warren, who truly loved her, had steered clear of her mother, never mentioning her unless Alex brought her up.

But now they were all questioning her about her mother, wanting her to recollect memories of her despite how hard she had tried not to in the past. Alex constantly had to fight the heat blooming on her neck when Chloe asked about her mother's family. When she tried to explain how her mother had been disrespected by her father's family because she had not come from the same background as them, the group fell hushed. Warren almost looked ashamed, as if pained he had never thought to see it that way before.

"It was the little things. I remember speaking in Spanish with her at the park," Alex had said, the memory still vivid, though years of denial had pushed it to the depths of her mind. She must have been seven or eight. "And an elderly couple came up to us and asked if she was my nanny. I didn't know enough to be bothered, but my mom was sad. She only cried when we left, and then I cried too. I thought I had done something wrong."

Everyone had avoided looking at her, frowning. She knew that this story disheartened them more only because it provided a very obvious reason for her mother's disappearance that did not include anything about an Emerald Stone or a magical city. But none dared say it to her face.

Only Zeb looked straight at her, startled. "You speak Spanish?"

She held his gaze. "Not anymore, but I understand it perfectly."

Zeb fell silent, probably remembering his snide comment on the first day they met. He had assumed, like most people do, that she did not understand. But in the end, though he was wrong in that, he was right in what he had said. She led a very privileged life, thanks to her father, and that made her all the more disconnected from the life her mother had led here.

But their conversation had ended on a good note, deciding to regroup later in the afternoon to start discussing Alex and Ari's night in the city in more detail, as they had spent most of their time painting a more solid picture of her mother. Chloe, Owen, and even Warren at times had brought a new energy, a different perspective, to their pursuit, for which Alex was surprisingly grateful.

Penélope was looking at her with a thoughtful air from across the dorm room. Alex stood up and walked from her desk to the now empty space on the bed where Chloe had just been. The three of them had returned to Alex's room together. It was nice to be in a group of girls for once, a sentiment she knew Penélope and Chloe shared as well, though perhaps for different reasons. Chloe had just left to organize her room, since after arriving yesterday she barely had time to unpack and had gone to bed early.

"What?" Alex asked.

Penélope continued to study her, but not in the way Ari did. She looked at Alex like one might look at a painting from another time and place, curious, thoughtful, and maybe a bit confused.

"You said earlier that your mother may have fallen in love in more ways than one," Penélope said. "You meant Alexandros, didn't you?"

"Yes." Her voice was barely a whisper. Alex cleared her throat. "At first, I thought it was a coincidence that we have the same name. But now..." She looked at the *Iliad,* resting in the golden case, which sat on her desk. "Now I don't."

"Paris and Helen," Penélope said, nodding her head.

"Alexandros and Elena." Alex sighed. "Exactly. It would explain her disappearance, wouldn't it?"

Penélope shrugged, but her eyes were dark and serious. "There are a thousand myths explaining why Helen left with Paris."

"How do we figure out which one is the right one?" Alex asked.

"Maybe that's not our job. Maybe that's something only Helen knows the answer to."

Alex appreciated Penélope's confidence and trust in other people's reasons, but right now she only wanted the truth. "What if it could explain what happened to her? She's my mother." Alex did not voice the unspoken, *I have a right to know.* Did she really have that right?

"But she was also just a girl, once, like you," Penélope said, eyeing her meaningfully. "Sometimes we do unexplainable things."

Penélope was clearly referring to how Alex had up and left her friends and family without a single goodbye, perhaps to feel closer to her mother than she had ever felt before. But she did not leave to feel close to her mother, not even to find her mother, not really. In all honesty, she could not explain why she left, just like she could not explain why her mother had left.

She remembered Warren's frustration, his head pressed against a shelf in the library when he had asked her why she left him and she could not give him an answer.

Why can't you accept that I had to do what I did?

Now Alex could ask the same question of herself about Elena's choice to leave. Maybe she had no right to know. But then Alex thought of the city, the gleaming gate by the shipyards, the rowdy Academy boys wrestling on the street. Had Alexandros attended the Academy? Was that how they met?

More questions, and never any answers.

Warren's eyes returned to her, pain bright in the blue, a reflection of her own pain, the question repeating itself over and over again, like the persistence of a blue sky each morning. *Then why? Why?*

Because of her mother. Because a bird had told her to. Because she would never move forward unless she closed the door on the past. But none of those answers were the truth. Because sometimes there was no answer, and that was the only truth.

The door swung wide and clanged against the wall. Chloe walked inside and looked at the two of them on the bed. "What are you two gossiping about?"

Alex looked to Penélope, unsure she should share their conversation with Chloe. Penélope only smiled and nodded encouragingly. Always hoping for the best in others. But she did not know Chloe very well.

"My mother," Alex said, trying to sound flippant and failing. "I think she fell in love with someone named Alexandros in the city."

Chloe looked at her for a moment, before laughing. "Is that why you both look so serious? Honestly, I thought you were talking about something more important, like how I might murder Owen."

"This *is* serious," Penélope said, looking startled but not yet offended, perhaps hoping Chloe was simply joking. "The *Iliad* acts as a parallel, maybe even more than a parallel. You were the one who told us to understand who she was as a person. This could explain why she disappeared."

Chloe shrugged off her words. "Alexandros could be anyone. Do you know how many people I've dated? In the end, she married your father, Alex. Don't forget that."

"But she also left him," Alex argued.

"Why are you so determined to think your mother left for love?" Chloe asked, almost snarling the last word. Penélope's eyes widened, but Alex was used to her sharp tones and merely crossed her arms.

"We're not saying that."

"Yes, you are," Chloe said, sounding more bitter than accusing.

"Well, what if she did leave for love?" Penélope asked. "There's nothing wrong with that."

"Her mother was a scholar," Chloe countered. "You read the second to last entry. She loved the New Academy."

Penélope's eyes flashed. "Her mother was a teenager. Besides, a woman can be a scholar and in love."

"If she was so in love why did she marry someone else?"

Alex stood up. "What is your problem? I know you're still upset I just up and left but we are trying to find my mother, and if that means considering she left my father for someone else—"

The moment the words left her mouth, Alex understood why Chloe had resisted the idea so much.

Chloe flinched at the words, and said viciously, "I will not waste my time on another cheater. If your mother is even the slightest bit like my father, you'd be better off pretending she's dead and moving on."

With that, Chloe whirled out of the room, as she hated to be seen in any state of emotion. They heard a door open and slam shut down the hall. Alex sighed and returned to her place beside Penélope, who was staring at the door with her mouth slightly open.

"I'm sorry about that," Alex said after a silence passed unbroken. "I shouldn't have pushed it. I knew how she felt about these kinds of things."

"She is right about one thing," Penélope said with a sigh.

"She is?"

Penélope shook her head wryly. "Don't worry, Zeb is the same way. But she's only right in that we should not forget who your mother married."

Alex could not forget that, even if she tried. "She married my father because she was pregnant with me. They eloped before she even finished finals, moved to New York, and I was born a few months later."

"Wait." Penélope's brows furrowed. "When were you born?"

Her stomach dropped as they both turned to each other. "July twentieth."

"That's only three months after April. She was already pregnant for six months."

Alex racked her memory for any mention of it in her mother's diary, but she knew she would remember if her mother had mentioned something as important as that. While this information did not contradict what her father had told her, six months was a long time to be pregnant before deciding to elope. It would have been harder to hide, harder to convince people that the baby was conceived in wedlock, especially Elena's parents who were religious enough to warrant an elopement in the first place.

But why would she wait so long when her father had sounded so willing to marry her? So in love? Unless...

Unless she did not want to marry her father. Unless the baby was not even his.

"What are you suggesting?" Alex asked, her heart stuck in her throat.

"I don't know." Penélope looked away, carefully avoiding Alex's searching gaze. "A lot can happen in six months."

46

"Three, two, one...go!" Penélope cried out excitedly.

Owen bolted from the starting line a hair of a second early, but Alex did not say anything as Ari, Warren, Zeb, and Chloe were only a breath behind, their arms and legs a blur on the dusty track.

It was a hot day, the air baking the ground beneath them. Alex and Penélope watched as the others sprinted past, leaving a light cloud of dust behind. She tried not to stare at Ari, who had taken his shirt off along with Warren and Owen, his muscles shifting under the gleam of the sun as he ran, his dark hair caught in the wind.

Owen quickly fell behind as Ari and Warren surged ahead, with Ari pushing past the finish line a few steps ahead of Warren, who finished second. Owen finished third, rolling onto the grass nearby with a groan, his chest heaving. Then Chloe bolted across the line, followed closely by Zeb, who hadn't wanted to race but who had not been able to ignore Owen's taunts. Penélope hated to run, so she took the job of the starter, while Alex had offered to watch the finish line.

"Owen started before the signal," Zeb said to Alex, still out of breath, pointing at Owen. "That's not fair."

Owen had already gotten up from the ground, his dark skin shining with sweat. He grinned at Zeb, his eyes flashing a clear sea green in the light like small glass stones found washed ashore. "Relax, love, I lost anyway."

Zeb glanced at him under lowered lashes, then turned away angrily, ignoring Owen and Alex as he walked towards Penélope. "It's cheating." But he no longer sounded as certain as before.

"So who won?" Chloe called beside Warren, who was leaning forward with his hands on his knees. Chloe, of course, looked impeccable in her sports bra and spandex, with barely a bead of sweat on her skin, her black hair remaining straight and glossy in a high ponytail.

"Ari won by a few seconds," Alex said. "Warren came second."

She saw Warren shoot Ari a resentful look, but Ari was already walking back to Alex and Penélope. Chloe met Alex's eye and she raised a brow, as if to say, *Well, well, Alex, is there something you need to tell me?*

Owen came over to Chloe and draped a sweaty arm over her shoulders, which she shrugged off with a shout. "I'm surprised you weren't distracted with so many shirtless men around you." He looked at Ari. "Are you a runner, Ari? You wouldn't think it looking at all that muscle."

Chloe rolled her eyes. "Are you sure *you* weren't distracted?"

"I was," Owen said promptly. "And that's precisely why I lost."

"I've run on this track since I was twelve. I had home advantage," Ari said, then after a quick flicker of his eyes toward Alex. "But I mostly box."

"Oh you'd love to see that, wouldn't you Owen?" Chloe said icily, but Owen only brightened at the thought.

"I saw him wrestle in the city," Alex said without thinking, and all of them looked at her except Ari, who frowned at the ground.

"You didn't mention a wrestling match," Zeb said, looking at Ari accusingly. "I thought you didn't interact with anyone."

"They were Academy students," Ari said, shrugging. "It was unimportant."

"You don't get to decide what is important or not," Zeb countered.

Owen, who had waltzed up to Zeb, ruffled his blond hair until the strands stuck up, much to the shock of Zeb. "I must agree with my mate Zeb here. A wrestling match between you and another attractive man is very important."

Zeb ducked away from Owen's hand, glaring at him. "It could have been a girl."

"Both are fine by me," Owen said with a smirk.

"Enough," Warren interrupted, stepping forward. "What happened?"

Alex fought a blush. He asked the question as if he had found out she had cheated on him. "We might as well explain everything from the start."

So Ari and Alex attempted to describe the events of that fateful night as they stretched out on the track. They recounted finding the door to the city behind the Squatting Scribe, how large the library had been and the white veiled women talking about a tyrant king, and the streets filled with extravagantly dressed men and women.

Everyone listened enraptured as they described Ari's fight, though Alex noticed how he still avoided explaining what they had said to him. They described the docks, the main street and the gate, the soldiers in their armor and how the city changed at dawn. Their story ended with their narrow escape from the Brother in the library, though neither of them offered the exact details as to how.

"This Brother who almost caught you," Owen said, being the first to break the silence. "You didn't recognize him?"

Ari shook his head. "I didn't get to see his face, but I've never met him at the New Academy. Ever. He must live in the city. Maybe he teaches at the Academy."

"Then why was he here?" Zeb asked pointedly.

"Probably watching the entrance," Penélope said, realization followed quickly by worry passing across her face. "They know someone is trying to get into the city."

Alex knew she was right. It was a nagging feeling she had been ignoring for some time, hoping that they had somehow evaded the watchful eye of Sister Stella. But then why had she not said something?

"Whether Sister Stella suspects or not, that doesn't change the fact that we have to find a way back to the city," Alex said firmly.

"We can't just waltz into a magical city we know nothing about," Ari protested. "They wear different clothes, speak different languages, and follow different laws. We'd have to sneak in undetected and miraculously discover where your mother might be, and we don't even know where we'll sleep if we have to spend the night. It's impossible."

Warren looked up. "You said you understood them. That they spoke Ancient Greek."

Ari glanced at Warren in annoyance. "Yes."

"Then why can't we just learn a few phrases?" Warren asked. "That's what I do when I travel to a country where I don't speak the language. We can also buy clothes that will be less conspicuous. Then we try to sketch a map of the city based on your memory and we come up with a plan."

It was the most concrete, logical solution, spoken with the confidence of someone who was naturally analytical and usually right. Everyone looked at Warren, then at Alex, as if she was the only person who could approve the plan.

But Ari was staring at the ground, his jaw tightening, and Alex felt a slight pity despite herself. Then she remembered how Ari had brushed past her at the bar. She didn't owe him anything.

She nodded, locking eyes with Warren. "Then we come up with a plan."

47

The following afternoon, Alex, Chloe, and Penélope drove to Chula Vista to look for clothes that might help them blend in with the strange citizens she had seen in the city at night. They left the boys behind with the hope that they would get along for enough time to find some useful information before they planned their return to the city.

They took Alex's car into town, Chloe sitting in the front seat automatically, Penélope sliding into the middle seat in the back. If Alex did not look too hard at the desert mountains and glaring sun, she could almost be driving in the countryside of New England, carpooling with Chloe back to their suburban havens in New York.

She took the freeway exit to Chula Vista, snatches of a blue bay on the horizon, and the feeling faded. Chloe was scrolling on her phone, bookmarking various thrift stores and shops they could visit that might have what they needed. After a mostly silent hour and a half drive, they finally pulled up in front of a massive Goodwill.

"Let's do this," Penélope said, hopping out of the car confidently.

Chloe raised a mildly impressed brow and stepped out onto the sidewalk.

Together they entered the Goodwill and began working through the rows. They started in the dresses section to see if they could find any brightly colored tunics. After a few minutes rifling through dresses, Penélope pulled out a long silk nightgown with frilly cuffs.

Chloe lowered her sunglasses and eyed the dress before shaking her head. "Too see-through. We don't want to give the wrong impression."

"They wore colorful clothing," Alex said. "With a lot of fabric. Like togas or tunics."

"Colorful?" Chloe echoed, holding out a lime green romper in dismay. "Are you sure?"

Alex nodded. "At least at night, everyone was wearing colorful tunics with shawls and jewelry."

"And during the day?"

"I didn't see many women during the day," Alex said, suddenly embarrassed. She hadn't seen much of the city in general during the day, and had not paid attention to those few women chaperoned on the docks. "Maybe we should buy veils and cloaks to hide our faces."

"Do you think it will be dangerous for us?" Penélope asked hesitantly. "In the city?"

"I don't know."

"If what you say is true," Chloe said slowly, "then we won't find anything here."

"What do you mean?"

"We'll need to go to a fabric store and make tunics ourselves."

"Do you even know how to sew?" Alex asked with a laugh.

Both Chloe and Penélope looked incredulously at her. "Of course."

It turned out Penélope had a sewing machine at her parents' house that they could bring to her dorm. So Alex drove them to the nearest fabric store. They walked around the stacked and hanging fabrics, Alex pointing out various colors she had seen and Chloe determining which could be best transformed into a simple dress or tunic. Penélope thought it would be a good idea to assign each person a color so that even cloaked they would know who was who.

"I like this royal blue," Penélope said, grasping the soft silk fabric that Chloe held.

Chloe nodded, holding up the fabric in front of Penélope. "Yes, this would look good on you."

Alex had to bite her lip to prevent a smile. It was rare for Chloe to hand out a compliment like that, and Penélope seemed to sense this, shooting Alex a playfully shocked look afterward. Then Alex pointed to a heap of emerald green fabric.

"I like that color," she said.

"Really?" Chloe said, glancing between the fabric and Alex.

"Yes," Alex said defensively. "Green is my favorite color."

"Ooh, this one would look great with Owen's eyes," Penélope said, pointing to a rich teal color.

Chloe cut her a sharp look. "Yes, it would."

"You would look good in this red," Alex said, holding up a bright red silk to Chloe's red-lipped frown.

"Actually," Chloe said, waving the red fabric away, "I'd look much better in this burgundy. Bright red washes me out."

"What about this one for Zeb?" Penélope asked, pulling out a roll of black fabric. "There's no way Zeb will wear anything with color."

"How about a charcoal gray?" Chloe asked.

Penélope shook her head. "Black only."

Chloe sighed irritably. "What's his deal anyway?"

"Zeb?"

"Yeah, he's in love with your other friend—what's his name—Aristotle, right?"

"Ari," Penélope corrected, her face suddenly hardening. "And I don't know what you're talking about."

Chloe gave Alex a quizzical look. "Am I the only one who noticed? Alex, tell me you also hadn't noticed since you're clearly drooling after that Aristotle guy too."

Alex nearly choked. "What—Chloe—I have—"

"Warren," Chloe interrupted, rolling her eyes. "Trust me, I know. But don't think I haven't noticed how you look at Aristotle."

"It's *Ari,* for the last time," Alex said in annoyance, suddenly conscious of Penélope's wide eyes on her. "And don't worry, even if I did he doesn't like me like that. Trust me."

Chloe stared at her, then suddenly smirked. "Oh my god."

Alex's stomach dropped. "What?"

"Oh my god." Chloe laughed. "You two *kissed,* didn't you?"

"What? No, of course not." Alex's cheeks burned, and Chloe smiled triumphantly. "Okay, maybe we did. But it wasn't like that!"

Chloe patted Alex's arm. "Sure, babe."

"Wait, you and Ari kissed?" Penélope asked, her voice terse.

Alex shook her head. "It wasn't like that, I promise." She sighed when Penélope raised an expectant brow. "Remember how I said we almost got caught in the library when we came back from the city? Well, we *did* get caught, but we didn't get in trouble because Ari pretended to kiss me so that the Brother couldn't see our faces. Then we ran. That was it."

Penélope's face was pale. "Oh no."

"What?" Alex asked, a fear gripping her. Had it been that wrong of her?

"Zeb is going to kill you when he finds out," Penélope whispered, sitting down on a bench covered in fabric. "He's been in love with Ari since he was ten years old."

"I knew it," Chloe said, crossing her arms.

"It didn't mean anything," Alex said quickly, though she knew deep down that it was a lie. "Besides, is Ari even into guys? It's not my fault Ari doesn't want him back."

"Oh this is bad," Penélope whispered, and her eyes shone with tears, making Chloe and Alex freeze. "You can't say anything. Not about the kiss, or that you know he's in love with Ari, or anything. Okay? You both have to promise me he won't know."

To Alex's surprise, Chloe stepped forward and settled a hand on Penélope's shoulder. "Of course. We promise."

"He'll never know," Alex whispered, her throat closing up.

Then Chloe looked at Alex. "When are you going to tell him?"

Alex looked at her, startled. She didn't understand. "What? I thought—"

"No, *Warren.*" To her surprise, Chloe looked grim. "When are you going to tell him?"

48

As the sun set behind the mountains, Alex drove them into Tierra del Sol, parking her car in the church lot.

Chloe and Penélope exited the car with several bags of fabric and new sewing supplies. She seriously doubted their ability to make several tunics and cloaks in a short amount of time, but both Chloe and Penélope reassured her that they knew how to sew very well thanks to their grandmothers.

"You know, I'm surprised you never learned," Chloe had said in retort to her disbelief.

Alex didn't tell her that her grandmother never sewed a day in her life and that she had never met her mother's parents. She wondered if her mother had stayed, whether she would have taught her how to sew. A part of her knew that her mother had never liked sewing very much.

They found the boys still in the library, piles of books around them, interspersed with several cans of beer. Alex was surprised to find them all laughing and talking with each other animatedly. The girls all shared a look before they dumped the fabric on the table.

Chloe gestured to the beers. "Having fun are we?"

Owen raised a brow, pinching a piece of fabric and lifting it carefully. "Please tell me we're not *making* our clothes."

"We thought it was the best way to recreate what Alex and Ari saw in the city," Chloe said, crossing her arms. "Unless *you* want to go shopping at Goodwill?"

Alex stepped in before they began arguing again. "Did you guys find anything?"

Ari, who had been seated in the far corner beside Zeb, stood up, a book held loosely in his hand. "Actually, we did." He showed them the book with what looked like a plan of an archaeological site. "We did some research into the Temple of Apollo and its history. In ancient times, the Temple of Apollo was considered the navel of the earth and was highly associated with Gaia. Technically this temple is located at Delphi in Greece, but many ancient cities had temples dedicated to Apollo."

"And you think the city has one too?" Alex asked doubtfully.

"It's very possible," Ari said. "And we found something else." He moved another very large book open on the table toward Alex. A hand-drawn map was spread across the two pages displaying a gridded plan of a city. "Remember how the city was divided by two main streets? According to where the sun rose, I believe one ran north-to-south while the other crossed it east-to-west. One of the most famous ancient cities to have this layout was...the city of Alexandria."

A hush fell over them and everyone looked at Alex. She felt hot and then cold all over. It seemed impossible that it was merely coincidental.

Penélope was the first to speak. "How does this help us navigate the city? As far as we know, this is not the ancient city of Alexandria."

"Well, based on my memory I drew a map of the city." Ari placed a sheet of lined paper on top of the book which had a rough sketch of two streets crossing at perfect right angles. He pointed to the northwest quadrant. "Here was the library. Across the main street was the Academy. At some point past the library we turned left down an alleyway and ended up at the docks. Then we walked along the boardwalk until we reached the other main cross-street. At that point, the sun began to rise in the east over the mountains. Then we walked all the way back to the library down the cross street. Essentially we walked in a large circle."

"That means we only saw one quadrant of the city," Alex said, pointing a finger at the other three quadrants. "We have no idea if these other quadrants have a temple dedicated to Apollo."

"This is the best you're going to get," Zeb said sharply. He had moved to his usual perch on the windowsill, his black hood pulled over his head. "I say we go to the city, ask around for the temple, and check it out. What's the worst that can happen?"

Ari and Alex shared a worried glance, recalling the squadron of soldiers they had seen patrolling the boardwalk.

"How are we sure that we'll find the Emerald Stone in the temple?" Penélope asked, frowning at the large blank spaces on Ari's map.

"Elena was searching for something," Ari said, lowering his voice. "She considered this hymn very important, enough to hide a piece of it in her diary. If she believed in the myth, she might have tried to find the Stone herself. It's the only lead we have. The Stone might hold a clue to what happened to her."

But Alex still felt uneasy. She had read Elena's diary from front to back and there had never been a single mention of an Emerald Stone or any kind of search. If her mother had indeed wanted to find the Stone, then she had clearly gotten distracted along the way. The city, after all, was much more than a mere place to her. It was an escape, a belief, a reason to live. She had met someone, possibly the love of her life, in the city, and then something happened that made her leave it all behind.

Suddenly Warren spoke, his calm blue eyes on her. "The choice is yours, Alex."

"We'll enter the city Saturday night," Alex said at last. "Then we find the Stone."

49

THE REST OF THE week Chloe and Penélope worked together to sew their new clothes, with the others helping to cut the fabric and act as models.

Ari compiled a list of helpful Ancient Greek phrases that they had to memorize in case they needed to explain themselves in the city. There was the obvious χαῖρε for *hello* and *goodbye,* συγγνωθί μοι to say *I'm sorry,* and ἐπαινῶ to say *thank you.*

As they were practicing these phrases one afternoon, Owen leaned over to Ari and smirked. "How do you say *you're hot* in Ancient Greek?"

Ari fixed him a hard look and did not respond. He rarely found Owen amusing.

"Εἶ κάλλος," Zeb said suddenly. "But it's more like *you're beautiful.*"

Owen winked at him. "Ἐπαινῶ."

Soon it was Friday, a day before they had planned to return to the city. Everyone seemed on edge. Chloe snapped at anyone who touched the fabric without her permission. Penélope rarely smiled and was quiet most of the time, hard at work tailoring the fabric to fit each person. Owen bickered with whoever would entertain him. Zeb was even more snarky than usual. And Alex avoided being alone with either Warren or Ari, which only caused them to be more irritated.

They had begun taking turns in the library. All of them would show up at nine in the morning to begin class. Ari would pretend to teach a bit of Ancient Greek in case Sister Stella decided to snoop or quiz them on what they were learning. Then Chloe would return to her dorm to work on the clothes, with one person visiting her at a time to make any adjustments to the sizing. After lunch, Penélope would go to her dorm instead of Chloe. At night, they all snuck into Penélope's dorm and continued discussing their plan.

Ari thought they should enter the old library at nine o'clock at night, since they needed enough time in the city to explore before they got too tired. They hoped no one would be guarding the library, but if there was, they decided it safer to leave the old library and regroup than to risk a confrontation with a brother or sister. If they made it to the city, Ari would ask a student of the Academy where to find the temple of Apollo. If this proved successful, they would go to the temple and find the Stone, hopefully returning to the New Academy by dawn. If not, they would return the way they came before anyone was the wiser.

"Alexandria," a familiar accented voice said behind them. "May I have a word with you?"

They had just returned from lunch, Penélope having already snuck back to her dorm. Zeb was about to leave to try on his tunic for the final time. Alex's heart beat loudly at the voice and turned around to see Sister Stella standing by their desk, her wrinkled hands folded in front of her.

"Of course," Alex said quickly, glancing at her friends. Ari kept his eyes trained on the book in front of him—thankfully the Hansen and Quinn textbook—and merely nodded his head at Sister Stella.

"I trust you are finding your stay at the New Academy acceptable?" Sister Stella asked as she led Alex outside to the courtyard. "Professor Melamed tells me that your friends have made very good progress."

She tried to keep the nervous waver out of her voice. "Yes, they have."

"It is unusual for so many people to be enrolled in the summer intensive here," Sister Stella continued. "You are very lucky to have such...supportive friends."

Alex was silent. She did not know what to say and they were now on the other side of the courtyard. At last, they came to a stop, and Sister Stella turned to her with a sad smile, her blue eyes heavy.

"I did wonder how long it would take for you to find it," Sister Stella said.

"What?"

"The city." Sister Stella raised a brow. "Did you think I would not know?"

Alex stared at her, uncomprehending. "I-I'm not sure what you mean."

"My dear, I am the Guardian of that door. I know every soul who walks in and out of it." The words struck Alex like a slap. "I knew Mr. Melamed had the key to the old library and together it was only a matter of time before you found the door. I had hoped visiting the city would be enough, that it would perhaps satisfy you, or you would come to me for answers. But it seems I was wrong. As I said before, you are a lot like your mother."

"I heard you," Alex said, feeling dizzy, "in the library. You were supposed to keep an eye on me. Because of my mother. Because she knew something you didn't want me to know. You *lied* to me."

Sister Stella shook her head softly. "Consider this a warning, Alexandria. The city is dangerous. I tried to warn your mother, but alas, she did not listen, and you are paying the price all these years later."

Alex felt a sudden white-hot rage in her breast. "Then you know what happened to her."

"Unfortunately, I do not," Sister Stella said calmly. "There are powers at play here that you do not understand. I have closed the door of the Squatting Scribe, just like I once did with your mother. You and your friends may continue the intensive course if you wish." She paused. "Please do not blame me, Alexandria. I only want to save you as I could not save Elena."

The words fell on her ears from far away. Alex stumbled back, then she turned and raced back to her dorm room. Her hands were trembling. She wanted to scream. Stinging tears welled up in her eyes. Sister Stella knew she had been to the city all this time? She knew that Alex would try to return? This was a worse betrayal than the one in the old library that fateful night. Sister Stella had let Alex believe she was one step closer to finding her mother, only to take it away when she knew too much.

I have closed the door of the Squatting Scribe, just like I once did with your mother.

Alex paused, breathing hard. She sat on the edge of the bed, wiping the tears away from her face. Somehow the words had tickled her memory. It had to be in her mother's diary. If Sister Stella had blocked the entrance into the city, Elena would have been devastated. She grabbed the diary from her desk and flipped through the pages furiously.

It took her almost an hour to find the entry, which was near the end of the diary. She did not know how she had not noticed it before.

March 17th. She closed the door. They say there are many doors, some guarded, others not. There is one in the valley when the moon is full, they say. There I will find the Cave of the Nymphs. The full moon is next Monday. I shall go once Sister is asleep. She will not prevent me this time.

Alex stared at the words which only made sense to her now. She wondered if her mother had sat on her bed in a dorm room just like this one, with tears in her eyes as she realized she would not be able to go back to the city. Had she run to the library in her anger, determined to find another way in? Had she gone into the valley and found a door against all odds? Did she even make it back into the city?

The next entry only had a single angry scrawl.

March 20th. Do not eat or drink anything.

She did not understand. The entry after that was the second to last one in the entire journal, the two bare sentences as familiar to Alex as if she had written them herself.

April 23rd. I am to leave the school. Final exams considered unnecessary.

What happened between March and April that caused her to leave the New Academy, the city, Alexandros—everything—behind? It could not have been her pregnancy alone, which she should have realized by December or January, if not earlier. How come there was no mention of it? Did she truly not know she was pregnant? Why the obsession with returning to the city if it was as dangerous as Sister Stella said? Was she so in love with Alexandros that she would risk everything for him?

There was a knock at the door.

Alex wiped her eyes one last time. "Yes?"

"It's Chloe."

"And Penélope!"

She almost smiled. "Come in."

The door opened, revealing Chloe with a hand on her hip and Penélope looking into the room worriedly. Both their eyes widened when they saw Alex crying.

"What happened?" Penélope asked, taking a seat on the bed. "We were all wondering why you never came back."

"It was Sister Stella," Alex said softly. "She knows I went to the city. She knows I'm trying to go back so she closed the door of the Squatting Scribe."

At first, they were both startled, and Penélope frowned as she thought this new revelation over. Even Chloe paled, and she took a seat on the bed, staring into space. Alex had the sense that neither of them had truly believed the city existed until now. But Sister Stella's confirmation was enough.

"Who does that nun think she is?" Chloe said viciously. "I should slap some sense into her."

"Chloe," Penélope reprimanded softly.

Chloe ignored her, turning to Alex fiercely. "What are we going to do now? We have to find a way there."

Alex huffed a laugh and showed the open diary. "It turns out the same thing happened with my mom. And I think she found another way in. But..."

Penélope leaned forward anxiously. "But what?"

"I have no idea where it is, how to find it, or what will happen if we do."

Chloe raised a brow. "That's not a lot to go on."

Penélope took Alex's hand in hers. "We will find a way back to the city no matter what. We will find your mother, Alexandria."

Alex squeezed her hand. "Promise?"

This time Chloe placed her hand on theirs, and Alex looked up in surprise. Chloe's eyes were steeled. "We promise."

50

"So let me get this straight," Zeb said, crossing his arms. "We go into the valley on the next full moon and we magically enter the city?"

They regrouped later that afternoon in the library, where Alex told them everything Sister Stella had said. Ari had wanted to speak with Sister Stella himself, but Alex refused. She didn't want her to block off any more doorways into the city. If they were going to find a way in, it had to be without her help.

"Supposedly we will find the Cave of the Nymphs," Alex said. "That's all my mother said in her diary."

Zeb raised a brow. "And we're just going to believe her?"

Suddenly Warren turned and glared at Zeb. "Yes, we are. Do you have a problem with that?"

"Zeb does have a point," Ari said quietly. "Her instructions are minimal at best. We have no idea where this door is or what we are going to find if we do. It could be dangerous. Sister Stella herself said there were powers at play here that we don't understand."

"And we're just going to believe her?" Chloe sneered. "Because she's been *so* honest already."

Alex stood up, ready to grab her bag and leave. "The full moon is next Thursday. If you don't want to come, you don't have to. I won't force anyone."

"Wait," Penélope said, her eyes worried. "We've trusted Elena this far. I think we should give it a shot."

"Your mother said that in the valley we will find the Cave of the Nymphs," Ari said quietly. "Legend says that Odysseus was abandoned there by the Phaeacians. Legend also says the cave is on the island of Ithaca. We're in the middle of a desert."

"We have both seen more impossible things," Alex said coolly, and Ari lowered his eyes.

Owen clapped his hands together. "While I am very excited for this full moon excursion, I know just the thing to ease the nerves."

"And what could that be?" Chloe asked, rolling her eyes already.

He grinned. "Getting wasted, of course."

So it was decided that after dinner they would all meet up outside the church to walk to the local bar. Alex was nervous for multiple reasons, the main one being how her friends would react to the bar. She only hoped they didn't manage to offend everyone in the entire town by the end of the night.

A few hours later they were walking down the main street of town. Penélope linked arms with Chloe and Alex, and together they walked ahead of the boys, taking turns sipping a homemade cocktail that had way too much tequila in it. Behind them Warren walked next to Owen, looking dejected, Zeb and Ari a ways off to the side. Soon the familiar *El Sol* sign appeared and they entered the bar.

It was Friday so the bar was packed. There was a full band in the corner and the dance floor was filled with older couples dancing to the music. They all came to a stop, surveying the scene. A few locals came forward with excited cries and pulled Penélope, Zeb, and Ari toward the bar.

Owen slid a pair of sunglasses on his face and smiled. "Now this is my kind of party."

They gathered at the bar and ordered shots of tequila.

"Here's to finding Elena," Owen said with his shot held high, and then they all downed their glasses. He grabbed Chloe's hand before she could protest. "Come dance with me, love."

Alex thought she saw Zeb sneak a curious glance at Owen as he slid away with Chloe, her glossy black hair flung over a bare shoulder. Penélope dragged Ari and Zeb to the dance floor after them. That left Warren standing beside Alex, his gaze on the dancers as they moved across the floor effortlessly. Owen and Chloe laughed as they tried to keep up with those dancing, tripping over each other. It was the happiest she had ever seen them together.

"Do you want to dance?" Alex asked before she changed her mind.

Instead of responding, Warren held out his hand. She took it and followed him to the dance floor. Alex swore she felt Ari's eyes fixed on her, but she tried to ignore him. Warren brought his hands hesitantly to her waist. *Now you're dancing, Alexandria.*

Alex shut her eyes and placed her hands around Warren's neck. She couldn't remember the last time she had kissed him. A part of her dreaded ever kissing him again. The ghost of another touch still lingered on her lips, and her cheeks burned with the memory of it. *Kiss me.*

"Look at me," Warren whispered. They were barely dancing, simply swaying to the beat. Alex opened her eyes and realized too late that they were filled with tears. "I love you. You know that, right?"

She bit her lip, the tears sliding down her face regardless. Then she nodded, and let Warren pull her close to his chest, the warmth of his embrace an echo of another person she used to know, the person she left behind to follow a different path, a different life.

The bass marched a steady rhythm throughout the bar. Alex wished this moment could last forever, but she sensed the moving tides and knew that whatever happened on the night of the full moon, everything was about to change.

She opened her eyes and met Chloe's warning glance across the dance floor. *When are you going to tell him?*

Alex closed her eyes and pretended one last time.

51

Alex stared in the mirror. Her emerald green tunic draped over her body, cut close to the neck and leaving her arms bare. The hem fell near her ankle, covering every inch of her body. She wrapped a matching shawl around her shoulders and slipped into her sneakers. No one wanted to risk having to run in sandals.

She looked like a stranger from another time once she lifted her cloak over her hair. The mesh veils they had made hardly obscured her face, nor the dark eyeliner she had impulsively drawn around her eyes as she had seen on those women in the caravans.

Penélope and Chloe met her in the hall, and all of them stared at each other. Alex had a small backpack of spare clothes, her mother's belongings, and other essentials slung over her shoulder just in case. Penélope tightened the straps of a large backpack nearly bursting at the seams, while a black designer purse hung from Chloe's arm. Despite the rather imperfect, handmade clothing, they both looked caught in the wrong century, Chloe's burgundy dress clinging to her body tightly so that she looked like a princess, Penélope's thick curls cascading over one blue, silk-clad shoulder like a regal queen.

"Ready?" Alex asked weakly.

They nodded silently. No one spoke as they descended the steps to the courtyard and crossed in complete darkness to the side gate. They met the boys near the track, where they were already dressed in their colored tunics, Ari in white, Warren in dark purple, Owen in a subtle turquoise, and Zeb in his signature black. Against the large silhouettes of the mountains they seemed like figures pulled out of a dream.

When they approached, the boys all turned and looked at them. Owen's mouth fell open at the reveal, Warren stared at Alex with wide eyes, and Ari raised a brow in approval. Even Zeb half-smiled at their costumes.

"Where do we begin?" Owen asked, glancing around the dark valley.

"First," Alex said, shouldering her bag and turning towards the mountains, "we walk."

Alex led the way with Penélope by her side. The faint light of the streetlights in town and the lamps around the courtyard faded as they picked a path through the valley. They shined flashlights ahead of them so that they did not trip on rocks or bump into cacti. While they had all brought their phones with them and portable chargers, they would need to preserve their batteries for emergencies, since the city had no electricity and certainly no cellular service.

"Shite," Owen hissed from behind. "I think I touched a cactus. Look? Is that a spine?"

"It's just a leaf," muttered Zeb.

"How will we know when we get there?" Penélope asked her worriedly.

"I was hoping we'd just...know," Alex said, shining her flashlight among the sand and bushes. "Maybe we'll find a cave near the mountains."

They continued hiking down into the valley, the decline turning steep at times before climbing up once more. The mountains remained far out of reach no matter how many miles they walked toward it. It seemed that hours passed, but when Alex checked they had only walked for forty minutes.

"How much longer?" Owen asked, panting slightly. "We're still far from the mountains. Maybe we should have driven there."

"If my mother didn't need a car, then neither do we," Alex retorted over her shoulder without breaking her stride. She still heard Owen grumbling about the pace, but she ignored him. This was her only chance to find a doorway back to the city and she was not about to give it up.

"I think we're lost," Chloe said, out of breath. "And we're in the middle of a desert. What if there are wild animals out here?"

"There are," Penélope said quietly. "Let's just hope we don't run into any."

At her words, Alex felt a shiver down her spine, as if she were being watched. She lifted her flashlight and scanned the horizon.

A shadow flitted across the beam of light.

"Stop!" Alex came to a halt and felt Penélope bump into her as the group came to a sudden stop. Her heart hammered fast in her chest. "Nobody move."

"What is it, Alex?" Warren asked darkly.

Alex shined the flashlight everywhere, but the shadow was gone. Perhaps she had imagined it. She almost released a sigh of relief when something moved near the light, a streak of shadow like a small mouse or a bird. *The bird is only a messenger after all.*

"I think I saw—" Then she heard it. A low, mournful tune on the wind, a bird cry, or a song. Alex swiveled around, searching for the source of the sound. "Do you hear that?"

All of them shook their heads silently, staring at her worriedly.

"Hear what, exactly?" Owen asked.

"There it is again!" She strained her ears, but the song drifted until it was faint, and she began to move towards it. "We have to follow that song."

The others followed after her without protest, though she caught a few of their doubtful glances. She swung her flashlight around, hoping to catch a glimpse of that shadow again. But there were no more shadows, only the song drifting on the wind. At times the song would cease altogether, and she would stand still, forcing the others to be quiet, until she could pick up those strained notes once more.

They walked and walked for a long time, until Alex suddenly looked up and went very still. Her vision swayed like the ocean from the deck of a ship. They were nearly at the foot of the mountains. While they had hardly gained any ground in the first hour of walking, since hearing the song they had somehow picked a path closer to the looming, rocky masses.

"I feel drunk," Chloe said, stumbling on the path.

Zeb was touching his face. "What's happening to me?"

Alex heard their voices as if she were underwater.

"We've been walking for too long," Warren said, his face rigid but his words slurred together. Alex turned and saw him slouched where he stood, half-asleep.

"We need to keep moving," Alex said, but her tongue felt heavy in her mouth as she spoke, and she was not sure anyone heard her.

"Am I hallucinating or is that a light?" Owen asked, pointing across the valley.

She squinted in the direction he was pointing and saw a small, flickering flame, as though someone were burning a fire very far away.

"Wait, I see it too," Penélope said slowly, followed by murmuring agreement from the others.

"They could be campers," Owen said dreamily, already heading towards the light.

"I don't think so," Ari warned, though he still followed after him.

They all began walking towards the light without another word. Alex's pulse raced as they ambled closer to the fire, her skin turning cold and then hot as if she had a fever. Something clutched her arm. She looked down in slow motion.

Penélope was grabbing at her, staring ahead with a pale face. "Look."

Alex looked, ignoring the way the world swayed before her.

The light had grown bigger, and she realized belatedly it was a bonfire, piling high into the sky. Dark shadows moved about the fire in a strange dance, but the longer she looked the more clearly she saw that they were only strange because they were not human. There were men with legs like a goat and women with long hair and lithe, naked bodies that hardly touched the ground as they moved.

She heard that song again and saw that it came from a flute that was being played by one of the goat men as he danced around the bonfire. As they came close and entered the ring of light from the fire, a group of women dragged a dead goat to the fire and threw it atop the flaming branches.

"*Alexandria,*" a voice whispered, but the name was spoken as if in her mind.

Alex stood frozen on the spot. A shape floated toward them, their feet never touching the ground. It was one of the women, her long hair an inky black like the night sky. She did not open her mouth, her lips stretched in a smile, and her silvery eyes shone from within like two small moons. The woman extended a long arm, and Alex realized it was scaled a translucent blue.

Someone left her side. Alex saw Penélope take the hand of a man with goat's legs and begin to dance with him as she once had with Zeb at *El Sol.* Following close behind her was Owen, then Chloe, and finally Warren, all of them stumbling into the dance circle, the music of the flute drowning out their shouts of delight.

"Alexandria." It was Ari, who stood beside her. His face was pale, with beads of sweat lining his brow, as though he were trying hard to focus. "What are you doing?"

Alex smiled as she took the woman's hand. "Dancing."

Then she was swept off her feet as the quick pace of the flute filled her head like a sweet dream. The woman danced ahead of her, and though she never opened her mouth, Alex could hear her laugh in her head like small bells tinkling on a sleigh.

"This is wonderful!" Owen exclaimed, prancing and twirling on his goat's legs. Alex blinked and shook her head. They were human legs once more. Her stomach heaved.

"Here," said the voice again. *"A drink."*

The valley spun in front of her. Her mouth was dry and scorching as if she had not drunk water for days. A hand held out a blurry cup which she saw was actually a cactus, cut in half and filled with a red liquid like cherry soda.

Her head felt heavy. Alex squeezed her eyes shut, then opened them. For a moment, the red liquid looked like blood. She gasped as it came to her in a rush of clarity, as though someone had blown air into her mind and cleared her muddled thoughts.

March 31st. Do not eat or drink anything.

"No!" Alex stumbled backward. "Don't eat or drink! Don't do it!"

She saw Owen turn to her in a daze, his hand already gripping his cactus drink. Penélope was reaching towards a cut of smoked meat on a silver platter. Warren had begun dancing closely with one of the women, while Zeb leaned drunkenly against Ari, who still looked pale and flushed.

Suddenly a booming noise like thunder shook the valley in an angry shout, and Alex felt rather than heard a deep voice thundering around them in a language she did not understand. Then a flash of light struck the bonfire so that the fire roared to the sky, its tendrils white and blue against the starry night. Alex shrunk away as a rippling wave of heat rolled off the fire and lifted her hair off her neck.

Then she heard a strangled scream.

Alex looked around wildly.

Owen had his hand held up, his face contorted in ghastly pain. The spines of the cactus cup in his hand pierced through his skin, blood flowing from the wounds in bright streams. Penélope gasped and keeled over as if she were about to vomit, her hand grasping a bloody raw steak. Warren shoved the woman away, whose lips had lifted to reveal razor-sharp teeth in a terrifying grin.

Another scream rose up into the sky, but it was not human, and they all turned to see the goat on top of the pyre bleating out in pain as the flames burned him alive.

"Alex, look out!" Chloe screamed, pointing behind her.

She turned, her heart pounding once in her chest at a glimpse of a tall, cloaked figure approaching before darkness swallowed her up and her thoughts drifted into sleep.

52

ALEX'S EYES OPENED STIFFLY at the light shining behind her eyelids. Dimly she saw tall shadows on the horizon. She looked harder and saw that it was the dawn rising behind unfamiliar mountains in a fiery red.

A figure approached slowly out of the light, the shape of a man growing bigger as it drew closer.

"Rise, Alexandria."

The voice was deep and melodic, yet tender, and she tried to move her aching muscles in a desire to obey the command. Stones dug into her back and dirt tickled her skin. At last, she struggled to her feet and the others did the same, all of them staring at the figure approaching in silent awe.

The figure came to a stop and Alex saw that it was a young man of strong stature, dark curls billowing in the wind around a serious, youthful face, a purple cloak fluttering across his shoulders.

"You seek a doorway."

He spoke without speaking, as the strange woman had at the bonfire. Alex shivered at the voice in her mind, but nodded, unable to find the words.

Ari stepped forward, his jaw set. "What is happening? Who are you? What were those creatures?"

The young man merely smiled, but the smile was unlike any Alex had ever seen, at once intimate and cold. *"I think you already know the answer to that, brother."*

Ari paled at the words but did not waver. "It was a revelry. Those creatures were nymphs and satyrs. Then you must be...Dionysus."

His cape whipped in the wind, and Alex thought she saw his eyes glimmer like the sun on ocean waves. *"I am many things."*

September 9th. The Prince of Thieves. He said he was many things but I think he is just a god with too much time on his hands.

"You can show us the way to the city," Alex said, failing to keep her voice from trembling. The young man did not answer, staring at her as if he might read the very secrets in her heart. "Tell us where we can find the Cave of the Nymphs. It is the only way we can go back to the city."

"There are many ways to come and go from the city, not all of them unseen." His gaze wandered ever so slightly to Ari. *"My cloak shall hide your mortal friends from unfriendly immortal eyes."*

Alex glanced at Ari, who frowned. Then from one blink to the next, the purple cloak that had graced the god's broad shoulders appeared at Ari's feet. Ari bent down and picked it up carefully.

Before they could ask any more questions, the young man turned and began to walk away.

"Come."

Alex took a step, then another. The others followed after her hesitantly. They walked and walked, the wind hot on the desert sands. She glanced behind her but she could no longer see the white stucco walls of the New Academy or the tower of the Lighthouse Church, though she doubted they were still in California at all. Wordlessly Penélope took Chloe and Alex's hands in hers as they stumbled after the young man.

The wind picked up in force, kicking sand into their eyes. Alex had to squint until she saw that it was not sand but water, spraying off the ocean that lapped in front of them. She stumbled, realizing that they were not in the valley of a desert any longer but on the white shores of an unfamiliar beach entirely surrounded by clear blue water, as if they were on an island in the middle of the ocean. The young man stood before them, the gentle tide foaming around his bare ankles.

"Until we meet again."

Dionysus inclined his head, the gesture as weighty as a mountain moving, before he turned and walked into the ocean. Except he was not walking in the water but on the water, his feet stepping firmly on the rippling waves as they rolled to shore.

"Where are you going?" Alex called out, suddenly afraid that he would abandon them there. "Wait!"

The figure faded on the horizon as the light of the approaching dawn pierced the sky from behind them. Alex let go of Penélope and Chloe and rushed to the water, her feet splashing as she tried to call after him again, her hand stretching out towards the empty air.

"Wait! Don't leave us! We need to find the Cave of the Nymphs!"

His deep voice returned to them across the water. *"Surrender to the waves and you shall find what you seek."*

Then he was gone. There was no one there. Alex swiveled around, breathing hard. Everyone looked wide-eyed and fearful at the horizon, and then at Alex. She turned to Ari, who wrapped the cloak around his neck with shaky fingers, not meeting her eyes.

"What do we do?" Alex asked, her voice trembling.

Penélope gripped the straps of her backpack. "You heard him. We have to go into the water."

"You're kidding," Zeb said flatly, shaking his head. "I'm not going in."

"What if it's the only way to find the Cave of the Nymphs?" Ari asked pointedly. He suddenly appeared much like that young man, his dark curls framing his face and the purple cloak caught in the wind. "We have to try."

"Scared of a little swim, Zeb?" Owen asked, flashing a grin.

Zeb paled and looked away without speaking.

"The good news," Penélope said, her voice oddly calm, "is that I don't think we'll have to swim at all."

They all stared out at the ocean waves as though they would drown in them now. *Surrender to the waves and you shall find what you seek.*

Ari grimaced. "There's only one way to find out."

He took a step forward, then another, until he reached the edge of the tide. Then he took a deep breath and ran into the waves, diving under the water. Chloe screamed and Penélope gasped. Alex felt her heart clambering into her throat. Ari never resurfaced.

She turned and Penélope and Chloe took shaky steps toward her. "Together?"

Both girls nodded and they held hands as they waded into the water until the waves lapped their waist, Alex hissing at the cold.

"Wait!"

They stopped. Warren strode into the water, his teeth gritted together. He made it by their side, his chest heaving with the effort or nerves, Alex could not tell.

"I'm going in with you," Warren said quietly, his eyes meeting Alex's.

Alex nodded, then all of them took a deep breath and dove forward into the water.

Instantly the water sucked them into its current, the heavy fabric of their tunics and bags weighing their bodies down. Alex's lungs strained, but she fought the urge to swim back to the surface. She felt Penélope and Chloe's hands slip out of hers. Her chest burned and her face was ready to burst.

After what felt like several long, torturous minutes, her vision darkened so that she no longer saw anyone else around her. She closed her eyes against the pounding in her head, her body growing still as the energy left her body, unable to fight against the growing pressure of the sea that sank her to the sand-bed below.

Her throat shriveled without air, her chest squeezed as though someone was strangling her body, then she felt distantly her lips open just a sliver and water poured into her mouth, sloshing cold in her throat, filling her lungs and choking her.

But Alex had no more strength to move and welcomed the darkness as a final reprieve from the roaring pain.

The Lady of the Golden Blade

And at the head of the harbor is a slender-leaved olive
and near by it a lovely and murky cave
sacred to the nymphs called Naiads.
Within are kraters and amphoras
of stone, where bees lay up stores of honey.
Inside, too, are massive stone looms and there the nymphs
weave sea-purple cloth, a wonder to see.
The water flows unceasingly. The cave has two gates,
the one from the north, a path for men to descend,
while the other, toward the south, is divine. Men do not
enter by this one, but it is rather a path for immortals.

—Homer, *Odyssey* 13.102-12, translation by Robert D. Lamberton

53

WATER LAPPED AGAINST HER cheek. Soft voices echoed around her. Alex stirred. Sand brushed her skin as she moved her head, which felt laden as though she had slept for several days.

She blinked open her eyes. A cave arched overhead made of layers of white sandstone. The voices were coming from the far side of the cave.

Alex sat up. Her hands sank into wet sand. The tide ran across the cave floor and underneath her body in thin tendrils before retreating to sea. Penélope and Chloe lay near her, unconscious, along with Warren. Zeb and Owen were sprawled a few feet away, their hands grasping each other tightly, still asleep. Only Ari was awake, his hair wet and sprinkled with sand. He locked eyes with Alex, looking grim.

Soft whispers echoed once more from the back of the cave. Alex turned and saw the shapes of women lounging in shadow, their hands working large stone looms weaving dark cloth the color of the sea. Surrounding them were large painted vases filled with sweet-smelling honey, small bees humming around them dutifully. The women looked the same as those dancing with the satyrs around the fire. *Nymphs.*

One of them glanced at Alex and flashed her a smile filled with sharp teeth. Alex shivered and stood up. She was soaked to the bone. She shook Chloe and Penélope awake, both of them groaning and coughing as their eyes flew open, looking around them wildly.

"So this is the Cave of the Nymphs," Ari said quietly.

Alex nodded. "We drowned." She hesitated. "I thought I died."

Ari's face darkened. "Me too."

A scuffle drew their attention away. Zeb and Owen were awake. Noticing their clasped hands, Zeb scrambled to his feet, his face flushed, wrapping his cloak tighter around him despite the water running off of it in streams.

"No need to get all fussy," Owen said, standing up and reaching to ruffle Zeb's hair.

Zeb shoved his hand away. "Don't touch me."

Owen looked slightly offended, narrowing his eyes. "Easy there, mate."

But Zeb stalked off towards Penélope, his teeth clenched and his wet blond hair stuck to his forehead. His skin looked as white as marble, tinged with gray. Alex raised a brow at Owen but he merely frowned and moved towards Warren, who was the last to wake. He jostled his shoulder, and Warren's hand shot out and gripped Owen's wrist as he gasped awake.

"Alex," he whispered hoarsely. "Alex."

Alex rushed over to his side without thinking, grasping his hand in hers and helping him up. He clutched at her, bringing her close into his arms. He was trembling. She kissed his cheek, then glanced back at the others, but everyone was averting their gaze.

"Warren, I'm right here." She took his face in her hands and his blue eyes softened in relief as they fell on her. "I'm okay. We're all okay."

He nodded, his tight grip on her relaxing, and he cleared his throat. "I'm sorry. I thought—"

"I know. Me too. But we're alive. We're all alive."

Warren looked embarrassed as he released Alex and they stood up together, still holding hands. For the first time, he looked around the cave, staring at the nymphs as they quietly wove in the shadows.

"Is this it?" Warren asked.

"This is the cave," Alex said with a sigh. "The question is how we get to the city."

Ari took a few steps toward the nymphs, but they did not look over and continued murmuring with each other while weaving. He cleared his throat. "We seek the city."

Their murmuring rose and fell like gurgling water in a stream. *"There is no city.*"

Alex exchanged startled glances with Ari. "We've been there before," Alex said, half-angrily. "The city is real. It has a library, and an Academy, and two roads—"

"A road do you seek?"

Then she remembered what her mother had written. *The city is not a place, he says, but a road. One for mortals, the other for the gods.*

"Yes," Alex said quickly, ignoring the strange glances her way. "A road."

The nymphs began to laugh, a terrible, eerie laugh, like seagulls as they glided across the ocean before they dove for the kill. Around their feet the tide surged, rushing across the cave and rising steadily.

"Not again," Chloe whined as the water level climbed and soaked their clothes once more.

"Look!" Penélope pointed at the wall of the cave. The water had rushed against it, and the sandstone caved into a tunnel that disappeared into darkness. "It's a door."

"I hope you're right," Owen muttered, but followed after her nonetheless.

Together they waded across the cave as the water continued to rise, walking single-file into the tunnel which seemed to go on and on forever in darkness. As they trudged further into the tunnel the water lowered until it clung to their ankles and eventually sunk into the sand. Still, the sandstone tunnel carved a deeper and deeper path.

"The sand is drier now," Ari said quietly. "We must be getting close."

A few minutes later the tunnel began to incline, the sand warm and soft beneath their feet, until the end of the tunnel grew bright with sunlight. They climbed out of the tunnel into a cloudless blue sky, the sun directly overhead. Once they were all outside, the tunnel crumbled in on itself so that there was no evidence of where they had come from.

Alex took in her surroundings. Behind them was a wide beach with white sand and clear waters as blue-green as a turquoise stone. In the east stood a tall gleaming gate of bronze across a stone bridge, built over a wide, deep canal. Beyond the gate, they could just glimpse a widely paved street bordered by buildings on either side.

"The Western Gate," Ari said under his breath. "The city."

All of them stared at the gate, the sun glancing off the bronze. It took Alex a moment to realize that meant the night had passed and they were entering the city during the day. She met Ari's eyes and knew he was thinking the same thing.

"Is that a guard?" Owen asked, squinting at the gate. "He looks...asleep."

Alex could just see the guard leaning against the wall by the gate, his head lolling to one side.

"Yes," Ari said gravely. "We'll need to take him out if we want any hope of entering the city undetected."

"I'll do it," Warren said, standing tall. Then he gave Ari a subdued look. "And you know how to box, right?"

Ari nodded. "Warren and I will take out the guard. Once it's safe, the rest of you can follow us inside."

"What about me?" Owen asked. "I'll have you know I wrestled for two years in secondary school."

Warren shook his head in disbelief. "Then you can stand watch."

So the three of them crept up to the gate, the hoods of their cloaks over their heads. Before he left, Warren had kissed Alex's cheek, and the real possibility of his injury or death suddenly swept through her, followed by immense guilt, and she had to clench her hands in fists to keep herself from crying out and stopping them.

But it was over almost as soon as it had begun. Ari and Warren each snuck behind the guard and slammed his head from behind with a large rock. Dazed, the guard could hardly resist both Ari and Warren as they gagged and tied him up, then dragged his body to the side. Owen stood nearby, anxiously looking down the street, but no one ever came.

Alex led the rest of them to the gate, which they unlocked with one of the large keys slung on the guard's belt. It seemed they had not expected anyone to sneak into the city through this particular gate, especially not the poor guard.

As they walked down the street they remained silent, their hoods lifted up, obscuring their faces. But there was no one to be found roaming the street or even making noise, as if the entire city had been abandoned. Those who had not seen the city yet were looking around with dazed, wide eyes, like they were caught in a daydream—or a nightmare. Penélope held onto Alex's arm as they passed the library where Ari and Alex had walked out of only two weeks ago.

Suddenly they come to a stop. Ari was standing a few feet away, staring at the building across the street. The Academy. It looked the same except for the gate, which was barred with huge iron chains. No students walked across the courtyard, nor did any lights shine out of the windows in the buildings.

Alex remembered what they had overheard the last time they were in the city. *...the decrees have become absurd. The King must watch himself, lest the people revolt.*

She wondered if the King had forced the Academy to shut down, or even decreed a ban on education altogether.

Ari turned to her. "We are not safe here."

Before she could respond, a blaring noise sounded throughout the city. For a beat all of them stood frozen, staring at each other, before their eyes lit up in panic at what could only be the city's alarm ringing out as if a thousand bells had been struck at the same time.

She heard that drumbeat again, the stamping in the ground like an army on horseback. Soldiers poured out from every alley, rushing down the street and straight toward them. Her throat turned dry, and she wondered if she was going to die.

Then a deep voice called out. *"Run!"*

Alex ran without thinking, the rest of them following her frantically as they turned down an alleyway and sprinted to the other end. They exited onto a smaller street, but soldiers were there, already trying to cut them off.

A hand grabbed her arm. She hardly had time to shout when someone was dragging her across the street and down another alley, her friends only a few steps behind. A hooded figure was running beside her, though she swore he hadn't been there a moment ago.

"This way!"

The voice was shockingly familiar, but in her state of panic, Alex could not place where she had heard the voice before. It was at once the voice of a boy but smooth and elusive, like a song drifting on the wind. She allowed the hand to guide them through the city, traversing one of the major streets before plunging once more in a maze of buildings, crisscrossing alleyways and side streets until the soldiers fell far behind them.

At last, they came to a stop, panting. The cloaked figure pointed them towards a small, nondescript door on the street, which opened a sliver as they approached.

"Here you will be safe."

Alex helped the rest of them inside before her. One by one they disappeared inside without question, Chloe and Penélope hurrying in first, with Zeb and Ari behind them. Warren entered with one last glance at Alex to make sure she was coming too. But before she reached the door, Alex paused and turned around.

The figure stood in the middle of the street, staring at her from beneath his hood, his face covered in shadow. Alex's heart beat fast, and she swore the figure's eyes gleamed beneath that hood as he cocked his head, just like the bird once had on her windowsill.

"Who are you?" she asked.

"If you are ever in need of help, you need only wield this."

She flinched at the words spoken so quietly in her mind before she registered their meaning. Something heavy and metal was in her hand, gripped tightly by her fingers, though she had been holding nothing before.

Alex looked down. In her grasp was a polished gold wand the length of her forearm, with two snakes twisting around it and crowned by a pair of wings. She looked up to speak, but the street was empty. When she looked back down at her hand, the wand had already begun fading into air, so that she wondered if she had imagined it.

Voices shouted down the street. More soldiers. She swiveled around and ran through the door.

54

ALEX IMMEDIATELY SKIDDED TO a stop behind Warren. She looked past him to see what they were all staring at.

A woman stood across from them in a small living area. In fact, there seemed to be no other rooms in the house. The woman was ancient, her hair a stark white beside her wrinkled brown skin. Her back was hunched, with one hand gripping the head of a wooden cane, but when she swept her gaze across them Alex saw that her eyes gleamed a bright green.

She spoke and everyone stared blankly as the words did not register. It was Ancient Greek. Somehow Alex had completely forgotten that no one in the city spoke English.

Ari stood up straight. "*Ξένοι ἐσμεν.*"

"What is he saying?" Warren asked Alex in a low voice.

"She is asking us who we are," Ari said loudly, cutting Warren a warning glance. "I said we are foreigners."

The old woman shook her head and wagged her cane at them, speaking again in Greek. Even though Alex could not understand, she could tell just by her tone that she was berating them.

Ari's mouth quirked. "She says it is dangerous in the city for foreigners. The king passed a new decree that foreigners are banned from entering the city."

"Is she going to turn us in?" Owen asked suspiciously, but Ari shushed him.

"Tell her we are just visiting," Alex said. "And that we need to hide."

Ari translated and the old woman's white brows raised. She nodded slowly, then she gestured towards the low couches in the middle of the room.

"She is telling us to lie down," Ari said. "And she will bring food."

"Brilliant," Owen said, before plopping down on the nearest couch. "I'm ravenous."

Chloe rolled her eyes but took a seat beside him. "Good to know that's all it takes to convince you to trust an absolute stranger."

The rest of them followed suit with nervous laughter, and Alex found herself lying down between Chloe and Warren as the old woman hobbled to the other side of the room, where Alex saw a cauldron hanging over a low fire in the hearth. She used iron tongs to pick up the cauldron and began hobbling back to them.

Ari got up and murmured something to her, before taking the tongs himself and carrying the cauldron to the low table in the center of their couches.

The old woman held out a small stack of flatbreads to Alex. "Ἔδετε."

"Eat," Penélope translated with a pleased smile. "Now that's a word I can understand in any language."

Alex took the flatbreads, which were warm to the touch. She grabbed one before passing the rest to Chloe, then peered into the pot and saw shredded meat in a stew. When no one moved to grab the meat, the old woman gestured with her hand, pinching the air.

"Ah," Owen said with a grin. "Allow me."

Owen reached into the cauldron and pinched some meat with a torn piece of his flatbread before expertly wrapping it up. He took a bite and gave an exaggerated moan, which caused Chloe to slap his arm. The rest of them took turns pinching meat with their flatbreads and wrapping them as Owen had. Alex took a bite of hers and was shocked by the burst of spice and smoke that filled her nostrils as much as her mouth. All of them devoured their flatbreads in silence, too hungry to speak.

Then the old woman spoke, leaning on her staff. Ari listened with a frown which grew deeper the more the woman said. Alex tried to hone into the sounds, remembering what she had learned of the alphabet, but the words were strung together in incoherent syllables.

At last, Ari turned to them. "I had trouble understanding everything, but I believe she said that the King has shut down the Academy and most of the city. He has an alliance with pirates and controls the ports so that no one comes in or out. The alarm means someone breached the city illegally, which means the King knows we are here. But she says we will be safe with her."

Alex pushed down a wave of annoyance, if only at the fact that she could not understand the Greek as her mother must have. "We can't stay hiding here. We need to find my mother. She could be in danger. Ask her where we can find a temple to Apollo."

Ari paused, thinking for a moment before speaking in what sounded like much more halting Greek. He struggled to find the words at times, but eventually he ceased speaking, and the old woman nodded slowly.

"Πρὸς ἠῶ." She spoke more slowly and pointed her cane across the room at the wall. "Παρὰ τείχεσι."

"She says it is in the east. Near the city walls."

"I think I understood that," Zeb muttered to himself, sharing a subdued smile with Penélope.

"Then what are we waiting for?" Alex asked, sitting up. "We should go there now."

The old woman brandished her cane at Alex, speaking rapidly. Alex looked at Ari in frustration, but he did not meet her eyes, listening intently. The woman took a deep breath and stopped speaking, though she continued to shake her cane at Alex.

Ari's brows furrowed, as though he had barely understood. "She said the temple is guarded by armed men and we cannot go inside without an appointment. We will need a plan. I think she said that the guards have rotations. Maybe if we learn them over the next few days, we could sneak in."

"Days?" This time Chloe spoke, her voice terse. "I thought we wanted to be in and out in one night."

"Obviously that's not possible anymore," Ari said cuttingly.

There was silence. Even the old woman waited to see what they would decide. Alex sighed and rubbed her eyes. She was exhausted. At this rate, they would have to spend the night at the very least.

"I'm sorry I brought you all into this," Alex said quietly. "If you want to leave before things get dangerous, I would understand."

"If you haven't noticed, love," Owen drawled, "things are already dangerous."

"You're not helping," Penélope said in annoyance.

Suddenly Warren took Alex's hand in his. He looked at her with those blue eyes, as solid and unwavering as a cloudless sky at midday. "I'm with you, no matter what. We'll find your mother together."

Penélope nodded. "Me too."

"And me," Ari said, followed by Zeb's murmuring agreement.

Owen glanced around and shrugged. "Then I'm in too."

Chloe hesitated, then sighed. "Well, I'm not going home alone, am I?" At everyone's silent faces, she rolled her eyes. "And I'll help you find your mother, Alex. Is that good enough for you guys?"

Alex could not help but laugh, though it was mainly in relief. "Thank you."

Ari stood up, looking at the eastern wall of the house as if he could see the Temple of Apollo somewhere beyond it. "Then we start after the sun sets. Until then, we should all get some sleep. It's going to be a long night."

55

Alex shifted her weight carefully to get a better view over the edge of the roof. She spotted a lone guard strolling before the temple doors, his back stiff and a spear leaning against his shoulder. His eyes darted around cautiously at the stragglers crossing the street.

"It's the same every day," Chloe muttered with a sigh, rolling onto her back away from the edge so that no one would see her from the street. "A single soldier guards the entrance for six-hour shifts. Then at nightfall, they increase it to two guards. God, this is boring."

Alex glared at her. "Keep your voice down. We might get caught."

But Chloe was right. This *was* boring. For the past few days, they had done nothing but scout the Temple of Apollo and the surrounding area. Ari and Penélope were on another roof nearby to keep track of the squadrons of soldiers that patrolled the area.

So far they have determined that two small squadrons patrolled the southeastern quadrant of the city—which was where the old woman lived—and that at every ring of the bells a squadron passed the temple of Apollo. The bells did not mark the hours, however, but chimed at different intervals that they could not explain, the closest interval being almost exactly an hour and a half and the longest just shy of two hours.

Just then the bells rang, clanging loudly through the air like a single terse note that remained vibrating after being plucked. Chloe jostled her shoulder and pointed. A moment later a squadron of soldiers marched around the corner and passed the Temple of Apollo, their bronze armor gleaming in the sunlight and their swords dangling at their hips. They passed down the street, turned, and were out of sight once more.

"I don't know how we're going to get past that squadron once, let alone twice," Chloe said, shaking her head.

"We'll just have to get in and out of the temple before the next bell," Alex said, sounding more confident than she felt. She had no idea what to expect inside the temple, not to mention how they would be able to enter and leave without alerting the authorities.

Chloe gave her a pointed look. "We don't even know if the Stone is in there."

A grating noise filled the air before Alex could respond, and then a carriage rolled before the temple, its windows covered by curtains, manned by two royal guards and a coachman.

"Here comes the rich lady for her daily prophecy," Chloe said sarcastically.

They had first noticed her daily appearance on the second time scouting, when the same carriage with the same woman rolled before the temple at the same time as the day before. Ari had asked the old woman about her and they learned that wealthy citizens frequented the temple to ask the priestess inside about the future, concerning everything from marriages to business ventures to deaths. This woman visited the temple without fail at the same time and left before the next bell rang.

The carriage doors were opened by the two fancily dressed guards, who helped the woman descend to the ground. A purple veil covered her face, and she was quietly followed by two handmaidens similarly veiled. The woman and her handmaidens entered the temple, passing the guard, who merely stepped aside and bowed his head.

"It's easy for her to get in," Chloe complained. "I guess all you need is money. Too bad my savings don't transfer. Maybe if we looked like her..."

Alex watched the three women disappear behind the tall white columns as a thought occurred to her. She turned to Chloe, who was already staring at her, eyes wide in realization.

"That's it," Alex whispered. "That's how we get in."

"But how?" Chloe asked, glancing at the guards and coachman nervously.

"It would be impossible to trick the guard if we don't arrive in the carriage."

"Then we make sure to arrive in the carriage." Alex counted the entourage and smiled. "It's perfect. Warren, Owen, and Ari can take out the guards and coachman. You, me, and Penélope will pretend to be the woman and her handmaidens. Then Zeb can keep watch for a squadron. We'll go in and out before the next bell rings."

"What about the priestess inside?" Chloe challenged.

"We'll deal with her," Alex said, though her stomach turned uneasily at the thought. "Maybe she knows about the Stone. We get to ask her a question, don't we?"

"It's a risk. She could alert the guard outside."

Alex was silent.

"But it's the only option we have," Chloe said reluctantly. "And no one else will come up with a better plan any time soon."

"Then you're in?" Alex asked doubtfully.

Chloe nodded. "Let's tell the others."

They returned to the house, quietly jumping over the roofs until they could hop down into an alley and turn onto the street of the house.

Compared to the large, decorated houses in the northeastern quadrant that Alex had seen on her first visit with Ari, the houses in the southeastern quadrant were blocks of grimy apartments stacked on top of each other in three to six-story buildings. Smoke rose from the fires inside each house, kindling the air with the sweet smell of burnt wood.

Alex and Chloe entered the door to the old woman's house. Ari and Penélope were already back from scouting and were taking their seats on the couches for dinner next to the others. The old woman was in the corner, eyeing Alex and Chloe as she prodded the stew in the cauldron hanging over the fire.

"I wish she would cook something different," Chloe muttered.

"Chloe." Alex cut the old woman a worried look, who was staring back at them, her eyes flashing with the light from the fire. "Sometimes I think she can understand us, don't you?"

Chloe just rolled her eyes and took a seat beside Owen, before announcing loudly, "Alex and I have a plan."

Ari glanced up at Alex in surprise. "Really? Since when?"

"You know the rich woman who comes to the temple every day at the same time?" Alex took a seat beside Warren on the couches. "Chloe and I came up with a plan to hijack that carriage. One of us is going to pretend to be the woman. The rest will be her entourage. We just need to be in and out before the next bell."

None of them spoke at first. The old woman hobbled over to the couches and set down the stew and flatbread. Before she walked away, Ari called out to her.

The old woman stared at each of them curiously as he spoke, her mouth lifting into an amused smile as Ari continued speaking. Once he finished, she nodded and spoke excitedly, pointing to herself and then behind her shoulder.

Ari turned to them and smiled. "I asked if she might have any fancy clothes for us to disguise as the woman and her guards. She said we could use her old wedding dress. Us boys will have to steal the clothes of the guards."

"Who will be the woman?" Penélope asked.

"Obviously me," Chloe drawled.

"Actually," Ari said with a smirk, "you're too tall. The old woman is half your height. If you walked into the temple as that woman you would draw too much attention to yourself."

Chloe crossed her arms. "If I'm too tall, then so is Alex."

At the same time, everyone turned to look at Penélope, whose eyes widened, and she began shaking her head.

"No, no, no," Penélope said. "They'll know right away."

"How many times have you lied straight to Sister Stella's face?" Zeb asked, raising a brow. "This isn't any different."

"This *is* different," Penélope said, her voice hardly a whisper. "She never had a sword and spear to kill me with!"

"Your head will be veiled," Alex said calmly, despite the quickened beat of her heart. "Chloe and I will be right behind you as your handmaidens. We won't let anything happen to you."

"You have no choice," Warren interrupted tersely. He rarely spoke in conversation these past few days and mainly hung around Owen. Alex got the sense that out of everyone he felt as though he belonged the least. "We need to find Alex's mother, and this might be the only way."

Alex ignored Warren's eyes burning into her. She felt helpless against that look, exposed and bare as a rock beneath the sun. Chloe caught her eye and Alex saw the warning written in that fierce gaze. *When are you going to tell him?*

"Perhaps I missed this small detail," Owen said, breaking up the silence that followed, "but how did you say we were going to hijack the carriage?"

"That is where you come in, *love*," Alex said with a smirk. "You, Warren, and Ari are going to stop the carriage before it reaches the temple. Two of you will replace the guards while the other will drive. Chloe, Penélope, and I will swap with the woman and her handmaidens. Zeb will keep watch to make sure we don't get surprised by a roaming squadron. Then together we will arrive at the temple."

"And once you guys get inside?" Zeb asked dryly.

"Then they find the Stone," Ari said, his gaze heated, lingering on Alex. "Then we find your mother."

For the rest of the dinner, they formulated the plan. They would need to scout the route of the carriage for one more day before deciding when they would perform the swap. The hardest part would be handling the guards and coachman and stealing their uniforms without someone hearing the commotion or one of them running off to warn a nearby soldier. If they made it to the temple, Alex could only hope the temple guard did not look too closely at the faces beneath the veils.

Once inside the temple, their plan became less certain. The hymn to the Prince of Thieves spoke of a chasm and a rushing stream where Hermes found the Stone. But the old woman had no idea if there was a chasm in the temple as she had never visited. While there was definitely a priestess inside, it was impossible to predict how she would react if they began snooping about the temple.

As the night wore on, they filed off to bed. The girls had silently claimed the couches as their beds while the boys rolled out mats and rugs the old woman had given them on the floor. Most of them had already nodded off to sleep, but Alex found she could not fall asleep, turning over on the couch and looking up at the painted red ceiling.

She sat up. The old woman was asleep across the room in her corner by the fireplace, which was nearly turning to embers, casting the room in gloomy shadows. Her gentle snores filled the small house like a running brook. Alex hopped off the couch and tiptoed across the floor towards the mats.

Warren had his mat separate from the others, near the wall. Alex ignored the warnings in her head and crawled onto his mat. His eyes flew open, and he stared at Alex uncomprehendingly.

"I couldn't sleep," she whispered, suddenly embarrassed.

But Warren only nodded and lifted the end of his blanket. She slipped under his arm wordlessly, closing her eyes as the familiar heat of his body sank her into sleep.

Warren held her close. His hand found hers and she held it tightly. Then from one breath to the next, she fell asleep.

56

Alex woke up and forgot where she was. Then she saw the dirt floor, the close walls darkened with soot, and her friends milling about the couches, eating small cakes and fruit, and the plan they had formed at dinner last night came rushing back.

She sat up swiftly, then felt the space beside her. Warren had already gotten up with everyone else. Alex stood up, raking her fingers through the knots in her hair. Ari glanced over at her from his spot on one of the couches with a frown, before saying something to Zeb.

Warren sought her gaze from across the couches and she forced herself not to look his way. She sat beside Chloe and Penélope, who were holding a heap of very long and sparkling purple fabric in their hands.

"What's this?" Alex asked.

Chloe held up the fabric and Alex saw that it was a dress. "This is the old woman's wedding dress. She has two other dresses that might fit us to look like the handmaidens." She stroked the loose folds of the dress, which Alex realized as she took a closer look were woven with fine threads of gold. "It's a beautiful dress."

"It must have cost her a fortune," Owen muttered, joining their conversation and brushing the fabric between his fingertips. "Though it smells a century old."

Chloe narrowed her eyes at the old woman who observed them from across the room. "How old *is* that woman?"

"Old enough to know when you're talking shit about her," Ari retorted from the other couch. He sat up, swinging his legs around so that they dangled in the center of the couches. All of them turned, sensing that the time had come.

"We'll have three groups posted at different points near the temple to look out for the carriage. Take these maps to find your scouting position," Ari said, handing Zeb a stack of loose parchments cut into small squares.

Alex took hers and passed the rest on. The small parchment had the now familiar grid of the city, the main streets crossing perpendicular to each other and the Temple of Apollo in the far southeast corner starred and circled, with small alleys and roads shooting off from it.

"If the woman comes at the same time," Ari continued, "she should appear on one of the marked streets a little before the next bell. Once we have the exact location, we'll reconvene here. I'll take Zeb and Penélope to the street marked A. The rest of you form pairs and scout the other two."

Before Alex had the chance to ask Chloe, Warren tapped her shoulder. She turned, feeling the reluctance build in her very bones. "Yes?"

"Can we talk?"

"Right now?" Alex asked, glancing at Chloe for help, who studiously avoided her gaze as she stood up and joined Owen.

"We're going to street B," Owen called over his shoulder. They followed after Ari and the others out the door, which shut quietly, leaving them in a heavy silence.

Warren sighed. "Fine. We can talk after."

Alex ignored a twinge of annoyance and followed Warren outside, feeling the eyes of the old woman fixated on her long after she left. They quickly turned the corner into a narrow alleyway and Alex pulled out the map. The street marked C branched off from the temple horizontally on the west side.

She folded up the map. "This way."

Warren followed Alex up a towering pile of crates that had been stacked by the old woman to help them climb to the ledge of the second story, where a rope dangled off the roof. He placed a protective hand on the small of her back as she hauled herself up the side of the wall. Soon Warren joined her and he fell into step beside her as they ran across the roof, their backs crouched to make themselves less visible to passersby below.

Every few blocks she consulted her map to make sure they were going the right way. Warren would then silently peer over her shoulder to look at the map, his eyes intermittently flickering to her face. Soon they reached the street that veered from the temple, parallel to the city wall which bordered the city to the south. From this close, she could hear the rushing waters of what must be a river on the other side of the wall.

"The bell should ring any minute," Alex said finally in a hushed voice as they took their places on the roof, the tiles poking her stomach as she lay down. Warren joined her, lying beside her uncomfortably. She scooted closer to the edge of the roof and looked down both directions of the street. There was not a soul creeping anywhere in sight.

"I'm not stupid, you know," Warren said suddenly, cutting her a harsh glance. "I have eyes."

"What's that supposed to mean?"

Warren shook his head in exasperation. "What are we doing, Alex? Do you still want to be with me?"

Alex stared at him, a lump pressing against her throat. Tears pricked her eyes, the words overwhelmed by the truth she felt running through her. Somehow she had never expected him to say it. His words settled between them like dust, more impossible than the magical city surrounding them.

"I love you, Alex," he said quietly. "And if you need time, I'll wait. I'll wait until you're ready."

"That's not..." Her voice trailed off, strained. She did not know how she was going to end it anyway. *That's not what I was going to say. That's not what I want. That's not fair.*

But before she could make up her mind, there was a loud clamor in the air. The bells were ringing. Warren met her eyes, his hardened and weary. The carriage must have already arrived at the temple, though it had not passed their way.

"We should go," he said.

"Wait." She wanted to tell him, to say the words now so that she never had to say them again. "Just hold on a second."

Warren gave her a strange look, caught halfway between scorn and embarrassment. "You don't have to say it."

"I do," she said firmly, then took a deep breath in. "This is not just about my mother. This is about my *life*. This is about finding out what I want. And I can't do that when I'm with you."

"Then you want to break up? You want to give up everything we've built together for what? Some guy you hardly know?" He shook his head when she tried to interrupt. "Don't deny it, Alex. I've seen the way Ari looks at you."

"This has nothing to do with Ari," Alex said angrily. "Nothing happened with him. I've been trying to understand what I want to do with my life since the day my mom left and this is the closest I've come to figuring it out. I can't pretend to live a life that I'm not even sure I want anymore."

"I don't think you'll ever know what you want, Alex," Warren said bitterly. "And if you truly loved me, you wouldn't need to leave me to find out."

Alex knew he was right, that the reason she began questioning her life and what she wanted was only because she knew it was not the life she was living. Warren reached out and took one of her hands, his eyes reluctantly softening, perhaps at the tears that silently rolled down her face.

"You know I will always love you." He brushed his knuckles against her cheek, wiping away the tears as they fell. "I'll wait, but I won't wait forever."

"What if I don't find her?" Alex asked, her voice trembling. "What if my life will always feel like chasing someone that doesn't exist?"

"Maybe that's what life is all about," Warren said, gently pulling her into a hug. They had known each other too long to act like strangers. "Chasing someone until we find ourselves."

He sounded like he was speaking from experience. They pulled apart and walked back to the house in silence. There was nothing more to say.

Alex let Warren help her down the side of the building to the alleyway. His touch on her waist felt like a long-lost memory that she once treasured, but it paled in the face of the city, the rambling, foreign-colored roofs, the distant harbor glinting on the horizon.

The others had already returned by the time they arrived back at the house. Chloe and Owen had spotted the carriage as it drove down from the north directly towards the temple. Tomorrow they would wait in the alley where soldiers were least likely to patrol at that time of day and then surprise the carriage on its route to the temple, taking out the guards and coachman and swapping places with the three women.

Everyone went to sleep after dinner, hoping to rest before the big day. Alex did not go to Warren's mat, forcing herself to remain on the couch. She closed her eyes, hoping to fall asleep quickly. The murmuring whispers in the room disappeared and Alex's mind swam in half-formed dreams, snatches of a phrase from her mother's diary, deft hands reaching into a rushing stream.

She awoke to a deep silence. It was still night. Chloe and Penélope were asleep. Warren was curled up on his mat, facing the wall. The old woman's familiar snores came from the other side of the room. Alex turned. The other three mats were empty.

Ari, Zeb, and Owen were gone. Alex's heart beat clumsily in her chest. She looked around the room but there was nowhere for them to hide inside. They had to have left. Had they given up so soon to finding the Emerald Stone?

Alex hopped off the couch quietly and tiptoed toward the door. She glanced behind her one last time before stepping out into the night.

The city was quiet, as if the fog blanketing the streets brought a hush that silenced all else. Then Alex heard familiar murmuring voices coming from the next alley over. She took one step at a time, her instinct telling her not to be heard.

One more step. She pressed herself up against the wall, then slowly, slowly, peered around the corner.

Alex froze at what she saw. Caught between the wall and Owen's strong arms was none other than Zeb, their mouths locked together. She watched as Zeb hooked a wrist behind Owen's neck, kissing him with an abandon she had never seen in him before.

She felt a hand grab her arm and her breath left her as she whipped her head around, ready to scream.

Ari. He had a finger up to his mouth, then motioned with his head to walk with him in the opposite direction of Zeb and Owen. Alex nodded silently and together they walked to the next alley, where Ari showed her a stone wall at the back that had grooves they could climb all the way up to the roof.

With her heart in her throat, Alex followed Ari up the stone wall and heaved herself onto the roof. Ari held out his hand and she took it. When he did not let go, Alex could scarcely breathe, and she let him lead her across several blocks and up another story until they had a view of the main cross street, where the main bell tower chimed in the town square, and the grand library stood regal and silent across the intersection, and the glistening gates at the harbor could just be glimpsed afar through the fog. She wondered if she should pull her hand away, thinking of Warren and his hardened blue eyes, but she did not have the strength to fight against her own desires.

"Did you know?" Alex asked as they sat down together near the ledge. "About Zeb and Owen, I mean."

"I knew for a while. I already caught them once."

"Is that what you were doing up so late? Spying on them?"

Ari huffed a laugh. "No. I come out here to look at the city. And the stars." He looked up with a wistful smile. "I've never seen anything like them. Have you?"

Alex shook her head, but could not speak. The constellations peaking through the cloudy night sky were strange. She wondered if they were different from the ones on Earth, or if they were merely seeing them from a different perspective. Her head spun with the impossibility of the city, the fire of the lighthouse in the harbor flashing like a warning.

"This city..." Ari glanced at her keenly. "You. It's changed everything."

She didn't know what to say, looking out at the tall columns of the library so that she would not have to look Ari in the eyes. "I broke up with Warren."

Ari was silent, though his hand on hers tightened ever so slightly. He seemed to be waiting for an explanation.

"I thought if I did I would suddenly see everything clearly," Alex said, almost smiling to herself. "But I've never felt more lost. He was my future. He was my life. He represented everything I once knew about myself. Now I'm nothing."

"Maybe that's a good thing," Ari said, raising a brow. "You can start over."

Alex looked out over the city and tried to imagine her mother as a girl about her age, running through the foreign streets and meeting a stranger with dark hair and a mysterious smile, falling in love with a city that did not exist.

A shimmer from the moonlight above cast the streets in a dream-like vision. She felt so unreal. Time was slipping through her fingers. The stars above seemed close enough to touch. Her hand stirred at her side, and she nearly reached out to try and touch them, just to make sure they were real, before Ari spoke.

"I was so lost at Harvard. I used to love Ancient Greek. I used to love the myths, the tales about giants and wanderers and goddesses. When I was a child, I was always alone, but when I read Homer, there was Odysseus, sailing the seas for years, or there was Achilles, fighting Hector before the walls of Troy. I *believed* in them as if they were real. And they were real to me then. At the New Academy, I read the entire library before I was fifteen. I read Greek and Latin until I could recite entire passages in them. I wanted to know what it felt like to live in a time of magic, in a time of demigods, monsters, and nymphs. I think all that time I secretly thought that a door would open, and I would walk through it and actually see the fast ships of the Achaeans, I would see the towering city walls of Troy, and I would finally understand the meaning of life."

Alex smiled wryly. "There's nothing magical about Harvard."

Ari shook his head. "No. I quickly realized that there would never be a door, that Harvard was a road that led to nowhere and I would be stuck on it until I was old and died. The day I quit, it was snowing for the third month in a row and everything seemed so bleak. All I could think about was how I missed the sun. I cashed the rest of my stipend and booked a flight home and never told anyone at Harvard until I was back in my dorm room at the New Academy. All because I missed the damn sun."

"Would you call me crazy if I told you I left because a bird told me to?" Alex joked.

Instead of laughing, Ari stared at her with that familiar, unbridled intensity, a hand reaching up and brushing a strand of hair away from her face. "Then you showed up. And the next thing I knew we found a door to a magical city, to a world of gods and myth, as if fate had somehow brought us together. You made me *believe* again."

Alex nearly shivered. She wanted to kiss him, she wanted to know what it felt like to tug at those curls and hear him whisper her name against her mouth, coming undone beneath her hands. *Alexandria*. She wanted to be uprooted, shaken as tree branches were in a winter storm. But a part of her knew that the storm was only a distraction and that the only true freedom she would find was in flight.

I must follow the sad nightingale.

"What are you going to do after all of this is over?" Alex asked.

Ari looked out at the city, the stars reflected in his dark eyes, and he grinned. "I want to stay. I don't believe it was a coincidence that I found this place. I can't just leave it." He gave her a sidelong glance. "And you? Will you stay?"

"I don't know," Alex said truthfully.

"Well, you always know how to return," Ari said, a hand subconsciously touching the clasp of his purple cloak which he had not taken off since he arrived. "Sister Stella can't keep you out."

Alex nodded. "There are many doors."

"There are many doors," Ari echoed, though he frowned and did not speak again.

When the first rays of the sun lifted in the east, they made their way back over the roofs, climbing down the stone wall and slipping back inside the house. Zeb and Owen had already returned and were asleep on their own mats.

Ari shared an amused glance with her before sliding under his blanket. Alex bit back a smile as she closed her eyes.

And as sleep descended like clouds on the horizon of her mind, she dreamed that a storm ripped through the city, tearing up the roofs, shaking the branches of the palm trees, blowing sand across the ocean, and Alex was standing at the heart of it.

Thunder clapped and shook the earth, rain poured in heavy sheets, and then lightning flashed and Alex was rooted to the spot as the bolt struck her, filling the world with white until Alex woke up, gasping, the morning light pouring in through the window.

57

"THEY'RE LATE," CHLOE COMPLAINED, craning her neck around the corner. "Why haven't they come yet?"

"Be quiet," Ari whispered. He pulled his cloak around his arms, as the morning was still overcast. "Once they're here you might be saying otherwise."

Chloe scowled at him but remained silent. Penélope paced the alleyway, her fingers knotted together. Alex stood a few feet away from Ari, trying to breathe calmly. Somewhere on a roof near the temple was Zeb, who would look out for any approaching patrols.

Then they heard it. That grating clamor of metal on stone coming from a distance. Ari and Chloe waited at the edge of the street across which they had pulled several long, thick ropes stolen from a nearby alley to stop the carriage. They picked up the ropes, holding them tightly. The carriage would pass them any second.

"Now!" Ari shouted.

Ari and Chloe pulled the ropes taut, hauling their weight backward with all their might. On the other side of the street, Warren and Owen would be doing the same. A loud screech and a shout were followed by horse whinnies and girlish screams. Alex waited anxiously beside Chloe and Penélope as the boys dropped the ropes and scampered into the street to deal with the guards and coachman. Soon they heard the scuffles and grunts of a fistfight they could not see.

"Let's go," Chloe said, nodding her head in their direction, before taking off around the corner.

Penélope and Alex did not have time to stop her and quickly followed,

Alex's heart beating wildly in her chest. When they stepped out onto the street, the coachman had one of Chloe's arms in his grip as he shouted angrily in Greek. Behind them, Warren, Owen, and Ari struggled with the guards, who were putting up a fight.

"Chloe, watch out!" Penélope cried out, her hand outstretched.

The coachman had managed to throw Chloe over the side of the carriage, where she fell to the ground. But before the coachman could grab her again, Chloe popped up onto her feet and threw a clean punch into his face. The coachman instantly keeled over, and Owen rushed over to grab his thick arms and wrestled them behind his back.

"Good lord, Chloe," Owen said, whistling. "That was a good punch."

The coachman struggled futilely as Alex and Penélope wrapped his wrists in a rough rope before Owen gagged him with a strip of the old woman's rags.

Chloe rubbed her knuckles with a wince, though she was smiling. "Ari's not the only one who knows how to box."

Ari shoved the unconscious body of one of the guards to the floor, whom they had accidentally knocked out by slamming his head against the carriage. "Let's put them in the alley."

Beside him, Warren nodded, and together they grabbed the guard by the feet and the arms, dragging him to the alley where they had waited for the carriage. Behind them Chloe and Owen roughly shoved the other guard forward, bound tightly in one of the ropes and glaring at them, his teeth bared against his gag. Warren returned and helped Alex bring the coachman down from the carriage and into the alley with the guards, a similar scowl on his face.

"Tie them up with the other guard," Ari muttered, grabbing the rope from the middle of the road. "Then we should take care of the women."

They followed him to the carriage doors which had not opened since the tumult had begun. Alex couldn't remember hearing another scream from within the carriage. Ari held out a warning hand, then quietly walked to the other side of the door. Then he nodded at Alex to open it. She reached a trembling hand to the latch, then pulled back, holding her breath.

A hand shot out gripping a small dagger. Ari grasped the arm by the wrist and strangled the knife from her tight grip. He dragged the woman out, who whimpered as she was forced to the ground.

Her head was veiled, but Alex knew immediately she was one of the handmaidens. Alex called Warren and Owen over.

"Tie her up with the others," Alex said. "Ari, tell them we won't hurt them."

"οὐ ὑμᾶς βλάψομεν," Ari said as gently as he could.

The second handmaiden who stepped out of the carriage glanced at Ari resentfully. "Βάρβαροι," she spat at him, before Warren and Owen took her by the hands to lead her away.

Alex glanced at Ari. "What did she say?"

Ari huffed a laugh. "I'll give you a hint. It's the same word that gave us *barbarians*."

Before Alex could reply, the last woman exited the carriage. She held her head high and extended an elegant hand. Ari exchanged a doubtful glance with Alex, but he gave the woman his hand and helped her down from the carriage. Her face was hardly visible beneath her veil but Alex thought she saw the curl of a smirk.

The woman dutifully followed Warren and Owen, who brought her to the alley where the rest of her entourage already had their arms bound in rope behind their backs and their mouths gagged. The two handmaidens glared at Alex as she finished gagging the rich lady, who remained quiet and still when Ari bound her to the others. Ari and the other boys hurriedly stripped the coachman and royal guards of their raiment, ignoring their feeble protests at lying on the cold, hard alley in nothing but their underclothes.

"We're running late," Alex said, looking one last time at their hostages. She felt a prickle of guilt at their helpless bodies, one of the men's heads lolling to the side, the women's faces lowered in submission. But then she remembered her mother, the Emerald Stone, and the king who would kill them simply for entering the city. This was her only chance.

She lowered her veil over her face, Chloe and Penélope doing the same, before they all climbed into the carriage. The inside was much smaller than she had imagined, with ornately patterned fabric lining every surface, even the ceiling. The thick curtains shut out the light and with their veils covering their faces, everything was cast in a murky darkness.

"How much time until the next bell?" Penélope asked quietly.

Alex shook her head, her entire body numb. "I have no idea."

They did not speak for the rest of the ride. The carriage trotted along as it usually did, with Owen at the reigns, since he had been the only one among them with experience riding horses. Warren and Ari stood on the sides of the carriage as it drove precariously down the winding streets.

At last, the carriage came to a stop. Alex grasped Penélope and Chloe's hands and squeezed. Suddenly everything they had spoken about and planned—the hymn, her mother's diary, the city, the Emerald Stone, the king—all of it felt as real and dangerous as walking on a tightrope and realizing too late that you were no longer tied to safety. Penélope walked out of the carriage first. Then Alex took a deep breath in and stepped out of the carriage, allowing Warren to help her down.

The bright sunlight flooded her vision, though everything was still tinted purple from her veil. Ahead of her were the towering fluted columns of the temple, the statues on the frieze larger and more detailed up close. Alex could make out a statue of a man at the very top of the temple roof, with dark curly hair, a gold flowing cloak, and a lyre tucked into his side.

Standing at attention before the massive wooden doors was a single soldier, his posture erect, a spear held up by one hand resting on his right shoulder. He saw Penélope and immediately began marching towards her.

Alex stuttered to a stop behind Penélope, wondering if their plan would fail so soon. He must have noticed their late arrival, or else that the guards or coachman looked different, even though Owen had covered his head with a cloak. But the soldier only stopped at the base of the steps and bowed deeply, before stepping to the side.

Penélope started forward again and Alex and Chloe followed after her. Together the three of them made for the temple doors. They walked up the stairs and passed the rows of columns until they reached the entrance. The soldier marched beside them, seemingly oblivious to the swap they had done, and opened one of the doors wide in perfect obedience.

They entered the darkness of the temple, which only grew darker when the door shut with a bang behind them, making Alex flinch. She peered into the shapeless room but could see nothing save deep shadows.

"Maybe no one is here," Chloe whispered.

A light flared to life across the room. Then another. Then another, until the entire perimeter of the small room lit up with torchlight. Alex inched subconsciously closer to Chloe and Penélope, then nearly gasped at the beautiful wall paintings around them. There were scenes of gods and mortals in battle, of ships sailing across oceans, and a herd of cows strolling in a valley. On one of the columns, there were three Ancient Greek phrases written in blood-red paint. And below those phrases was the letter E, just like the one on the Squatting Scribe.

"῎Ελθετε, ὦ πότνια."

A female voice echoed against the marble floors and all three of them jumped. Ahead, shrouded in darkness, was a woman, flanked by two robed men and standing before another door. She was dressed plainly in a simple white tunic, her long brown hair falling loosely around her shoulders. Alex realized she could not be older than fourteen. In one hand she held a stalk of laurel leaves, in the other a glittering bowl filled with liquid. Alex could not help glancing at Penélope and Chloe in alarm, as they had not anticipated anyone else besides the priestess being inside the temple.

When none of them moved, the priestess beckoned them over with a questioning look. "Πότνιά μου?"

Penélope stepped forward hesitantly. "Χαῖρε."

The priestess cocked her head. "῞Επευ μοι, πότνια."

She turned with a swish of her dress and opened the doors, slipping inside the room. Penélope started, then looked at Alex worriedly. Alex nodded for her to continue, and with a deep breath Penélope continued walking, Alex and Chloe close behind her. They passed the two priests, who bowed their heads and remained at their posts.

Alex squinted as they entered the inner room which was flooded with light from the opening in the ceiling above. The priestess took a seat on a tripod at the far end of the room before the altar, where a jagged crack in the floor revealed a chasm of bare rock, steam curling up from the crevice.

"Τί ζητεῖτε, ὦ πότνια?"

Her voice hissed like a snake as she leaned forward and breathed deeply from the fumes cloaking her seat, where she seemed to float above the chasm.

Penélope cleared her throat nervously. "Βούλομαι τὴν σμάραγδον λίσπην."

Alex didn't understand the unfamiliar syllables, but they had practiced before and she knew what those words meant. *I want the Emerald Stone.*

At this the priestess straightened up, her eyes narrowing. She hopped down from the seat and strolled over to Penélope. Alex shared an anxious glance with Chloe, who shrugged. The priestess stood before Penélope, her eyes roaming her face and down her dress.

"Οὐ πότνια εἶ," the priestess purred before she ripped the veil from Penélope's face, smiling in triumph when she saw that it was not the Queen. They had been caught.

Alex's heart jumped to her throat, and she stood as still as a statue. Before she could decide what they should do next, the priestess let out a yelp and was dragged backward. Chloe had her arms behind her back and was dragging her away, the priestess twisting helplessly in her grasp. When the priestess began to scream, Penélope lunged forward, pressing a hand against her mouth and muffling her cries.

"Quick!" Chloe whispered harshly, struggling to drag the protesting priestess away. "Help me tie her up!"

Alex ran towards them and helped Chloe tie the priestess' wrists with her veil. Chloe then used hers to gag the priestess, whose eyes widened in fear and indignation, her muffled noises spitting past the fabric. In case one of the priests heard the commotion and entered, they hid the priestess behind the altar and hooked her tied wrists to a stone carving of a serpent jutting out from the sculpted relief.

"We have to start looking," Penélope said grimly, glancing around the walls painted with intricate decorations of green wreaths, gold candelabras, and marble vases, their two-dimensional lines and colors seeming to come alive in the flickering light of torches along the walls.

Chloe crouched beside the chasm and tried to look inside. She shook her head. "It's completely dark down there."

"I don't even think we could fit our hands inside," Penélope said, crouching down and probing the crack with her fingers. Some of the crumbling rock fell and echoed loudly as it bounced down and down the chasm to some unseen stream. "It runs deep."

Alex got on the floor and pressed her face to the crack. A moment later a rush of fumes rose and nearly choked the breath from her lungs. She sat up and coughed harshly until tears blurred her vision. The smoke stung the back of her throat and she felt dizzy.

"That is toxic," Alex said between coughs.

"There's nothing around the altar," Chloe said in a hushed voice, hurrying around the stone block and peering at the floor where the priestess mumbled her protests. "There are no drawers, just this fire with bones on it. Gross."

"Sacrifices," Penélope explained as she walked around the perimeter of the room, searching the walls with her hands and examining the corners. "This room is empty."

A wave of anger choked Alex. She wanted to break something. She wanted to kick the chasm and watch the stone floor crumble in, but she was afraid the noise would alert the priests. All of their planning, all of their hard work spying on the temple and hijacking the carriage, all of it was for nothing.

"We should go," Alex said angrily. "It's not here."

"What?" Chloe asked, her head shooting up. "You're just gonna give up?"

"We knew it was a long shot. Now we can all go home." Alex looked up at the sky as if the harsh sun looking down upon them could give her the answers. She closed her eyes tightly and whispered under her breath. "Please, Mom, help us. Help us find you."

A shrill noise sounded outside the temple and Alex thought it was the city alarms until she realized they were the bells of the tower, ringing out at the next interval.

"We should be gone by now," Penélope said, her face pale. "What if the next person comes in?"

Right on cue, a loud knock resounded throughout the temple. The doors rattled as someone pounded a fist on the wood, followed by concerned shouts.

"I have an idea," Chloe said quickly. She lifted the old woman's dress over her head in a swift motion, throwing it onto the floor behind the altar. All that clothed her now was a small slip of thin white fabric that they had put under their dresses in case the fabric tore.

"What are you doing?" Alex asked in disbelief.

"I'm going to pretend to be the priestess." Chloe grabbed the laurel leaves and water bowl by the priestess' feet and walked over to the tripod, ignoring her muffled cries. "How hard can it be? Then when the guards see everything is alright, I change back and we get the hell out of here."

"I don't like this," Penélope said, right before the knocking and shouting at the door resumed. Her eyes widened. "But it might be the only option we have."

Chloe sat on the tripod, holding the laurel leaves and the bowl of water. Cloaked by the white smoke rising from the chasm she looked almost like the priestess. As she took her seat, the doors burst open, and the priests entered. But they hardly glanced at the priestess, instead stepping aside to allow an old man to limp inside.

"Πάντως χαῖρε, ὦ βασιλεῦ!" exclaimed the priests.

The gray tufts of hair on the old man's head were crowned with a circular band of gold leaves. He wore a robe of rich purple, his feet clothed in bejeweled slippers, and he used a gold cane to walk, one old, gnarled hand gripping the golden head. Then Alex saw his eyes, a milky white with a lingering tinge of blue. He was blind.

Penélope and Alex stood stiffly as the old man entered the inner room. It was clear he had an appointment. He hobbled across the stone floor, then glanced at the two of them. For a moment, Alex thought he would realize that they were imposters, but he merely bowed his head.

"Χαῖρε, πότνια." His voice was gravelly and made him seem more ancient than he looked. Then he turned his aged, blind face towards Chloe and a pleased smile etched across his mouth. "Χαῖρε, ἱέρεια τοῦ Ἀπόλλωνος."

Chloe merely inclined her head.

The old man seemed to wait, and Alex realized they were expected to leave. She bowed her head once more, then followed Penélope to the door, which the priests held open for them, exiting the room with one last glance at Chloe, who did not betray a single emotion as she was left alone with the old man.

They walked in silence to the carriage, where Warren, Ari, and Owen were waiting. When they saw them, they stood at attention, though their eyes widened when they realized that one of them was missing.

Warren helped Penélope into the carriage. He took Alex's hand. "Where's Chloe?"

Alex shook her head silently, then slid into the carriage seat. Penélope let out a shaky breath once the carriage jolted and drove off. She grasped Alex's hand and squeezed.

"Alex," she said, still in a whisper. "I think we just met the King."

58

"We have to go back!" Owen said angrily.

"How?" Warren demanded. "It's guarded."

Alex fixed him a look. "We have to go back."

Ari stood up from his seat on the couch, where they had gathered after returning to the old woman's house. "What if we caused a distraction? Then when the guard is lured away a few of us sneak in and pull her out. No one will be the wiser."

"What if she was imprisoned?" Penélope asked. "They would only need to look at her for a second too long or find the real priestess behind the altar."

"Zeb is watching the temple," Alex said. "He will see if she's taken away. The old woman already said that only the priestess and the petitioners are allowed in that inner room."

"Hopefully," Warren muttered.

Alex paced the room. She saw the old woman observing them from her seat by the fire, a woven blanket thrown over her feeble legs. But her sharp eyes fastened themselves on Alex, the green eyes glowing with red and orange from the fire.

"Ari," Alex said suddenly, "can you ask the old woman if there's any other way out of the temple?"

Ari nodded, then after a moment's consideration began speaking to the woman while pointing in the direction of the temple. The old woman cocked her head to the side, then grinned. She spoke as her hand made a swooping motion.

"Yes, there is," Ari said, then pausing to let her add more instruction. "In the inner room of temples, there is usually a cellar door in the corner made of stone which leads to a supply room that has an exit out the back."

"Then we wait for nightfall," Alex said firmly. "Warren and Owen, you two will pretend to fight near the temple. Penélope, Ari, and I will sneak inside when the guard is distracted. Ari can speak with the priests and distract them while we go inside and grab Chloe. One of us will sneak Chloe out the back of the temple. If something goes wrong, we improvise and run."

"That sounds like a horrible plan," Owen said, raising a brow.

"Yeah, why does *he* get to sneak into the temple?" Warren asked while pointing at Ari, his harsh tone hardly hiding his jealousy. Ari raised a brow at him but remained silent.

"Do you know how to speak Ancient Greek?" Alex asked irritably. When he was silent, she nodded. "Then that's settled."

No one contradicted her. She let out a breath as they broke up the meeting and Penélope sat down beside her on the couch.

"The King," she said quietly. "There was something off about him, wasn't there?"

They had briefly mentioned their suspicions to the others that the old man was the King of the city, but there was no other proof besides what they had witnessed at the temple. They could only hope he had not noticed anything unusual about Chloe.

Alex nodded absently, remembering his blind eyes and eerie smile. "If he was the King, then he's the one that was trying to arrest us."

"The priestess usually never gives coherent prophecies," Penélope said. "She can speak gibberish if she wants, and the priests will interpret what she says. As long as Chloe doesn't draw too much attention to herself, then there's a chance they won't notice the swap."

They spent the rest of the time practicing more Ancient Greek phrases that could get them out of trouble and eating flatbread with honey for dinner since the old woman had run out of meat. At some point, Ari switched places with Zeb on a nearby rooftop until it was time for the rescue. Zeb entered the house and immediately passed out on one of the couches. As night descended and the old woman dutifully lit the small hanging lamps around the house, they grew quiet and restless.

At last, Alex stood, her stomach turning in anticipation as all eyes swiveled on her. "We should go."

The old woman's gaze lingered on them as they filed out of the house and checked both directions of the street for a patrol. When the coast was clear, they tiptoed down the street where Zeb broke off to replace Ari on lookout duty. Once they neared the temple, Owen and Warren turned down a cross street and disappeared around the corner. Ari met Alex and Penélope hiding in an alley across from the temple and together they waited.

Soon they heard shouting nearby. Ari peered around the alley and beckoned with a hand. Alex and Penélope followed him onto the street, staying close to the house fronts on one side where the shadows were darkest. In the distance were two figures swinging punches and wrestling each other, with the guard of the temple quickly approaching and leaving the door unguarded. They ran towards the temple door, not looking back to see if the guard had noticed them.

"Go, go," Ari grunted as he opened the heavy wooden door.

They slipped inside. Alex and Penélope lowered their heads as they had practiced, while Ari stepped towards the two priests, who eyed them suspiciously. He began speaking in Greek, pointing towards the door to the inner room.

"Οὐ εἰσέρχεσθε," one of the priests said, shaking his head. "Ἐκείνη νυστάζει."

Before Ari could explain more, Penélope stepped forward, holding her head up high and ready to speak with her usual confidence. When the priests saw her they immediately bowed their heads. Penélope's face flickered with surprise but she didn't waver.

"Χαῖρε, ὦ πότνια," the priests said hurriedly, before opening the doors and allowing them to pass without protest.

"What was that?" Alex whispered once they were inside.

Penélope nearly replied when she came to a sudden stop, looking across the room. "Chloe!"

Alex turned. Chloe was slumped over the tripod, her white dress torn and dirtied. She had a bruised eye and red marks on her arms. Alex rushed over and tried to bring her down, shaking her shoulders when Chloe didn't move. She seemed unconscious but her hands gripped the edges of the tripod and refused to let go.

"What happened to her?" Ari asked, glancing around the room as if the culprit was still there. But they were alone, save the real priestess, who must still be tied behind the altar.

"Chloe, please," Alex said, trying to lift Chloe from the tripod, though even in her unconsciousness she resisted, her eyes half open and rolling to the whites. "Please wake up, Chloe."

"Alex..." she groaned, her voice hoarse.

"Chloe, yes, it's me, Alex!"

Suddenly Chloe's body tensed up, shuddered, then convulsed as she arched her back, her face staring up unseeing at the night sky. The ground seemed to tremble with the beginnings of an earthquake and smoke rose thicker and stronger from the chasm as though it were about to explode.

"We need to get out of here," Ari said, starting forward to help Alex bring Chloe down. But before he took a step, Chloe opened her eyes, and they were clear white, as though she had gone as blind as the old man.

Then Chloe's voice rang out slow and deep throughout the room, her lips moving stiffly as her body shuddered, her face contorted in pain.

"Quarts to diamonds,
Copper to Iron,
Lead to Gold."

"Chloe?" Alex asked worriedly, sharing terrified glances with Ari and Penélope. They all looked at Chloe again when she continued to speak in that strange, slurred voice, as if she were drunk, or as if someone else were speaking through her body.

"First is black, second white,
Third is gold, last is red,
So the new restores the old.

Hidden in her caverns deep
Lies the seed of his defeat,
A song the Fates uphold.

The King of the Gods,
Fallen from his throne,
By one of his own mold.

Death will birth life,
Life will birth death,
Thus his end has been foretold."

When the room fell silent once more, Chloe fainted and fell into Alex's arms. Alex scrambled to feel her neck as she gently lowered Chloe to the ground, her vision blurred with tears, and she could only catch her breath when she felt the steady pulse beneath her skin.

"Chloe, Chloe, come on, wake up," Alex whispered, lifting Chloe into a sitting position.

Penélope grasped Chloe's hand and closed her eyes tightly as tears fell down her cheeks. *"En el nombre del Padre, del Hijo, del Espirito Santo..."*

Chloe's eyes cracked open and she groaned. "A-Alex?"

"Yes! Chloe, I'm here. We're here. You're going to be okay." She hugged Chloe close to her chest, relief flooding her body. Chloe tensed in her arms, then relaxed.

"Thank you," Chloe whispered, her voice raspy. She still clung to

Penélope's hand.

"What happened to you?" Alex asked, her voice breaking. "What were you saying?"

Chloe's brows furrowed. "I don't know."

"Did someone hurt you?" Penélope demanded fiercely.

"I don't remember," Chloe said, though she did not meet their eyes this time.

"We have to move," Ari said quietly, glancing back at the doors. "Do you think you can stand?"

Chloe nodded and let Alex and Penélope help her up. Then they transferred her to Ari, who supported her weight over his shoulder.

He gave Alex a crooked grin. "Meet you on the other side."

Then with his help, Chloe limped across the room to the corner where there was indeed a slab of stone with a small iron hook on the floor that Ari lifted carefully, revealing a dark hole. Once they disappeared down a wooden ladder leading to the underground chamber, Alex and Penélope took a deep breath and walked towards the doors. They could only hope to escape the temple before the priests noticed their missing companion.

Alex opened the doors for Penélope, who walked out with a feigned air of confidence, Alex keeping in step close behind. The priests remained with their heads bowed as they exited the temple. Outside there was no guard and no sign of Warren or Owen. With panic in their eyes, Alex and Penélope ran off towards the house.

As they turned the street where the old woman lived, someone rammed into Alex from the side and she gasped, spinning around and ready to fight. Warren had his fists up in front of his face, then lowered them when he saw it was her. A few seconds later Owen ran up to them, breathing hard.

"Quick...chasing...us," Owen said between deep gulps of air.

"Who?"

But then she heard the familiar clanking of swords and armor and the heavy footsteps of a patrol squad. Without another word, they all sprinted down the street, not bothering to look behind them. They found the small door to the house and barreled inside.

Ari and Chloe arrived a few minutes later, having waited for the soldiers to move from their street. Chloe's face was flushed and she moved her body weakly as she lay down on the couch. Owen froze when he saw her, then rushed to her side, dropping to his knees and taking her hands in his.

"Chloe, my love," Owen said, kissing her forehead. "What happened to you?"

"She doesn't remember," Ari said, though Alex could tell he didn't believe her.

Chloe's face looked more terrible outside of the darkness of the temple, with blue and green bruises around one eye and a grayish tint to her skin. The old woman hobbled over and shooed Owen and the others away to give her space. She patted a damp cloth on Chloe's face and rubbed a sharp-smelling oil on her temples, muttering to herself.

"She says Chloe will be fine," Ari said with a sigh. "She just needs to rest."

"I think we should address the elephant in the room," Owen said, looking around sharply. When no one answered him, he threw his hands up. "The Stone, remember? That's what this was all about. That's what got Chloe—"

His voice broke and he frowned harshly before turning away. Alex's heart burned with guilt. She was the one who put Chloe in danger. It was her fault that they had all risked their lives for something that did not even exist.

"I'm sorry," Alex said, biting her lip when the tears rushed to her eyes. "I'm sorry this was all for nothing."

"It wasn't," Penélope said, taking a step forward. "Don't you remember what Chloe said in the temple?"

"She was delusional," Alex protested. "She had no idea what she was saying."

"What if..." Ari said, his eyes lighting up, "What if she didn't know what she was saying because she—"

"—wasn't the one saying it," Penélope finished, smiling triumphantly. "She was giving a *prophecy*."

Alex's whole body trembled at the words. "I can barely remember what she said."

"I do," Ari said. "It started with a basic belief of Hermetic Alchemy. *Quarts to diamonds. Copper to iron. Lead to gold.*"

Penélope nodded eagerly. "Then the next verse had colors in it."

"Oh, I remember!" Alex closed her eyes as she recalled Chloe's shuddering body sitting on the tripod, her back arched towards the sky and her voice echoing in the temple while her lips hardly moved. *"First is black, second is white..."*

"Third is gold," Penélope said, then fell silent with a groan. "I can't remember what came next."

"Last is red!" Ari shouted, then calmed himself when the old woman gave him a stern look. "So *first is black, second is white, third is gold, last is red*. What does that even mean?"

"I get it! How could I not see it before?" Penélope said in barely contained excitement. "It's the fourfold way!"

"The what?" Zeb asked, raising a concerned brow.

Owen winked at him. "Better than three, I always say."

"The fourfold way," Penélope continued with an annoyed look at Owen, "is written in the Emerald Tablet. It's part of Hermetic Alchemy too. The transmutations of the metal are just symbolic of the spiritual transmutations. Don't you remember reading this when we were researching the Emerald Stone?"

"I can't say I retained any of that information," Owen drawled.

"I remember reading about the metals," Ari said slowly, "but not about anything spiritual."

"Don't you see? It's a *rebirth,*" Penélope said excitedly. She sighed when everyone looked at her blankly. "Hermetic Alchemy believes that certain minerals can change in the womb of Mother Earth. So that's where *quarts to diamonds, copper to iron, and lead to gold* come in. But there is also a belief that the spirit can be reborn, much like a metal. So first is black. That's the descent into the Underworld, or the earth. The second is white, literally for white-hot temperatures but it's also symbolical of purity. The third stage is gold to symbolize an ascent to the Sun. Then the last is red, for rebirth on Earth."

"That's like the *Book of the Dead,*" Owen said with a hint of surprise in his voice. All eyes turned to Owen after he spoke, who leaned against the wall with his arms crossed. He shrugged at their shocked faces. "What? I was obsessed with Egyptian mythology when I was younger. You know, the spell book that guides you in the afterlife—"

"We're familiar with the *Book of the Dead,*" Ari said impatiently. "But how is it related to this?"

Penélope nodded in agreement, while Zeb stared at Owen as if he were looking at him for the first time. Alex and Warren shared an amused glance, since they were the only ones besides Chloe who had no idea what they were talking about.

Owen rolled his eyes. "I thought this was supposed to be your thing. The *Book of the Dead* is not just about how to die. It's also about rebirth. The whole point is to become united with the sun god Re in this endless cycle of death and rebirth."

Ari frowned. "That's an interesting comparison, but—"

"Let's debate this later," Alex interrupted. She had to know what the rest of the prophecy said. "What came after the colors?"

Penélope began pacing the floor as she tried to recall the words. *"Hidden in her…in her caverns deep, lies the seed of his defeat…a song the Fates uphold.* Then the next verse started with the King of the Gods. That's obviously Zeus."

"The King of the Gods, fallen from his throne…" Ari continued.

"*…by one of his own mold!"* exclaimed Penélope and Ari at the same time, though they quickly apologized when the old woman shushed them again.

"The last verse was strange," Penélope said, her eyes growing troubled. *"Death will birth life, life will birth death…"*

"Thus his end has been foretold," Ari finished grimly. "The prophecy is talking about the end of Zeus' reign as King of the Gods."

"Hidden in her caverns deep, lies the seed of his defeat…" Alex repeated slowly, her heart racing ahead of her thoughts as she sensed rather than knew what this meant. "Do you think it's talking about the Emerald Stone?"

"It makes sense," Penélope said hesitantly. "But why refer to it as *a song the Fates uphold?*"

"Could be metaphorical," Owen suggested. "Or it's not referring to the Stone at all and we have no idea what any of it means."

Alex glared at him. "Not helpful, Owen. What did it say about Zeus falling from his throne?"

"The Kind of the Gods, fallen from his throne, by one of his own mold," Ari said, then paused. "Could it be a descendant of Zeus?"

"That narrows our list of options," Zeb muttered sarcastically.

"Why would anyone want to overthrow Zeus?" Owen asked doubtfully. "I thought he was the main guy."

"Not always," Penélope said, a growing smile on her face. "He overthrew his father, Kronos. And before that, Kronos overthrew *his* father, Ouranos."

"Ouranos..." Ari's eyes kindled like a fire come to life. "Ouranos who is married to Gaia!"

"And according to Hesiod," Penélope continued urgently, "Gaia is the first god born out of Chaos."

Alex felt a rush of clarity run through her at these words. "It all makes sense. The Emerald Stone was hidden in her caverns. That is what the hymn said and now we see it in this prophecy too. She's supposed to be the Queen of the Gods, not Zeus."

"Hermes stole the Stone to overthrow Zeus," Ari said in realization. "Hermes is the son of Zeus! One of his own mold!"

"So Hermes is going to overthrow Zeus?" Zeb asked. "If he already has the Stone, shouldn't the prophecy be fulfilled?"

They were silent at this new flaw in their logic. Alex felt helpless, her heart aching at how little she understood, about this city, about her mother, and the world she had lived in. Did she hear the prophecy trying to find the Stone? Was that why she came to this city in the first place, not only to find the Stone but to overthrow Zeus? It seemed absurd to think it, but Alex would believe anything if it meant discovering the truth.

"Hermes was a thief," Penélope said, breaking the silence at last.

"Remember what the hymn said? Gaia told Hermes not to waste her precious gift. She knew he was going to steal it. She let him steal it. The question is why?"

"The question, my dear girl," came an old, deep voice from behind them, "is *for whom?*"

They all stared at each other in alarm, before slowly turning towards the old woman. She stood before Chloe with a knowing smile, her wrinkled hands grasping her small wooden cane.

Alex gazed upon her face, the eyes that seemed to flash an unnatural green for a split second so that Alex always thought she imagined it. *"You."*

The old woman laughed, a rich, deep rumble like rolling hills. "Hello, Alexandria."

59

The old woman carefully walked over to them, her cane loud in the silence as it hit the stone floor. Everyone stared at her in shock. The woman only looked amused, glancing at each of them in turn.

"You speak English," Owen said at last, shaking his head in disbelief.

"I do," she replied, though now Alex could detect a slight accent in her voice. "It is not commonly spoken here, but many of your people pass through this city. I have known enough of them to learn it."

"Why didn't you say anything?" Alex demanded. "We could've used your help."

"Am I not helping you?" the old woman asked, raising a white brow. "Why do you think I am letting you stay in my home?"

"I don't know," Alex said honestly. When she really thought about it, she had no idea why she let them stay at all. "We only wanted to be safe from the King."

"And so you are," the old woman said sternly with a thump of her cane on the ground. "I have long known you would be coming. The prophecy you heard once spoke of seven disciples from a faraway land who would herald its fulfillment."

"How come you never spoke English until now?" Ari asked, rather embarrassed. "I've been having so much trouble translating."

The old woman's eyes glittered like stones in a riverbed. "Oh, you were doing just fine, my dear boy. There were some things you needed to understand on your own and others that I knew must be told to you at the right moment. Besides, I have lived alone for many years and found you all quite amusing."

"So I'm guessing this is the right moment?" Zeb asked impertinently.

"Ah, the boy who lives with one foot in the dark and one foot in the light," the old woman said, narrowing her eyes at Zeb, who went very still at her words. "Do not be so quick to cast judgment, lest it be cast upon *you*."

"What my friend is trying to say," Owen interceded quickly, "is that any help right now would be very much appreciated."

"Then you, my boy, better learn how to listen." Owen flushed. The old woman beckoned for them to follow her to the couches, where she sat down expectantly beside Chloe. "Let me tell you a story." They all hurriedly sat down on the couches opposite her and waited. "This is a very old story, a story that was once told to all children in this city before the Old Faith was forgotten. It begins with the prophecy you just recited, that one day a descendant of Zeus shall wield the Stone of Gaia and the power of the Stone shall overthrow the King of the Gods. But Zeus, hearing of this prophecy long ago, wished to prevent such an end and ordered swift-footed Hermes to steal the Stone for him. Hermes, being the trickster that he is, indeed stole the Stone, but did not return it to his divine father, instead hiding it in the mortal world. To this day Zeus hunts for the Stone, seeking to use the power himself. Those who still practice the Old Faith believe that a mortal descendant of Zeus shall one day find the Stone and restore Gaia to her rightful place as Queen of the Gods."

Once the old woman finished, no one spoke for a long time. This changed everything. Alex felt dizzy with the full force of this realization, the truth in all of her mother's words glaring like the sun on water. She had been so blind to it all, so blind to the deeper story behind her mother's disappearance.

"So if the Stone is not in the Temple of Apollo," Penélope said slowly, "where is it?"

"If it was hidden among mortals it could be anywhere," Ari said, his eyes seeing far away. Suddenly they snapped up to Alex. "No, not anywhere. What if Sister Stella was not just guarding an entrance, but something more?"

Alex nodded, remembering her last conversation with Sister Stella. "I think she knows more than she lets on. She tried to warn me about coming here, that it was too dangerous." She paused. "We need to find out who she is and what she is hiding."

"Then we need to go back to the library," Penélope said. "That's where you said there is an entrance to the city, right? If she guards it, we can find her there and maybe find the Stone too."

"The Great Library?" the old woman asked, then she shook her head. "Have you not heard? The King has banned all education and scholarship in the city. No one is to enter the Great Library or the Academy without his permission. When kings wish to control the minds of their citizens, they need only control their access to knowledge." She paused, looking at each of them in mild amusement. "If you do not want to get caught, you must know more about the city."

"I have only been here once before," Alex said, feeling defensive. "The last time we visited, things did not seem as dangerous."

"Ah, yes," the old woman said, her voice growing sad. "The King was not always like this. Once upon a time, he was happy, kind, charitable even, and he would spend time among his people and aid those in need. But since his son abandoned his post for piracy and other base pleasures, the King has become quite a changed man. He never reveals his face in public anymore and has become greedy for more power and ruthless in dispensing punishments."

"If only we could keep the whole city distracted for a day," Owen muttered. "Then maybe we would have a chance of sneaking into the library."

The old woman pointed her cane at Owen. "You are in luck! Soon the city shall celebrate The Feast of the Beautiful Meeting. I hardly doubt the King can stop it, for this festival is sacred to our people. There shall be crowds and noise and chaos all across the city. That is your best chance of entering the library unnoticed, for most people will be too intoxicated or excited to care, and the guards will be too busy watching the procession to watch the library."

"When is the festival?" Alex asked.

"In three days' time," said the old woman.

"Then we need a plan," Ari said gravely. "We won't have another shot at this."

"Now that," the woman said with a glimmer in her eyes, "I can help you with."

The rest of the day consisted of filling in the details of Ari's map with important landmarks and streets according to the old woman's knowledge of the city. She explained that each quarter of the city was different, with the southwest quarter mainly inhabited by the Academy and its students as well as the Royal Society. The northwest quarter was for the Mouseion, which included the Great Library, a museum, a theater, a park, a temple, and even a zoo.

The northeast quarter was split into the Royal Quarter, with a large palace and neighboring houses for nobility, while the rest was reserved for citizens of various trades who worked for the royal family. The quarter the old woman resided in was called the South Quarter, which was inhabited by ordinary citizens and poor laborers. They also learned about the shipyards by the public walkway called the Neoria, as well as the Necropolis island off the bay where she had seen the Lighthouse, which was a city built for the dead and has been haunted for centuries by pirates.

The city as a whole was bordered by the Great Harbor in the north and in the south the Southern Wall built along the Notus River and the Sun Harbor. The Eastern Wall protected them from the hot wind of the Valley of the Palms, right beside which the Temple of Apollo had been constructed over the Eastern Canal, explaining the rushing stream underneath the chasm. The Nereid Beach and Western Canal hemmed the city in from the western end, which was where they had entered the city.

The two main roads—Priam Boulevard running north to south and the Meson Pedion running east to west—were guarded by the Gate of the Moon in the north, the Gate of the Sun in the south, and the so-named Western and Eastern gates. In the center of the city was the forum, where the Tower of the Winds stood, which, the old woman explained, told the time based on the movements of the heavens and had been built by their founder, King Helenus, a son of King Priam of Troy who had fled the famous battle and established the city as a safe haven.

"Our founder also bequeathed his name to the city," the old woman said.

She spread her arms wide, her cane lifted in the air. "Welcome to the city of Helena."

Alex met Ari's eyes, the impossibility of it all coursing through her veins, and she felt that familiar shiver run down her spine. *Helena*. Like Helen of Troy, and her mother, Elena. Like a story that never ended, spinning the threads of a tale again and again, only to be unraveled before it was finished.

As it was well into the night and nearing dawn, they decided to rest until the next day, when they would come up with their plan to sneak into the Great Library. As the others returned to their beds, still exhausted from the disastrous events at the temple, Alex went over to the old woman, who sat by the fire and poked the wooden scraps inside the hearth with an iron rod.

"Pardon me," Alex said quietly. The old woman looked at her sharply. "When you said many of our people pass through the city, do you mean those from above? Those on Earth?"

The old woman shook her head in amusement. "Above? On earth? You speak as though we do not stand on the ground beneath us." She paused, scanning Alex's face as if to read her hidden thoughts there. "You are lost, child, but I am not so sure you know what you seek."

"I'm trying to find my mother." Alex paused, wondering how much of the truth she should divulge to this strange old woman. "She came here once, and I think she might have returned. That's why we are searching for the Stone, because we think she tried to find it too."

"Many come to the city hoping they shall find answers," the old woman said gently. "But the city is just like anything in this life—it is more like a road, between this world and the next."

"Her name was Elena de la Fuente," Alex insisted, hoping that her name might trigger the old woman's memory. "I think she fell in love with someone in the city. His name was Alexandros. That's all I know."

The old woman's eyes brightened. "Ah, but everyone knows this story! Helene and Alexandros, a tale as old as the earth!"

Alex's heart beat faster. "I'm not sure what you mean."

"Yes, you must! Ἑλένη καὶ Ἀλέξανδρος! The face that launched a thousand ships! Their love is legend. Surely you must have heard the story, even where you come from?"

She nodded as disappointment sank into her stomach. "Yes, I have heard that story."

The old woman brought a shaky hand up to her chin, gently turning Alex's face towards her. She peered into her eyes intently. "Curious! You have the mark of Gaia, my dear. Did you know?"

"What?"

"Your eyes," she said with a smile. "One green, one brown." Then she patted Alex's cheek affectionately like a grandmother might and returned to her seat by the fire. "Now get some rest, Alexandria. There is much work to be done tomorrow."

Alex began to walk away, then stopped. "What is your name? I forgot to ask."

The old woman pulled her quilted blanket above her shoulders. "You may call me Mother. It is custom among my people."

"Thank you, Mother," Alex said softly, before she returned to her bed.

60

"WHERE ARE YOU TAKING us?" Chloe asked worriedly, looking back down the street. But there was no sign of any soldier, only a young woman carrying a basket on her hip. "We could get caught."

The old woman walked ahead of them, her head covered by a cloak. "Not here, we won't."

Alex shared a concerned glance with Penélope as they struggled to keep up with the old woman's surprisingly fast pace. The morning sun peeked over the city from behind the mountains, bathing the city in light as the citizens awoke and began their day. Very few people roamed the streets carelessly or lingered in plain sight, preferring to walk quickly to their destination and not draw attention to themselves.

When they had woken up this morning, the old woman had given instructions to Ari on where to take the boys to bathe and led the girls herself, as none of them had the chance to shower in the chaotic days following their arrival in the city. While they were grateful to have the chance to clean up, they had no idea where the old woman was taking them.

"This better not be a river," Chloe muttered. She held onto Alex's arm, still weak from the events at the temple.

As they turned the street corner, Alex saw a large building across the way with a long line of women standing outside its entrance. She saw that most of them covered their hair or even wore veils, but they seemed livelier than usual, greeting each other with kisses. At the door sat an elderly woman who controlled how many women entered at a time based on how many left.

They joined the line silently. Once more women stood behind them they blended in with the crowd, so that Alex could finally breathe again.

Penélope stared at the large building again, the columns framing the entryway and the steam that wafted from the door. Her eyes lit up and she whispered excitedly, "It's a bathhouse!"

The old woman smiled. "This bathhouse is for women only. In these waters, we shall cleanse body *and* soul."

Chloe gave Alex a doubtful look. They waited in silence for another few minutes until it was their turn to approach the elderly door-woman. She seemed even older than Mother, her skin wrinkled tightly around her eyes and mouth so that they looked small in her round face, her gray hair twisted in elegant braids around the crown of her head. When she saw Mother, she cried out and brought her in for a hug and kissed her cheeks.

"Φίλη θύγατερ!"

"Πότνια μήτηρ," Mother said warmly, kissing the elderly lady's hands.

After exchanging a few more words, they were let inside the bathhouse, where they found a small changing room with carved cubicles in the walls to store their belongings. Several other women were slipping out of their dresses and sandals, happily walking naked to the next room.

"That woman," Penélope said quietly to Mother as they finished undressing. "You called her Mother."

"We call all our elders Mother, for in this city we raise our children together," Mother said. Then she took Alex's hand in hers and a small glass flask in the other and led them all down the hall and into a spacious room with a large pool in the center, the light from an opening in the roof shining on the water.

The old woman's hand was firm but gentle as she guided them down a set of stairs half-submerged in water, so that Alex could not help feeling a swelling gratitude in her chest as they entered the pool.

"Is this sanitary?" Chloe asked, raising a brow at the rather clouded waters.

Penélope shushed her, and together they submerged their heads underwater.

The water was warmer than Alex had expected, but still felt refreshing as they found a corner to stand in where they could wash their bodies. Alex expected to feel self-conscious without any clothes on, but none of the women seemed to notice them, lounging in small groups in the water or beside the pool, conversing as old friends and laughing easily.

"It is custom to wash each other's hair," the old woman said, cupping water in her hands and gently pouring it over Alex's head.

Alex shivered as the water splashed down her neck, followed by a trickle of warm olive oil. She closed her eyes when the old woman began gently massaging the oil into her hair. Chloe began washing Penélope's hair in the same way.

"There. Now we switch."

Alex turned and washed the old woman's hair, the snow-white curls surprisingly soft under her touch and the olive oil silky smooth beneath her palm. Beside her, Chloe let out a pleased sigh as Penélope rubbed circles across her scalp.

"I could do this more often," Chloe said, her eyes closed and her head drooping.

"I thought this wasn't sanitary enough for you?" Penélope asked, adding a little extra force as her fingertips reached Chloe's temples.

"Oh I take it back," Chloe murmured. "I take it all back."

After they rinsed the oil from their hair, Mother led them out of the water and across the room to another pool, this one much smaller in size, with steam rising from the water and the lamps lining the perimeter bathing the room in an eerie glow.

"Be careful," Mother warned. "This water cleanses more than just the body."

The three of them shared identical concerned glances before they joined the old woman in the pool.

Alex took one step inside and hissed. The water was scalding, if not boiling, and she wondered how she would submerge fully without pain. Mother had already slipped under the water with a sigh, closing her eyes as the steam clung to her face.

"Oh this is what I'm talking about," Chloe said as she slid easily under the water until it reached her chin. “I love bathhouses.”

Alex gently lowered herself into the water. She had to close her eyes as the burning water consumed her in licking flames of heat. Penélope crouched in the water beside her, leaning her head back against the side of the pool.

“Mother, what do you mean that the water cleanses more than just the body?” Alex asked.

The old woman smiled knowingly. “Bathing is an act of rebirth when we purify the body *and* soul. In the water’s reflection, we can see more than just ourselves.”

“What else can we see?” Chloe asked suspiciously, eyeing the water where her face was reflected on the rippling surface.

“The truth.”

Alex stared at her face mirrored on the water, the features warping along with the ebb and flow of the bath as other women ascended or descended the steps at the other end. Her face looked as she remembered, a round face, short brown hair, and those two different colored eyes. She swore the green one glimmered like an emerald stone at the bottom of the bath.

You have the mark of Gaia, my dear.

She looked up. Mother was looking at her with those same flashing green eyes. “I thought I saw...”

Beside her, Penélope breathed in sharply. “My face...”

Alex’s heart dropped. “What?”

Penélope shook her head, letting out a breath and forcing a smile. “For a second, I thought I saw something. But it was just a trick of the light.”

Alex turned to Chloe. “Did you see anything?”

Chloe crossed her arms, her eyes hardened. “Of course not.”

They turned to Mother, who did not try to hide her amusement. She climbed out of the pool and beckoned for them to follow. “Now we wash ourselves in lavender oil and scrape away the dirt. Then we will sit in the steam room. And while we do so, I am going to tell you the plan.”

As they walked out of the room, Alex turned to look back at the pool. In the depths of the steaming water, she saw a winking light, as though the lamplight glanced off a stone at the bottom of the bath, a green stone filled with magic and secrets.

Then she blinked and it was gone.

When they returned from the bathhouse smelling of lavender and olive oil, they found the boys freshly washed and chatting together in the house. It was already early afternoon, and there was much planning to do before the festival tomorrow.

Chloe waltzed into the room, feeling much refreshed after the baths. All the boys seemed relieved that she was feeling better, and Owen even threw an arm around her shoulders and kissed her cheek.

"So how did you boys enjoy the baths?" Chloe asked.

"Oh they were *marvelous*," Owen drawled, earning him a pinch in his side from Chloe. "Ow! What? It's true. We bathed with other naked men—"

"—who were all middle-aged and balding," interrupted Zeb, glaring at him.

Owen threw him a wink. "Not all of them."

"Enough flirting," Ari said coolly, and this time both Zeb and Owen glared at him. "We have very little time before the festival begins and we still don't have a plan."

"Actually," Alex said, and all eyes turned to her, "we do."

Ari raised a brow. "Since when?"

Penélope stepped forward and stood beside Alex. "Mother told us the plan in the baths. It's very simple, actually. As we already know, tomorrow is The Feast of the Beautiful Meeting, where Horus, the Egyptian god of the Sky, meets his bride, Hathor, on the river. It is a celebration of love, marriage, and procreation. Apparently, there is a procession on the Meson Pedion that reenacts this meeting, along with a ceremony. The entire city will be caught up in the festivities."

"That's where we come in," Alex said, locking eyes with Ari, and she forced herself not to stutter when they lit up in surprise. "Throughout the city, there will be small plays based on the meeting, so many actors and citizens will be dressed up as the gods Horus and Hathor. It would not be suspicious if we were dressed up as them too, which would also get us close to the library. Since we are the only ones who have been inside the Great Library before, we thought it made the most sense if only we two went."

An uneasy silence followed before Warren broke it. "Absolutely not."

Alex turned to him, her cheeks heating up. "Why?"

Warren steeled his face. "You can't go alone just with him. It's too dangerous."

She raised a brow. "It's more dangerous for you to come."

"You'd stick out like a sore blond thumb," Chloe said mockingly. "They would worship you as the sun god or something and the King would imprison you for it."

"Hey, what about me?" Zeb asked, touching his blonde hair.

"You wish, *Zeb Hades*," Owen teased.

Zeb blushed and forced a smile into a frown. "It's pronounced *Hay-dz*, for your information, not *Hay-deez*."

"Well, Zeb *Hades*," Chloe said, "you look more like a very pale ghost than a god."

"An attractive ghost," Owen muttered with a sly smile. Zeb paled at this and they all laughed except Warren, who still looked like he disagreed with the new arrangement.

"You still didn't explain the plan," Ari said, crossing his arms over his chest. Alex was reminded of that day she saw him wrestle, the broadness of his chest and the solid muscles of his arms. *Now there's a man,* she remembered thinking, so different to her tall and lean Warren, his embarrassed, awkward smile whenever she kissed him and they were not alone. She tried to push the thought away.

"First we dress up as Horus and Hathor," Alex said, "then when the processions meet at the crossroads, we sneak through the crowd and into the Great Library where we'll look around for Sister Stella and where she might be hiding the Emerald Stone. If we find her, we find the Stone."

"Just one question," Ari said slowly after a moment of thinking over the plan. "How are we going to dress up as Horus and Hathor?"

Alex paused. Mother had not given them instructions on that part. She turned towards the fireplace to ask her but the words died in her throat.

She was gone.

61

A ROUGH HAND ON her shoulder shook her from a deep sleep. Alex opened her eyes and saw the old woman standing above her. The house was dark and there was no movement from the others, who were still asleep.

"It is time," the old woman whispered. She motioned for Alex to follow her.

"Where have you been?" Alex asked rather angrily.

Once they had realized that the old woman was gone, they thought she had abandoned them, and when she never returned they went to bed and decided to carry out the plan regardless.

Instead of explaining, however, Mother merely shook her head. "You shall see."

She led Alex to the fireplace, which faintly illuminated a pair of dresses laid out on the floor. One was a long, woven red dress while the other consisted of a rich green top with a white and gold skirt, a long tail sewn to the back. Both were adorned with an elaborate neckpiece of alternating rows of green, red, and black stones. Beside the green dress was a bust of a falcon, its beak sharp and yellow in a white and black feathered face.

"Come, come," Mother whispered.

Alex turned. She hadn't noticed the old woman leaving to retrieve Ari, who she led still half-asleep to the fireplace. Alex met his eyes, but neither of them spoke.

"What are you waiting for?" Mother asked, gesturing to the clothes. "It is nearly dawn. You must dress."

"In those?" Alex asked. "But those are both dresses."

"No, no, no." The old woman stooped to the ground and lifted the red dress. "This here is for you, Hathor. You shall cover your face with your veil."

Alex took the red dress in her hands, feeling the soft stitch of the fabric. It seemed a hundred years old and a size too small. "I won't fit in this."

The old woman nodded encouragingly at her as she picked up Ari's costume. "Dress, dress!" She handed him the green top and white and gold skirt, which Alex realized were two separate pieces. "And for you, Horus, god of the Sky."

Alex and Ari shared a worried look before they slipped out of their tunics and white slips. Ari avoided looking at Alex as she stood in her bra and underwear, quickly shrugging on their costumes.

The red dress hardly fit over her head, but as she squeezed into the opening, she found that she fit well enough, though the fabric pressed tightly on every inch of her body. She found her veil among their pile of cloaks at the door and pinned it to her hair. When she glanced back at Ari, he was already dressed, falcon headdress and all. The green shirt fit snugly across his chest, and there were thin sleeves that looped around his biceps, leaving his shoulders bare. He held up his gold and blue-feathered tail in amusement as they made for the door.

"The procession has already started," Mother whispered as she opened the door. "Soon they shall converge at the crossroads. Hide behind the Tower of the Winds until you may slip into the crowd and make for the Great Library. I wish you luck in your endeavor, and we shall be anxiously awaiting your return."

Inexplicably, Alex felt her eyes prick with tears. She grasped the old woman's hands tightly. "Thank you, Mother."

Mother squeezed her hands. "And one more thing! Not all in this city are who they seem. Trust only each other."

Then her hands withdrew and the door shut behind her. Sure enough, the sky in the east lightened with the oncoming dawn. Alex lowered her veil over her face.

"We should hurry," she said.

Without another word, Ari led the way, turning right down the street and then into an alleyway. It was best to keep out of sight, even if most of the guards would be deployed for the procession.

Though she knew the city was celebrating a festival, the streets were strangely hushed and deserted. Their zigzagging path led them to the forum, directly in line with the Tower of the Winds, which shielded them from prying eyes on the main streets. Alex had not yet seen the tower up close, so now she leaned her head back and took in the full height of the tower.

The tower was octagonal in shape, the pointed roof rising above the forum like a lighthouse at sea. Gold sheets plated each wall, engraved with constellations and names written in Ancient Greek. Around the top ledge were carvings of flying figures in high relief, their wings white and their robes red. At the base of the tower was a single wooden door nailed with rusting iron bolts, though it seemed that no one had entered the tower in years.

Ari pointed to the painted plaques. "Those are the eight winds. There is a similar tower in Athens, but it's only ruins now. That one ran on some kind of water machine and was advanced technology for its time."

They moved from the edge of the alleyway to the base of the tower and crouched down in the shadows, hidden from the main street of the procession. There was not a soul in sight, not even soldiers, as if the city had been suddenly deserted.

"Do you think Mother got the date wrong?" Alex asked.

Ari smiled wryly. "We'll just have to wait and see."

She looked at her long red dress and his revealing green top, those bronze shoulders that had once wrestled another boy to the ground for her. "I still can't believe what we're wearing."

"At least you don't have to wear this on your head," Ari murmured, glancing up at his falcon headdress that covered his dark curls, then at Alex, his gaze traveling down her dress before reluctantly looking away. "You make a beautiful Hathor."

Alex ignored the heat that rose to her cheeks at his words. "Thank you."

Ari met her eyes, his brown ones growing serious. "Remember the night we kissed?"

Her breath hitched. How could she forget? "Yes."

"I never told you this, but—"

Before he could finish, the earth began to tremble, and they froze. Then they heard the beating of drums, followed by heavy footsteps, as if thousands of soldiers were marching their way.

The sun had already cleared the mountains and shined on the Tower of the Winds so that the walls soaked the streets in a shimmery gold haze. They could now hear many voices chanting in unison, growing louder and louder. Alex dared not peek out from behind the tower, standing as close to the wall as possible where the sunlight had not yet reached.

"Are they close?" she whispered.

Ari pressed himself against the tower beside her, then leaned ever so slightly around the corner before quickly returning beside her. "Two processions. A lot of soldiers. They are meeting in the middle."

The drumming crescendoed and the pace of their chanting quickened until the entire city seemed to shake with the beat. Their passionate chanting grew to a feverish pitch before suddenly everything fell completely silent.

Alex gave Ari a questioning glance. He leaned over the edge once more, but this time he returned with a half-smile. "Hathor and Horus have kissed."

She had no time to respond before the crowds erupted into cheers and music flooded from everywhere at once, and for the first time, Alex felt like she was at a festival. Couples and groups in costume poured out across the streets, passing their hiding spot behind the tower.

Without a word, Ari grabbed her hand and led her out onto the street before she could protest. They were immediately swallowed into a bustling crowd of costumed men and women wearing veils and similar falcon headdresses. Alex could not help a small smile. They fit in perfectly.

At the center of the crossroads was a large platform carried by at least fifty men, where a beautiful veiled woman in a long red dress sat beside a handsome man with a falcon headdress. They appeared to be in a long, carved wooden boat, with attendants pretending to row them down a river. A large procession of soldiers and singers stood on both ends to the west and east, surrounded by citizens craning their necks to get a better view.

Now that the bride and groom had kissed, it appeared everyone was eager for celebration, with vendors setting up shop on the side of the road selling food and costumes. Small, makeshift stages were already popping up all over the wide streets, with puppets and actors replaying the procession and final kiss as well as other myths and stories of the gods.

"Come on," Alex said, nodding her head towards the Great Library. "While they are still distracted."

They wove through the thick crowds of people singing and crying out in delight as they rushed to the vendors and plays and flocked around the procession. A few people noticed their costumes and threw coins and flower petals at them as they pushed a path through the crowds.

At last, they reached the other side of the street and stood in front of the Mouseion. The Great Library towered before them in its familiar tall columns painted red, its many white stone steps leading up to a pair of massive wooden doors. They glanced around to see if any guards were watching, but all of them were busy keeping the procession in order and berating troublemakers who tried to get on stage or steal from the vendors.

Alex's heart began racing. She met Ari's eyes. "Now."

They both darted up the stairs, beelining it for the large wooden doors. Surprisingly, they opened easily with hardly any force, and they slipped into the gap and shut the door behind them without a sound.

Once they were inside, they took the right staircase up to the second level, retracing their steps from the first time they came to the city.

Ari paused at the beginning of the hallway and looked around, but there were no women in white prowling the corridors. He motioned with a hand for her to follow, and together they crept down the hall, passing the many branching passageways leading to more unknown rooms, the niches carved in the wall stacked with ancient-looking scrolls and books. All of the walls were still streaked with black soot, with some niches crumbled and disused, their fallen stones blocking entire corridors now doomed to darkness. She wondered how long it would take them to search every hallway, especially when they had no idea what they were looking for.

"This is the door to the old library," Ari whispered. "Maybe if we hide out here, we'll catch Sister Stella on her way here and follow her to the Stone."

They slowed down as they reached the small opening in the wall where they had exited from the staircase connected to the old library. Ari moved to hide behind one of the large columns lining the wall. Alex glanced down the hall one last time and paused. Her heart stuttered in her chest and she grabbed Ari's hand.

"Wait."

He stopped and turned to her questioningly.

"Look." She pointed to a door that she had never noticed before at the far end of the hallway. It appeared to be made entirely of gold, but that was not what had drawn her attention. "Look at the symbol."

Engraved on the door was a rod, entwined with two serpents and capped with a pair of wings. She recalled that strange hooded figure who had guided them to Mother's house, rescuing them from the soldiers.

If you are ever in need of help, you need only wield this.

"It's the wand of Hermes," Ari said, staring at it strangely.

The words repeated themselves in her head ominously. "It can't be a coincidence, Ari. What if that's where they hide the Stone?" Alex asked urgently, then lowered her voice. "We need to try."

Ari nodded and followed her down the hallway, glancing over his shoulder every so often to make sure no one was there. Alex quickly reached the door, which gleamed even brighter up close. She touched the carving of the wand. It was so much like the one she had grasped, the gold wand that had come and disappeared like a dream.

She pushed it and the door swung open silently, revealing a twisting staircase spiraling down into darkness. They shared uneasy glances before beginning the descent.

The staircase wound down and down several flights, with a small torch on the wall every ten steps, only illuminating where their feet landed. Soon they reached the bottom and entered a lofty, circular room, its domed roof decorated with a blue and green mosaic of the earth surrounded by gold stones. In the center of the floor was another mosaic mirroring the ceiling, a flaming sun woven with several straight lines of gold that crossed the mosaic at equal intervals. Around the sun were small circles in different sizes and colors, which Alex guessed were planets.

Alex walked to the center of the room, Ari following hesitantly. She circled the mosaic on the floor, staring at the small red, gray, blue, and orange stone planets around the sun, the torchlights lining the room illuminating the cut stones so that it seemed a fire was lit from within the sun itself.

Ari stood beside her and stared at the mosaic. "This is strange. Very strange."

She followed the gold lines that cut up the mosaic. "What are these lines?"

"Strings," Ari said softly. "From the seven-stringed lyre. Like the one Hermes makes from a tortoise shell."

"But what does it mean?" Alex asked, walking around the circle. "If this is the sun, then those other circles must be planets. But why are they connected with the lyre?"

At the far side of the room was a white altar, half-hidden in shadow. She approached the altar hesitantly, and as she neared Alex saw that lying in the center was a large book, bound in weathered brown leather. Was it the Bible?

"Look at this," Alex said. Ari joined her at the altar. "It's a book."

She gingerly picked up the book, which was heavy and thick, the leather soft and worn from use. She opened to the first page.

ὕμνον ἄειδέ μοι, μοῦσα, λόγοισι μελίφροσιν ἀλλά
ἡδυτερεῖ φωνῇ κλέπτην διὰ νυκτὸς ἄειδε...

"It's the Prince of Thieves," Ari said, sounding shocked. "It's your mother's hymn."

She turned to him. "But how—"

Murmured voices floated down the staircase. Alex and Ari glanced at each other in alarm, then Ari swiftly steered Alex behind the altar. They crouched down, hoping that they could not be seen from the winding staircase. Alex clutched the large book to her chest, having accidentally forgotten to put it back.

The voices grew louder as their footsteps rattled the stairs, and Alex realized to her horror that she recognized one of them. Ari's face grew ashen. He recognized it too.

It was Sister Stella.

"...festival shall not cease until the sun sets," Sister Stella said. "We shall have to keep our eyes and ears open."

"Agreed," said another voice.

"I shall speak to Brother Ezra. If anything goes awry, he shall know what to do."

Suddenly it came to her, and Alex struggled not to gasp aloud. *Brother Ezra.* The E on the Squatting Scribe, the E on the Hymn to the Prince of Thieves, and then the E in the Temple of Apollo! The E stood for Ezra! He must have strong ties with the city, just like Sister Stella, and perhaps he even taught at the Academy. Alex wondered if he guarded the Stone too.

Sister Stella and the other voice continued to converse about trivial news from the city and then about certain scrolls of ancient philosophy which had been discovered deep inside the library among the archives. After what felt like an eternity, they began to say their goodbyes, when Alex's knees were beginning to ache.

"I shall be just a minute, Sister Theresa. There is something I must attend to."

Footsteps could be heard on the staircase. "Until tomorrow, Sister Stella."

The clanging footsteps faded, followed by a deep silence. Alex wondered why Sister Stella was not leaving too. Had she noticed the book was missing? Beside her, Ari placed a hand on her shoulder, keeping her crouched down.

Then suddenly a voice spoke in the quiet.

"I know you are here, Alexandria."

62

Alex's heart stopped. She stared at Ari, who stared back with equal dread. How had Sister Stella known they were there?

"Please come out," Sister Stella added when neither Alex nor Ari moved.

Alex slowly stood up, her head growing faint when she looked across the altar and saw Sister Stella standing there, dressed in her usual black skirt and pale blue sweater. Her white curls framed a disappointed but stern face as she looked between Alex and Ari. It seemed impossible that she was here, and yet there she stood, as if she had been plucked from the New Academy and plopped here beneath the Great Library.

"And you, Ari," Sister Stella continued, her voice sharp, glancing at the book and then at Ari. "I taught you better than to be a thief."

"A thief?" he asked, his voice tight. "I am no thief. But you, Sister, are a liar."

Sister Stella flinched, her blue eyes turning cold, and she clasped her hands in front of her. She seemed about to respond to his insult before thinking better of it and turned her attention towards Alex. "I cannot say I am surprised, Alexandria, that you found your way back here. After all, your mother did the same thing when she was your age, though I am sure you already knew that."

"Ari's right," Alex said, her voice wavering. "You are a liar. You knew my mother went looking for the Emerald Stone."

"You speak of things you do not understand," Sister Stella said coldly.

"Like the prophecy?" Alex challenged.

Sister Stella's eyes snapped to her. "How do you know about that?"

"See?" Alex smiled tightly. "I'm smarter than you think."

"Oh no," Sister Stella said, shaking her head. "You are young and headstrong. This will only put you in more danger. I must ask you to leave the city at once."

Alex let out a strangled laugh. "I'm going to find my mother, with or without your help."

"If you continue down this path, I cannot protect you." Sister Stella sighed wearily. "The city is more dangerous than you realize. You do not know who people truly are here."

"I could say the same about you," Alex shot back. Then she glanced down at the book she still clutched in her arms, and back at Sister Stella, who appeared unfazed by the strange domed room, hardly glancing at the intricate mosaics made of gold or the staircase that wound up and up to a city of wonders. "Who even are you? And what is this place?"

Sister Stella lifted her chin. "This is the Great Library and I am one of the Seven Sages. We are guardians of the city of Helena and the Emerald Stone. Your presence here is a threat to all of the hard work we have put in to protect them."

Alex stared at her, her mind spinning with realization. "Then you have the Stone."

"No." Sister Stella smiled without mirth. "It was destroyed. In fact, your *mother* was partly responsible. If not for her, the Stone would have remained a secret, unknown and unseen to the prying eyes and greedy hands of gods and mortals alike."

"My mother..." Alex could hardly comprehend what she hearing. "So I was right. She *did* try to find the Stone. She did try to fulfill the prophecy."

"Not exactly," Sister Stella said, eyeing Alex carefully. "She was led into a trap, thinking she had met the one who would fulfill the prophecy. But she was wrong. That mistake nearly burned this library to the ground, destroying centuries of collected and preserved knowledge. She herself hardly survived, and then she left, unable to face the consequences and wishing to have nothing to do with this world."

"Then why did she leave me ten years later?" Alex demanded. "She had to come back. I know it. It's the only explanation that makes sense. You must know where she is. Tell me or I'll never leave this city until I find her."

Sister Stella's eyes grew sad. "That I cannot tell you, though I wish I could. I know you may not believe this, Alexandria, but Elena was like a daughter to me. Once I had even hoped that she would join the Seven Sages, but she took a different path." She paused. "Now, I have told you quite enough already. I warned you not to go searching for your mother, for there are far worse dangers here than a mere city guard. The next one who catches you will not be as kind as I am. Now go and leave the city at once."

Alex stared at her, disbelieving. She shook her head. "Maybe my mother left because of *you*."

"Leave the book," Sister Stella said softly. "Or I shall turn you in to the King myself."

Without thinking twice, Alex left the book on the altar and ran towards the staircase, Ari following close on her heels. They both knew this was the only chance they had to escape Sister Stella, and they weren't about to waste it. This time Alex did not care about getting caught, taking the steps loudly two at a time and barreling out of the golden door.

"She knew," Alex said angrily once they were back in the main hallway. "She knew this whole time and never said."

Ari looked livid. "I should've known."

Then Alex remembered her realization and groaned. "I forgot to ask her about Brother Ezra. She mentioned the name. We keep seeing the letter E everywhere and I think it's connected to him. Maybe he knows more about my mother and what happened to the Stone. We have to speak with him."

"How?" Ari asked. "We have no idea where to find him."

"I'm not sure," Alex said, hurrying her pace across the hall. "We should get back to the others and tell them what we learned. Then we make a plan."

Ari nodded and they quickly descended the steps to the front door. They exited the library and slipped back into the raging crowds of festival-goers that had not let up since they left. Alex lowered the veil over her face and Ari pulled on the falcon headdress as they struggled to cut across the surging sea of people.

They hardly got far when rough hands grabbed her shoulder in the crowd, and Alex was yanked backward along with Ari and directed in the opposite direction. Behind them, a man with a round belly and tufts of greasy hair shouted at them, though he was not dressed in a soldier's uniform and was not arresting them. She shot a panicked glance at Ari.

"He says we're late," Ari said incredulously, trying to move away from the man, but his strong hand kept them walking forward until they were shoved through a curtain and into a small tent. Inside several people were standing around half-naked. They looked up in surprise when Alex and Ari stumbled in.

"Στέλλεσθε!" the man barked behind the curtain before he was gone.

Ari turned to her slowly. "He said to get ready."

"Get ready for what?" Alex asked.

They looked at the other people in the small cramped room. Most of them were dressed as sailors, with oars in their hands. A man in the corner struggled to pull on a pair of trousers, a theater mask by his feet.

"This is a play," Alex whispered, having the strange urge to laugh. "And he thinks we're playing Hathor and Horus."

Ari grabbed her hand. "We need to go."

Then he pulled her out of the tent and they ran down the street, ignoring the shouts of the greasy-haired man when he noticed their escape. A few moments later they heard the telltale sound of soldiers in armor running their way.

Now Ari shoved his way through the crowd without caring if they attracted attention. Alex breathed hard to keep up with his fast pace.

They stopped in front of the gates to the Academy which were still barred with large iron chains. Ari shoved the gate open and the chain gave way about a foot, enough space for them to squeeze inside. Alex went first, struggling to squeeze herself between the iron bars. Ari followed with a grunt.

"Come on," Ari whispered once he was on the other side, pulling Alex after him, his hand holding hers in a tight grip. He led them across a wide stretch of grass, then down a walkway between two large, silent buildings that led to an inner courtyard. Across the courtyard was a squat building, much like the library of the New Academy, with tall wooden doors and a red-tiled roof decorated with painted clay figurines.

Ari glanced behind them. Distant shouts of soldiers could be heard from the street. "We can hide in there."

They crossed the courtyard towards the wooden doors. Ari shook the bronze handles and one of the doors jerked open with a loud creak.

Inside grew dark when they closed the door behind them. Alex quickly realized it was a library, though this one appeared much older than the one back at the New Academy. Here the shelves were made of stone painted with geometric designs in red and purple. Instead of books, there were heaps and heaps of scrolls piled on the shelves and on wooden tables towering up to the ceiling.

In the middle of the library stood a large statue of an old man in a cassock, bald and hunched on a cane, his face wrinkled but otherwise nondescript as he gazed forward.

As they neared the statue Alex froze. Ari came to a stop beside her and looked at the bald man, his eyes widening when he saw what she had seen. Carved into the chest was the same letter E.

Brother Ezra.

Suddenly they heard shouts outside. Ari dragged Alex in between one of the stacks, their backs pressed up against the scrolls. Then the voices faded, as though they had moved away from the library.

Alex let out a breath. They stared at each other, then they began to laugh softly. Ari removed his falcon head, shaking out his curls with a grin. She leaned her head back against the stone shelves, taking another deep breath in and out to calm the racing of her heart.

Ari turned to look at her, his eyes lowered but kindled with amusement. "We need to stop hiding in libraries or we might have to kiss again."

She stared at him and any response died in her throat. He was silent, his smile fading as they both looked at each other. Alex did not move from her spot beside him, her cheeks growing warm from that same heated gaze Ari always gave her, from the moment they had met and he had called her Alexandria. *Remember the night we kissed?*

The truth was that Alex hadn't stopped thinking about that kiss, the arm sliding around her waist, the leap of her heart in her chest as their lips met and she forgot why they had needed to kiss in the first place. Besides, they were dressed up as Horus and Hathor, so they might as well play their parts. Alex placed her hands on the front of his shirt and leaned in to kiss him.

Before their lips met, she saw Ari's eyes widen, the falcon headdress in his hands dropping to the floor with a lone thud. He remained still beneath her touch, so still she wondered if she had misread everything, every glance, every blush. But then he smiled against her mouth, and so she kissed him again, winding her arms around his neck to bring him closer until she could feel the heat of his body through the thin fabric of her dress, her pulse drumming at the base of her throat.

"Gods above," Ari whispered, laughing nervously when she moved her mouth to his neck and sifted her fingers through his curls as she had wanted to do ever since that night she first found him lounging on a library table, a wine bottle and a book held loosely in his hands, his unruly dark hair spread recklessly across the wood.

She had never kissed anyone like this before, with such abandon, such confidence, her hands searching his chest, wrapping around his back, savoring the muscles as they shifted beneath her skin. It was intoxicating, and she was afraid she'd never want to stop.

Ari held her hips loosely, his fingers brushing the small of her back, pulling her closer to him. Alex was so used to Warren making the first move, his controlled desire, his peculiar self-restraint, as though all their moments of intimacy had to be planned or measured for him to want them, their relationship penciled into his life like another check-mark on the path to adulthood.

But Ari was none of that. He leaned back against the bookshelves helplessly, as though he had no strength save to hold her close and kiss her. His strong muscles she had seen countless times were tender and malleable beneath her touch as she pushed him up against the bookshelves. Her stomach grazed the sharp indents of his hips and she felt a wave of pleasure roll through her. His hands moved lower, cupping her from behind, a low groan reverberating from deep in his chest as he kissed her again and again and again.

At last she placed her hands on either side of his face and pulled away, their chests rising and falling against one another. Ari cracked a smile and shook his head, a dazed look in his brown eyes. He looked so handsome then that Alex could not help leaning in and kissing him again, this time more slowly, so that she could feel his tongue move gently, hesitantly against hers, her heart skipping a beat as his hands passed lower, burning a path down her thighs and up once more over the smooth fabric of her dress.

Ari trailed kisses across her jaw, down her neck, letting out another shaky laugh against her skin, his voice breathless. "I've wanted you to do that for a long time."

"Me too," Alex said, her eyes fluttering shut as Ari's touch swept down her spine, the fingertips brushing her lightly, too lightly, sending a rippling desire across her skin.

She never wanted to stop kissing him. They remained wrapped in each other's arms, unable or unwilling to move, Ari's mouth still against the curve of her neck, as though he were content merely to be embraced in her touch forever, as marble lovers in a courtyard.

Suddenly a loud noise echoed in the library, followed by low voices. A door on the opposite end of the library had opened. Alex and Ari quickly unraveled themselves from each other's arms and shared a panicked look. Before she knew it, Ari had dragged them both under the large oak table between the aisles and they crouched there as quietly as possible.

"Ὦ σεβαστέ βασιλεῦ," said an old, hoarse voice into the quiet. "Οἱ κακοῦργοι πρός τῷ θεάτρῳ ἐοίκοτες τῷ Ὥρῳ και τῇ νύμφῃ βεβλέπαται."

Footsteps fell softly on the tile floor, along with an intermittent clack of what sounded like metal. Alex saw that this was true when a pair of leather sandals sewn with jewels and the bottom of a gold cane came into view under the table, his purple robes cut off from view.

It was the King.

He spoke with a loud knock of his cane on the floor. If the other voice sounded old, this one was ancient, like a mountain of weathered rock, like a fabled serpent coiled on hoards of gold for centuries.

"Ὠς δεξιοί!" said the King, amusement clear in his voice, though underneath it Alex thought she heard a lurking anger. "Σφᾶς ὠφελεῖ τις. Χρή τὴν κόρην εὑρίσκειν."

Alex nearly gasped as the realization struck her like a bolt of lightning. This was the same Brother that had been speaking to Sister Stella all those nights ago. This was the same Brother who had almost caught them in a different library, when they had to kiss not to get caught. She didn't know how she hadn't realized it before at the temple.

The other man answered hurriedly in a meek voice. To Alex's surprise, the King laughed in response, a cackling, derisive laugh that nearly made her flinch. He walked a few steps closer to their desk, and for a moment Alex held her breath. The King only needed to lean down and all would be lost.

Instead, he turned around and began walking away, his cane clicking ominously in the silence. Then he paused and spoke softly into the deathly silence. "Καῖε." The other man stuttered a reply, but the king's vicious hiss interrupted him. "Καῖε νότου τὸν πρός τὴν χθόνα. Ὁρῶμεν εἰ σφέτερος θεὸς τότε ὠφελήσοι ἄν."

The purple cloak swished behind him as the King walked away, the other old man quickly following after him while muttering in a submissive tone. Alex waited until the door shut behind them and there was not a sound in the library before crawling out from under the table, taking in a deep breath to steady her racing heart.

She turned towards Ari and her stomach dropped. His face had gone pale and fearful, and he could hardly look her in the eyes.

"What is it?" Alex asked in a whisper.

"They saw us," he said haltingly. "On the street, dressed as Horus and his bride. He knows someone is helping us. And—" He broke off, looking at her with pain bright in his eyes. "And he's looking for you."

"Then we need to go back to the others—"

But he placed a hand on her arm, silencing her. "He's going to burn it."

"What?" He didn't answer her at first. "Ari, tell me. Tell me what he said."

"He said to burn the South Quarter, to see if our god will help us then."

63

ALEX STARED AT ARI, uncomprehending. She felt a pang of guilt that they had kissed without a thought for their friends and the danger they were in because of them. Because of *her*.

"We have to go," Alex whispered, the words barely escaping her lips. "We have to warn them."

This jolted Ari out of his shock and he nodded quickly. "This way."

They exited the library through the opposite door, entering another modest courtyard with browning fruit trees, as though no one had bothered watering them in weeks. Surrounding the courtyard were two-story buildings with windows blocked by curtains. They looked like the dormitories at the New Academy.

"We should avoid the main street," Ari said, taking her hand in his.

Alex pointed to a small gap between the dormitories, where she thought she spied grass. "That way!"

They ran through the narrow alley and emerged into a sloping stretch of green grass peppered with gnarled trees, as ancient-looking as the blind King.

Ari paused, looking around in dawning awe. "I can't believe it. This must be the sacred olive grove, just like in Athens."

Shouts from behind the dormitories broke up his reverie. The soldiers must have heard their voices and returned to scout the area. They didn't have much time.

"The history lesson can wait," Alex said, pulling him away by the hand. "We have to get back to the others."

Beyond the grove was a high stone wall that had to be the Southern Wall, the Notus River flowing directly behind it. There was no jumping over it, more so for its lofty height than the spikes jutting up from the top ledge, not to mention the swift currents they would face on the other side.

Alex glanced to her left and saw a low iron fence lining the edge of the grove. On the other side was the widely paved Priam Boulevard, which came to an abrupt end before the towering Gate of the Sun, its tall golden rods wedged in a gap of the Southern Wall, the Sun Harbor flowing out to sea behind it. Alex had never seen the gate so up close before, but she didn't have time to stand and gawk.

"We need to hop the fence," she said.

Ari raised a brow but did not protest when they heard shouts yet again, this time definitely closer. The soldiers seemed to be checking the buildings and had not thought they would risk the dead end of the olive grove. Ari held out his hands when they reached the fence, cupping them low enough for her to use as a foothold. She grasped the fence with both hands, her heart beating fast.

"On three," she whispered. "One, two, three—"

She jumped up, Ari using his strength to lift her higher as she careened over the spiked fence and stumbled onto her feet. Only once she teetered to a stop did she see the rip in her dress down the length of her right thigh and the blood that spilled from the gash. She hardly blinked, nor felt anything until she took a step and winced at the deep, knife-like pain.

Ari was still on the other side of the fence. Suddenly a crowd of soldiers poured out into the olive grove several yards away. He glanced at them in alarm, before he took a few large steps back and ran towards the fence at full speed.

The soldiers shouted and charged at them as Ari cleared the fence and rolled on the ground, before quickly jumping to his feet. He grabbed Alex, leading them across Priam Boulevard towards the South Quarter.

They sprinted down a narrow street and turned into the first alley they found, weaving through the apartment blocks until they no longer heard the shouts of the soldiers behind them. Alex could barely run any further, her leg screaming in pain with every step.

Ari noticed her limping as they took another alleyway and froze when he saw the gash. "You're bleeding."

"I'm fine," Alex said, her voice hoarse.

"Alexandria—"

"Oh no." Alex came to a sudden stop, her vision swaying dizzily. "We're too late."

She stared down the street they had just turned on, the nearest apartment walls black and gushing smoke from the iron-grated windows, the roofs burning up with red-hot flames. More fires were visible down the street, and large clouds of gray ash choked the sky. Somehow in their escape they had not noticed the fires or smoke until they were right before their eyes.

Ari ran down the street. Alex followed, ignoring the pain in her leg as a numbness washed over her. She coughed on the smoke engulfing the street, and when she heard the distant cries of children her eyes filled with tears.

Soon they neared the apartment and saw that Mother and all of their friends were huddled outside with their belongings cast at their feet.

When they saw Ari and Alex, all of them appeared relieved, and even Chloe broke down crying. Penélope rushed forward and hugged Ari and then Alex, leading them back to the group. She looked down at Alex's limping leg and gasped.

"You're hurt! We have to get a bandage—"

Mother gathered them into the group, shushing them. "No time for that. All wounds shall heal. But first, you must get away. You are no longer safe here. I will bring you to a friend of mine. She will keep you safe for now."

Alex grasped Mother's arm and felt the tears rolling down her cheeks. "But what about you? Aren't you coming with us?"

The old woman smiled at Alex, and somehow it tugged at her heart in its familiarity, like a true mother's caress. "Do not worry about me, my child. I have survived much worse than a mere fire. Now let us go before the king's men begin to round us up like pigs for slaughter."

They followed the old woman down the next alleyway and towards a part of the South Quarter that had not been victim to the worst of the fire. Alex shared confused glances with the rest of them as they approached a familiar intersection near the Temple of Apollo.

A few moments later they heard the screeching sound of metal on stone, before a carriage could be seen flying down the road, coming to a sudden stop before them. The door of the carriage opened and the same veiled woman they had assaulted only days before appeared.

"Quick!" she whispered, peering down the street. "All of you, inside!"

They all stood and stared. Then Mother shooed them inside from behind and closed the carriage door before they could even say goodbye. No handmaidens were accompanying the woman this time, but the inside of the carriage was still cramped, and they struggled to all fit inside. Chloe and Penélope sat on Owen and Zeb's laps beside the woman, while Alex was squeezed between Ari and Warren across from them.

As the carriage took off once more, Alex struggled to focus on the strange turn of events, her leg continuing to throb in pain.

"I just want to say that we are very sorry," Ari said quietly. "We had no intention of hurting you."

The woman smiled. "Do not worry. I am quite alright."

"You're the Queen, aren't you?" Penélope asked suddenly.

The woman raised a brow. "Yes. I heard you did an excellent impression of me at the temple. The King did not notice a difference."

"Where are you taking us?" Alex asked, remembering the horrible laugh of the King. She had a hard time believing this woman could be his wife. "How do you know Mother?"

The Queen gazed at her steadily before responding. "We have been friends for a long time."

"But you're the Queen," Alex continued, ignoring the warning glances from Penélope and Ari. "Won't we get caught?"

Instead of being defensive, the Queen continued gazing into Alex's eyes until Alex had to look away. "No, you will not. I am taking you to a place that no one except myself and my…and my late husband knows about."

"You're not married to the King?" Zeb asked suspiciously.

The woman glanced at him with an air of being highly offended. "Of course not, though I am sure he would like you to think so. The true King was sent far away on business and has not yet returned. This imposter used that to his advantage and took his place. I had to send my son Leandros away so that he would not kill him. I was allowed to live only not to arouse any suspicion."

"He's burning the city alive to find us," Ari said urgently. "He will kill you if he finds out you helped us."

Alex could see a faint smirk on the Queen's face beneath her veil. "That is why he will never find out."

They remained silent for the rest of the ride. Alex closed her eyes, the searing pain of her leg and the twists and turns of the carriage sending rolling waves of nausea through her stomach.

Soon the carriage jolted to a stop, and they gratefully exited the cramped carriage. They were parked in an alley branching off of Priam Boulevard, very close to the Gate of the Moon, but there were no guards around, perhaps all preoccupied with burning the South Quarter. The Queen glanced around anyway before procuring a ring of silver keys. She approached the wall and inserted one of the keys into a small indent in the stone, which Alex realized was the lock of a small door that had been painted to blend in with the wall.

They all ducked inside the door after the Queen and ascended a steep staircase in the dark. Alex used her left leg to climb up, an arm slung around Owen's shoulders, who helped her up the stairs. They entered a spacious living area with plush couches in a similar circle to the one in Mother's home, though these were twice their size.

A large fire roared at the other end of the room, where small windows looked over the harbor, the Lighthouse shining a glimmering light on the City of the Dead. Several doors around the room appeared to lead to private quarters, and what Alex hoped would be nicer latrines and a washroom.

The Queen looked around the living area with a sad smile. "This was my husband's safe house when he wished to sneak out on a ship during the night without anyone knowing. He loved the ocean. The last time I was here was to see him off. I never thought..." She trailed off. Alex thought there were tears in her eyes. "You shall be safe here. There is food and clothes. Please, rest."

The boys had already found a trunk full of provisions, as well as fresh clothes and blankets, and were passing them out excitedly. But Alex could not rejoice. She kept hearing the King's ancient, horrible laughter resounding in her mind.

"And where will you go?" Alex asked, then winced at how rude she must sound to a Queen. "My Lady?"

"I will return to the palace before the King grows suspicious," the Queen said, walking towards the stairs. "I shall come back tomorrow night. Until then, stay out of sight."

64

"I STILL DON'T UNDERSTAND how you two ended up in the Academy," Warren asked, crossing his arms.

Warren stood near the fire he was tending as the rest of them piled onto the couches and ate the hot rice and pork that Penélope and Ari had cooked up in the fireplace.

Alex shifted uneasily and winced at the shooting pain in her right leg. Penélope and Chloe had helped her bandage it last night before going to bed, cleaning the gash and wrapping it in strips of linen, but it was still sore to the touch.

"We went over this already," Ari said, slightly annoyed. In the morning they had explained their encounter with Sister Stella, the old man mistaking them for actors, and overhearing the King in the library before their narrow escape from the soldiers. "Someone thought we were actors and tried to push us into a tent. Then we ran away."

"But why not run straight home?" Warren pressed. "Why hide in the Academy where someone could find you?"

"There were too many soldiers on the street. We didn't want to lead them straight to our doorstep," Alex interrupted. She sensed his jealousy and refused to admit that perhaps he was right.

"You did that anyway," Warren muttered.

Alex wanted to bite back a response, but Owen spoke instead. "Let's all calm down. We made it out alive, that's all that matters."

"Besides, there's something else we learned," Ari said, his voice dropping. "The King."

"What about him?" Zeb asked.

"We already know he's an imposter," Alex said, "but I realized something when we overheard him in the library. He has the same voice as the Brother who was speaking with Sister Stella about me and the same one who almost caught us in the New Academy after coming back from the city the first time. Somehow he's the king now."

"Are you sure?" Penélope asked.

Alex nodded. "I'm positive. His voice is exactly the same. But I never saw him at the New Academy, only at the Temple of Apollo pretending to be the King, so I had no idea how the Brother looked. And he only speaks Ancient Greek in the city."

"Chloe, he never spoke to you in English when he visited the temple, did he?" Owen asked.

Chloe glanced up, half-distracted. She shook her head slowly, her eyes clouding with the memory. "No."

"So Sister Stella is working for the King?" Zeb asked doubtfully. "I thought she was a protector of the city."

"The first time Ari and I came to the city, we overheard some of the women working in the library complain about the King's decrees," Alex said, her thoughts working like rapid-fire as she connected the dots. "Which also explains why they were speaking in English! They must be part of the Seven Sages, like Sister Stella."

"And that's why Sister Stella was warning us about the city!" Ari continued excitedly. "She told us that people aren't who they seem here."

"How are you so sure she's not working for the King?" Warren asked pointedly. "He told *her* to keep an eye on Alex. Isn't that suspicious to you?"

"Sister Stella called him Brother," Alex argued, "not King. Besides, she would never allow him to burn the South Quarter, I know it. The King is not just an imposter. He's a *spy*."

"Let's not forget why we came to the city," Warren said darkly. "This is about finding your mother, not involving yourself in something that could get you killed."

"What if this is all connected to my mother's disappearance?" Alex asked, anger kindling in her chest when Warren's face hardened at her words. "Why do you question something that might lead us to her? Why do you always insist on fighting me?"

"Because this place has only brought us closer to death and farther away from actually finding her!" Warren shot back. "And you don't want to see that because it's your mother, and I get that. But we almost died in that fire. The fire that the *King* ordered because of *you.* How many more near-death experiences do you want to have until something goes wrong?"

Alex stared at Warren, his blue eyes dark and teeming, his nostrils flared. She knew he wanted to hurt her, sensing somehow that she and Ari had shared a moment that excluded him. And yet, he was right. She was so selfish, turning a blind eye to the mounting dangers in the city only to find nothing substantial of her mother in the end. But she couldn't just agree with him, not when she had come so far, not when there was so much still at stake.

"What about the prophecy?" Alex asked in disbelief. "And the Stone? And the fact that Sister Stella said my mother tried to find it? And there's more! Ari and I discovered that the E we keep seeing everywhere is actually—"

"There you go again," Warren interrupted. *"Ari and I.* Does no one else think it's strange that every time you two are alone together you discover yet another way to almost get us killed? It's like you don't really want to leave this place even though some of us have actual *lives* outside! I have an internship this summer with a job riding on it. I have a family I actually like to be around. I *want* to live my life, unlike you!"

"Then I'm sorry I dragged you into this!" Alex shouted angrily, the words that she had always held back pouring out now. "I'm sorry that your boring life plan is more important than anything else! I'm sorry I couldn't fit into it like a box you wanted to check! I'm sorry my family isn't perfect like yours! And I'm sorry that I don't love you anymore. I truly am! And if you want to leave, you can go ahead and leave, I won't stop you."

Warren stared at her, his eyes wide. Everyone around them sat silently, glancing between the two of them. Alex felt a wave of dizziness hit her before

Warren abruptly turned and stalked towards the stairs. She tried to call his name, to tell him to stop, but the words got caught in her throat.

"Warren, mate," Owen said uneasily as Warren stormed down the stairs.

Warren opened the door, and the realization of what he was about to do hit Alex like a slap to the face.

"Wait!" she cried out, springing to her feet despite the pain that lanced up her leg, her voice half a sob. "Wait, Warren, come back! I didn't mean it!"

She ran down the stairs, hardly hearing the voices calling after her, shoving through the door and out into the alleyway.

"Warren!" she screamed at the empty lane.

He was gone.

A cold fear gripped her. Alex began to run toward Priam Boulevard when strong arms wrapped around her chest.

"Don't." It was Ari. He held her close against him. "It's too late. He's made his choice."

"Warren," she cried softly. "Warren, come back, please come back."

Ari's arms tightened around her. She could hear Owen cursing behind her, but it was distant to the roar in her head, the rushing between her temples like the night she stood beneath Niagara Falls.

"We have to find him," she whispered, the words choked with her tears.

"It's too dangerous," Ari said, his voice low. "You can't risk getting caught. We both know you're the one the King is after."

"It's all my fault," Alex said, but she wasn't sure the words even made it past her lips, the alley shrinking before her as though passing through a tunnel, and before she could call for help she was sinking down, down, down, swallowed by the depths of the earth.

65

Alex stared into the fire, watching the flames blacken the wooden logs and crackle into ash. She wrapped the wool blanket closer around her body, as though there were an ever-present chill in her bones that she couldn't shake.

"Are you feeling okay?" Penélope lingered behind her.

Ever since she woke up after fainting in the alleyway she had been attended to like a baby they were afraid would start crying again.

"I'm fine," Alex said, perhaps a little too harshly. She sighed. "Sorry. I'm just..."

Penélope sighed too and sat beside her. "I know. Me too. I can't believe Warren left like that. I hope he's safe and made it back to the New Academy."

Alex shook her head. "I was too hard on him. He's right. I'm risking everyone's life. And for what? To find my mother? Who left me when I was ten? I'm being selfish."

"I would do the same," Penélope said warmly, placing a comforting hand on her arm. "Besides, it's not every day you find a place like this."

They were silent. Alex looked out the windows, at the harbor that unfurled to the distant horizon, the Lighthouse an orange streak on a black sky filled with foreign stars. Where were they? Was this a place? A road? Or was it all a dream, an illusion, and when she woke it would all slip away like sand between her fingers, her mother and the past Alex kept searching for fading into memory?

Before she could respond, Ari spoke loudly from across the room. "I know we don't want to think about it, but there's more we have to discuss."

Alex and Penélope turned around. Owen and Chloe were lying together on the couch, while Zeb exited one of the small bedrooms he shared with Ari, looking around to see who had spoken. Alex tried to catch Ari's eye but he firmly refused to look at her.

"We overheard Sister Stella speaking about someone she called Brother Ezra," Ari continued. "Alexandria put two and two together and realized that the E we kept seeing must refer to him. We saw it on the Squatting Scribe statue, we saw it on the parchment of the Hymn to the Prince of Thieves, Alexandria saw it in the Temple of Apollo, and we saw it on the statue of a brother in the library at the Academy. We had no idea what the E meant until we heard the name. At this point, it doesn't feel like a coincidence."

"Even if it's not," Owen said, sounding tired, "what does it mean?"

"It means that there's someone out there who also knows about the prophecy," Alex said quietly. "Someone important enough to have their statue in the Academy. Someone who discovered the Hymn to the Prince of Thieves. Someone who might know more about my mother and the Stone and where to find it."

"How are we going to speak with this mysterious Brother Ezra?" Chloe asked, raising a brow.

"We'll go to the Academy," Ari said firmly. "If he has his statue in the library, there's a good chance he's the Headmaster or at least teaches there. We find Brother Ezra, we ask about the prophecy, and then we leave."

"That sounds easy enough," Zeb said dryly. "It's not like you two were almost caught in that same library a day ago."

Alex met Ari's eyes and saw the heat of that memory mirrored there. She struggled to keep her focus on the conversation as she recalled those hands pressing into her hips, his chest and strong thighs flush against her, and his helpless groan as he kissed her again and again.

"I won't ask you to risk your life for me," Alex forced herself to say. "I can go alone. It will be easier for me not to get caught anyway."

"I'm coming with you," Ari said immediately, ignoring the sharp look from Zeb. "It's too dangerous for you to be roaming the city alone." He paused. "But the rest of you should wait here. If something goes wrong, we might need your help."

The others began to protest when a rattling at the door echoed in the house and everyone went silent. Alex got to her feet, her heart pounding as the door swung open.

"Warren?" she asked, breathless.

From the stairs emerged the purple-veiled head of the Queen. She glanced around the room steadily before walking up the remaining steps. They did not speak as she came forward and paused, as if she were waiting for something.

For a moment, no one knew what to do, but then Ari bowed, and Owen quickly followed, then Zeb. Chloe, Penélope, and Alex stood up and wobbled a curtsy. It all felt so foreign and nearly comical in its formality, but the Queen inclined her head and swept her gaze over them once more.

"One of you is missing," she said, her voice soft but sure, and everyone stiffened at her words. "It is as I feared."

"What do you mean?" Alex asked quickly, momentarily forgetting her manners. "My Lady?"

"Your friend has been taken into custody," the Queen said. "They found him sleeping in an alley behind the Tower of the Winds."

Alex's mind went blank. "We have to rescue him."

"I am afraid that is impossible." The Queen paused. "He is as good as dead."

Chloe gasped and Penélope choked on a strangled sob. But Alex felt strangely calm. She walked towards the Queen, not caring if she was being rude. *How many more near-death experiences do you want to have until something goes wrong?*

"I don't care," Alex said angrily. "I'm going to rescue him or die trying."

The Queen met her gaze and seemed to almost smile. "Very well."

"Alexandria, are you sure?" Ari asked her. "If you do this, we may never have the chance to find your mother."

Alex stood up straight, keeping her voice level despite the urge to cry. "We have to rescue him. He would do the same for me." She breathed in deeply and turned to the Queen. "Where is he being kept?"

"In the King's palace," The Queen said calmly. "There are prison rooms there. But it will be impossible to breach the palace. Guards are watching every room and every hall at all hours of the day. You would hardly last five minutes past the front door without getting caught."

For a moment, Alex struggled to sift through the panic humming in her brain. She tried to think of the palace and how they could possibly get past all those guards. But the Queen was right. No matter how hard they tried, there was no world in which they took out enough guards to make it to the prison rooms without getting arrested as well.

The others were debating possible plans of attack. Owen suggested making a distraction like they did with the temple guard. Chloe argued that they should sneak inside the palace through a back door. Zeb said they could dress as soldiers or servants of some kind, while Ari thought they could scale the wall and come down from the roof.

Then it occurred to Alex as if the thought had been there all along. "But it's not impossible," she murmured, more to herself.

Ari looked up at her. "What?"

Alex couldn't help but smile. "It's not impossible to get in, only impossible not to get caught. But he *wants* to catch me. So we let him, and it won't matter because I'll be inside the palace. Once I'm in, all I have to do is break him out."

"So you *want* the King to arrest you?" Chloe asked flatly. "That sounds like a suicide mission."

"Do you want to save Warren's life or not?" Alex demanded.

"Yes," Owen responded firmly, cutting Chloe an irritated look. "We do. Let's face it. None of us are going to be able to scale a wall like Ari, and it's probably inevitable that we'll get caught any other way. At least once we get arrested it's *part* of the plan."

"I agree that this might be the only shot we have," Ari said slowly, "but we have no idea what to expect once we're inside the palace."

The Queen smiled in amusement. "But I do."

66

Alex kept her eyes focused on the ground, the stone walkway tinted purple behind her veil. She could hear Chloe's short breaths beside her as they followed Penélope up the long path to the palace gates. Behind them were Ari, Owen, and Zeb fitted as their royal guards.

"Χαῖρε, ὦ πότνια!"

Just as the Queen predicted, the guards at the palace gate hardly gave them a second glance, swinging open the gates and saluting them as they walked past. They entered the palace with measured steps, though Alex thought her heartbeat was so loud the guards would hear it and know they were imposters.

While they had planned the rescue down to the last word and movement, using the Queen's memory to sketch a map of the palace and the best routes of escape, Alex still feared that something could go wrong.

They had entered from the South Entrance off the Meson Pedion, which led up a slight incline past craftsmen workshops and houses reserved for relatives and nobility to the inner palace gate, where they would visit the King in his throne room. It was nearing evening, before dinner, when most of the palace staff would be preparing a great feast and would be less likely to notice that the Queen did not appear like herself.

Once they reached the smaller iron gate leading to the Central Court, Ari, Owen, and Zeb broke off down another hallway which would lead them to the prison room. While they were in constant danger of being caught by other guards, they were in less danger than Alex, Penélope, and Chloe were about to be.

As they approached, trying hard not to walk at an abnormally fast pace, the guards at the gate looked at Penélope, before sharing skeptical glances. Alex held her breath. Penélope was almost at the gate, not breaking her stride. Her confidence at last won the guards over, who hurriedly opened the gate for her, bowing their heads and muttering a salutation.

Breathing quiet sighs of relief, they walked across the Central Court bathed in the soft glow of a setting sun, the several-story-high palace climbing up into the sky around them so that Alex felt both exposed and trapped.

All of the walls were painted with beautiful scenes of gods and goddesses, as well as carvings of battles both on land and at sea. Everywhere she looked there were colorful statues of men and women she did not recognize, and at the center of the open space was an elaborate, mosaic-tiled fountain gushing with water. Guards clothed in bright tunics and bronze armor stood at attention around the courtyard, staring vaguely before them, sharp spears resting on their right shoulders and swords strapped to their hips. It was only a matter of time before they were caught. They just needed to reach the King.

Alex and Chloe followed Penélope toward the throne room, which was adjoined to the Central Court facing east. Two guards stood on either side of a grand wooden pillar, as thick as a tree trunk, which held up the roof of the throne room and hid the King. When they saw Penélope, they immediately bowed their heads and allowed them to pass.

They walked around the wooden pillar, Alex's heart beating fast. Suddenly they came to a stop in front of a large throne carved into the stone wall, and seated there in the same purple robe and bejeweled slippers was the King, his blind eyes staring ahead and his mouth a harsh line on his face.

The King seemed to look down upon them and his face grew angry. "Tί οὐ ἐν τῷ θαλάμῳ του εἶ?"

Penélope was silent, merely lowering her head submissively as the Queen had told her to. She had predicted that the King would be angry at her late arrival, as she had orders not to wander the city past sundown.

"Οὐ λεγείς?" he asked, half-growling, so that Penélope flinched.

Out of the corner of her eye, Alex saw the guards lining the room share questioning glances, a few even taking hesitant steps forward. Their time was up.

Alex took a step forward and lifted her veil. "There's no need for theatrics, *Brother*. We know who you really are."

The King looked at her in surprise, and though he was blind, his eyes seemed to fix on Alex with those milky irises. Then he smiled, slow and sly. "*Alexandria*. What a pleasant surprise. I suppose the Queen put you up to this? You should not trust that woman, nor anything she has said about me. She is weak, easily corrupted, and a skilled liar."

His voice was silky smooth and persuasive. The words ran through her mind with dreamlike power, and she stood still, a small part of her mind already half-believing, as if the King had cast some spell on her. She shook her head, trying to rid herself of his words.

"*You're* the liar," Alex said angrily through clenched teeth. "You sent away the true King to seize power. You lied to Sister Stella and pretended to care about her cause. You burned the South Quarter and left the people there to die."

At her words, a flash of wrath spasmed across the deep wrinkles of his face, before he pointed to them and shouted, "Σφᾶς συλλαμβάνεσθε!"

Guards rushed upon them and Penélope screamed, while Chloe struggled to escape the soldiers' unyielding grip as their arms were pinned behind their backs. The King laughed, a raspy, grating sound like stone against stone.

"You know, you are so much like your mother, Alexandria," the King said with a sharp grin of crooked teeth. "Headstrong, arrogant, emotional, but above all, predictable. Sister Stella was quite concerned when you discovered the prophecy, but I told her not to worry. You are your mother's daughter after all. She tried to find the Stone, just like you. She thought she figured out the prophecy, the answer to a centuries-old riddle, but she was wrong, like so many before her."

"Where is she?" Alex cried out, trying to yank her arms from the guard's strong hands which only caused him to tighten his hold on her. "Tell me where she is!"

The King looked upon her with a curl of disgust. "Dead."

Alex felt the breath leave her chest despite every part of herself screaming that what he said was not true. "You're lying!"

"Believe what you wish," the King drawled, "but I saw your mother's dead body fall to the ground. Elena made a mistake when she threatened the supreme power of Zeus, King of the Gods, and she paid the price. Now you will too."

"I don't understand," Alex whispered, her legs buckling beneath her. The guard held her upright so that she would not fall to the ground. "She left when I was ten years old."

The King stared at her coldly, and the guards began dragging them away. "That is impossible. She was struck down by Zeus, her shade sent to the Halls of Hades. And there is no returning from the Netherworlds lest you strike a deal with Death himself. "

Just then a guard ran into the throne room shouting and waving his arms hysterically. Alex didn't understand what he was saying, but she didn't have to. She already knew exactly what was going to happen next.

Suddenly a huge crowd of people flooded into the throne room, trampling the shouting guard, some rushing towards the throne and others escaping down the halls. They were prisoners, all of them, unlocked from their cells by Ari, Owen, and Zeb while the King had been distracted.

The soldier holding Alex let her go to save the King from certain death as the vengeful prisoners aimed for the throne. Alex didn't hesitate. She grabbed Chloe and Penélope's arms and together they ran back to the Central Court. They took the hallway left towards the prison rooms, all of them empty save a few straggling prisoners trying to escape. And waiting for them in the last open cell were the boys, including Warren, who was dressed in a simple dirty white tunic and whose wrists were bloody and raw from the chains.

Alex ran towards him and hugged him as the sobs rose. Warren tried to calm her, kissing her hair and saying her name soothingly. She didn't care that everyone was watching her.

"I'm so sorry, Warren," Alex said between a sob. "I didn't mean—"

"Save the apologies for later," Owen interrupted. "Let's get out of here."

Without another word, they ran down the hall toward the north entrance, where the Queen had managed to remove the guards with the help of some loyal friends inside the palace. Her carriage awaited them by the small theater attached to the palace. Owen ran to take the reigns while the rest of them crammed inside.

No one spoke as the carriage rattled down the street, for all the world transporting the Queen away from a very dangerous situation in the palace. Soon enough they were turning down the same alleyway by the harbor and entering the Queen's safe house, where she stood in the center of the room waiting for them.

67

No one spoke as the Queen set down the large pot of stew in the middle of the couches. When they first arrived from the palace, they had all collapsed on the couches exhausted, and instead of asking them any questions, the Queen simply went about making food.

While Alex knew it was perhaps very rude to allow a queen to cook for them, her aching limbs and still-throbbing wound were grateful as she swallowed the steaming hot stew. The others seemed to be in agreement, finishing their bowls hurriedly.

Once they began pouring out seconds, Warren spoke. "Thank you all for rescuing me. I shouldn't have run away like that, and you have every right to be angry with me. Even though I didn't mean to get caught, I still wanted to apologize."

"How *did* you get caught?" Owen asked, raising a brow.

Warren's gaze clouded, and he frowned. "I regretted leaving, but I thought it would be easier for all of you if I wasn't there. But the Great Library was too well guarded to sneak inside. So I hid in an alley behind the Tower of the Winds, hoping to sneak into the library at night." His cheeks colored pink, and he brushed his fingers against the bandages on his wrist where the iron shackles had chaffed his skin. "Obviously I was caught before I could."

Alex felt that same guilt again and she tried to push back the tears. "It was my fault. You were right. I have been putting all of you in danger for someone that might not even be alive." She paused, taking a deep breath. "That's why I am going to stay in the city alone, and all of you will return home. What I'm about to do next is too dangerous for any of you to risk your lives anymore."

"What are you talking about?" Chloe demanded. "What are you doing next?"

Ari was staring at her, while the rest of them looked confused. Alex ignored them all and turned towards the Queen, who merely looked back at her, as though she knew all along that it would come to this.

"I want to go to the Underworld," Alex said. "The King said my mother's shade was sent to the Halls of Hades. *And there is no returning from the Netherworlds lest you strike a deal with Death himself.* If my mother died that night as the King said, then maybe I can find my mother in the Underworld. Maybe she made a deal with Death."

For a moment, all was quiet, and Alex held the Queen's gaze, undaunted. Then Owen burst out into a mocking laugh, while Chloe sputtered her disbelief along with Zeb, demanding Penélope tell her if Alex was serious. Ari and Warren remained quiet.

"Have you gone mad?" Owen asked when he realized Alex was not joking. "This isn't *Percy Jackson*. You can't just *go* to the Underworld."

"But you can," Penélope said, her eyes lighting up. She looked at the Queen. "Odysseus did once. And so did Aeneas. Why couldn't Alexandria?"

The Queen shook her head. "Not everyone can travel to the world below. You must have a guide, lest you lose your way and remain trapped in the Underworld for eternity."

"Oh, we're seriously considering this," Owen said in disbelief. "I don't know why I question anything anymore."

"I'm not asking any of you to come with me," Alex said sharply. Owen frowned and averted his eyes. "But this is my mother. I knew from the start she could've been dead all along. But if she made a deal with Death once, then maybe I can too." She paused, her throat closing with coming tears. "This might be my only chance to save her."

"I'll come," Warren said. Alex looked at him in surprise. He nodded at her, as if this was his forgiveness for all the harsh words she had said to him. "I'll come with you."

"Me too," Ari said quietly.

"Then I'm coming too," Penélope declared, her eyes fierce. "I know what lengths I'd go to bring back someone I love."

Suddenly Zeb spoke. "I'll come too."

Owen stared at Zeb in surprise, then rolled his eyes with a dramatic sigh. "I'm not going to let all of you go without me and miss all the fun."

The only one who hadn't agreed was Chloe. She glanced at Alex, that familiar hesitation in her dark eyes. *Only search for answers if you are willing to find them.* "What if you can't bring her back?" she asked.

Alex felt that familiar dread return, but she forced herself to say the words. "Then I find the Emerald Stone and finish what my mother started."

Chloe paused, then nodded. She would come.

"So now all that's left to figure out is how to get to Hell," Owen said happily, clapping his hands together. He looked around the room at all their silent, serious faces. "She said we need a guide. Maybe we can ask around for a tour?"

No one laughed. Suddenly Alex gasped. They all looked at her in alarm. "The *Book of the Dead.* You called it a spell book—"

"—that guides you in the afterlife!" Owen finished, his eyes widening. "And it's about rebirth!"

"We just have to find the *Book of the Dead*—" Alex continued, then she looked at Ari, who was already up on his feet.

"—in the Great Library!" Ari concluded, a smile on his face.

"Unfortunately," the Queen said, her soft voice cutting through their excitement, "you shall not find any spell books in that library. They are too potent to be lying around for just anyone to read."

"But if they're not in the Great Library..." Penélope said, her voice faltering.

"It is forbidden to speak of their location exactly," the Queen said, standing up, "but I may tell you that the spells you seek lie buried in the city of the kings. This is the last advice I will give you, for I must return to the palace, and I am afraid the King shall not let me leave again."

"The city of the kings?" Ari repeated. "Do you mean the Necropolis, where past kings are buried?"

The Queen merely smiled, glancing keenly at Penélope, who frowned and thought over her words again.

Penélope stood up, her face bright. "The Valley of the Palms! Mother told us about the desert beyond the Eastern Wall. She called it the Valley of the Palms." She looked around at the others, but they all stared at her blankly. "You know, *King* Palms? That's the name of those kinds of palm trees. So it's literally the city of Kings!"

"You are clever, Πηνελόπη, just like your namesake," the Queen said, inclining her head towards Penélope, who blushed in surprise. "Before I go, however, a warning I must impart. Many have gone missing in those sands searching for the spells of the dead. My people tell the story of a woman who wanders the Valley of the Palms and guards her secrets from those who are unworthy. But if you wish to find what you seek, you must first face her wrath."

"How do we find her?" Alex asked.

The Queen looked at her steadily and a shiver ran down Alex's spine before she said the words. "She is called the Lady of the Golden Blade, and she will find you."

68

Water lapped against the small boat creaking on the rolling waves. Alex held onto the side of the boat and prayed they wouldn't tip over as Owen jumped inside, swaying the boat even more.

"Stop that," Chloe snapped nervously, her hand reaching out and clinging to Alex's arm. She hated being anywhere near the water, least of all on a small rickety rowboat.

Owen flashed her a grin. "Sorry, love."

Warren was the last to jump in the boat after pushing it away from the dock and onto the water. At this hour, all of the fishermen and traders were out at sea or sleeping, and would not return until the early hours of the morning. The boys sat at the oars and quietly rowed them along the coastline. The darkness of the night blended with the black waves of the bay without a light to guide them, but luckily the moon and the Lighthouse shed enough light on their surroundings to follow the vague shape of the coastline up to the Valley of the Palms.

"Why couldn't we have just gone through the East Gate?" Chloe complained. "I'm gonna be sick on this boat."

While Alex would have preferred to walk to the valley as well, the Queen had insisted that they would not breach the Eastern Gate after the King increased his security measures. Instead, she had prepared a small rowboat to take them up along the harbor, past the Port of Pirates, and beyond the Eastern Wall where the Valley of the Palms stretched in a sea of golden sand peppered with tall, majestic palm trees.

Unfortunately, the tighter security measures meant that they could not use a lamp in the boat, because that would be seen from the shore, so they had to rely on Warren and Owen's boating skills to smoothly row them to the sandy banks of the valley.

"What are those rocks in the water?" Penélope asked, frightened, pointing up ahead near the Necropolis Island where the people of the city buried their dead.

"Easy now," Owen said, standing up to get a better look. The boys eased up on their oars and the boat glided to a stop. "They look like boulders."

"Must be the Path of Sphinxes," Ari murmured, peering over the water. "Mother mentioned them, but I almost didn't believe they existed."

Alex squinted over the water. The boat continued onwards once the boys began rowing again, this time more slowly. To the side of their boat, she saw a large boulder jutting out of the water, close enough that if she jumped out she would land on the curved, dry surface. As they passed, she noticed carvings across the stone. Beyond it similarly carved boulders emerged from the water, forming a straight line to the Necropolis Island.

"Are they statues?" Penélope asked doubtfully.

"Of sphinxes," Ari said, nodding his head.

"They must be huge if they reach the bottom," Zeb said, awe creeping into his voice. "I wonder how they got there."

Alex shivered, trying to imagine the massive sphinx statues standing on the ocean floor, only the tops of their heads visible above the water.

"Are we almost there yet?" Chloe asked.

"Now we're in the Port of Pirates," Warren whispered, glancing around warily.

The Queen had warned them of the dangers of the Port of Pirates, which had become so named in the last fifty years due to the pirates roaming the eastern side of the Necropolis Island, which they had long brought under their control. To this day, many ships that wandered too close to the island were pillaged.

Despite the warnings, their boat slid by unharmed, with not a single pirate ship in sight. Soldiers did not roam the streets this close to the Port of Pirates, so they could breathe easier as they neared the valley.

Soon the tall palm trees came into view, the moonlight glinting off their shiny palm leaves swaying in a slight breeze off the ocean. Once their boat rowed close enough to shore, Warren and Owen jumped out into the shallow water and pulled the boat up onto the sandy bank. The rest of them hopped out and trudged their way to dry land.

"Now my feet will be all wet and sandy," Chloe complained, slipping on her socks and shoes that she had taken off before jumping from the boat.

"If what the Queen says is true," Ari said, wringing water from his tunic, "we'll have greater things to worry about soon enough."

Once they were all ready, they walked into the valley together, Alex, Penélope, and Ari taking the lead while Chloe stayed behind with Owen, Warren, and Zeb. The journey reminded Alex of the time they walked deep into the desert behind the New Academy, when after hours of searching they stumbled upon the revelry and its subtle horror, then drowning to death afterward.

"Ari," Penélope said hesitantly, "do you think the woman we are meeting—the Lady of the Golden Blade—is actually..."

Ari's face darkened. "I was thinking the same. For all our sakes, I hope not."

Alex nearly shivered, though at the words or the wind on her wet clothes, she did not know. "Who is she?"

"Someone who loves revenge," Ari said, sharing a knowing look with Penélope.

They walked in silence once more, hiking deep into the valley, the desert sand marching for miles and miles up to the mountains looming in the east, even farther away than those in Tierra del Sol.

Alex's neck prickled with that peculiar sensation she has become familiar with in the city, of eyes peering out of shadowy places, as though someone were watching her. She walked closer to Penélope, hoping that the feeling was her paranoia and not a possible truth.

"Do you think we're there yet?" Chloe asked from behind them. "We've been walking for at least an hour."

"Remember what the Queen said," Alex replied, sounding more confident than she felt. "*She* will find *us*."

"Then maybe we're doing it wrong," Penélope whispered. She came to a sudden stop and turned around, forcing the others to stop and gather in a circle.

"What do you mean?" Ari asked, looking around the dark rolling hills of sand. "You want to wait for her to find us?"

"That's what the Queen said, isn't it?" Penélope said hesitantly. "If we stop searching for her, maybe she will come to us."

"So you just want to sit in the middle of a desert and wait for a random woman to show up?" Owen shook his head. "Sounds like bogus to me."

Penélope glared at him. "This isn't a *random* woman. This is a goddess we're talking about. If she wants to find us, she will."

Ari nodded slowly, then sat down on the sand with a sigh. "Then we'll wait."

Owen stalked over to a nearby palm tree and sat down with his back leaning on the trunk. "I'll just get some sleep then. Wake me up when she's here, will you?"

"I think I'll do the same if you guys don't mind," Warren said quietly, taking a seat beside Owen and leaning his head back, his eyes closed.

Alex lowered herself to the ground beside Penélope and Ari. Chloe and Zeb joined them in a circle. They stared at each other, wondering if they should take the time to rest or keep an eye open for a wandering woman.

Then Pénelope looked up at the sky and sucked in a breath. "Oh look! The stars..."

All of them looked up and even Zeb laughed in delight. The stars crowded the night sky in different colors, and streaking right down the middle of it all was a shower of meteors with fiery tails trailing behind them.

Alex could not help but lean back on the sand and look up with wide eyes. She had never seen anything so beautiful in her life. All those years blanketed under the smog of cities, Alex had yearned for a sky full of stars. She remembered staring up at the constellations in New Mexico and wishing that she could fly up there, leave behind the clambering weight of her mortality and watch humanity rise and fall into oblivion.

The black of the night sky grew wider and wider above them like a blanket pulled taut over the earth, hugging the valley in a sweet, enchanting embrace. Distantly she saw the stars wink out one by one, and felt the desert sand tickling her cheek, her breaths evening out and becoming one with the wind of the valley, her heartbeat pulsing to the same beat deep beneath the sand. All was dark for a long, long time.

She felt rather than heard her name, a voice as old as the changing seasons whispering to her in a dream. Alex lifted her eyelids, heavy from sleep, and saw the sky once more, still filled with stars, the fiery tails of the meteor shower already fading into darkness.

All at once Alex realized she had fallen asleep without meaning to. Her heart pounded frantically as she sat up, looking around at the others who were shaking themselves awake, also startled to have fallen asleep. How long had they been sleeping?

Then Alex saw Chloe's face go rigid, looking behind her into the valley. She turned and her own heart skipped a beat. A hunched, cloaked figure slowly hobbled towards them across the sand, ragged black robes unmoving in the wind. Owen and Warren had already scrambled to their feet, while Ari and Penélope stood up slowly, as if any quick movement would frighten the apparition away.

The figure held up a lamp that glimmered amidst the long, shadowy trunks of the palm trees. As the figure approached, Alex thought she glimpsed a pair of flashing eyes in a wrinkled face, like a white glow deep inside ice.

"O strangers, why do you disturb my grief?"

The voice was unmistakably that of an old woman, yet Alex felt the bottomless sorrow etched into the hoarse words, the voice crackling as dead leaves crunch beneath careless footsteps or upon snow packed deep in the heart of winter.

Penélope shared a glance with Ari before she stepped forward and spoke, her voice steady save the slightest tremble. "O Holy Queen, we do not wish to disturb your grief, but we came here seeking the *Book of the Dead*."

The old woman laughed, low and cold, like an arctic wind ripping leaves from branches, the barest hint of wrath in each gust. "You seek to bring back a soul from the Halls of the Dead."

"Y-yes," Penélope said, her voice faltering. "We were told that you guarded the spells of the dead."

"Guarded? *Guarded?* Stupid girl! I am no watchdog! I am no Cerberus! I am no Sphinx!"

The old woman's hunched back heaved with more mocking laughter, until the frail body seemed to curl into itself, her laughter growing deep and loud until it boomed one with the wind, shaking the palm trees and the desert sands alike, before the hunched cloak crumpled to the ground in an empty heap.

Penélope gasped and Chloe huddled closer to Alex. They watched in horror as the sand around them began to swirl in the air, the wind picking up in a storming cloud, and they had to shut their eyes against the flying sand.

A voice rang out deep and guttural, brittle as the whipping grains of sand, raging as the heaving layers of the earth when it erupts, cold and stinging as the blue ice piercing deep beneath the sea.

"I am Demeter, daughter of Kronos and Rhea, keeper of the seed, destroyer of the crop, who shall forever roam the earth alone, severed from her child, who was plucked from the fields like a flower in bloom by the very hands of Death!"

Alex squinted open her eyes through the wind and sand, struggling to keep herself standing upright in the storm. She cowered away from the glowing figure before her, as tall as the tallest palm tree, in the body of a woman but with eyes like molten steel, her skin burning in the flames of eternal white fire, her hair streaming like the fiery tails of comets in the sky, and in her right hand she gripped a golden sword, as terrifying and blinding as an exploding star.

"I am the Lady of the Golden Blade, mother of vengeance, reaper of Death, giver of Life! My blade shall sever your souls from your mortal limbs as the scythe cuts down the stalk!"

Demeter lifted the blade above her head, ready to strike, the divine gleam of revenge burning in her eyes. Alex held her breath as she brought the blade down—

"No!" Penélope shouted, standing tall before Demeter with her hands in fists by her side, her eyes open despite the sand whipping around her, facing the goddess unflinchingly. *But if you wish to find what you seek, you must first face her wrath.*

Suddenly the wind ceased, the sand dropping heavily around them and the glowing light shrinking rapidly like a breath exhaling until all that stood before them was the old woman once more, cloaked in black robes and hunched against the cold wind off the harbor.

They were all breathing harshly, staring at the old woman in a daze, who mere moments ago had taken the shape of an undying goddess, ready to kill them where they stood. She laughed once more, a low cackle that sounded more like the slice of a blade through a thick field of grass.

"Your courage, daughter, is admirable," the old woman said hoarsely, "but it shall be your doom."

Penélope lifted her head high, tears clearing a path down her dusty cheeks. "We seek the *Book of the Dead*."

The cloaked head bowed silently, and a wrinkled hand shot out of her robes, the knobby, scarred fingers yearning for the sand. Below where her hand reached the sand began to bubble like a soup boiling, and a sand-colored snake coiled out of the ground, as a worm is pulled by a bird's beak. Not a snake, Alex realized belatedly, but a long, thin linen now brown and flaky, with faded black marks drawn on both sides.

"Long ago, the dead were embalmed in the *Spells of Coming Forth by Day* and buried in the sands of the desert." The old woman reached down and plucked one end of the linen, holding it out to Penélope, who grasped it reluctantly. "It is not easy to resurrect the dead. Your journey shall lead you to the darkest and loneliest corners of the world, from which few are allowed to return."

Penélope bowed her head, the hand holding the linen trembling as she took a step back. "Thank you, Holy Queen."

The old woman began to turn away, then paused. Alex held her breath. Demeter looked up at the mountains in the east, their dark peaks piercing the night sky.

"Rosy Dawn approaches," she said, her voice suddenly lighter, almost younger, soft as grass weighed down with morning dew. "You shall need this, daughter, though you shall rue the day you ever have to wield it."

Penélope gasped, stumbling back. Standing before her, the long tip buried inside the sand, was a golden sword. The length of the blade glowed from within as though it contained a burning fire. Penélope hesitated, taking a step towards it.

"Take it! But be warned—"

With her right hand, Penélope had grasped the golden sword, pulling it out of the ground in a single motion. In the same instance, light flooded from the sword, blinding them, and they all cried out. Alex shut her eyes against the light, as white as the whitest star in the sky, flashing against her eyelids. The voice of Demeter echoed in her head, already more of a fading memory than words, and Alex thought she heard the distant scream of a girl floating in the wind, a fair maiden untimely snatched by Hades.

"Never make a deal with Death."

Then the light faded and Alex opened her eyes slowly. Everyone was blinking and rubbing their eyes, except Penélope, who stared at the sword in her hand in astonishment, the golden blade no longer glowing, though the moonlight caught the sharp edge from above.

Penélope looked up, her face grim, the scrolls of the *Book of the Dead* in one hand, the Golden Blade in the other. "Now we go to Hell."

The Lord of the Dead

O ye who make to enter souls perfected in the house of Osiris may ye make to enter the soul perfect of Osiris, the scribe Ani, victorious, with you into the house of Osiris. May he hear [as] ye [hear]; may he see as ye see; may he stand as ye stand; may he sit as ye sit. O givers of cakes [and] beer to souls perfected in the house of Osiris, giv eye cakes [and] beer at the double season of Osiris Ani, victorious before the gods all of Abydos, victorious with you. O openers of the way [and] openers of the roads to souls perfected in the house of Osiris, open therefore ye to him the way, open therefore ye the roads to the soul of Osiris the scribe [and] accountant of divine offerings of gods all, Ani [triumphant] with you. May he go in with confidence, may he come forth in peace from the house of Osiris. Not may he be repulsed, not may he be turned back, may he go in [as he] pleaseth, may he come forth [as he] desireth, may he be victorious. May be done his commands in the house of Osiris, may he walk, may he speak with you, may he be a glorified soul with you. Not hath been found his defect there. The scales have been emptied of [his] trial.

—From the *Book of the Dead* for the Scribe Ani, translation by E. A. Wallis Budge

69

WHILE IT HAD FELT like hours to reach the Valley of the Palms, they quickly made it to the shore where they had left their small rowboat, as though some god was helping them pick the shortest path through the desert.

Soon they were rowing into the harbor, still empty of fishermen and merchants at this time of night save a few shadowy figures walking furtively at the edges of the street. They steered their boat near the far end of the Neoria, Warren quickly tying the rope to the dock. The earliest light of Dawn kissed the eastern skies when they reached their safe house.

All of them were relieved to lock the door behind them and spill into the house. Warren and Owen immediately went to the fireplace and began piling logs into the hearth, and soon a fire sputtered to life, orange sparks floating in the air just like that night roasting marshmallows with her father, Simona, and baby Malcolm. That felt like years ago now.

Since they had all fallen into a deep slumber while in the desert, none of them felt tired in the slightest, and in fact, Alex had never felt more awake. They sat on the couches in a big circle, while Penélope unwrapped the long coils of linen.

"Do you think that was really wrapped on a dead body?" Zeb asked, eyeing the linen warily. "You know that's what the Ancient Egyptians did with the *Book of the Dead*."

Penélope glared at him. "It was wrapped on their mummies. And we have no choice but to use it." She turned to Ari, who had picked up the right end and was squinting at the markings. "Can you read it?"

He nodded slowly, tracing the faded hieroglyphs with his fingertip. "It's definitely Ancient Egyptian."

Owen scoffed. "Now he knows Egyptian too?"

Ari glanced up at him and smirked. "I know some Sanskrit too, if you ever wish to read the Vedas. Or do you *fancy* a tale of dragons and witches? I'm not half-bad at Old English. Let's not get into Linear B and the fascinating world of ancient Mycenaean economics."

"Show off," Owen shot back. "I bet you can't speak something useful, like Mandarin Chinese."

"Can you?" Ari asked, raising a brow.

Owen rolled his eyes as Chloe began to laugh. "No, but that's not the point."

"Back to the *Book of the Dead*," Penélope interrupted. "We need to be able to read what it says."

"Okay, okay," Ari said, bringing the linen closer to him. "But I'm going to need a minute to decipher it completely. My Ancient Egyptian is...rusty."

Owen mimicked Ari as they left him in silence to read the text. Alex followed Chloe to the trunks full of food, grabbing some dried meat and unsalted flatbread, since they were too lazy to cook a full meal.

A half-hour passed, some of them lounging by the fireplace, grabbing small snacks, or retiring to a bedroom for some much-needed privacy. Ari remained at the couches, working his way through the text and conversing with Penélope, who nodded her head and pointed to a specific hieroglyph here and there.

Alex was dozing off by the fire when Penélope called out to them. "We're done!"

They all staggered to their feet from around the house and returned to the couches, where Penélope excitedly held out the linen.

"Ari figured it out!" she said, nudging Ari's shoulder. "Right?"

"As best I could," Ari said, sounding somewhat embarrassed. He waited for everyone to settle around the couches. "The text begins with a spell for entering the Underworld."

"Can you translate it?" Zeb asked, trying to peer over Ari's shoulder. Alex swore she caught Owen shooting Ari a jealous glance.

"It begins with this hieroglyph, supposedly addressing the god who guards the entrance to the Underworld," Ari said. He motioned toward a section of the hieroglyphs etched with black ink in vertical, lined columns. "I'll try my best to translate it fluidly."

"O you who make to enter souls perfected in the house of Osiris may you make to enter the soul perfect of Osiris, victorious." Here Ari paused, motioning towards the blank space in the column. "The blank spaces are usually where the deceased's name would be. ...*with you into the house of Osiris. May he hear as you hear; may he see as you see; may he stand as you stand; may he sit as you sit. O givers of cakes and beer to souls perfected in the house of Osiris, give you cakes and beer at the double season of Osiris, victorious. Before the gods all of Abydos,*

victorious with you.

"O openers of the way and openers of the roads to souls perfected in the house of Osiris, open therefore you to him the way, open therefore you the roads to the soul of Osiris the scribe and accountant of divine offerings of gods all, triumphant with you. May he go in with confidence, may he come forth in peace from the house of Osiris. Not may he be repulsed, not may he be turned back, may he go in as he please, may he come forth as he desires, may he be victorious. May be done his commands in the house of Osiris, may he walk, may he speak with you, may he be a glorified soul with you. Not has been found his defect there. The scales have been emptied of his trial."

After a long moment of silence, Warren spoke. "Where do we say the spell?"

"At the entrance of the Underworld." Ari hesitated. "And the instructions clearly state that only tombs can be entrances."

"The Necropolis," Zeb said, his voice grim.

"Let me guess," Owen drawled, "we have to be buried alive."

Ari cut him an irritated look. "Not necessarily. It says that you must spill blood on the tomb and say the correct spell and the doorway to the Underworld will open. It says nothing about being buried alive, though they assume the one reading the instructions is already...deceased."

"That part sounds easy enough," Alex said hesitantly. "But what happens next?"

"That's when things get...complicated," Ari said, sharing a look with Penélope, who bit her lip. "Once we enter the Underworld, it says to find the river of Forgetfulness and drink from it. I'm assuming that's like the River Lethe in Greek mythology. Only then will you be able to speak with the dead."

"Why is that complicated?" Warren asked, raising a brow.

Ari and Penélope shared one of those uneasy looks again.

"Oh no," Owen said with real dread. "You're not thinking of the monsters at the gates, are you? Because that's not going to be good."

Penélope nodded her head. "In Ancient Egyptian mythology at least, the journey into the Underworld is a difficult one. There are seven gates you must pass through. At each gate, there is a monster that must be pacified with a spell. But the only problem is that this text doesn't mention those monsters or any spells to ward them off."

Alex nearly winced at the thought. "Let's assume we all make it to the river and there are no monsters. What do we do then?"

"Not *we*," Ari said quietly. "Since *you* are the one who is going to speak with one of the dead, you have to drink from the river. But to speak with someone specific means you have to bring an object with you that means something to them."

"What about bringing them back to life?" Alex asked, her voice tight in her throat.

Penélope shook her head. "It doesn't say anything about that. Besides, by that point...we'll technically be dead too. But if you can speak with your mother, maybe she can tell you how to bring her back."

Alex nodded, taking a deep breath to calm the knots in her stomach that had instantly formed at the thought of speaking with her mother. Even though everything she had sacrificed, every decision she had made since that day she took off in her car, had led up to this moment, Alex still couldn't fathom the idea of *seeing* her mother ever again, let alone speaking with her. It was as though her mother was a ghost she kept chasing, but one that she was never supposed to catch up with.

"And then?" Alex forced herself to ask. "How we do return? How do we make it out alive?"

"You have to drink from the Lake of Memory," Penélope said when Ari did not speak. "That way you retain the memories of your life and can return to the world of the living. From there, I guess we retrace our steps back the way we came."

"And what happens if we don't make it?" Zeb asked darkly.

This time Ari spoke, his voice hardly a whisper. "We die."

70

Without the Queen's help, the next few days consisted of hashing out a plan. The first step was escaping the city and making it to Necropolis Island. But there was just one problem. While the first time the Queen had provided them with the small rowboat in the harbor, this time they would have to steal one themselves.

Once they were on the island, it was only a matter of finding a gravestone and performing the spell. Alex didn't know which part she dreaded the most, stealing a boat without getting caught or trying to find a doorway to Hell.

"How are you feeling?"

Alex turned, the hands that were adjusting the hood of her cloak falling to her sides. They would be leaving within the hour while it was still dark. Ari stood in the doorway of the bedroom she shared with Penélope and Chloe, who were busy in the living room with Zeb packing provisions and getting ready for the journey. Owen and Warren were still out scouting the harbor one last time to decide which boat they should steal.

"I'm good," Alex said. Ari raised a brow and walked inside the room with a leisurely step, making it hard to think. "Nervous, too. And terrified. I can't believe we're doing this. I never even believed in Hell before this."

Ari searched her face intently. "What about finding your mother?"

Alex shrugged. Her mind was so, so far away from her mother right now. "I try not to think about it."

He nodded slowly. "And...what about us?"

She nearly choked. "Us?"

"You know," Ari said, his voice lowering with an undeniable taunt, "when you kissed me."

"When *I* kissed *you?*" Alex asked, unable to help a slight smirk when Ari frowned. "Are you sure that's what happened?"

Ari narrowed his eyes at her. "Don't deny it, Alexandria."

Before Alex could come up with a witty reply, she saw a head of blonde hair pass by and her stomach dropped. Then she saw it was just Zeb walking back to his room, his eyes firmly fixed on the ground. Alex let out a breath, but she couldn't shake the feeling of being caught red-handed.

Alex cleared her throat and moved past Ari. "We should help the others pack up."

She almost reached the doorway when a hand caught her wrist, pulling her back towards him and into his arms. Instead of protesting, as she half-wanted to do, her arms automatically wound around his neck and her fingers found the soft curls of his hair that she loved, right as he leaned down and kissed her.

Suddenly nothing else mattered, their looming departure and descent into Hell falling away like waves breaking against the prow of a ship. His mouth moved slowly on hers, the pace dizzying, as if she were slipping out of reality. She ran her hands down the strong slope of his back, a reckless passion taking hold of her, made all the more tantalizing by the possibility of getting caught.

They were kissing passionately now, Ari's hands clenching the fabric of her dress, and Alex wondered distantly if she should close the door in case this escalated further. Ari pulled her close with a new strength as if he were thinking the same, until she felt all of him beneath her, the sharp hips, the hard rope of his belt, and under that, nudging the soft curve of her belly—

Alex leaned back, out of breath. Ari's hands clenched around her waist, digging into the skin as though afraid she would let go, keeping them close together. His eyes were shut, and he didn't open them, his dark lashes trembling against the blushing curves of his cheeks.

She shifted against him so that he bit his lip. "Ari, Ari, Ari..."

Then she let him go and turned away, slipping out of his arms. She nearly didn't hear his voice, a rough whisper in the dark, enough to make her face hot as she turned quickly down the hall as though fleeing from the scene of a crime.

But the words repeated in her head long after she had left. "You'll be the death of me, Alexandria..."

Alex ignored the quick beat of her heart as she walked into the living room where Penélope and Chloe were filling Owen's backpack with carefully wrapped provisions.

Chloe looked up at her, studying her face for a moment before her mouth fell open. "Oh my god."

Penélope glanced at her, then almost smiled.

Alex fought a blush. "What?"

"Oh my god," Chloe said again. "Did you two just have sex?"

"Be quiet, Chloe!" Alex whispered urgently. "And no, of course we didn't."

Even Penélope raised a disbelieving brow, while Chloe crossed her arms.

Alex rolled her eyes. "Fine, we kissed. Again."

"Again?" Chloe demanded. "Did you kiss him since the first time?"

"We kissed at the Academy when we almost got caught," Alex said, then quickly added, "but it's nothing. Warren and I just broke up. This is a nice distraction. But there are more important things to worry about."

"Right," Chloe said slowly. "Whatever you say. But you should fix your hair. You're a mess."

As Alex hurriedly adjusted her hair beneath her cloak, Penélope sighed. "If only I could meet someone who would fall in love with me and we could get married and live happily ever after."

"Be careful what you wish for," Chloe muttered, earning her a glare from Penélope.

"You want love just as much as I do, Chloe," Penélope said, lifting her chin haughtily as Chloe usually did. "You're just too proud to admit it."

Instead of denying it, as Alex expected, Chloe laughed and patted Penélope's arm affectionately. "Maybe. But Alex is right. There are more important things to worry about, like the fact that we are literally going to Hell."

"Who's going to Hell?"

They all turned. Owen had appeared at the top of the steps, a silent Warren in tow, though he had a small smile on his face, probably from one of Owen's jokes.

"You are," Chloe replied immediately, earning stifled laughs from Alex and Penélope, "in this life *and* the next."

"Oh is that so?" Owen asked, before noticing Alex and Penélope sharing an amused glance. "What are you two snickering about?"

"Nothing," Alex said quickly, unable to stop a smile. "Nothing at all."

"Did you hear that, Warren?" Owen asked, glancing back at Warren, who looked at Alex keenly before walking towards the fireplace, causing her smile to fade. *"The lady doth protest too much, methinks."*

"You two were late," Chloe drawled, placing a hand on her hip. "Can we talk about that?"

Owen ignored her. "Where's Zeb? And Ari?"

Alex felt her face heat up despite herself, and Penélope and Chloe shared the briefest glance. Warren continued to poke at the logs in the hearth, the silence nearly stifling. They were saved from answering by a voice across the room.

"You're back."

Ari entered the room. Alex refused to look at him, in case laying eyes on him caused her to give them away completely. Instead, she joined Penélope and Chloe, helping them to fill up the rest of their bags.

"How did the scouting go?" Ari asked. "Did you secure the boat?"

"Well, about that..." Owen began with a grimace.

"Oh no. What happened this time?" It was Zeb, sauntering into the room.

Alex swore she saw Owen stiffen ever so slightly at his voice. Chloe did not notice, so Alex knew she had not figured them out yet. Her heart ached for her, since Chloe had always loved Owen much more than she let on, despite Owen's clear rejection of her. This would only be the salt rubbed into the wound.

"We found a boat," Owen said defensively, narrowing his green eyes at Zeb. "But it might be...trickier to steal than we anticipated."

"What Owen is trying to say," Warren said, standing up from his crouched position by the fireplace, "is that the boats are heavily guarded at all times.

Someone must've seen us coming back on the rowboat and warned the King."

"How are we going to steal it now?" Penélope asked worriedly.

"We're going to have to run," Owen answered with a smirk, as if that were any explanation, ignoring the pointed looks his way.

"There's a guard change," Warren said. "Every hour and a half. While one squadron marches into formation and leaves, the other arrives. Owen and I counted exactly a minute and twelve seconds before the change was completed. That gives us a small window to steal a boat before the next squadron blocks off access to the docks. Hopefully, they are too surprised and unprepared to chase after us."

"But doesn't that mean there will be *double* the guards on site?" Chloe asked sharply. "Why can't some of us cause a distraction while the others steal the boat?"

Warren shook his head. "There are too many guards. They line the docks from end to end. Even if we caused a big enough distraction, not enough guards would be deployed fast enough to clear the harbor, and then we'd have to fight our way to the boats from two different directions. This is the only chance we have for all of us to get on a boat and row away before the guards can stop us."

There was silence. The plan was convincing, but there were so many things that could go wrong in a window of seventy-two seconds. But no one was going to come up with a better plan any time soon.

"I think we should do it," Alex said firmly. "It's either that or give up on our plan entirely."

"I agree," Ari said, and Warren glanced at him suspiciously. "We'll be in the boat and on the water before they know what's happening."

Zeb sighed. "I'll do it. But if something goes wrong..."

"It won't," Owen interrupted, his face oddly serious. "I promise."

Penélope nodded. "Then let's do it."

"I don't like boats," Chloe said, "but I trust Owen and Warren. If they know anything, it's how to get on the water."

"Never thought I'd see the day," Owen murmured in false shock. "Was that an actual compliment from Chloe Zhang?"

Chloe glared at him. "Keep talking and it will be the last you ever hear."

"So..." Zeb said loudly. "When do we leave?"

71

Alex lowered the hood of her cloak over her face as they crept down the alleyway. A cold wind off the harbor tunneled between the buildings on either side of them, chilling Alex's skin beneath her clothes.

Up ahead Warren lifted a fist in the air, signaling them to come to a stop. Alex huddled with Penélope and Chloe against the wall.

The plan was simple but dangerous. Since the docks on the North Quarter were reserved for royalty and luxury goods and thus more heavily guarded, they had to cross Priam Boulevard in front of the Gate of the Moon to the other side of the docks, where fishing boats and merchant ships were allowed to unload. They only had a small window to cross the wide boulevard and secure a boat as the guards changed shifts.

From Alex's place in the alley, she could just glimpse a shaded park and the public walkway that she and Ari had walked along on their first visit to the city. At night, citizens were no longer allowed to stroll among the fruit trees or linger near the harbor. The only people out at this hour were soldiers lining the perimeter of the docks, their stiff backs facing the waves rolling like black hills under the moonlight.

Beside her, Penélope gripped the handle of her gold sword until her knuckles grew white. They had found a few old swords in leather sheaths stored at the safe house, so Penélope had strapped one of the sheaths that fit her sword around her waist. The sword itself was surprisingly heavy, as though it were truly solid gold through and through, and its edge was sharp enough to cut with hardly any pressure applied.

Chloe jostled Alex's shoulder. Warren had once again put up his hand, this time with all five fingers splayed, his face leaning a sliver over the edge. This meant they had five seconds to go until the squadron at attention began to make their formation. Alex breathed in, then out, unsuccessfully calming her nerves.

Warren lowered a finger, leaving four. Then three. Two. Alex tightened her hands on the straps of her backpack. One.

He made a fist. Alex nearly sprinted forward, but stopped herself, her shoes scraping the stone street. All of them held their breath, and then Warren flattened himself against the wall and the rest of them did the same. The sound of boots slamming on the ground echoed across the pavement, followed by the first row of soldiers marching in unison down Priam Boulevard.

Once the last row of the squadron was visible marching with their backs turned towards them, Warren pointed a finger in the direction of the docks. They all ran.

Alex clutched the straps of her backpack as they sprinted across the boulevard, past the shining Gate of the Moon towering at the end of the street, and straight toward the docks. Farther down the public walk Alex could glimpse the other squadron marching to replace the one leaving.

Suddenly there were shouts. The soldiers had spotted them, but they still had much ground to cover if they were going to catch them. Soon the other soldiers would be alerted by the commotion and in seconds they would be surrounded.

Ari was already in the boat, helping Chloe, Zeb, Penélope, and then Alex inside while Owen and Warren worked on unraveling the cables that tied down the rowboat to the docks. They were almost free.

Alex could see the soldiers closing in behind them. She held her breath as Warren and Owen pushed the boat together and jumped from the dock, a soldier's outreached hand a hair's breadth away from Owen's arm as he landed on the planks.

The boat floated away from the docks, but no one celebrated, everyone grabbing an oar and rowing furiously, including the girls. They knew the chase would not end there, and sure enough, the soldiers piled into other rowboats tied to the same dock and rowed after them in terrifying unison, shouting orders at each other.

"Faster!" Chloe shouted as one of the rowboats inched closer.

Alex's arms burned with the effort, her oar splashing into the water, the current seeming to strain against them. They passed the Gate of the Moon and flew past the Royal docks, where there were no soldiers to stop them thanks to the squadron change.

Their boat passed precariously close to the jutting rock of a Sphinx head, but soon they rowed clean out into the Port of Pirates. Alex glanced back, and to her surprise, the soldiers' boats had slowed to a stop before the Path of Sphinxes, a few of them standing tall and arguing with each other.

"They must not be allowed into the Port of Pirates," Ari said quietly, the arms in his chest tensing with each stroke of his oar.

"Who cares," Owen said, slightly out of breath. "We made it."

Their boat landed on the shore of the Necropolis Island a few minutes later. The boys all jumped down into the shallow waves to haul the boat on the sand until they couldn't pull it anymore.

Ari stood by the side of the boat and gave his hand to each of the girls as they climbed out and onto the shore. Alex saw the tall tombs ahead and nearly shivered. The Necropolis seemed an abandoned city, the tombs rising like houses, the paintings on their walls faded from weather and neglect. Many were carved with faces of the deceased, along with the name of the family and other decorations. The silence was deafening, and even the waves lapped eerily quiet on the shore.

Alex stepped forward to guide them into the city when a shadow up ahead caught her eye. A moment later, hooded figures were leaping out behind trees and large rocks by the shore. Penélope screamed, and others shouted. Alex tried to run back to the boat but strong hands grasped her arms and something rough and smelling of damp covered her head in darkness.

"Chloe!" she cried out. "Warren! Penélope!"

"Alex!" It was Chloe, but her voice sounded muffled.

There were other voices too, deep, guttural voices who jeered and laughed. She could hear sobs and cries around her, and thought she heard Penélope calling out her name. The hands on her arms shoved her forward and forced her to walk, though she could not see where she was going.

"Owen!" she called, tears sliding down her face. "Ari! Zeb!"

"I'm here!" Zeb cried, his voice hoarse. He sounded as though he was somewhere behind her. "They're pirates!"

"No shit, Sherlock!" It was Owen's voice, from somewhere close by, followed by a grunt as if he were in a tousle.

"Don't fight them!" This time it was Ari's voice, near where Alex had heard Owen. His voice was terse. "They might kill you if you do."

This silenced them. Her next step landed on a rocking surface, and the strong hands on her arms forced her to sit down on what felt like a wooden plank of a boat.

Alex blinked away the tears as they were rowed onto the water, the sound of oars splashing around them. As the boat sailed away from the shore, the sounds of creaking wood and wind whipping against large sails grew louder.

There were more orders shouted around them, some from far away, and she heard ropes straining and their boat knocking against something, the sound of water dripping below. They must be boarding a ship.

Once again she was forced to her feet. The hands shoved her forward, then she stepped—into thin air. She fell and landed painfully on her knees upon a slippery wooden surface, her kneecaps aching from the impact. Hands grabbed her arms again and lifted her, shoving her forward.

They walked for a few paces and then suddenly came to a stop. The grip on her arms yanked her hands behind her back. She felt something cold and hard encircle her wrists and heard the jangle of keys.

Alex tried to move, but her wrists caught on stinging metal, followed by the rattle of chains.

They were prisoners.

72

Before she could call out to her friends, the sack over her head was lifted in one swift motion, leaving her squinting into the bright flame of a lamp. She blinked, then saw the face behind the lamp and nearly screamed.

A scarred, one-eyed man with rotting teeth and yellow nails sneered at her. "'Εκείνη καλός ἄνθος ἐστι!"

She heard others laugh. Her face burned despite not understanding what he had said. His roaming eyes and sly smile said enough.

Alex glanced around. She was chained to the large mast at the center of a strange-looking ship. On either side of her was Penélope and Chloe, the sacks on their heads lifted one by one. She heard Ari speak in a low voice beside Chloe, followed by Owen and Zeb arguing behind her.

"What are they saying, Ari?" Alex asked, her voice trembling. "What did he say about me?"

"Nothing important," Ari said in a tight voice.

"Tell them to let us go!" Owen said furiously. "Tell them I have money! Gold! Lots of gold! I can pay our ransom!"

Ari shouted a translation, followed by another bout of laughter from the pirates. One of them stalked toward Owen, pointing a long-nailed finger. Alex saw that his right leg was gone from the knee down, replaced by a wooden peg. He growled something and spat on the ground.

"He said they don't need gold," Ari translated quietly.

Although she had heard of pirates and seen many renditions of their ragged, sea-worn appearances, nothing had prepared Alex for the grime and reek, the scars and ugly mutilations, and those crazed, reckless eyes, as though life at sea had chipped away both their body and sanity.

Alex craned her neck, trying to count how many pirates there were on deck and sitting at the benches beside long oars, but she stopped counting once she got to twenty-five. There was no point. Even if they did manage to break free of their bonds, they could hardly expect to fight off so many men at once. Besides, the ship had long drawn up her anchor and was sailing swiftly away from the island, the wind and the force of fifteen oars on either side carrying them across the water.

"Just tell them not to hand us over to the King," Penélope said frantically. "We'll give double what the King offers."

Ari translated this quickly. This elicited an even greater roar from the crew, and the peg-legged pirate laughed before replying in his guttural voice.

"He says they don't work for the King," Ari said slowly. "They're pirates, not...prissy merchants."

Chloe shook uselessly at her bonds. "What? That doesn't make sense. The King allied with the pirates. The Queen told us that."

When Ari translated this, the pirate answered him with a smirk, and they exchanged a few more words. They all waited impatiently for Ari's translation.

"For now the King turns a blind eye to their operations," Ari said, pausing when the pirate added something else. "They wouldn't turn his protection down, but they do not serve the King."

"Who do they serve then?" Owen asked dryly. Ari translated.

The pirate whispered, but Alex could hear the word echo in the sudden silence from the crew. "Ο πλάνης."

Ari hesitated. "The Wanderer."

"Who?" Chloe asked, exasperated.

This time the pirate seemed to understand her, limping towards her with a malicious grin of yellow and silver teeth. He spoke with a clear reverence and threw his hands out as though he could embrace the endless seas.

"He's their captain," Ari said. "The most dangerous man to sail these waters."

"That clears it up," Zeb muttered.

The pirate narrowed his eyes at Zeb as though he could hear the insult in his voice, but instead of berating him, he suddenly stood up straight, his hands behind his back and his face staring straight ahead. He shouted a word and the rest of the crew did the same, going very still.

Footsteps followed on cue, heavy and sure. Alex turned her head toward the back of the ship.

A tall, bearded man walked down a narrow wooden staircase from the raised deck. He had a broad chest and towered over the crew in height and authority. When his gaze swept over them, Alex was surprised to see a pair of gentle brown eyes in a youthful face, though grim and hardened. His dark, curling beard was the same length as his hair, which fell around his shoulders in dark, messy locks, making him appear older. He was almost handsome, though a single red scar ran across his face, over the bridge of his hooked nose, and through both his lips, so that they appeared slightly mismatched.

He paused before the mast, then walked around it slowly, eyeing each of them in turn. Up close he seemed even larger, the leather of his vest stretching tightly around his muscular chest, the angular cut of his biceps visible even through the thin, brown tunic he wore underneath, the hem falling just above thick, strong thighs, another scar running white down the knee and slicing past the shin.

Then he spoke, and his voice was deep, a voice accustomed to giving orders and being obeyed, though Alex thought she heard a hint of weariness. "Tί πρᾶγμα ἒν τῇ Νεκροπόλει?"

"He's asking what our business is in the Necropolis," Ari translated.

At this, the captain looked at him sharply, and after a long moment pondering said in a thick accent, "You speak a foreign tongue I have not heard in many years, stranger."

"You understand us?" Alex asked incredulously. She nearly flinched when the captain's gaze landed on her, his perceptive glance sweeping over her cloak and down to her shoes with a curious, detached look.

"I have traveled to many distant lands," the captain said in his thick, lilting accent that immediately sounded familiar. Alex realized it was like Mother and the Queen's accents, somewhere between a fluid Spanish accent and a halting Arabic one. "I have seen many cities and met many people."

"You must let us go," Alex said firmly. "We are traveling to the Underworld."

His face turned dark and thunderous, an unhidden fear lurking in his eyes. "What business do you have there other than death?"

Alex was suddenly afraid that if he knew the truth, he would somehow prevent them. "We cannot tell you. How do we know you won't report us to the King?"

"The King?" he spat. "He is no king of mine. He is an imposter. Only a fool would bow to that wily snake."

"Then why do you work with him?" Owen asked suspiciously.

A slow smile spread across his face, the scar slicing his lips turning white. "Better a good enemy than a bad friend." Then he straightened up and continued walking around the mast, eyeing them keenly. "But I know who you are. Oh yes, I have eyes and ears in many places, and there are those in the city still loyal to me. They told me of a band of criminals who the King was hunting down. I am sure he would pay a pretty price to see you all in his prison cells."

"No!" Owen growled. "I can pay you three times the gold the King can give you."

The Captain waved him away with a large, scarred hand fitted in leather straps, glinting metal on the knuckles. "I do not need or desire your money, stranger. I am only interested in information. I want to know why the King is hunting you down. You must all be very important people if that is the case." He looked Chloe up and down, placing a fingertip beneath her chin and peering into her face. "Are you royalty from another kingdom?"

"We come from a land that has no royalty," Zeb said quickly.

"Speak for yourselves," Owen retorted. "I am descended from noblemen!"

Chloe yanked her chin from the captain's grasp, glaring at Owen though he wasn't in her line of sight. "Oh, and that makes the rest of us what? Peasants?"

The captain backed away, eyeing Owen and then Chloe with some hesitation. "I wish to have no trouble with your people. I only wish to know why the King would have such an interest in children."

"Children?" Owen repeated incredulously. "You can't be much older than us."

"Perhaps," he said, stroking his long beard, "but I am old at heart. Troubles weary the spirit and turn a youthful hope into the despair of the aged."

Owen huffed disbelievingly. Alex turned to Penélope to see her reaction, but she was merely staring at the captain with a mixture of surprise and curiosity.

At the sudden silence, the crew members began to shout, no doubt wanting to know what all the talk was about. The captain settled them with a hand and a few calm words in Greek. He then grasped the handle of a small sword Alex had not noticed hanging on his leather belt and withdrew the blade, which gleamed sharp in the dim light of the lamps. The captain swung the blade around until the end pointed at where she guessed was Ari's chest.

"No!" Alex cried out before she could think. "This has nothing to do with my friends!"

"Alex, stop," Warren said fiercely as the captain pointed the blade at her.

Alex ignored him. "It's true! I'm the one the King wants! This has nothing to do with them. Don't hurt them!"

"What do you mean this has nothing to do with us?" Owen asked angrily, yanking at his handcuffs. "Aren't we in chains like you?"

Alex wished she could glare at him properly. "You know what I mean. You shouldn't die for something that doesn't involve you."

"A bit too late for that, isn't it?" Zeb sneered.

"Yeah, you don't get to decide that for us," Chloe added angrily.

The captain swung the blade around and pointed it again at Ari. They all fell silent. "What are they squabbling about?"

"It is not my place to say."

"Coward," Warren hissed.

"It's the truth," Ari replied, keeping his voice even.

"You'll get her killed!" Warren shouted, struggling in vain against his bonds until the peg-legged pirate stalked over to him and pushed him, rattling the mast and forcing Warren into silence.

"This is her mother, not mine," Ari continued. "She can speak for herself."

The captain walked around the mast back towards Alex, the tip of his sword pointing directly at her. He stopped when the blade was an inch from her chest. She imagined the blade sinking in, the blossoming pain, and then the darkness that would follow. Would she see her mother on the other side? Or would she face the emptiness of eternity alone forever?

"You," the captain said, looking at her carefully. "Who are you?"

She ignored the racing of her heart and the nausea that rose in her stomach at the sight of the blade so close to her chest. "I am Alexandria. That man pretending to be king got my mother killed. Now I'm trying to bring her back."

"Bring her back?" the captain repeated slowly, as though the words were foreign to him. "That is impossible."

"Impossible for some," Alex said, "but not for those who know the way."

The captain looked troubled at this. "Why did that man wish to kill your mother?"

Alex knew she would have to tell the truth or risk her death and the death of her friends. This was the only chance they had to convince the pirates to spare their lives if they would not grant them freedom. Alex recalled the words of Mother on the night they heard the prophecy, which felt like years ago instead of mere days. "She was searching for the Emerald Stone. She wanted to restore Gaia to her rightful place as Queen of the Gods."

There was a long, terrible silence, before the captain fell to his knees, bowing his head before her and sheathing his sword. "I did not realize you were of the Old Faith."

Alex looked at him incredulously, her head spinning from the sudden change in demeanor. "The Old Faith?"

The captain looked up. "There are few who still believe, but my family descends from a long line of those who practice the Old Faith. In absolute secrecy, we have worshiped Gaia, Mother and Creator of All Things Living and Dead, Queen of Gods and Mortals."

She felt his words sweep through her like a premonition. "My mother believed in the Old Faith. She died for the cause. I plan to bring her back so that she can finish what she started and restore the old order as it was foretold in the prophecy."

"I apologize, my lady," the captain said reverently, bowing his head once more before standing up. "I did not know." He looked around and called to his men. "Ἄνδρες! Λύετε ἐκείνην!"

The first pirate she had seen hobbled forward with a key and quickly unlocked her handcuffs, staring at her strangely with the single eye he had left. But he did not question his captain's orders, and Alex stepped away from the mast, rolling her aching wrists.

"Hey, what about us?" Penélope asked the captain loudly, who was now speaking in a low voice to the peg-legged pirate, rattling her chains to catch his attention. "You can't just leave us here!"

The captain seemed to look at Penélope as if he had not noticed her before, dragging his gaze up and down her blue dress with a raised brow. "That is no way for a woman to speak to a man who has her in chains."

Alex stared at him in shock, and Penélope's mouth fell open. The others were looking at the captain in mingling fear and anger.

"But it's right for a *man* to put an innocent woman in chains?" Penélope shot back indignantly. "Or do you plan on treating me as any common barbarian would?"

"Penélope, be quiet," Zeb whispered.

But the captain was staring at Penélope, unmoving. Alex was surprised to see a flush creep up his neck. When it did not appear that he was going to speak, Alex sighed and stepped forward, dragging his attention away.

"Please, captain," Alex said quietly. "They have helped me all this way. I can't do this alone."

After a moment's pause, the captain grudgingly nodded. "Very well."

With a single motion of his hand, a few men came towards them and unlocked the rest of their handcuffs, releasing them from the mast. Penélope rushed forward and hugged Alex, then Zeb, and soon all of them were hugging each other and laughing in relief.

"Where shall I bring you, Alexandria?" the captain asked, watching them with an odd look in his eyes that Alex realized belatedly was jealousy.

Alex smiled grimly. "The Necropolis Island. We're going to the Underworld."

73

ALEX LEANED OVER THE side of the ship, wind and water spraying into her face as the oars propelled them across the ocean. She closed her eyes and breathed in the smell of salt and the sharp burning of the oil lamps on board.

The wood of the deck creaked with footsteps.

"My lady." The captain stood beside her, resting his arms on the same wooden plank. "What do you ponder with so solemn a face?"

"My mother," Alex said in surprise, a small smile at his proper English speech. She glanced sidelong at the tall, bearded man beside her, the stark contrast between his harsh silhouette and those kind, brown eyes, the graceful way he carried his strong, weather-worn stature. "You know, you're a very strange pirate."

The captain glanced at her, amused. "And you are a very strange woman, Alexandria."

"You never told us your name."

His face grew solemn. "Like you, I hold many sorrows in my heart. Long ago my name became a reminder of what I left behind."

Alex shook her head. "I left behind a lot when I came here. Never thought I would be kidnapped by pirates when I did."

"You must be prepared to see many things when you lift the anchor of your ship and sail away from home," the captain said gravely. "I was around your age when my father left, never to return. I have been searching for him ever since, while my mother waits at home, growing older and more weary with each year that passes. But sometimes those who are lost do not wish to be found, and those who wander seek only that which they cannot find in themselves."

"Sometimes I wonder if I even want to find my mother," Alex said, her voice hardly more than a whisper. "Sometimes I think I just want to escape who I am becoming."

"Ah." The captain grinned ruefully. "Then you are a wanderer like me."

She began to smile when a loud call tore her attention away. The crew moved swiftly into their positions, the first mate calling out orders. On the horizon she could see the Necropolis Island rapidly approaching, the familiar skyline of the city behind it, where the Gate of the Moon stood proudly at the center of the docks like the prow of a ship.

"We have arrived," the captain said. He glanced back at Alex's friends, who had begun gathering their belongings. "There is one more thing I must attend to before my duties." He paused. "Has the lady a suitor?"

"What?" Alex stared at him, but the captain's face was serious and unsmiling.

"A suitor," he repeated, then nodded his head towards Penélope. "Has the lady a suitor?"

Alex couldn't help but laugh, which she realized rather offended the captain, and the laughter quickly died on her lips. "Well, no. She doesn't have a *suitor*."

With a short bow of his head, the captain took his leave and stalked across the deck, disappearing inside a wooden door below the raised deck to his captain's cabin. Alex sighed at the strange proceedings and rejoined her friends in the center of the deck. She met Ari's eye, and he gave her an imperceptible nod. Chloe and Penélope were debating something while Zeb stood a few feet away from Owen in silence, who was talking animatedly to Warren about the ship.

Soon they anchored off the island's shore and the crew prepared the small rowboats attached to the side of the ship in which they had initially been brought up. Alex's knees throbbed with the memory of falling on the deck. She was grateful that at least she would be able to see this time.

The first mate—the pirate with the wooden leg—ushered them towards the rowboats. Chloe volunteered first, eager to be off the ship and back on dry land. But before she could climb into the boat, the captain reemerged from his cabin, his hands behind his back and his face flushed above his beard.

"Halt!" he said loudly. They all paused and turned to him in surprise. "There is something I must declare before you go."

Chloe groaned. "What could it be this time?"

The captain ignored her, coming to a stop before Penélope, who looked up at him in alarm. "I must ask for your name, my fair lady."

Penélope blinked. "Penélope."

"Πηνελόπη," the captain repeated in Greek, nodding his head. Then he looked her firmly in the eyes and began a soft, rehearsed speech. "Κάλλιστα παρθένος εἶ ἣν ποτέ βέβλεφα. Ἠράσθην σε ἀπό τοῦ πρώτου καιροῦ εἰς σε εἶδον. Ἐρᾷς καί με?"

Before Ari could translate, the captain moved his arm. Alex realized only after Penélope caught it that he had thrown something. They all stared in astonishment at the red, round apple cradled in Penélope's hands.

"Oh, Penélope," Ari said with a growing smile. "I think he's in love."

Penélope looked aghast. "What?"

"The tradition comes from the myth of the Judgment of Paris," Ari explained. "The goddesses Hera, Athena, and Aphrodite are fighting over a golden apple meant only for the most beautiful. Zeus appoints Paris as judge, and the three goddesses attempt to bribe Paris into choosing them. Hera offers him kingship, Athena fame and glory in battle, and Aphrodite the most beautiful woman on earth...Helen of Sparta."

They all looked at Alex, recalling the similarities between Elena and her lover Alexandros with the myth of Helen and Paris. She wondered if it had been mere chance that they were captured by these pirates, or if they were meant to meet this strange captain all along.

"In the end," Ari continued, "Paris chose Aphrodite. From this story arose a tradition that to seduce a woman, a man would throw an apple at her. And if she caught it..." he trailed off, looking in unconcealed amusement at the captain's beaming face, to the growing horror of Penélope. "It meant she accepted his advances."

Penélope made a noise of protest and threw the apple back at the captain, who caught it with some confusion. "I do not accept anything! We just met. You can't fall in love with someone you don't even know!"

The captain's face was grave. "I knew the moment I laid eyes on you."

She stared at him in silence. The words had been spoken with such sincerity it was hard not to believe him. Penélope glanced around at them as if she were asking for their help.

"I thought this was what you wanted," Chloe said dryly, though her words sounded more serious in the quiet as the captain waited for an answer.

Penélope's eyes were wide as she looked at the captain. "I-I can't. I'm sorry."

At first, the captain's face fell, as though he had waited years for her answer only to be utterly disappointed. Then he bowed his head, a grim look on his face. "Then I will keep your name in my heart like an oath and never seek the arms of another woman unless that woman is you."

Penélope looked mortified now. Owen choked on a laugh, and Zeb stared at the captain as though he had proposed in marriage, which Alex was not sure he hadn't. The others were shaking their heads in disbelief. But out of the corner of her eyes, Alex saw Ari's gaze flicker over to her before settling firmly on the ground.

"Well," Chloe said loudly, "you're going to have to wait a long time. We have things to do and we don't have all night."

With that, Chloe hopped over the side of the ship and into the rowboat. Warren, Owen, and Zeb were the next to join her. The first mate followed after them. They were lowered into the water, their heads disappearing below the hull, though Alex thought she could still hear Chloe complaining, her voice swallowed by the crash of the waves.

Alex began to walk away, followed by Ari, but Penélope remained where she was, staring at the captain helplessly. She fumbled a curtsy, her cheeks red before she turned on her heel and ran after them.

They piled into the other boat, joined by the first pirate Alex had seen, though by now his single eye and gnarled face had become oddly comforting to her. After the captain had explained who they were, the crew had begun to look at them with respect, treating them as guests instead of prisoners. Now they were dutifully lowered onto the water and rowed to the island without a single nasty comment or glare.

Once they were back on the shore, they took one last look at the ship, its curved prow painted with a large eye staring back at them, where Alex could just glimpse the tall, broad figure of the captain gazing out across the water, before he turned and disappeared among the crew.

"Can you believe that guy?" Owen asked with a snort of laughter. "Falling in love at first sight? Who does he think he is? Romeo?"

"It's not a crime to fall in love," Zeb shot back, glaring at him before slinging an arm around Penélope, who still had not spoken a word since leaving the ship. She appeared completely absorbed in her thoughts and had not taken heed of Owen's jest.

Owen stared at Zeb with a strange look, then shook his head. "Maybe, but kidnapping us and *then* declaring his love definitely must be."

"Let's focus," Ari interrupted. He looked up the hill at the rising graves. "We still have a long road ahead of us."

They followed Ari up into the Necropolis in silence. Alex walked a few paces behind him, her heart quickening its beat as they approached the center of the Necropolis where they found a wide, paved road, crossed by another similar path, as though they were at the intersection of the graveyard's two main streets, a mirror to the City of Helena across the water.

"The *Book of the Dead* never specified which grave we were supposed to choose," Ari murmured, as though he were afraid to wake the dead if he spoke too loud.

"How should we choose then?" Alex asked, looking around at the names on the graves. At times, it was difficult to read the Greek letters etched into the stone, worn from rain and blackened with dirt.

Ari walked closer to one of the graves, peering at the carved figures sitting across from each other under a temple-like roof, their eyes eternally open. "I was hoping we would just...know."

They continued walking down the street slowly, the silence of the island growing heavier the deeper they tread into the City of the Dead. Alex found herself ahead of the group, reading the names above the various steles and statues. Some were carved to look like vases, others like temples housing the dead, others blank or very sparsely ornamented, the farewells of the deceased to their families inscribed forever on the stone. Σοφία, Ἀνάσσων, Κασσάνδρα, Ἰωσήφ...

She stopped before a tall structure, the largest grave they had seen yet. The grave was built like a miniature house with four walls, a flat stone roof, and two carved slabs of stone facing her that seemed like doors. But that was not the only thing that caught her eye. Every inch of the stone walls was carved with Egyptian hieroglyphs, and on the bottom of the carved doors were two painted figures standing guard. A painted niche above the door showed a familiar scene of overlapping ships, their sails forever blowing in the invisible wind. Across from them was a large fortified city, a winding river cutting through the fields before the city walls.

Above this scene were large, carefully inscribed letters that she could clearly see despite how high they had been written. She read the name and her stomach dropped.

Ἀλέξανδρος Φιλοξενίδης

Alexandros Philoxenides

"Ari," she whispered, her throat constricting. She forced herself to speak louder. "Ari, I think I found it."

He came to her and looked at the name on the grave, his face paling. The others joined them in silence, staring at the grave nervously. Ari brushed the stone door, his eyes glancing down at the single, square stone step built before it.

"It's a false door," Ari said in surprise. "Like the ones built inside Ancient Egyptian temples. It was believed that the dead could leave their graves through the door to receive the offerings placed on the altar stone in front of it." He turned to Alex grimly. "This must be it."

No one spoke as Penélope stepped forward and handed Ari the linen scrolls. He took them wordlessly, looking closely at the hieroglyphs.

"The first step is to spill blood on the tomb," Ari said quietly. "Then I'll say the spell and the doorway should open."

Alex knew what she had to do. She held out her hand. "Penélope. Your sword."

Penélope hesitated, then unsheathed her sword. The gold shined dully in the moonlight. "I don't want to hurt you."

"It's the only way," Alex said, her voice trembling.

She reached out and covered Penélope's hand that gripped the sword. Then she lowered the blade to her left palm, the metal kissing her skin. She slid the sword down until she felt a sting, then stepped away.

In the center of her palm, the blade had left a thin, red cut, already welling with blood. Alex met Ari's eyes, who nodded for her to continue. She placed her palm against the flat wall of the grave above the doorway, the rough stone stinging her skin where it had been cut. When her hand fell, leaving a bright red stain on the stone, Ari began to speak the spell written at the beginning of the linen, his voice a low chant of foreign syllables.

"ȧ setekeni baiu menχu em pa Ȧusȧr seteken-ten ba ȧqer en Ȧusȧr, Alexandria, maāχeru ḥenā-ten er pa Ȧusȧr setem-f ten maa-f mȧ maa-ten āḥā-f mȧ āḥā-ten ḥems-f mȧ ḥems-ten..."

As he spoke, the words fell softly at first, then louder, echoing in the silence of the tombs like a bell clanged in the dead of night. When he finished, the silence was stifling, as though Alex's ears had suddenly been stuffed with cotton—or worse, with dirt, the words alone seeming to bury them alive.

A scraping noise like a knife on stone split the silence. Alex realized the stone door of the grave had cracked around the edges and then fell backward, pushed inside the house by an invisible hand.

Where the door once stood yawned an endless darkness. She approached the doorway hesitantly and nearly gagged at the thick, hot smell that wafted out of the opening.

Alex couldn't look back, fearing that if she saw a single face, if she heard a whisper of fear or doubt, she would not walk through the door, and she would leave behind the city without ever finding her mother or fulfilling the prophecy.

She took another step forward, crouching her back to fit inside the narrow doorway. Before she took her last step into the darkness, Alex thought distantly that she did not recall hearing the stone door hit the floor.

She slipped inside the opening, her foot passing through empty air, and then she gasped silently and her stomach dropped as her body pitched forward and fell into the darkness.

74

The sickening smell of sulfur stirred Alex from a dreamless sleep. She was lying on the ground at an awkward angle, her arm tucked beneath her chest and her cheek lying on a bed of rocks.

She tried to sit up and felt the emptiness on her back. Scrambling to her feet, she looked around and saw her backpack lying a few feet away. Then it occurred to her that she was not inside the tomb at all, but in a lofty cavern, as if many miles beneath the earth. Even though the cavern was untouched by the light of the sun, the rock around her seemed to glow from within, an eerie, foggy blackish-green like sea glass.

The bed of rocks she had felt was the sloping bank of a river pouring out of a wide, ominous hole at the other end of the cavern, slithering across the black soil and disappearing into a rocky tunnel. Alex shivered, her hands rubbing her arms which she noticed were uncovered. Her cloak must have ripped off in the fall along with her bag. She hardly remembered what had happened, but when she had stepped inside the grave there had been no floor, and the next thing she knew she had been falling for a long, long time, until the darkness seemed to swallow her whole and she woke up here.

Alex looked around the cavernous space but there was not a living soul to be found. *Or dead,* she thought to herself uneasily.

"Ari?" she called out. "Chloe?"

The names bounced around the cave like stones falling down a cliff, skittering across the barren soil. She was alone.

Once we enter the Underworld, it says to find the river of Forgetfulness and drink from it...Only then will you be able to speak with the dead.

The only thing she could do was to follow the plan and hope she found her friends on the way out. Alex walked hesitantly down the slippery rocks and knelt by the river's edge. The water was murky and dark green, as though some poisonous plant thrived in this dark, cavernous world and had even stained the rocks in colors of decay.

She reached a trembling hand down and scooped a pool of water into her palm. Then before she could think too hard about the floating green bubbles and flecks of dirt swirling in the water, Alex leaned down and drank.

The moment the water passed her lips, her head exploded in clamoring voices and wails, and she saw silvery shapes of people swarming her, their hands reaching out. She screamed, backing away, but the hands passed through her, their bodies insubstantial as the wind.

Alex could not hear anything over their pitiful cries, a horrifying mixture of terror and pain, as though they were being tortured in death. Alex shut her eyes tightly so as not to see the shapes of the dead, scrambling away from the river.

Her mind felt muddled, crowded with voices, her mouth bitter with the taste of the water. That sickly smell of sulfur filled her nostrils sharply, erasing all thoughts from her mind until her stomach heaved and she gagged, spitting up the water on the shore.

"Mom..." she whispered, her gags turning into sobs. "Mom, please..."

Then she remembered. Her backpack. Her mother's diary. She heard a voice in her head, but this was unlike the others. It was familiar, though she could no longer name it, and she heard the deep voice as a distant dream, already escaping her once it passed through her mind. *But to speak with someone specific means you have to bring an object with you that means something to them.*

Alex crawled up the bank to where she had left her backpack, ignoring the hands that clawed at her body and face. With shaking fingers, she opened up the bag and pulled out the diary, her muscles aching with the effort, as if they had long forgotten how to move.

Gripping the diary in her hand, Alex inched her way back to the river, even as each second drained the life from her, and she wondered distantly if the dead were sucking her very soul from her body. She craned her neck towards the still edge of the water, hardly rippling against its rocky banks. At last her lips reached the tide and she swallowed a sliver of the icy cold water.

The voices around her instantly faded. As the clamoring shapes of people dissipated back into air, Alex felt the life returning to her limbs, her heart thumping inside her chest, and she struggled to her knees.

And there, standing beside her, was her mother.

Alex stared.

She was beautiful, just like Alex remembered, but younger than she had imagined. Her hair was long and dark, falling over one shoulder. She wore a simple white dress similar to the tunics they had made before coming to the city and her feet were bare on the rocky bank.

"Mom," Alex whispered, before she clambered to her feet and threw herself into her mother's arms—and fell on the sand, the rocks biting into the heel of her hands. She looked up. Her mother was gone.

"Alexandria."

She turned. Elena stood behind her, looking down at her with a sad smile. This time Alex understood. Her mother was no different than the apparitions that had swarmed her the first time she drank from the river.

"Mom," Alex said, her voice hoarse. "Can you hear me?"

"Alexandria, my love," Elena said, her voice smooth and steady like polished stone, not a hint of the carefree, willful girl she had read in her diary. "Why have you come here?"

Of all the questions her mother could have asked her, this was the last she expected. Alex wanted to reach out to touch her, but she knew what would happen if she did. Her mind raced with a million answers to that question, along with the million questions she herself had. How much time did she have before her mother disappeared into thin air again?

"I came to find you," Alex said, watching as her mother continued to look at her vaguely. "You disappeared when I was ten years old. I thought you chose to leave me. But then I found your diary." She held the book out, but her mother did not look at it. Alex's voice turned desperate. "You wrote *I must follow the sad nightingale,* remember? You didn't want to leave. I know it! I found the New Academy. Sister Stella. The Squatting Scribe. The Prince of Thieves. I found the city of Helena! The prophecy! Everything!"

Elena began to turn away. "You should not have come."

"What?" Alex followed quickly after her mother, who had turned her back on Alex and walked along the bank. "Aren't you happy to see me? I came all this way."

"I sacrificed everything to get you as far away from this city as possible," her mother said coldly. "I sacrificed everything to keep you safe."

"You abandoned me!" Alex cried out in disbelief. The shock of her mother's words hit her like a punch to the gut. Her mother stopped walking and turned to face her angrily. "You left me and Dad alone! He's never been the same. He loved you!"

"Love? Love?" Elena's eyes blazed, as though burning with an inner fire. "Do not speak to me of love. I died for love! I lived for love! No, my child, do not speak to me of love."

"You left me," Alex said, her voice breaking as she cried, and she covered her face with her hands. "You left me."

"Listen to me, Alexandria." Her mother spoke more gently, and Alex uncovered her face. Elena was looking at her with an intensity that sharpened her soft features. "It is no coincidence that you found the city of Helena. Though hard I tried to change your fate, the gods keep their own counsel."

"The Prince of Thieves," Alex whispered, recalling the bird she had first seen on the windowsill of her bedroom, the knowing gleam in its eyes as it seemed to ask, *Are you listening?*

"Yes," Elena said, though her eyes grew clouded. "And others."

"Does this mean you're really dead?"

"Oh, my love." Her mother smiled. "You already knew that."

Distantly, Alex felt a tear slide down her cheek. Of course, she knew. She knew from the beginning. Somehow, she had always known. Except that was not true. She had known, but she had not believed it. She would sooner believe in a city of gods and magic stones than the death of her mother who had disappeared into thin air ten years ago.

"Can't I bring you back?" Alex asked. "Isn't there some—some spell I can say? It's unfair. You shouldn't have died. You should have stayed. I can't live without a mother! I can't! I can't!"

Elena shook her head. "There is no escape from Death."

Alex took a step back, a coldness washing over her, as if she had truly died. She nodded numbly. "Then I did all this for nothing. I came here for nothing."

"Nothing?" Elena repeated slowly. "No. You are here because you had questions and there was no living person on earth who could answer them. I would have done the same if I were you. I, too, sought the answers to many questions when I was your age." She paused. "Sometimes I wonder if this city was nothing more than a story I told myself to pass the time, a reality I invented to bring all of those gods and heroes that I loved to life. But all stories come to an end, and this time you must finish it."

"Just tell me this," Alex said tersely, knowing that there was only one question that truly mattered in the end. "Did you want to leave? All those years ago, did you want to leave me and Dad?"

Elena looked at her, and for a moment she did not speak, her eyes glazed with visions of the past. "There are some things that no other mortal being knows besides me. Not even Sister Stella. When I found the Emerald Stone, I had unknowingly revealed its location to Zeus. I died in the process, sacrificing myself for the protection of the Stone." Elena smiled suddenly, and it was like a ray of gentle sunshine in the dark, and her gaze was soft upon Alex. "But what no one knows—not even myself, at the time—was that when I died, I was pregnant with you. As a reward for my sacrifice, I was allowed to live ten years to raise you. But when the time came..."

"You had to die." Alex could hardly believe the words she was hearing. They were the answer to everything she had wondered, all those missing pieces in the grand puzzle of her mother's past. But still, Alex felt as though the real question she had always asked herself over the years, the question that still echoed in her heart, remained unanswered. Perhaps that question did not have an answer.

"Yes," Elena said. "On the appointed day I was guided to the Halls of the Dead by a messenger between worlds."

"Hermes," Alex whispered. "The sad nightingale."

Her mother nodded. "I knew the less I left behind, the better chance I had to protect you from the dangers of the prophecy."

"But I thought..." Alex's head spun. "I thought you would be the one to fulfill the prophecy. I thought if I brought you back, you would know how to restore the old order."

Elena laughed, a rich, musical sound that warmed Alex through the chill of the cavern. "My sweet Alexandria. But of course not."

"Then who?"

"The day I died, Zeus tried to destroy the Stone, along with the man I thought would fulfill the prophecy." She paused. "His name was Alexandros."

"You were in love with him, weren't you," Alex said quietly. "He was my real father."

Elena did not speak for a long time, looking at Alex as if she were very far away. "Alexandros was the son of King Philoxenos, descended from King Helenus, founder of the city of Helena, who was the son of Priam, King of Troy, and a descendant of Zeus."

Alex nearly gasped. *"The Kind of the Gods, fallen from his throne, by one of his own mold.* Alexandros was a descendant of Zeus. You thought he would be the one to fulfill the prophecy."

"But I was wrong," Elena said, her voice heavy with sorrow. "And then I had you. *Death will birth life, life will birth death, thus his end has been foretold.* I realized then that you would be no ordinary child. The secret of the universe lives on in you, Alexandria. *You* are the only one who can fulfill the prophecy. You must be the one to restore the old order."

"How?" Alex asked in frustration. "I thought the Emerald Stone was destroyed?"

"Destroyed? No," Elena said with a wry shake of her head. "Not destroyed. Lost, perhaps. And I cannot tell you how to find it. But if you do, tell no one. Do not lead *Him* to the Stone."

Elena took one last look at her before she turned around again, but this time she walked into the water, her feet disappearing in the dark swirling currents.

"Mom, wait!" Alex shouted from the edge of the banks, but Elena did not look back, wading into the depths of the river until her head sunk below the water. "Mom!"

She was gone.

Alex stumbled back, tears streaming down her face and blurring her vision. She had not expected to see her mother again, but to see her like this was almost too painful, close enough to see but not to touch, like trying to grasp the fragments of a dream before awakening. Her head began to pound, her body ached all over, and she struggled to remember what she had to do next.

A part of her no longer cared. She longed to lie on the banks of the river and sleep. Sleep until she forgot everything her mother had told her, everything she had seen in that infernal city, everything in her life that she had suffered. All of it would be forgotten if she simply lied down and closed her eyes.

She dropped to her knees, the diary falling from her hands. The pages fanned out and opened to a random entry. Alex glanced at the words. *November 22nd. I cannot stop smiling. Today Alexandros took me to the Academy and we walked all across the city. I am going back tomorrow.*

The Academy. She paused, her heart beating fast, the memories rushing back to her like coming up for air. The E on the Squatting Scribe's cassock. The E on the hymn to the Prince of Thieves. The E on the statue in the Academy. The E in the temple. Maybe all this time the answer was right in front of her and she had been too blind with the desire of finding her mother to see it. Brother Ezra was the missing link. *He* was the hidden figure behind all of the puzzle pieces.

Alex mustered up all of her strength and limped to her backpack, shoving the diary inside. As she slung the bag over her shoulder, she saw a glimmer on the other side of the cavern, like heat shimmering on desert sands. Was it real? Or another apparition? She squinted her eyes and saw the clear, glassy surface, as still as a mirror.

It was water.

She moved. The water did not disappear as she was afraid it would. Instead, the closer she got the wider the water reached, until she realized it was a lake, stretching from one end of the cavern to the other, disappearing into darkness.

Then she remembered. *The Lake of Memory.* She had to drink from the Lake of Memory.

Alex nearly ran to the lake, her legs giving out once she reached the water's edge. She used both hands to scoop up as much water as she could and drank. The water was pleasant, sweet as a fresh spring in the mountains, and Alex drank more. She hardly noticed that the water had risen until she felt the cool ripples of the tide against her thighs. All around her, the lake had steadily climbed, flooding the cavern silently.

She stood up, but her dress was already half-soaked, clinging to her skin and weighing her down into the water. Her pulse quickened as she began to panic. When she tried to move back towards the dry ground the water only rose faster, sloshing up her waist and climbing to her chest. She tried to swim but her backpack and her dress made it difficult to move her arms and kick her legs fast enough.

The water had floated her up and up as the lake flooded the cavern, the ceiling quickly approaching from above. At that moment Alex realized she was going to drown.

"Help!" Alex screamed, though she knew no one was there. "No! Mom! Help!"

She took one last gulp of air before the water covered her face and clawed its way into her mouth, the weight on her back dragging her down, until it felt like she was falling, falling, falling into darkness and she remembered no more.

75

Alex gasped for air, choking and spitting out water. Her hair was plastered to her face and she shivered beneath her cold, wet clothes, her eyes unwilling to open.

"Alex!"

It was Chloe. Alex thought she had truly died this time and had rejoined her friends in the afterlife, whom she had come to accept were long gone.

"Alex, it's me!"

She forced her eyes to open, and they stung once the air hit them. Chloe's tearful face swam before her.

"Chloe?" Alex's voice was hoarse. She looked around and her head spun as though she were drunk. "Where am I? Where is everyone?"

She was lying down beside a river, not unlike the one she had first seen upon waking up in this strange, cavernous place. Chloe helped her up on her feet, looking at Alex worriedly when she staggered to the side and struggled to find her balance.

"We're all here. This is where we ended up after we...fell." Chloe hesitated. "But you were gone. We thought you died."

Alex raised a brow. "I thought we were all already dead."

"Look who finally made it to the party!" Owen had his arms crossed, but when Alex reached him, he pulled her into a tight hug. "You scared me there for a second, Alex."

"I'm fine," she whispered, surprised to feel tears spring to her eyes. "I'm here."

The rest of the group was huddled together a ways off from the river.

Warren immediately strode up to her and hugged her, followed by Penélope, and even Zeb. Ari was the last to see her. He didn't hug her, but he stood there with an odd, almost angry look on his face. It took her a moment to realize it was fear.

"Where were you?" Ari said roughly, as though he had been crying. When Alex looked around, she realized all of them had red, slightly puffy eyes. They had thought she died. They had accepted that she was gone forever.

"I woke up by the river," Alex said. "Alone. I spoke to my mother. Then I drank from the Lake of Memory and...and I drowned. And woke up here."

"Wait," Zeb said sharply. "You spoke to your mother?"

"Yes."

"What did she say?" Chloe demanded.

"A lot of things." She turned away from their prying eyes and shook her head. "We can discuss it later. First, we have to get the hell out of here."

"Agreed," Owen said. He looked around the cavern, which was the same as the one Alex had been in save for the empty stretch of dark soil where the Lake of Memory had appeared. "And how do we do that?"

Alex looked down the dark tunnel where the cavern disappeared into darkness. She sucked in a breath. In the deepest shadow, she saw a wink of light, like the glint of sun on metal.

"I think we go that way," Alex said, pointing to the tunnel.

"No way," Zeb said, shaking his head.

"Are you sure?" Penélope asked with a sniffle. She hadn't stopped crying since Alex appeared on the shore. "We have no idea what's down here."

Alex was silent. Penélope was right. They had no idea what they could encounter in this underground cave. But it was either go through the tunnel or stay here forever.

"It's the only option we have," Warren said, coming to Alex's side. "Otherwise...we stay dead."

At this, no one argued anymore. They marched together in twos and threes towards the tunnel, which grew larger and larger as they came closer. The darkness persisted, but Alex had long gotten used to that faint, greenish glow in the black stone that provided enough light to pick a path in the dark.

Warren remained at her side, and after a minute of walking in silence, he spoke, his voice quiet so that the others wouldn't hear. "You don't have to tell me what happened with your mother, but if you ever need someone to talk to, I wanted to let you know that I'm here."

Alex nodded, her throat closing up. "Thank you, Warren. That means a lot."

"I know things have changed," Warren continued, a slight tremor in his voice. "I didn't want to believe it at first, but now I do. You are meant for something greater. You always were."

"Was I?" Alex shook her head. "I always felt like I never did enough."

"It was the world that was not enough for you," Warren corrected. "And when that happens, the world tries to blame you for it. It's no wonder that you had to leave that world behind."

Alex wanted to deny it. She wanted to tell him that she hadn't meant to leave, that she hadn't wanted to leave *him* behind, but just like her mother, the words never came. Instead, she said, "I wish things could've been different." *I wish you could've been enough for me,* were the words she did not say.

Warren half-smiled. "Me too. And maybe one day they can be. But first, you have to find out who you are and what you want, and no one can tell you that but yourself."

She nearly took his hand in hers on instinct when out of the corner of her eye she caught that same glinting light. It was a gate, far off in the distance, built into a lofty gap in the stone and guarding a shrouding darkness beyond.

"Wait," Alex said, holding up a hand. They all came to a stop behind her. "Do you guys see that?"

"Oh no," Penélope whispered.

Owen groaned. "We're doomed. More than we already are, at least."

"What is it?" Chloe asked anxiously.

Ari answered with a grave face. "It's one of the gates of Osiris' house."

"Osiris?" Zeb repeated. "Like the God of Death?"

No one replied. The answer was obvious enough. Together they approached the end of the tunnel and exited into a large cavernous space. Across stood the iron gate, blocking the next tunnel. Alex looked around cautiously, but there was not a single movement or shadow flitting across the dark rock.

"It's unguarded," Ari said in surprise, but he didn't sound happy about it. "Something is not right."

"Shouldn't we be glad there isn't a dancing blood monster waiting for us?" Owen asked, raising a brow. "Maybe we were *meant* to pass through the gates."

"That's what I'm afraid of," Ari said darkly. "That *someone* wants us to pass."

They walked across the floor in silence, their footsteps echoing in the cavern until they stood before the black, iron gates. When they came to a stop, the gates creaked loudly, before swinging wide open as if by magic. Alex shared an uneasy glance with Ari before leading the rest of them through the gate.

The dark tunnel continued carving into endless black rock, spitting them out into another ominous cavern, guarded by yet another iron gate. Same as the gate before, the next gate opened of its own accord for them, and they passed through unmolested. Again, they reached a third gate and it opened silently. A fourth gate. A fifth gate. A sixth gate.

"There are only supposed to be seven gates," Ari murmured as they passed through the sixth gate.

"And what is beyond the seventh?" Alex asked.

Before Ari could answer, a deafening screech rang out. They looked down the tunnel to the next cavern where the final gate loomed even greater than all the others. And before the gate, a slithering, black creature was heaped in thick coils, a massive head with glinting fangs rearing back and crying out in that terrible screech.

"That's going to be a problem," Owen said, his voice faint. "I say we run."

"What? No." Ari shook his head. "This is the only way to make it back out alive. We can't give up now."

"But how are we going to defeat it?" Penélope asked. "We don't have the spells."

Ari smiled at her. "No, but we have the Golden Blade of Demeter."

Penélope stared at him, then slowly dragged her gaze down to the sword strapped around her waist. "You've got to be joking."

"Demeter gifted that sword to *you,*" Ari said quietly. "You were meant to wield it."

"I-I can't." Penélope looked around at all of them, but when no one contradicted Ari, she paled. "Ari, I don't know how to wield a sword."

Owen patted her shoulder. "Just stab the snake with the sharp end, love."

Penélope glared at him and opened her mouth to snap what would have been a well-deserved retort when the large serpent let out another howling screech. She froze, her right hand automatically reaching for the hilt of the sword.

"We go together," Alex said firmly, though her voice betrayed her nerves. If they did not manage to kill the monster, they would be better off turning back and staying here forever. She didn't want to imagine what would happen when the dead were killed.

"Maybe we can sneak past the gate without the snake noticing," Owen offered. "We can throw a stone far away and distract it like in *Harry Potter.*"

"The snake was blind by then," Chloe said flatly. "And Harry almost died."

Owen grimaced. "Fair point."

"It could still work," Zeb added. "The sound might distract it long enough for us to get past the gate."

Warren knelt and picked up a large, black rock that had chipped away from the tunnel wall. He tossed it once in his hand. "Will this do?"

"It's good enough," Alex said grimly.

They crept closer to the end of the tunnel that opened on the large cavern, the gate gleaming at the other end, blocking them from going any further. Black shadow swirled menacingly on the other side of the iron bars, as though this gate had something to hide. Alex shivered.

Warren crept to the edge of the tunnel, his arm raised. He kept his eyes trained on the monstrous snake, whose head swung back and forth attentively, its black, slitted eyes closing and opening rapidly, a red forked tongue flicking out between its fangs.

"Now," Alex whispered.

Warren wound up his arm and threw the rock, putting the weight of his body behind the throw. The rock sailed high through the air and then skidded across the cavern's stone floor, landing close to the far wall.

At the noise, the serpent coiled up and hissed in the rock's direction, before sliding its hefty, scaled body towards the far wall to investigate. Warren motioned with his hand and they ran for the gate as quietly as they could.

They made it halfway across the cavern when the serpent swiveled around and screeched hideously, its eyes fixing an evil glare on them.

"Run!" Ari shouted.

Alex sprinted towards the iron gate and was the first to stand before it. "Open, open, open..."

But the gate would not budge, remaining tall and aloof. She stared at it, the call for help dying in her throat as the rest of them crowded around her. Alex turned. The monster was slithering towards them, its black, scaly head craning forward with its jaws slightly parted, ready to pounce—

A blinding light exploded inside the cave, and Alex heard the creature screech as she shielded her eyes. The light pulsed, then subsided into a hazy shine which Alex saw encircled Penélope, who stood before the serpent, her hands gripping the Golden Blade in front of her.

The snake reared back with a cry of pain or indignation, its head swinging wildly in the air as though the very light of the sword hurt him.

Penélope let out a shout and ran towards the monster, ramming the length of the blade into the twisting body, the sword sliding past the scales like a knife slicing through water. The sunken sword glowed hot inside the serpent, the golden color heating up to a bright red visible even outside the shiny black scales.

Suddenly Penélope screamed and let it go, falling back on the ground, her palms a mottled red. The sword was burning with the same holy fire that had consumed Demeter's womanly shape. Flames licked out of the serpent's open jaws, its piercing screeches dying as its lifeless, coiled length collapsed to the ground, the cavern shaking from the impact.

Zeb rushed forward and helped Penélope up to her feet. The Golden Blade had burned her palms, which were already blistering from the fire. She curled her hands inside her chest and leaned weakly against Zeb.

Then behind her Alex heard the gate swing open with its telltale creak. She turned around slowly, dreading what she would see. The shadows curled like smoke beyond the gate, obscuring the path ahead.

Alex met Ari's eyes, but he only looked at her, waiting. It was her decision. She took a deep breath and walked inside the shadows.

76

As Alex stepped into the darkness, the shadows parted around her, leading her blindly forward. The others followed, eyeing the curling shadows fearfully. She flinched when the iron gate clanged shut behind them.

Just when she thought the shadows would never end, a cold blast of wind rushed past her, clearing the shadows and leaving them all shivering in a lofty, polished room, white-flamed torches lining the perimeters.

Seated before them on an elevated, ornately carved couch made of the same rock as the cave was the statue of a man and a woman, lounging together in an eternal lover's embrace. The man's skin was painted dark green and he wore an elaborate feathered white crown, while the woman donned a long, red dress, her black hair adorned with a miniature carved throne atop her head.

A deep, cool voice echoed softly in the room. Even though no one's mouth moved, Alex knew it was the green-skinned statue who spoke.

Osiris.

"Who comes forth by day before the victorious Osiris and his wife Isis?"

The stern mouth and dark eyes stared them down with a tangible haughtiness, the lack of a moving mouth and eyes giving the impression of a mummy, its trapped soul lurking beneath the painted mask.

Alex's heart pounded before she spoke. "I do."

The words fell meekly before the high throne of Osiris, who sat still in his stone carving, his wife equally immobile, though Alex felt the power brimming within their unmoving figures, as though this was the tomb that chained their restless spirits forever.

At last, Osiris spoke. *"Then you have come to die."*

Alex heard Chloe suck in a breath and Penélope let out a feeble protest. She felt her hands shake at her sides, the sudden possibility of death choking the air from her lungs.

"We came to speak with the dead." Ari was at her side, facing the still head of Osiris undaunted. "We request your permission to return to the world of the living."

A low laugh reverberated in the ground and the stone walls of the room, growing louder and louder until it seemed others were laughing, hundreds and then thousands, all of the dead souls laughing that horrible, derisive laugh, even though there was no one else in the room.

"If you wish to return to the living, you must pay the price," Osiris sneered.

"No," Ari said firmly.

"What's your price?" Owen called out, ignoring their whispered commands to be quiet. "I can pay it."

"Not you, boy," snapped the god, his green-skinned face seeming to glare at them. *"The girl. A life to balance a death."*

"Me?" Alex asked doubtfully.

"No." Penélope stepped forward. "He means me."

"Penélope, stop," Zeb whispered, trying to pull her back. But Penélope only shook him off, taking another step forward and facing the throne.

"I killed the snake," Penélope said. *"A life to balance a death.* It's the only way."

"Penélope, no," Alex whispered, horror pooling in her stomach at what she was suggesting. "We'll find another way."

"There is no other way," declared Osiris. *"If you pay the price, the way is yours."*

With his last words, a cold wind blew once more from the throne, followed by the splash of ocean waves.

Alex looked back and her breath left her at the familiar scene. It was Priam Boulevard, as seen from the edge of the docks, and the iron gate was now the silver Gate of the Moon. All they had to do was step through the gate and they would find themselves back in the city. Then she remembered Demeter's warning.

Never make a deal with Death.

"No," Alex said, turning back towards Osiris. "No deal."

"It's the only way," Penélope protested, tears falling from her eyes. "If not, then we *all* die."

Alex shook her head. "Then I'll stay. I'll take her place."

"No," Warren said fiercely.

Penélope walked before the throne, looking up at the silent, unmoving figures of Osiris and Isis, their stone faces more eerie than if they were moving. "I will pay the price. It's my choice."

That low laugh returned. Osiris did not look at her, but Alex swore she saw a sinister smile curl the carved lips. Alex heard the gates swing open behind them. She turned and saw the boulevard stretching beyond it, the night sky filled with stars, and the golden Gate of the Sun glinting at the other end of the city.

Suddenly she had an idea. Alex met Ari's eyes and she motioned with a slight jerk of her head towards the gate. He nodded subtly, the muscles in his jaw tightening. She slowly closed the fingers of her hand at her thigh, counting down. *Three, two, one—*

"Go!" Alex shouted.

Several things happened at once. Ari sprinted towards the gate, grabbing Owen and Chloe's hands who were closest to him and dragging them to the other side. Alex ran towards Penélope and grabbed her arm. Warren and Zeb realized what was happening and ran towards the gate too.

But before they got far, Penélope was pulled back and Alex nearly lost her grip on her arm. To her horror, she saw a mass of faces and hands yearning towards them, just like those apparitions by the river, except this time their hands grasped Penélope and yanked her towards Osiris and Isis, whose faces were now carved in laughter.

"No!" Zeb appeared at Alex's side, grabbing Penélope's other arm and helping Alex pull her towards the gate.

Alex looked back. The others were shouting at them to run. Suddenly they broke free of the dead hands, and Alex shoved Penélope forward, the three of them racing towards the gate.

That same laugh shook the room so powerfully that dust and rocks fell from the ceiling. Out of the corner of her eye, Alex saw Zeb fall behind her. She skidded to a stop as Penélope sprinted through the gates to the other side. The faceless ghosts were dragging Zeb back into the room now swirling with shadow like the hole of a yawning tomb.

Alex ran back across the fissures cracking the tomb floor and grasped his pale hand, struggling to pull him away.

"Alex, the gate!" Warren shouted. "Run!"

She heard the gate creaking shut. Zeb struggled to kick against the bodies grasping at him, clutching at his clothes, his hair, dragging him into the abyss that was quickly consuming the very ground Alex stood upon.

"Alex, now!"

Then she heard it. A low, mournful tune, the same song of the nightingale she had heard in the desert.

She looked back, her arms straining to drag Zeb away from the dead souls, and saw Warren through the closing silver bars of the gate. He stood on the other side with a shining gold lyre in his hands, his eyes screwed shut in effort and his fingers plucking the strings. The gate strained to keep itself open, widening ever so slightly as if the music was holding the gates back. Warren shouted her name again.

"Go," Zeb said in a strangled voice, his eyes wide. "Save yourself!"

Suddenly Zeb let go of her hand and shoved her away, then a moment later he was sucked beneath the mass of dead spirits.

Alex could hardly think as she ran for her life. She felt fingers brushing her sides as she sprinted towards the gate which was rapidly closing, the gap narrowing on Warren's figure as she leaped in the air—

—and fell on the ground. Stone pavement peeked out beneath her splayed fingers. The gate clanged shut behind her. She saw familiar shoes in her vision. Warren lowered his hand and she grasped it, stumbling to her feet.

"No, no, no!" Penélope cried out. She grasped the bars of the gate, shaking them, her sobs torn from her throat like a wild animal. "Zeb! Zeb! No! We have to go back! We have to go back..."

With a terrible sob, she sank to the ground before the gate, where the tomb of Osiris and Isis had disappeared, the lapping tide of the harbor now kissing the other side of the gate.

Alex looked around, her entire body numb. Owen stared at the gate in stunned silence, while Chloe had a hand over her mouth, tears filling her eyes. Ari crouched beside Penélope, holding her against him as she sobbed, his face rigid with pain.

Warren looked around the street. "We should get back to the safe house."

"There's no one here," Owen snapped back angrily, and Alex was surprised to see a tear slip down his cheek. "And Zeb is gone. Have some pity, Warren, for God's sake."

Warren flushed. "I wish I could have saved him too. But there's nothing we can do now. We have to get back to the safe house or risk getting caught and this will all have been for nothing."

Ari stood up, helping Penélope to her feet. "Warren's right. We have to go."

Warren hid his surprise, before nodding. Alex followed Ari and Warren, who led them across the deserted street toward the North Quarter. She and Chloe held Penélope on either side as she walked lifelessly to the safe house.

They reached the familiar stone doorway, which Ari unlocked with the keys the Queen had given him. Once inside the living room, Alex and Chloe carefully laid Penélope onto the couch, where Chloe remained to comfort her. Owen stalked off into one of the bedrooms and slammed the door behind him, Warren flinching at the sound.

Ari patted Warren's shoulder firmly as he walked towards Penélope and sat beside her. "There was nothing you could have done."

Warren nodded wordlessly, but he still seemed shaken.

"How did you do it?" Alex asked, remembering how Warren had stood there with a gold lyre before the gate, the song seeming to hold it open. She wondered if she had hallucinated it all. "How did you keep the gate open?"

"I'm not sure," Warren said honestly. "I think it was the lyre."

"The Seven-Stringed Lyre," Ari murmured, staring off into space with a pensive look as he stroked Penélope's back, who was still shaking with stifled cries. "It has the power to charm any living being, mortals and gods alike, including Death himself."

"How did you find it?" Alex asked in disbelief. "Did you have it all along?"

Warren shook his head. "The night I left, when I fell asleep in an alley behind the Tower of the Winds, I had a dream that I went inside the tower. At the center of the mechanics was a seven-stringed lyre. It was connected to the movements of the heavens somehow and made the most beautiful sound when the mechanics moved. When I woke up, I was holding the lyre in my arms. The next thing I know, I was found and arrested by soldiers, and the lyre...disappeared."

After a few beats of silence, Ari's head snapped up. "The Music of the Spheres! It's the same symbol we saw in the Great Library. A lyre connected with the movements of the planets." He stood up, so suddenly even Penélope stopped crying to look at him. "How did I not see it before? The Seven-Stringed Lyre! The Music of the Spheres! It's all connected!"

"Please explain," Chloe said wearily.

"The Music of the Spheres was an ancient philosophy claiming that the sun, moon, and planets move in harmony, and that according to their mathematical proportions, each celestial body emits its own song, or musical note, just like the strings on a lyre. Pythagoras included the theory in his own philosophies, but it is much more ancient than him. Sister Stella and the Seven Sages must practice the philosophy."

"It also explains the Temple of Apollo," Penélope said, and all eyes turned to her. "In the Homeric Hymn to Hermes, after being born Hermes turns a tortoise-shell into a seven-stringed lyre, which he gives to Apollo, who is also a god of music."

"My mother wrote about that in her senior thesis," Alex said, recalling the passionate words her mother had written, and how much Alex had changed since reading it. "The middle string of the lyre, sometimes personified by the muse Mese, was worshiped at Delphi along with Apollo. My mother believed that the power of Hermes as a messenger and thief was similar to song as a transitory power, giving the musician almost divine powers when they play."

"Power to hold back even the gates of Death," Ari murmured.

"How did the lyre come back to you?" Alex asked Warren, remembering the golden wand that had appeared in her hand and then disappeared.

He looked down at his now empty hands, as if the gold lyre might suddenly return to them. "I don't know. But when I saw you on the other side of the gate and it started to close, I had it in my hands. It was then I knew what to do. I played the notes from a memory I didn't even know I had...and the gates stayed open."

"Strange." Alex sighed, rubbing at her eyes. She felt drained of life, even though it seemed they had not even been gone a full night. "But somehow it's stranger that there were no guards on the streets. Where did they go?"

"Who knows?" Ari said, a glint in his eyes. "But this is our chance."

"What?"

He looked at her with a grim smile. "To find Brother Ezra. If guards are no longer patrolling the city, we can sneak into the Academy without getting caught and speak with Brother Ezra. We can finally know what happened to the Emerald Stone. We can figure out how to fulfill the prophecy."

Alex was silent, her stomach knotting with guilt. She recalled her mother's words. *The secret of the universe lives on in you, Alexandria. You are the only one who can fulfill the prophecy. You must be the one to restore the old order.*

"You never told us what happened with your mother in the Underworld," Chloe said suddenly, looking at Alex with a keen glance, as though she had read her thoughts.

But if you do, tell no one. Do not lead Him *to the stone.*

"She told me how she died," Alex said, and once the words left her mouth she felt the emptiness in her chest, as though the words had been carved from there. "Everything the King said was true. She wanted to find the Stone. She thought that Alexandros would be the one to fulfill the prophecy. But she was wrong, and Zeus killed him and then her. She was allowed to live ten years to raise me before she had to return to the Halls of the Dead."

"I'm sorry," Chloe whispered after a shocked silence. "I had hoped he was lying."

"Me too," Alex said, her voice hollow.

"What do we do now?" Penélope asked. The tears had dried on her face, though Alex saw a deep sadness in her eyes that had not been there before.

"I'm not sure." Alex hesitated. She knew what she had to do, but she could not risk divulging anything about her role in the prophecy. "I found my mother. I did what I came here to do."

"That's it?" Ari asked in disbelief. "You'd leave it all just like that? What about Sister Stella and the prophecy? The Emerald Stone and the Old Faith? You said if you couldn't bring her back you would finish what she started."

"The Stone was destroyed," Alex countered. "Sister Stella said so." Though she remembered distantly what her mother had said. *Destroyed? No.*

"Then we find another way," Ari said fiercely. "Everything keeps leading back to Brother Ezra. The Squatting Scribe. The Prince of Thieves. The Temple of Apollo. The Academy. It's like he's been helping us from the beginning, leading us to him. He may be the Headmaster of the Academy, just like Sister Stella is the Headmaster of the New Academy. He must have gone into hiding when the King rose to power."

Alex sighed. "I've been thinking the same thing. But what if Brother Ezra tells Sister Stella that we are still here?"

"We'll just have to take that risk."

"I don't want to risk anyone else," Alex said sharply.

Ari nodded slowly. "Then you and I can go. Alone."

"No," Warren interrupted. "We go together. We finish what we started and then we leave the city behind."

Penélope nodded. "If we don't, then Zeb sacrificed himself for nothing."

"I agree," Chloe said, taking Penélope's hand in hers. "We do this together."

"What if it's a trap?"

They all turned. The voice came from one of the bedroom doors. Owen stood there, leaning against the door frame, his face grave. He strolled inside the room and looked at all of them with a rare seriousness.

"There wasn't a single guard at the docks or on the streets. Don't you wonder why?" he asked.

"Maybe the King left," Chloe suggested.

"Or he thought we did," Penélope added. "If the pirates know our whereabouts, so must he."

"Or the King is baiting you to reveal yourselves," Owen argued. "He must've heard that we sailed away. Now he's trying to lure you back into the open by making you think he's not watching anymore."

"But how could he know we came back?" Ari asked. "We were captured by pirates. For all he knows, we might be dead or sold into slavery. Besides, we have no idea how long we spent in the Underworld."

"The only reason I think this is a good idea," Owen said, taking a deep breath, "is that this Brother Ezra person might know how to get Zeb back." They all stared at him. "What? If we could go to Hell once, then we can go back again."

"Then it's decided?" Warren asked. "We find Brother Ezra, ask him about the prophecy, and restore the old order. Then we rescue Zeb."

Alex nodded with the rest of them. Even Ari couldn't hold back a small smile. Penélope squeezed Chloe's hand, a tear slipping down her cheek. They were all in agreement.

"So where *can* we find this Brother Ezra?" Chloe asked.

Alex met Ari's eyes and she almost smiled. "We start at the Academy."

77

The city was eerily silent as the first day they arrived, when the city had seemed abandoned. Not even a single guard or soldier patrolled the main boulevards. Yet Alex still felt that familiar prickling on her neck, as though eyes watched her from the shadows.

Alex followed Ari down the side of the road where the light from the street lamps did not reach. Warren, Chloe, Penélope, and Owen followed behind her in silence. They approached the Academy from the east on the Meson Pedion. As they came closer, she saw that the Academy gates were still chained, and now the buildings looked even more abandoned, the grass growing high and unkept, rotting fruit from the trees peppering the ground.

Ari opened the gate as he had once before. She slid through the gap, and the others followed suit. Once they were all on the other side of the fence, they crept across a wide expanse of grass, weeds cropping up where the grass had died, until they came to the same courtyard facing the library.

"Where do you think he would be?" Alex whispered, squinting at the rows of windows lining the dormitories, but all of them were dark.

"Did you see that?" Ari asked sharply. He was looking at the library. "I thought I saw a light..."

Alex looked at the small slitted windows of the library, and sure enough, she saw a small orange glow pass by one of the windows. Could it be Brother Ezra? She nodded, and together they led the rest of them to the library. Ari listened with his ear resting on the wood, then grasped the handle.

Just like before, the door opened easily beneath Ari's hands, as if it wanted to be opened. A foreboding feeling stole over her. She glanced back at the others and lifted her finger to her lips. After all, this was the place they had almost been caught by the King.

Once they were all inside, Owen gently closed the door behind him. There was not a single light inside, the shelves of scrolls plunged into a thick, musty darkness. Alex walked forward quietly, looking around for that orange glow, but she saw nothing.

Soon she stood before the statue of Brother Ezra. She reached up, touching the carved E on his chest, just as it had been on the Squatting Scribe. The sight of it stirred a long-forgotten memory. Where had she seen that E stitched before? Soft clicking like the ticking of a clock nagged at her mind until it suddenly ceased. A horrible thought occurred to her, then, and she started in alarm, about to turn and call for Ari when she heard his voice, that familiar rasp like the grinding of stone against stone.

"Χαῖρε, Alexandria, daughter of Elena!"

She turned, her stomach dropping in dread. Limping out of the shadows on his golden cane was the King, except he was not dressed in his purple robe and bejeweled slippers, but in a brown cassock tied at the waist by a rope, just like the Squatting Scribe, just like the Brother that had almost caught them in the New Academy library, and just like the statue before her.

His blind eyes fastened on Alex, and he grinned viciously when she did not speak. Across the room, Ari and the others came to a stop, staring at the blind King in shock.

"Ah, expecting to meet someone else here?" the King asked. "Brother Ezra, perhaps?"

Alex understood. The words were bitter in her mouth. "You're Brother Ezra."

He laughed, which sounded more like a crow's cackle. "Did you think I do not know every move you make in this city? I have followed you since the day I learned of your existence. Do you think I did not know you were here that night, listening to my conversation?" When Alex looked quickly at Ari in alarm, he laughed again. "Oh yes. I may be blind, but I see everything. That is a gift from the *True* King."

"The True King?" Alex asked, his words and the feeling of betrayal stirring a wave of anger in her chest as she remembered what her mother had said, how she had sacrificed herself for the Stone. "You mean Zeus."

"Do not speak his name!" Brother Ezra spat. "Foolish girl! You heard the prophecy and believed in the *Old Faith*. But you do not understand the power He holds. It is folly to think a mere stone could destroy Him."

"But you wrote the prophecy," Ari said, stepping forward. "You believed in it then, didn't you?"

"Yes, I discovered the prophecy in my youth," Brother Ezra said impatiently, waving Ari away with a gnarled hand before settling it on the head of his cane. "I knew Hermes had given the Stone to the Seven Sages countless centuries ago. Those silly women guarded it like no other. I could never get close enough to it."

Alex almost laughed once she realized. "You wanted the power for yourself."

"I was young," Brother Ezra said reluctantly, "and naive. But once I was shown the truth by the King of the Gods Himself, I realized that the prophecy was wrong. It would never be fulfilled. The True King has eyes and ears everywhere. He granted me the Kingship in order to watch over the city."

"You mean you were afraid," Alex retorted. "He threatened you, and because you knew you could never be the one to fulfill the prophecy, you became his puppet."

Brother Ezra pointed his cane at her, his face livid. "Your mother had the same arrogance as you and she died because of it. If I had known she had a child, I would have hunted you down and killed you too."

At that moment, Alex realized that Brother Ezra did not know that her mother had died and come back to life, that she had been pregnant with Alex when she sacrificed herself for the Stone, and that now Alex was the only one who could fulfill the prophecy. *There are some things that no other mortal being knows besides me. Not even Sister Stella.*

Brother Ezra might see many things, but he was blind to one thing. He thought she was irrelevant, another nuisance blocking his path to power. His own fear and greed blinded him to the truth, to the sacrifice her mother had made the day Zeus tried to destroy the Stone.

"I trust my mother and what she believed in," Alex said quietly. "And I will not let you get in the way of what I must do."

He laughed and slammed his cane on the ground, then pointed it at Alex. "Σφᾶς συλλαμβάνεσθε!"

Shadows jumped out from behind the bookshelves, cloaked and armed. Soldiers. They sprang towards her as Alex ran back to Ari and the others, who were already running out the door and into the courtyard.

"You can't run from me!" Brother Ezra shouted after them. "I have the gods on my side!"

Alex dodged the soldiers' outreaching arms just as she had when they first arrived in the city. A small movement up ahead caught her eye, followed by the faintly familiar tune of the nightingale drifting in the air. Then she remembered. The cloaked figure who had led them to the old woman's house, his voice, the gleam in his eyes, and the cock of his head that had struck her as so familiar, like a thief in the night, like a bird on her windowsill. *If you are ever in need of help, you need only wield this.*

A heavy weight filled her palm. She looked down and saw a long, golden rod encircled by snakes and crowned with wings clutched in her hand, as if it had been there all along. Maybe it had.

The soldiers were closing in on them, circling the courtyard where more soldiers spilled out from behind the dormitories and from the streets.

Owen had been right. It was a trap.

They huddled together as the soldiers pointed their spears at them, inching closer in tight formation, leaving no room for escape. She heard Brother Ezra's laugh and his raspy voice bark out more orders in Greek. The soldiers marched forward in unison, the spear tips a few seconds away from killing them where they stood.

"Quick!" Alex said, holding out the golden wand. "Take it!"

No one thought twice. Their hands reached out for the golden wand and Alex closed her eyes, imagining the safe house in her mind, the shining flame of the Lighthouse visible from the windows.

She opened her eyes.

78

THEY WERE STANDING IN the middle of the safe house as if they had never left. Everyone stared at Alex in alarm. She looked down where their hands were joined, but the golden wand was gone.

"What just happened?" Owen asked as they all stepped away hesitantly.

"You were right," Alex said. "It was a trap."

"I meant how we got here all the way from the Academy," Owen muttered. "But thank you for *that* shocking revelation."

"I'm not sure how." She held out her palm as if the golden wand would appear there once more. "Remember the night we arrived in the city? How we were led by a hooded stranger to the old woman's house? *He* gave me the golden wand and told me to use it if I ever needed help. Then he and the wand disappeared and I forgot about it. Until now."

Chloe looked at her strangely. "Alex, no hooded stranger was leading us. You were."

Alex was silent. The others did not contradict her. All of them were staring at Alex as if she had told them she had magical powers.

"A golden wand," Ari repeated with a half-smile. "I think that was our Prince of Thieves."

"Then he was the one who helped us escape...Brother Ezra," Alex said. At his name, she felt that same anger return to her swiftly. He was the man responsible for her mother's death. He was the one who had betrayed both Sister Stella and her mother. All along, he had been the figure behind the shadows leading them to him—and to the King, like a spider stealthily crafting its web.

Ari seemed to think the same thing. "He's a traitor," he said fiercely. "We have to warn Sister Stella."

"How?" Chloe asked. "The entire city is crawling with those soldiers. He has this whole place under his control."

"It's the only option we have," Alex argued. "If we stay here, he might burn the entire city to the ground and us with it."

So it was decided that tomorrow they would plan their escape. All of them gratefully went to bed. They hadn't slept since the night they had left for the Underworld, and it felt as though days and days had passed with no rest.

Alex fell asleep swiftly, her exhaustion weighing on her eyes and pounding in her head. She drifted into a dream.

A desert rose around her in waves like a ship at sea. Ancient, gnarled trees reached for the blistering sun hanging over the far mountains. She was walking without knowing her destination.

Then she heard it in a slight breeze.

A low, mournful song, the song of the sad nightingale. She turned and saw a small brown bird perched on a nearby tree branch. Its small head cocked to the side, and its black, beady eyes looked at her knowingly.

The bird flew off and landed on another tree's low-hanging branch. Then another. And another. Alex followed it through the desert, its soft melody like a familiar lullaby, as if her mom had sung the same tune to her before she fell asleep. She wondered where he was taking her, but another part of her knew that the bird was just a messenger, a guide between worlds, not the answer but a question, and the question was, *Are you listening?*

Suddenly the bird flew to a tree directly in front of Alex's path, but instead of landing on a branch, the bird soared clean through the trunk and disappeared into thin air.

Alex stared. At the center of the tree, right where the bird had flown through, was the Seven-Stringed Lyre, the tree trunk having grown around it.

As she stared the lyre began to play a song, one note and then the other, the music ringing out in the sweetest melody Alex had ever heard. The sun arced swiftly across the sky in time with the music and the stars shone brightly as the blue faded to black and she saw the seven planets of the solar system swing around the earth like the mosaic in the Great Library, their movements a song sung in unison, before aligning above the tree in one straight line leading up to the sun, like the path of stone Sphinxes in the water, like a road between this world and the next.

As the song crescendoed around her, the Seven-Stringed Lyre illuminated every branch and leaf of the tree in gold, and at the base of the trunk, where the roots glowed red beneath the desert sands like molten lava, Alex saw the silhouette of a heart beating—but, no, not a heart—a stone, pulsing pure white light like blood in the veins of the earth.

Alex woke up with a gasp. She knew where to find the Emerald Stone.

79

THE NEXT DAY THEY came up with a plan. Warren proposed that they split up into two groups in order to cause two distractions and divide the King's forces, hopefully buying themselves some time.

Both groups would ultimately meet at the Great Library and find Sister Stella to warn her about Brother Ezra. The hope was that with her help, they would be able to end Brother Ezra's false reign, then somehow fulfill the prophecy and find a way to rescue Zeb. Surprisingly, no one had any disagreements about Warren's plan, and the rest of the day was spent hashing out the details.

It was decided that while Warren, Owen, and Chloe provided a distraction on the west side of the city, Alex, Ari, and Penélope would create a distraction in the east. If everything went according to plan, they would all meet up at the Great Library afterward.

The greatest risk was that one or both of the groups would be caught before making it to the Great Library. To avoid this, Warren suggested that they try to sneak in during the day when more citizens were out and about on the street. This allowed them to disguise themselves as common civilians and surprise Brother Ezra, who probably expected them to move by night as they had always done.

Once they were satisfied with the plan, the sun had already set and the room had grown dark. Warren tended to the fire while the others made dinner before they all filed off to bed. Tomorrow morning they would leave for the Great Library. No one spoke too much, their minds elsewhere. It was possible that things would go very wrong and this would be the last time they saw each other.

Alex tried not to think about it as she lay on her bed. She had not mentioned her dream or her plan to fulfill the prophecy to anyone. Penélope and Chloe were already fast asleep on the other small mats in the room. She closed her eyes, blocking out their soft snores, but a moment later she heard familiar footsteps in the hall. Without thinking, she got out of bed and tiptoed down the hall to the living room.

She found Ari crouched before the fire, jostling the logs inside the hearth with the iron poker. He glanced back when she approached and stood up.

"Alexandria," he said in surprise.

"I thought I heard you," she murmured.

Ari scratched at the scruff on his chin, which had grown dark after days of not shaving it. "Couldn't sleep."

"Me neither." Alex sighed and sat down in front of the fire. Ari did the same, sitting beside her. They both stared into the flames. "I can't believe Zeb is gone."

"We'll get him back," Ari said firmly. "I know we will."

Alex hesitated. "Will we? Tomorrow might change everything. The King might catch us and we'll be stuck in prison cells for life. Even if we do manage to warn Sister Stella, how are we going to fulfill the prophecy without her help? How are we going to rescue Zeb? If the summer ends before we do, what if I have to go back? What if I need to go home?"

Instead of criticizing her as she half-expected him to, Ari only nodded, though she thought his eyes were sad. "I understand. You left everything behind. We all did."

"I can't force my friends to throw away Harvard and their careers like I did, even to find Zeb," Alex continued. "At least Sister Stella might be able to help you and Penélope find him. But I doubt she'll let me near the city once I leave."

Ari paused for a long moment, then, "Are you sure you want to go back home? Wasn't there a reason you left in the first place?"

Alex nearly answered, *I left because of my mother and now I know she's dead.* But that was not entirely true. She left because she no longer recognized herself in the mirror. She left because the life she had planned for herself felt like running and running only to find herself in the same places. She left because she wanted to feel the wind in her hair, the road flying beneath her tires, her two hands gripping the wheel.

Or maybe she left because her mother had left all those years ago, and a part of Alex had wanted to know what it felt like to disappear into thin air too.

I must follow the sad nightingale.

"I don't know what I want," Alex said finally. "I don't think I ever have."

Ari reached out and took her hand in his. She looked down at their fingers laced together, ignoring the rush that his touch sent through her. "I've never felt like this about anyone, you know."

"Like what?"

He lifted her hand and kissed her knuckles. "Like with you I might discover the secrets of the universe."

Alex went still. She wondered if her heartbeat betrayed her. "What about Rosamaria?"

"She was only someone to pass the time. She was nothing. *We* were nothing yet." Ari nearly growled the words as he pulled her close to him, wrapping his arms around her waist and burying his face against her neck. "She's not *you.* She's not Alexandria. She doesn't make me want to punch anyone who insults her. She doesn't smile the way you do, so rarely that when it happens I feel like I've found a rare gem. She doesn't look at me like you do, as if you can see me for who I am. She doesn't remind me why I study dead languages. She never discovered doorways to other worlds that I couldn't have dreamed up in my wildest imagination. And I don't feel like I'll die if I never get to kiss her again."

She had no words to say once he finished, but it didn't matter anyway, because he was kissing her. She felt that kiss down to her toes, like a heavenly fire that burned her up from the inside. Ari lifted her onto his lap and she sank into his arms, finding those soft curls and tugging on them.

A creaking sound from across the room broke her concentration and Alex sat back quickly, her heart pounding in her chest. But there was no one there. She placed a hand on Ari's chest and kept him away at arm's length, which was still much too close for comfort.

"Are you sure you don't just love this city?" Alex asked, only half-joking, ignoring the hurt that flitted across his face at her words. "Maybe we are drawn to each other only because it was the right time and right place. If I hadn't left my life behind, if you hadn't felt so lost, or if I hadn't discovered this city and you hadn't kissed me that night, maybe I'd still be with Warren, and you'd still be seeing Rosamaria, never knowing the city even existed."

Ari had grown still around her as she spoke. "Is that what you truly believe? Or is that what you want to believe?"

Alex didn't answer at first, instead pulling away from his embrace and standing up. Her chest squeezed tighter and tighter, as though she were suffocating, drowning as she had in the Lake of Memory. "We should sleep. Tomorrow is a big day."

He didn't look at her, staring firmly into the fire, his face tense and red with embarrassment.

She felt a twinge of guilt, but there were things that he did not know, and tomorrow all their lives could change. "Goodnight, Ari."

Alex went back to bed.

80

"THIS ISN'T GOING TO work," Penélope whispered.

"We only need to distract them for half an hour," Alex said. She glanced at Ari, who was lying close to the edge of the roof and squinting at the buildings below. "Do you see anything?"

Ari pointed in the direction of the theater, which was a large structure with a wooden stage, inclined seating, and a three-tiered backdrop. "I can see two guards at the north entrance of the palace. We'll have to be really quiet."

"We only have one shot at this," Alex warned.

"Come on," Ari said, scooting back from the edge and crawling to where she and Penélope were crouched down further back on the roof. "It's time."

They had been scouting the Royal Palace since the early hours of the morning and the time had come to get moving. The others would be nearly ready to implement their part of the plan, so they would only have a small window to put their distractions to use. Luckily, the guards at this end of the palace were more at ease so tucked away from the public streets.

Ari helped them climb down the side of the building with a rope he tied to the roof. Once Alex and Penélope were both on the ground, the three of them snuck down the dark alleyway toward the palace theater, directly across from the north entrance of the palace.

This was the same entrance they had escaped from when they had rescued Warren, and it was generally one of the least guarded parts of the palace due to its distance from the main boulevards and the protection of the neighboring houses. By scaling the roof of their own safe house and carefully making their way across the North Quarter, they had avoided the prying eyes of noble families and their private guards as well as the soldiers marching the streets.

"I'll take the east end," Ari whispered as he unzipped his backpack. He handed Alex a few matches from the supply they had brought and a broken piece of concrete from an alleyway. Then he gave Penélope a pile of woodcut blocks. "You two take the stage end. Then we make the run. Don't wait for me. I'll catch up."

Alex and Penélope nodded. This had been the plan they agreed upon from the beginning, but to actually execute it was a different story. Alex gripped the matches and the stone tightly in her hands and met Penélope's fearful eyes.

Ari began to count down silently with his fingers. *Three, two, one—*

They ran towards the theater with their backs hunched down to stay out of sight. Alex and Penélope ran towards the west end where the facade of a three-story building rose behind the stage, while Ari ran east towards the seating. From this side of the theater, they could not see the soldiers guarding the entrance to the palace, but soon that would not matter.

"Quickly," Penélope said, taking the extra matches. "Light it."

Alex's hands shook as she grasped the concrete stone in one hand and the match in the other. They had practiced this at the safe house but it suddenly felt like the first time. She struck the match against the stone. Nothing. She struck again. A flame burst at the tip of the match.

Penélope held out the first wood block until the flame caught, then she threw it inside the theater, the flaming wood rolling across the stage. Alex managed to light another wood block before the flame kissed her fingertips and she let the match drop with a hiss of pain, stamping on it quickly.

"Another," Alex whispered. Penélope handed her a match. She lit it and Penélope held out another wood block. They threw a few more flaming blocks of wood inside the theater until a small fire spread across the wooden stage. They saw Ari's fire had already engulfed the lower rows of seating.

"Let's go," Penélope said. She ran towards Priam Boulevard and Alex followed after her. Ari soon joined them, out of breath but his eyes lit with determination, and together they headed in the direction of the Great Library.

A few moments later they heard the telltale shouts of alarm. Alex glanced back and saw the theater burning up in tall orange flames, the fire consuming the wood viciously. Soldiers rushed towards the fire, some of them already trying to douse the flames with vases of water, their backs turned towards them.

Once they were on the boulevard, they struggled to weave through the traffic of merchants driving their wares on wagons, sailors heading off to inns and brothels, and groups of men and women walking to the various shops and baths across the city.

Soldiers patrolled the Mouseion across the way where the entrance of the Great Library towered over the Meson Pedion, but if the others succeeded in their distraction, that would not be a problem for much longer.

Ari directed them behind a wagon of fruits and vegetables driving steadily along the Meson Pedion in the direction of the Mouseion. They walked close behind it to hide themselves from the scanning eyes of the guards on both sides of the street.

"Where's Warren and the others?" Penélope asked worriedly, looking around the street. "They should be here by now."

Their wagon was rolling steadily onward, quickly approaching the tall columns of the Great Library, and still, there was no sign of them.

Suddenly a scream pierced the air. Alex looked around but nothing seemed amiss. Then another scream rose in the street, followed by another, causing those walking to pause and look around. She turned and froze at the strange sight before her.

A herd of ostriches barreled down the street, heedless of those walking or pushing carts of food, knocking a few women down to the ground and scattering the baskets of food they carried on their heads. Behind them a pride of peacocks trotted down the road, their feathers fanning as they screeched. In all of the commotion, the soldiers guarding the Mouseion turned their attention toward the animals and began running them down.

"Come on!" Ari said. They stepped out from behind the wagon and ran towards the Great Library. All of the soldiers had left their posts trying to chase after the animals, leaving the lofty doors of the library unguarded.

They got to the top of the stairs and looked around before quickly hiding behind the large columns. Still no sign of Warren, Chloe, or Owen. A large shadow covered the street. Alex looked out and saw two large elephants stomping down the Meson Pedion, their trunks and tusks swinging and their heads shaking off flies as the citizens screamed and shouted in panic.

"Oh god," Alex said with a laugh. "What did they do?"

While it had been part of the plan for the others to break the animals out of the zoo on the northern side of the quarter, Alex had not expected it to work so spectacularly. She heard footsteps come up the stairs and froze. Had the guards seen them? Ari had heard it too and lifted his fists up.

"Oi!" said a familiar voice. "Anyone here?"

Alex stepped out from behind the column, and then Ari and Penélope did the same. Warren, Chloe, and Owen stood on the steps in the tattered sailor outfits they had found in the safe house. Behind them, the street was in absolute chaos, with every kind of animal imaginable wreaking havoc on the citizens and soldiers alike, everything from snakes and crocodiles to bears and giraffes.

Penélope gasped. "Owen, your arms!"

Owen looked down at his arms, which were cut up with huge red gashes running with blood. He winced as he gingerly lifted an arm. "Ah, yes. That would be the tiger."

"The *what?*" Alex asked.

Suddenly Chloe screamed, her arms and legs lashing out. A soldier had noticed them foolishly standing in front of the Great Library and had grabbed Chloe from behind, dragging her down the steps.

Before anyone could move to help, there was a loud *smack* and the soldier crumpled to his knees with a groan, clutching his face which was now spattered with blood. Chloe had elbowed him in the face and must have broken his nose.

She rolled her shoulders with a grin. "That felt good. That felt *really* good."

Owen shook his head. "You are terrifying sometimes, did you know?"

Then there was a shout. The soldiers on the street had taken notice of their fallen comrade and were pointing right at them. All of the animals had either scattered or were being tied down with large ropes and nets.

"Time to go!" Owen said, before bolting towards the doors.

They ran after him into the Great Library. Inside, Ari led them up one of the grand staircases and down the main hall. As they approached the staircase that would bring them back to the Old Library, Alex stopped, seeing that glimmer of gold from the corner of her eye.

She knew what she had to do. "Follow me!"

Ari hesitated, looking one last time at the staircase that would lead them up to the New Academy and Sister Stella, before he followed after her. The others did not protest and dutifully ran with them towards the golden door, the symbol of the Golden Wand carved down the middle.

"Where does it go?" Penélope asked, her voice filled with awe as she looked at the door and then around at the high ceilings of the library, the niches crammed with scrolls and books.

Alex brushed her fingertips down the carved wand, remembering the dream she had the other night. Then she heard the shouts of soldiers down the hall. They had followed them inside. She pushed open the door and raced down the spiral staircase.

The steep, metal stairs led them to the familiar domed room. As they entered, the torches lining the curved walls flared to life. Alex shivered, wondering if someone was watching them, or if the prickling on her neck was merely from the chill of the underground.

"This is where Sister Stella found you, isn't it?" Penélope asked, walking towards the altar where the strange leather book they had found rested as before, the first page beginning with the hymn to the Prince of Thieves.

The mosaic on the floor gleamed gold under the torchlight. Across the center were the gold strings of the Seven-Stringed Lyre, the planets circling the sun as it had in her dream, right before their movements aligned with the tree and the lyre, singing out a familiar song, the Emerald Stone beating in time at the heart of the earth, as though the planets themselves were a path, a road between worlds. *November 19th. The city is not a place, he says, but a road. One for mortals, the other for the gods.*

As if her thoughts were aligning as the planets had, Alex finally understood. The song she had heard, the familiar notes, they sang a song she had always known because it was a part of her. Because it *was* her. *The secret of the universe lives on in you, Alexandria.*

At last, she understood what her mother had truly meant, but could not say. All this time she had been searching for the Stone and the key to finding it had been within her since the beginning, if she had only listened.

Alex crossed the floor to the altar. The leather book was heavy in her hands as she flipped to the first page. Somehow the words came to her, as though they were memory, as though they were written on her heart.

Her voice bubbled up her throat with the foreign yet familiar words, ignoring the stares of the others, ignoring Ari's realization as she sang with a voice that was not her own but of the earth, of the seven planets and of the sun, all singing in unison through her, the secret of the universe.

"ὕμνον ἄειδέ μοι, μοῦσα, λόγοισι μελίφροσιν ἀλλά
ἡδυτερεῖ φωνῇ κλέπτην διὰ νυκτὸς ἄειδε
ἐρχομενῳ πρὸς δ' ἄντρα νεηνίῃ ἀνδρὶ ἐοικώς
ἔνθα πολύτροπος αὔτης ναὸν ἴεν πόδας ὠκύς
ὥς ἄδυτου φύλαξ ἔν χειμῶνι ἀπεβήσετο νόσφι·
κλέπτης εὗρεν χάσμα βάθη πέτρας πολύκαπνον·
ἔβλεψε φέγγος ἔν δὲ φάραγγ' ὅτε πρὸς τὸν ὄψ εἶπε
τὸν κλέπτην χαίρειν· τί σύ μου δόμον εἰλήλουθας;
ὥς ἔφατ' ἡ θέα· τῇ καὶ φωνήσας προσέφη φώρ·
τὸν λίθον ἀγνή πότνια· χεῖρ' ὀρέγων ῥόον εἶπε·
καὶ τότε γῆς ἄπο θερμὸν χλῶρὸν τὸν δ' ἕλε λᾶα
τὸν δ' ἀπαμειβόμενος προσέφη κεχολωμένα θυμῷ
οἶδας ἔχειν δύναμίν; σοι λεξω· κεῖνος λίθος εἶχε
τὸν κόσμου μυστήριον· ὥς ἔφατ' ἡ θέα τῆς γῆς·
κλέπτης παύσας ἔτρεψ' ἰδεῖν καπνὸν καταπίνειν
βωμὸν· καὶ τότε μορφὴν ὄρφνης ἐξαναδῦσαι
οὐδε γε γυναικὸς ἄλλὰ δράκοντος ἔθει δ' ὅ συνῆκε
ἡ θέα τὸν εἶπον· μή δῶρον θεῖον ἀφῆς μου."

When she finished, the room was deathly silent. Then a single note vibrated from below the ground, underneath the mosaic, as though one of the seven stone strings had been plucked by an invisible finger. A grinding noise followed and the ground beneath them trembled.

The planets around the mosaic began to move, circling the sun until they aligned with the middle string above and below. Then the sun mosaic lifted up and split at the center, before they began to slide apart, revealing a small opening at the center.

Once the floor ceased to tremble, Alex saw an emerald light glow out of the hole in the ground. She took hesitant steps towards it until she stood at the edge of the open circle where the sun had once been. At the bottom, inset into the base of a mechanical golden lyre, was the Emerald Stone.

As if still in her dream, Alex reached down to pick up the Stone, a small, unevenly cut emerald gem. It sprung from the lyre into her hand, warm to the touch, and if she paid close attention, Alex could feel a small pulse emanating from the Stone into her palm.

"Is that..." Ari whispered. Alex nodded. "How?"

"I saw it in a dream," she said, her hand grasping the Stone tightly, as if she still didn't believe it truly existed. "When I saw my mother, she told me that when she died protecting the Stone, she was pregnant with me and didn't know it. But the Stone was not destroyed, because its power lived on...in me. She named me after Alexandros, who was the son of King Philoxenos, descendant of Priam, King of Troy."

"Then you're the one who can fulfill the prophecy," Penélope said in realization.

"Yes." Alex hesitated, seeing the betrayal flit across Ari's eyes. "My mother told me not to tell anyone. She said if I did, then He would find me. I would lead Him right to the Stone like she did, and He would take it and destroy me."

"Lead who to the Stone?" Chloe demanded, looking around fearfully. "Alex, who are you talking about?"

Before she could say His name, the room shook with a terrible thundering sound overhead, as though a massive earthquake had hit the city at the same time as a storm. Alex heard a crack of thunder and she had the sudden foresight to jump back, narrowly missing a strike of lightning from the darkening ceiling that pierced the spot where the Emerald Stone had just been, leaving the ground scorched black.

A deep, thundering voice echoed from all around, and Alex went still.

"But child, I'm already here."

The King of the Gods

The mother of us all,
the oldest of all,
hard,
splendid as rock

Whatever there is that is of the land
it is she
who nourishes it,
it is the Earth
that I sing

Whoever you are,
howsoever you come
across her sacred ground
you of the sea,
you that fly,
it is she
who nourishes you
she,
out of her treasures

Beautiful children
beautiful harvests
are achieved from you
The giving of life itself,
the taking of it back
to or from
any man

are yours

—Homer, *Hymn to the Earth, Mother of All,* translation by Charles Boer

81

Thunder growled all around them while darkness descended on the room. A wind whipped through the air and snuffed out the flames of the torches.

Alex couldn't see anyone around her, as though the shadows had obscured everything save the Emerald Stone which still glowed in her hand. She thought the green light glanced upon a flitting white movement in the clouds above before it was gone.

"Don't come any closer!" Alex shouted shakily, looking around in the darkness.

"Alex!" It was Warren. She heard footsteps near her and then a grunt as something hit the floor and then was dragged back to the wall.

"Warren!" she cried.

"I'm fine," came a weak response from the edges of the room.

"It was foolish to think you could defeat me, girl. Give me the Stone and no harm shall come to your friends."

"Don't listen to him!" It was Penélope.

"Don't give him the Stone!" Ari shouted.

She heard their strangled cries a moment later along with thuds that shook the walls. Alex clutched the Stone and tried to suppress a sob. Her mother had watched Zeus kill the love of her life before killing her. If she gave Zeus the Stone now, then the deaths of her mother and Alexandros would be for nothing. But if she didn't, she risked the lives of her friends and herself.

"You killed my mother," Alex said bitterly, tasting salty tears on her lips. "You'll have to kill me too!"

The thunder crackled all around her in the darkness and lightning pierced the air in a white flash, briefly illuminating a massive, white eagle in the eye of the storm, its talons as long and sharp as spears and its powerful wings spanning the full width of the room, sending terrible gusts with every beat that nearly knocked Alex to the ground. Wind swirled around her, tugging at her clothes and throwing her hair across her face, until Alex had to crouch down, her arms shielding her face.

"I am King of the Gods!" Zeus bellowed from above at the same time as the eagle's caw pierced the air, his voice as loud as moving mountains and as wide as the caverns of the sky. *"You shall not defy my will else you shall be destroyed!"*

Alex held up her arms against the torrential winds that threatened to throw her to the ground. In the swirling darkness above she saw the crackling of another lightning bolt ready to strike, gathering in the clouds above the eagle's flashing white eyes and menacing beak.

Was this how it happened? Did her mother stand before the King of the Gods, struck to death by a fierce bolt of lightning? But her mother was not the one who would fulfill the prophecy, and neither was Alexandros. Only *she* held the secret of the universe, only *she* could wield the Emerald Stone, only *she* had the power to overthrow the King of the Gods and restore the old order.

Thus his end has been foretold.

A flash of blinding light descended upon her and Alex could only hold her hands up as if that would stop the pain. *Crack!*

The flash of lightning hit the Emerald Stone and exploded out in a flat burst of power and light. She let out a strangled scream as the burning heat scorched her skin and seeped through her hand and up her arm like a fire from within, the same fire that had shone out of Demeter's eyes, the same fire that had burned the monstrous snake in Hell from the inside, like the molten fire at the center of Mother Earth, its pulsing heartbeat growing stronger and stronger. Alex could not let go no matter how hard she tried.

The others called out her name, when the Emerald Stone suddenly burst forth with a glowing light through her hand, blinding Alex, the others crying out as the light engulfed the room, slicing through the swirling shadows and piercing the giant eagle's chest, its horrible caw protesting in pain as it fell and disappeared into darkness. The fire burned her up from head to toe, and she screamed at the pain like a thousand cuts to her skin, like her body would explode at any moment.

Alex screamed as the Stone blazed in her hand, the blinding light all that she could see, burning her eyes like staring straight into the sun. A familiar song could be heard through the pain like a ringing in her ears. She no longer felt her body, no longer felt anything at all, only the fire, only the song burning within, her vision tunneling despite the light.

Then the Stone splintered in her hand, crumbling in her grasp as she dropped to the floor, the light burning through the storm, the wind and the thunder ceasing in one fell swoop, her blurred vision returning when she hit the ground.

A hushed silence hung over the room. Alex looked around and saw the others flattened against the wall, looking around in fear as if the storm might return and finish them for good. But she saw no eagle, nor heard any thunder or bellowing voice.

Alex could not move a muscle, her whole body tingling and aching as though she were bruised all over. The ash of the Emerald Stone spilled from her open palm onto the floor. Alex saw through her gloomy vision that the floor was whole once more, the golden mosaic of the Music of the Spheres intact, with no sign of the charred floor destroyed by Zeus' lightning bolt.

The others rushed over to her. Ari gingerly held her hand where the Stone had been, looking at her with wide, panicked eyes. Chloe began to cry, stroking Alex's hair and apologizing over and over again, though for what Alex had no idea. Warren, Penélope, and Owen were silent, crouched over her with worried looks.

Alex tried to move her head, straining her eyes to look at Ari, whose face swam uncertainly in her vision. He cupped her face in his hand and sucked in a breath.

"Alexandria," he whispered in awe. "Your eye. It's glowing, just like the Stone."

She tried to speak, but the words would not come. The others circled around and looked at her with similarly shocked faces. There was a dull pulsing in her head, like the heartbeat of the Stone, that grew and grew until it was all she could hear, thudding ceaselessly in her head.

Then a flash of pain spasmed across her face and she fell into darkness.

82

"*Open your eyes, Alexandria.*"

The voice was familiar in its deep, lilting warmth, the strong accent of those from the city now apparent in the words. She was back at the old woman's house, being woken up for breakfast. *Mother.*

Alex's eyelids fluttered open. Indeed, before her stood the old woman, except she did not look old at all, her skin smooth and rich like earth and her white hair streaming from her head like water from snowy peaks. Her figure, at once supple and strong as tall tree trunks, was enveloped in a glow of sunlight, so that it hurt to look upon her for too long, though in her bright green eyes Alex glimpsed the same ancient depths, like the depths of a chasm carved in layers of rock formed before the dawn of humankind.

"She's awake," Chloe said in relief from somewhere behind her.

"Will she be okay?" Penélope asked worriedly.

Mother laughed, a deep laugh like the ripple of a field in a summer breeze. "Yes, my child. She needs rest, but she shall soon heal."

Alex looked around carefully, her head pounding with the effort. "What happened?"

"You fainted," Owen said hesitantly. "After the Stone exploded...and set you on fire."

She was helped to her feet slowly, and she cringed at the pain still lacing her limbs with every small movement like walking on a bed of needles. All of her friends looked on with mingling concern and relief. Mother stood before her, a deep power emanating from her tall stature, and now Alex noticed the white dress she wore. Her voice, too, unlike that of the other gods they had encountered, was spoken not merely in their minds as blossoming thought, but seemed to reverberate in the very ground they stood upon, echoing in the sky above, as though the physical shape of the woman before her could hardly contain the power held within, the power of one born from the depths of chaos.

"Who are you?" Alex asked weakly, though she had a feeling she already knew. Perhaps she had known all along.

Mother smiled and held out her arms joyfully, and everyone lowered their eyes, though out of respect or from the light that shone even brighter around her Alex could not tell. "I am Gaia, my child, and thanks to you I am once again Queen of the Gods."

For the first time, Alex saw the seven veiled figures lining the walls, dressed in white. One of the women stepped forward and lifted her veil. It was Sister Stella. She bowed to Gaia before addressing Alex.

"We are the Seven Sages, Daughters of Gaia, and Protectors of the City and the Stone," Sister Stella said. "I must apologize for my behavior before. I could not reveal what I knew of the prophecy or the Stone without risking its discovery, though I am sorry I ever doubted you. We are forever in your debt, Alexandria, for restoring the old order and fulfilling the prophecy."

"Then Zeus is dead?" Owen asked doubtfully.

"The Deathless Gods cannot die," Gaia said, looking sharply at Owen, "but his reign has ended."

"What about the Stone?" Alex asked weakly. "The secret of the universe. It was destroyed."

Gaia shook her head. "Destroyed? No, the Stone can never be destroyed, just as my power can never be destroyed. The Stone *is* power, as is every stone of this earth, as is every planet in the cosmos. For they contain the Music of the Spheres, the harmony of the universe, and within them resides the power to give life and to take it away. In his hubris, Zeus believed my power could be confined to a mere stone, and wished to take the power for himself. This was his downfall. For if he had never sought to take the Stone in the first place, you would never have found the Stone and used his own power against him, which could be the only force strong enough to defeat him in the end."

"We traveled to the Underworld to speak with my mother," Alex said hesitantly, though neither Sister Stella nor Gaia looked surprised. "She said that the night she found the Stone, Zeus killed her, but since she was pregnant with me, she was allowed to raise me for ten years."

Gaia nodded. "When your mother sacrificed herself for the Stone, she had not known she was pregnant with you. In gratitude for her unknowing sacrifice, I struck a deal with Death."

"Before Elena left the New Academy," Sister Stella said, "she made me swear not to tell a soul that she had survived the fire that burned much of the Great Library. To this day I have not told anyone, not even you. Nor, thankfully, Brother Ezra."

That explained why he had insisted that her mother had died, but it did not explain everything. "My mother also said that the power of the Stone lived on...in me."

"The power of the Stone lives in all things," Gaia said in amusement. "You simply listened to its song." She looked at each of them steadily, then bowed her head. Somehow, Alex knew this was goodbye. "Until we meet again, my children."

They all bowed as she turned and disappeared up the winding staircase. Alex felt her absence like the setting sun, when all warmth slowly seeped away beyond the horizon, and the cold of the night crept across the skin.

Sister Stella stepped forward. "Alexandria, Penélope, and Chloe. In light of your relentless courage and commitment to the Old Faith, we have decided to offer all three of you apprenticeships in the Order of the Seven Sages. Your decision should not be made lightly, however, for your vows are lifelong and devoted entirely to the Old Faith. But if you should accept, know that there is great fulfillment in a life of devotion, and your soul shall forever rest in the Halls of the Sages after death."

Alex stood in silent shock. She had not expected to be offered an apprenticeship as a Sage, and the offer from Sister Stella—who had continually discouraged her from coming to the city—was even more confounding. Then she remembered what Sister Stella had said to her the last time they were together in this room. *Elena was like a daughter to me. Once I had even hoped that she would join the Seven Sages, but she took a different path.*

Elena must have been an apprentice when she stumbled upon the Hymn to the Prince of Thieves. What if her mother had had the choice to stay instead of marrying Malcolm? Would she have continued her apprenticeship, training to be one of these white-veiled women? Would Alex have been raised like Ari, among the sisters at the New Academy, nearly fluent in Ancient Greek?

But in the end, her mother had left. She had left this life behind to forge a new one with Malcolm, the life that Alexandria had inherited, who had abandoned it the first moment she could. The city of Helena, the New Academy, and the Seven Sages, they were all part of Elena's story. They were written in a diary, treasured in an ancient copy of the *Iliad* and a silver dagger, and forgotten in a box with her name on it. If Alex had never found that box, where would she be? Still at Harvard with exams finished and starting an internship in New York City? Still dating Warren even when she no longer saw a future with him? Who would Alex be had she remained on that path instead of turning on a new one?

"I came here to find my mother," Alex said quietly. "Now that I have, there's nothing left for me in this city."

Sister Stella inclined her head. "Very well. But just know, there will always be a place for you at the New Academy."

"Thank you, Sister."

Next Sister Stella turned to Penélope. "And you, my dear Penélope Reyes? I am certain you would excel as an apprentice of the Seven Sages."

Penélope lowered her head, but not before Alex saw her face harden. "Thank you, Sister Stella, but I'm afraid I cannot accept." Sister Stella raised a brow, and they all turned to Penélope in surprise. Penélope looked up, her eyes glistening with tears. "I cannot abandon Zeb to the Halls of Death. He sacrificed himself so that we could survive, and I'm not leaving this city without him."

Sister Stella nodded slowly, her eyes holding a heavy sadness. "I am sorry to hear of our dear Zeb's fate. You have a dark and dangerous road ahead of you, filled with sorrow and loneliness, if this road you do choose to take."

"She won't be alone," Owen said loudly. "I'm going with her."

Ari stepped forward. "Me too."

"And me," Alex said.

"Unfortunately, Alexandria, you are too weak for this task, and to rescue your friend from the Netherworld shall not be as simple as your last deadly venture, for it shall require you to sail to the very ends of the earth." Sister Stella laid her heavy blue eyes on Ari. "And Professor Melamed, I must humbly request your assistance in other pressing matters. But I shall do all in my power to help Penélope and Owen on their quest, for the fate of more than one may rest on the success or failure of their journey," Sister Stella said. Then she turned to Chloe, who had not yet said a word, gazing off into the distance with slightly wide, fearful eyes, as if she were reliving a terrible dream. "And you, Chloe Zhang? Do you accept an apprenticeship among the Seven Sages?"

Chloe glanced up, pulled from her reverie, her lips moving stiffly as she answered. "Yes."

Owen stared at her. "What?"

Alex's stomach dropped. The rest of them struggled to contain their shock. They had entirely expected her to reject the offer, so that none of them had paid much attention to her response.

"Chloe, are you sure?" Penélope asked worriedly. "You can't back out once you take the vow."

"What are you doing, Chloe?" Alex demanded. "Don't do this because of me or Zeb or anyone else."

Chloe looked at her sharply. "I'm doing this for me. For once in my life, I'm doing something not for my parents, not for my career, not for a boy who will never love me back." She spoke the last part viciously and Owen flinched. "I'm doing this for *me.*"

Sister Stella was the only one who did not seem surprised, merely looking at Chloe with an air of curiosity. "Instructions shall be given to you in a week's time for the preparation of the vows. Until then, all of you shall be escorted to the palace by a very dear friend of mine. It has come to light that Brother Ezra has been secretly vying for the Stone and usurped the true King of Helena, hoping to gain power over the Seven Sages. He has since then escaped the city and shall henceforth live the rest of his life in exile." She looked Alex in the eyes, and for a moment, Alex knew Sister Stella was seeing Elena standing there instead, right before she said goodbye and left. "Until our paths cross again, my friends."

No one spoke as they walked back up the spiral staircase and towards the grand doors of the Great Library. Alex had to lean on Penélope and a stone-faced Chloe, her muscles screaming in protest with each step. Owen was uncharacteristically silent behind them, while Ari avoided her gaze and Warren had a pensive crease between his brows.

As they walked down the hall of the Great Library, Alex realized belatedly that none of the walls had any black streaks from the fire that her mother had caused. It was as if the power within the Stone had returned the library to its former state of glory, restoring the burned knowledge that the Seven Sages had so carefully collected over the centuries.

They walked outside the doors and paused. The sun had begun to set while they were in the library, and the sky now shone with a brilliant array of flaming reds, oranges, and pinks, as though the Emerald Stone's glowing light had left traces in the sky. But that was not the only array of color in the city.

Throughout the streets were crowds of citizens in their shiny, colorful tunics like the first night she had walked out of the Great Library, with birds folded from parchment and colorful bits of fabric catapulted from the roofs of the houses and song and dance breaking out everywhere they looked.

The city was celebrating. They were free from the tyranny of Brother Ezra, the false King, who was ultimately just the puppet of another usurping King who had finally fallen from his throne.

"Look!" Penélope exclaimed happily.

She was pointing at the bottom of the stairs, where a familiar carriage had rolled to a stop at the base of the steps. The door opened and a veiled figure stepped out, helped by one of her dutiful royal guards.

It was the Queen.

83

THE THRONE ROOM LOOKED the same as before, but Alex thought that the palace seemed brighter, the windows thrown open and the curtains pulled back to let in the early rays of the morning.

All of the soldiers were fitted in new royal garb and stood proudly beside the throne. And sitting on the throne in a long, purple robe, crowned with jewels and her face veiled, was the Queen.

They were lined up before her throne, freshly bathed and dressed in the palace's finest clothes, Ari and Penélope on Alex's right side, and Chloe, Owen, and Warren on her left. The Queen gazed upon them in her regal silence, the entire court waiting impatiently for her speech.

She stood, and a hush fell over the court. Then she began to speak in Greek, sweeping an elegant hand toward them, her voice amplified by the stone floor and walls of the large throne room. One of the Seven Sages—Sister Theresa, Alex had learned, the same one who was speaking to Sister Stella before they were caught—translated her words for them.

"We are gathered here today to honor the men and women standing before me. Their courage and resourcefulness saved this city from the reign of a tyrant and false King. My husband, King Leon, has been lost at sea for ten years and has not returned. In his absence, this imposter seized power against my will, forcing my son to be an exile of his own people." She paused, then beneath her veil Alex glimpsed a brilliant smile. "But in light of the false King's exile, my son has returned to take his rightful place by my side. Please welcome back our very own Prince Leandros!"

The Queen flourished a hand towards the courtyard, where a squadron of soldiers stood at attention. Everyone turned to watch as the soldiers shouted salutes and moved to the side in unison to allow a tall princely figure to walk through them. The court burst into applause and cheers as Prince Leandros walked forth, a thin gold crown atop a familiar scarred and bearded face.

"The Wanderer," Penélope whispered.

Prince Leandros stopped before them and bowed, his eyes lingering on Penélope. "It is a pleasure to see you all once more."

They returned his bow, speechless. It all seemed so clear now. The captain of the pirates was the son of the Queen forced into exile by Brother Ezra, whom the blind King had even accused of piracy. Alex felt that she should have made the connection sooner, remembering that strange, confident air about him that she could not quite place until now as royalty, and the fact that he was one of the few people in the city to speak English.

"Our honored guests have sacrificed much in the name of our freedom, including the life of one of their own," the Queen continued. "In gratitude for their sacrifice, each shall receive special honors of the highest degree. For the three brave men, they shall be granted knighthood, and for the three courageous women, damehood. For all, there shall be a seat at my table and henceforth shall be known as friends of this court."

Once the ceremony ended, the court dispersed for the evening festivities. The Queen approached them from her throne, along with Prince Leandros.

"Sister Stella has informed me," said the Queen, "that your personal sacrifices resulted not only in the final defeat of the city's tyrant but has also restored the old order. As a disciple of the Old Faith, if there is any favor I may grant as Queen, I shall do everything in my power to grant it."

Penélope stepped forward. Leandros' eyes flickered over to her. "Pardon me, my Lady, but if it is not too bold of me, there is one favor I would ask of you."

"Of course," the Queen said, bowing her head gracefully.

"In our effort to find Alexandria's mother, we ventured to the Underworld, as Prince Leandros may attest. Our friend, Zeb, sacrificed himself for the rest of us to return to the world of the living. If your Ladyship might allow, I would like to take a ship and a few brave sailors to rescue him."

A shadow passed across the Queen's face. "The Lord of the Dead does not grant return to souls who have so willingly wandered into his Halls. Your quest may be impossible if it does not end in certain death."

Penélope steeled herself. "I will not leave him behind."

"Neither will I," Owen said, a slight tremor in his voice.

The Queen nodded her head thoughtfully. "Very well. Your wish is my command. I shall seek a squadron best fit for this task."

Leandros stepped forward. "I will take you."

They all looked at the Prince, Penélope's eyes widening in surprise. The Queen glanced at her son keenly, before looking at Penélope once more. "It seems my son has volunteered himself, for better or worse, and I shall not hinder him. In his father's absence, he is free to make his own decisions. But one request I must make if I shall endure my son's departure once more. His father and my husband, King Leon, has been gone for many years. I have hoped for his return in my darkest hours, but the gods have kept him far from home. In your journey to the Halls of the Dead, I must ask you to seek answers and learn of his fate. Only then might there be a chance of his triumphant return."

Penélope bowed her head, but not before her gaze landed on Leandros. "We will do our best to learn of the King's fate."

Then the Queen looked at Ari. "I have also been told by Sister Stella that she is in need of a suitable replacement for Headmaster of the Academy. The last one, it seemed, had strayed from the Old Faith. As Queen, I am officially offering you, Ari Melamed, the position of Headmaster, which I hope you shall accept."

As the Queen spoke, Ari's lips parted, and his eyes kindled with excitement. He nodded his head vigorously. "Yes, I accept. Of course I accept. Thank you for the generous offer, my Lady."

"The pleasure is all mine," the Queen said warmly, "but it is really Sister Stella whom you should thank."

Ari bowed to hide the glimmer in his eyes at her words. Alex knew that for all his complaints and scoffs of his time spent at the New Academy, Sister Stella had been like a mother to him since a very young age. Her words in the Great Library had hurt him more than he had let on, so it was a relief that Sister Stella had once again regained trust in him.

The Queen invited them all to a banquet afterward to continue the festivities into the night. After, they would sleep in the luxurious guest bedrooms of the palace and send off Penélope, Owen, and Leandros by the docks in the morning.

As they walked across the courtyard to the dining hall, the Queen fell into step beside Alex, who still had to walk slower than the others. "Is there something I may do for you, Alexandria? I trust you are feeling better under the care of our nurses?"

"Yes, I am," Alex said, then hesitated, glancing at the Queen's mild smile. "I did have a question actually. Was there ever a prince named Alexandros that lived here?"

The Queen looked troubled. "Yes, there was, once. King Leon had an older brother named Alexandros. But he died in battle long ago, when wars plagued the city. My husband never quite healed from that wound. It is why he is king after all, for he was second to the throne after Alexandros."

Alex's head spun. If she was indeed the daughter of Alexandros, did that make her royalty here? "I see."

"I am told that you shall return home? Sister Stella tells me you traveled very far and left much behind to come here."

Alex nodded, though she felt slightly nauseous at the thought. "I left my family, my home, my education. Everything, really."

"So did I," the Queen said with a wistful smile beneath her veil. "I was only sixteen when I married Leon and left my family and everything I had ever known to come here. Shortly thereafter my mother died. I never saw her again and my father quickly remarried."

"I'm sorry." Alex looked at the Queen's graceful air in a different light. "The same thing happened to me." Then she added with an embarrassed laugh, "Besides getting married at sixteen, of course."

The Queen glanced at her thoughtfully. "I see a lot of myself in you. But my fate was already written, whereas yours is not."

"How can you tell?"

"It is just a feeling," the Queen said lightly. "The eyes tell much about a person. In them, one can often see the words written on their heart. In my son's eyes, for example, I see pain and loss, and he flees his home to escape his future. But there is a hardness in them, an unbending determination to chase the ghosts of the past, which has sealed his fate as much as mine." She paused as they came to a stop before the large oak doors of the dining hall. The others had already walked inside, leaving them alone. "But when I look into your eyes, I do not see any answers, but rather a question, one that you have been asking for all your life."

Alex stared at her, unable to speak. *Are you listening?*

The Queen grasped her hand tightly. "You *are* the answer, Alexandria. Never forget that."

Then she stepped away, her royal guards opening the doors of the dining hall for her. Alex took a deep breath in, her eyes stinging with unshed tears.

She glanced behind her, feeling that familiar prickling sensation on her neck. The courtyard was empty, but she thought she saw a small bird flitting in the shadows, the eyes of the gods watching her always, for they were the eyes of eternity.

The Prince of Thieves. He said he was many things but I think he is just a god with too much time on his hands.

Alex couldn't help but smile.

84

A SALTY BREEZE WAFTED over the docks, lightly billowing the sails of the familiar, two-eyed ship anchored beside the shining Gate of the Moon.

It was the same pirate ship that had kidnapped them off the Necropolis Island, but today it was fitted with royal flags, purple cloth, and green wreaths, as though the send-off were closer to a wedding than a journey to Death.

Penélope and Owen stood at the docks in front of them as Leandros' crew carried trunks of belongings and supplies on board. Leandros was somewhere on deck shouting orders and preparing the ship for departure.

Alex struggled to keep her tears at bay as she and Penélope stared at each other, unable to say goodbye. She recalled the first time she had seen Penélope, the kind eyes and subtle confidence that had impressed Alex from the start. While Penélope had changed since then, her eyes now mingled with sadness, she was still the first person to make Alex feel welcome at the New Academy and in her mother's hometown, Tierra del Sol.

"You know I would come with you," she said, her voice trembling. "If you say the word—"

"I know," Penélope said with a smile, a tear escaping down her cheek. "But you need to go home and rest. You need to see your dad. You've sacrificed enough for this city and the Stone."

"Besides," Owen added, "it's time you let others do some rescuing. Penélope and I will be just fine, right Penélope? She can't stop drooling over that pirate hunk anyway."

"Hey!" Penélope shoved him, reminding Alex that she was a sister of multiple brothers and could handle Owen and his antics just fine. "I don't drool. And he's a prince, not a pirate. You're lucky we don't talk about why *you're* coming."

Owen did not try to deny it and settled into a sullen silence. Ari shared a knowing glance with Alex, but she quickly turned away when she caught Warren looking at them.

Suddenly Chloe ran forward and threw herself around Penélope, hugging her tightly, her voice thick with tears. "I'm going to miss you so much. Please don't die or I'll kill you. Seriously."

Penélope laughed and hugged her. "What about you? One of the Seven Sages! You'll have to tell me all about it when I get back."

Chloe stepped away, wiping at her eyes. Then she turned toward Owen. They looked at each other in uncharacteristic silence, and all of them held their breath. Then Chloe hugged him, though Alex saw that she whispered something in his ear, to which Owen flushed and nodded silently.

Once Chloe backed away, the rest of them said their goodbyes and gave their final hugs. Ari and Penélope were laughing and crying at the same time while Warren hung back with Owen. Alex hooked her arm in Chloe's, something that had never felt right until now.

Chloe sighed and leaned her head lightly on Alex's as they walked back down Priam Boulevard. "What are we going to do without Penélope? And what am I going to do without you? Can't you stay? For me?"

Alex laughed, her heart warming at her words despite the sadness that lingered there. "You'll have your work cut out for you with the Seven Sages, I can promise you that." She hesitated, glancing at Chloe's sniffling face. "You are sure about that decision, right? You're leaving behind Harvard, law school, and family. Everything. The vow can't be taken back once you swear it. And I'm pretty sure it involves celibacy."

"I know," Chloe said, straightening up with an air of seriousness. "But I feel like for the first time, I have a purpose in life that I feel good about. For so many years I equated my self-worth with my career, or with men, or with what school my parents approved for me. But now...I'm a part of something greater that will live on even after I'm gone. Not many people get to say that."

"Look at you," Alex said, shaking her head. "Chloe Zhang all grown up."

"What about you, Alex Montgomery?" Chloe asked teasingly. "Are you going to continue studying at Harvard? Date Warren again? Apply to law school?"

"It'll be like I never left," Alex joked, but her voice fell flat, and she stared hard at the ground to avoid Chloe's sharp gaze that had always seen too much in her. "I don't know. I don't know what I want anymore."

Chloe jostled her playfully. "Did you ever really know?"

"I think at one time I thought I did," Alex said slowly. "But now I know that I don't."

"And what about Ari?" Chloe asked in a low, suggestive voice.

"What about him?"

"You two kissed!" Chloe whispered. "He's clearly into you and you're definitely into him. Don't deny it, Alex. I saw your face after you kissed at the safe house. You were *flushed,* as Owen would say."

"Maybe," Alex conceded with a small smile, though it quickly faded. "But my mom sacrificed everything for love. I don't know if I could do the same. Besides, I thought you didn't believe in love."

"I didn't think I did either. But I also didn't believe in a magical city filled with gods, kings, and pirates, but here we are!" When Alex remained silent, Chloe sighed, sensing that Alex's mind was made up for now. "You have to come visit me soon then. I don't say this often, but you're my best friend, Alex. I need you in my life."

Alex felt her eyes burn, and this time the tears came. "You're my best friend, too. I love you, you know that, right?"

"I love you too," Chloe said quietly, coming to a stop.

They had turned on the Meson Pedion and were approaching the Great Library where Chloe was expected to meet Sister Stella. Further back down the road were Ari and Warren, who Alex was surprised to see were having a civil conversation.

Chloe noticed them and smirked. "Oh, Alex. You're more like your mother than you know."

Then Chloe hugged her tightly, always uncomfortable with prolonged goodbyes, and hurried off towards the steps of the Great Library. Alex looked after her with a strange feeling, as though she were watching someone who should have been *her,* who was doing something that she should have wanted, but in doing so, realizing she never truly wanted it in the first place.

Ari and Warren soon neared her. Warren nodded towards Alex, then Ari, before walking towards the Great Library, where Sister Stella had already prepared their belongings for the return journey home. At last, Alex stood before Ari, and they were both silent for some time.

On either side of them, the people of the city walked by, hardly glancing at them except in quiet awe at their royal robes. Rowdy Academy students stood in clumps on the freshly cut lawn across the fence, dressed in their signature blue robes, while many walked in and out of the gates that had so recently been chained and abandoned. The city had come alive again, and it was thanks to her.

Ari smiled, though it was more bitter than sweet. "I spoke to Sister Stella before the send-off. She said you were welcome to study at the New Academy if you wanted. You could continue to learn Ancient Greek. I'd still be able to teach you. I do make a great professor, you know."

Alex nodded, unable to smile, scared to speak too much lest the tears threaten to fall. "I know."

"You're not staying." It wasn't a question. Ari looked at her with a longing that pained her. He glanced away briefly, collecting himself, before looking at her once more. "I hope you find what you're looking for, Alexandria."

"Me too," she said, hardly more than a whisper.

She looked down at the ground, unable to see him look at her like that, as if she were breaking his heart when all along it felt as though her heart was broken, searching for a mother whom she had never truly known, only to discover what she had always known but had never believed—that she was gone forever.

Alex looked up to try and tell him that, but Ari was already there, pulling her into his arms. She let the tears fall silently as she closed her eyes, the warmth of his embrace familiar and foreign at the same time, like a dream that often held both reality and unreality in the same breath. She didn't need to say the words. She never had to, because he already knew them, as if their fates had been intertwined since the beginning, even if the end had now come.

Ari stepped away, his hand passing over his face, hiding a glimmer of tears in his eyes. "I'll miss you, Alexandria."

"Goodbye, Ari," she said softly, then turned to walk away.

A hand grasped her wrist before she could take a step and pulled her back. Then they were kissing, his arms wrapped tightly around her, as if he would never let go, as if he could make this moment last an eternity.

Distantly she heard the gasps of those around them, and the shouts and cheers of the Academy boys. She kissed him like it might be the last, tugging at his curls, trying to brand his touch in her memory so that she would never forget the way he said her name, the curling desire deep within whenever his burning gaze found hers, and the magical city they had discovered one fateful night, the same night they first kissed.

They moved apart at last, and Alex walked away before he could change her mind, the familiar columned entrance of the Great Library rising above her.

At the top of the steps, her hands on the doors, Alex paused. She glanced back over her shoulder at the city bustling with noise and people, the colorful crowds speaking in languages she would never know, and the rambling buildings and gardens of the Academy, its black gate clanging shut behind a familiar dark-haired figure.

Ari was gone.

85

THE HOT SUMMER SUN shone down on the pavement outside the Lighthouse Church.

Warren leaned against Lady Montgomery—her forgotten white Audi streaked brown from the dust—with sunglasses on and fitted in a blue polo shirt, as if he were going golfing and not hopping on a plane.

Alex shoved her suitcase in her car and shut the trunk door. Sister Stella stood beside her in the same long black skirt and blue sweater she had seen the first day she entered the church. The same large silver cross also dangled on her chest, but this time Alex saw the carving of a stone at the center of the cross, which now more than ever reminded her of two streets intersecting the heart of a magical city.

Sister Stella's eyes twinkled knowingly. "Take care, Alexandria."

"Thank you," Alex said. "For everything."

"I said this once before to your mother, and I will say it again to you now," Sister Stella said, grasping Alex's hands. "You always have a home here at the New Academy."

Alex nodded her head, biting her lip to stop the tears from coming. Sister Stella let her go, and Alex moved towards the driver's side. Warren climbed inside the passenger seat as she opened the door.

"Your mother would have been proud," Sister Stella said, stepping away from the car.

Alex smiled. "I know she is."

Then she slid into the driver's seat, buckling her seatbelt and turning on the ignition by memory, savoring the familiar rush she felt with her hands on the wheel. She could go anywhere. She could be anyone or anything.

Warren glanced at her questioningly, so she pulled out of the parking lot and drove out of Tierra del Sol.

Neither of them spoke as the car rolled onto the nearest highway. There wasn't much to say. Instead, Alex rolled down the windows and turned on the radio, letting soft Latin music fill up the space between them.

Warren had booked a flight from Jacumba Airport—the closest airport to the New Academy, right along the Mexican border—direct to New York City. Luckily, his consulting internship only started in a few days. Their adventures in the city of Helena had taken almost a full two weeks. Including the weeks it had taken for her to travel cross country and for her friends to find her, she had spent about a month away from home. It felt closer to an eternity.

The drive, however, lasted less than twenty minutes. Alex pulled up beside the drop-off area of the airport, where sliding glass doors led to a small check-in area.

Warren sat there in silence for a moment. Finally, he turned to look at her, sliding his sunglasses off. His eyes still startled her to this day, the steady blue of them like a cloudless sky.

"I know it's over between us," Warren said, and the words were so final Alex almost flinched. "But I knew it most when we were escaping the Underworld through the Gate of the Moon, and I had to use the Seven-Stringed Lyre to hold the gate back so that I could save you. I knew that the reason I could save you was because I loved you and I would never stop loving you. It's a love that will always stay with me, even when I fall in love with someone else, a love that can hold back the gates of Death. But it was at that moment I knew we had stopped being *in* love with each other a long time ago, and you were just the first to see it."

Alex didn't know what to say, but it didn't matter. The tears were already rolling down her face, and she nodded wordlessly, hoping that he could see that same love she had for him reflected in her eyes.

"Good luck with everything, Alex." He touched her hand on the wheel briefly. "And drive safe."

With that, Warren got out of the car, slinging his Harvard crew backpack over his shoulders with his usual easy confidence. He pulled his suitcase out of the backseat and headed inside the airport with one last wave goodbye.

Alex watched him disappear behind the glass doors before pulling onto the road and driving away.

86

It took her another three weeks to drive across the country, though that was entirely her fault.

Instead of driving directly east, Alex drove up north impulsively, passing through Palm Springs and Joshua Tree, until the desert faded into valleys and forests cropped up where it rained.

She visited the Sequoia National Park, then cut across Death Valley to the Grand Canyon in Arizona. In each place, she spent a few days soaking up the desert and mountain views that she had still not gotten used to, though she was always eager to jump back in the car and drive.

When she reached Albuquerque, she spent two nights in the same campground she had stayed at just to look up at a sky full of stars, though they now appeared dull and incomplete compared to her memory of the city's sky and the meteor shower she had witnessed in the Valley of the Palms.

Once she reached Oklahoma, she turned north and drove through Kansas, where the flat fields of wheat made her feel like she was sailing on an endless golden sea.

At some point, Alex sent a text to her dad that she was on her way home, but that she would stop by her apartment at Harvard to get her things. Malcolm had heard from Warren much earlier that she was safe and that they were with her, but he hadn't heard from them until they returned from the city. She didn't explain or offer any excuses, and Malcolm didn't ask for them, merely stating that he was looking forward to her return.

From Kansas, she trekked north to Chicago. She walked along the lake, which glittered blue in the summer heat, families and groups of friends crowded on the shore. While she was enjoying the scenery, Alex knew she lingered on the road because she wasn't ready to go home yet.

After Chicago, the scenery grew familiar as she drove through Ohio and Pennsylvania back to Buffalo, New York. Alex revisited Niagara Falls and paid for the same tour of the Cave of the Winds, hoping to hear the song again, but the thundering water like a stampede of elephants overhead was all she heard, the chaos of the Falls reverberating painfully in her head and reminding her of the agony she had felt while holding the Emerald Stone.

With each mile closer to Harvard, Alex's chest tightened. New York passed in a blur, the East Coast states so small and quaint compared to the vast stretches of gleaming desert in the west and that vaulted blue sky that seemed to never end.

All too soon she was rolling into the driveway of her apartment. Chloe and Owen's cars were still parked there, though they would soon be picked up by Chloe's parents, who along with Harvard thought she was transferring to UCLA, while Warren would take Owen's car to his home for safekeeping until he returned. She had no idea what Owen planned to tell his parents or Harvard about his extended absence.

Alex unlocked the front door and stepped inside. The apartment smelled a bit musty from the recent heat of summer, but other than that, everything looked the same as she had left it.

She opened the door to her bedroom. It was empty, of course. A small part of her had expected to open the door and find another Alex sitting there, the version of her on that night when Warren recounted his time in New York City and she turned her head and saw the small nightingale perched on her windowsill. *Are you listening?*

Alex wondered how her life would have played out if she had chosen to stay and forget about her mother's strange box of words and treasures, if she had learned to love Warren and the life he had planned for them. Would she find peace in that life, in marriage and children, with a law degree and a prestigious career, following in the footsteps of her grandfather and his father before him?

Or would she wonder at some point down the line what her life would have been if she had dropped everything and left, exams considered unnecessary? Would the day have come when she could no longer bear the confines of her home, her loveless marriage, her mind lingering on a kiss in a library out west that she had once in a dream, in another life, and she would hear the sad song of the nightingale call to her, just like it had for her mother, a bird perched on the windowsill, cocking its head, and when she reached out would she, too, disappear into thin air?

Then the moment passed, and Alex stepped inside, dropping her bags on the floor. She took out her mother's diary—the *Iliad* in the golden case and the silver dagger having been returned to their rightful place in the Old Library—and put it back in the box with her mother's maiden name written on the outside, holding it close to her chest.

Alex sat on the edge of the bed, not knowing what she should do next. Her eyes wandered to her desk, where she had left her computer, her planner, and her textbooks for classes she never completed. Then it hit her, the memory of the stitched E on the statue's cassock. *I have followed you since the day I learned of your existence.*

Professor Ezra.

Somehow she had forgotten all about him when she reached the city, and even the name Brother Ezra had not sparked her memory. Without thinking, Alex left her apartment and ran across campus as fast as her body allowed to the Classics department building. She dashed down the hall to Professor Ezra's office, not bothering to knock before she slammed the door open.

At the desk sat the same middle-aged man with brown curling hair, glasses, and a startled smile, as though he had not expected anyone to barge into his office but was happy to see them anyway.

He raised a brow when she didn't speak. "May I help you...Alex, right?"

"Yes," Alex said, still out of breath. "You called me Alexandria before. How did you know?"

Professor Ezra looked completely puzzled at this. "I'm not sure what you mean."

Alex stared. It was clear that whatever had happened in that moment, coincidence or not, the Professor Ezra in front of her had no memory of it. The certain fear and panic that had driven her across campus instantly left her, and she knew that the time had come for her to move on.

"Have you perhaps reconsidered taking the Ancient Greek summer intensive?" Professor Ezra asked hopefully.

"Thank you, but no," Alex said, then added under her breath, "I've heard enough Ancient Greek to last a lifetime."

Alex turned around and left without bothering to explain. When she got back to her apartment, she packed up the rest of her clothes into another suitcase.

Then she went home.

87

Alex slowly pulled into the long, winding driveway of her grandparent's house, as though she were returning from her semester at Harvard and not a spontaneous two-month-long adventure following the forgotten memories of her mother's life.

Simona and baby Malcolm were waiting outside when she parked. Alex was surprised to see Simona sobbing as she set a confused baby Malcolm on the ground and rushed towards Alex, hugging her tightly.

"Oh, Alex," she said in her thick accent through the tears. "I'm so glad you came back."

Alex nodded, not knowing what to say. She stepped away to see baby Malcolm waddling towards her, his hands outstretched with that adorable frown on his face, a promise of a future tantrum if he was not appeased quickly. Alex leaned down and scooped him up into her arms, smiling when he squealed in delight.

"I think you've gotten bigger!" Alex joked, hugging him tightly to her chest.

When she looked up, Alex saw her dad standing at the front doors of the house. She handed baby Malcolm back to Simona, then walked up to her dad, wondering if he would start yelling at her or crying like Simona had. Instead, he simply brought her into a hug. Alex stood there, her hands limp at her sides, before hesitantly hugging him back.

"You don't need to explain," Malcolm said when they pulled apart, his eyes heavy with an understanding that surprised her. "We all have to leave sometimes. All that matters is that you came back."

Alex nodded, still at a loss for words. Her dad helped her carry her suitcases up to her room, then left her there and headed back to the kitchen where he was helping Simona prepare dinner.

At dinner, she learned that Harvard had de-enrolled her when she failed to finish her exams. Her dad had made some calls explaining the situation, and by that, he had manufactured some excuse about Alex grieving the news of her mother's death, which was not so far from the truth. Malcolm told her that Harvard would be willing to ignore her slip-up and allow her to return for the Spring semester if she made up her courses in the Fall at another institution.

Alex didn't know what she wanted anymore. She knew it would be easy, in some ways, to fall back into her old routine at Harvard, to continue her studies in economics, and apply for law schools. She would make new friends, forget about her mother and the city and Ari, find a new boyfriend, and eventually get married. They would buy a house somewhere near her father, and her children would grow up never knowing the strange city she had discovered or the truth about their real grandmother.

It was the last chance she had to make things right. Her father urged her to accept the offer, sensing her hesitation and hoping to convince her not to throw her life away.

At first, he was understanding and gentle, but as the weeks of summer wore on without her making a decision, he grew impatient and frustrated. He argued that she was wasting all the hard work he had put into providing her with this life, and the hard work of all the Montgomery men that had come before him. He called her selfish, naive, and depressed, and threatened to force her into therapy or even an in-person counseling group.

Alex pacified him with phrases like *I just need time to figure out what I want* or *I'm not depressed, but Warren and I just broke up.* They were almost the truth after all.

To avoid her father, she took long drives around Greenwich, sometimes disappearing for hours, and returning in time for dinner. She always felt more comfortable with a road beneath her, as though by tracing already made paths she was not in one place or another, but a road between worlds, existing outside of time and place.

Her twentieth birthday came and went and July bled into the late-summer heat of August. The Fall semester was quickly approaching. Alex half-heartedly searched online for courses at local community colleges, but she grew uninterested once she began reading the class descriptions, and she would close the computer, her breath shallow and her head dizzy. She wondered sometimes if it was a consequence of the Stone's fire. After a while, she stopped searching.

Her father knew she had given up, and soon he, too, stopped trying to convince her. He figured that eventually she would grow out of it, and he would weasel her into another university or some consulting job with the connections he had, and Alex would be fine. She would always be fine.

Now that the days were hot and the nights warm, Alex liked to bring a sleeping bag outside on the patio and lay down on a beach chair to watch the stars. They weren't as numerous as they were in Albuquerque or the city of Helena, but Alex had never taken the time to look at them before.

At last, August rolled into September, and already the trees were showing their first signs of reddening. Her father pulled her aside after dinner one day, a Scotch in one hand and silently handing her a glass of wine with the other, before leading her to the patio out back like he used to do with Warren. They sat down side by side and gazed out at the rolling countryside.

"I never told you this," her father said, looking down into the amber liquor of his cup, "but your mother wrote me a letter before she left."

"What?"

"She knew she was going to leave, it seemed. I only found the letter months afterward, tucked inside a book she had been reading at her bedside. I didn't want to tell you before because I thought it would only make you more upset. That was a mistake."

Alex couldn't believe what she was hearing. "What did it say?"

Malcolm took a sip of his Scotch. "She said she had to leave for reasons that she could not say, and that she herself did not understand fully. But she said she loved me, and she loved you, and if she could have stayed to raise you, she would have." He paused. "I never understood how she could love me and her daughter and still leave. But I think I understand now. I see a lot of her in you, Alex."

"Thank you for telling me this," Alex said quietly. She didn't know how much it would mean to know that her mother had left behind a letter in this world, even if she already knew the words were true.

Her father nodded. "I want you to know that no matter what you choose to do with your life, I will always support you."

Alex tried not to cry, taking a sip of her wine. The Montgomery house stood proudly behind them, reminding Alex of her father's legacy, the legacy of her family, their sacrifices and labor that built the life she lived, the freedoms she enjoyed, and the opportunities she had so often taken for granted. Yet that legacy was only half of her, while the other half yearned for more, for the song that called to her, for the road that never ended.

Why did her life always feel like being pulled in two directions, as though there were a crossroads in her heart? Why did Alex only know herself when she had her two hands on the wheel, driving without a destination in mind? If she did not want Harvard, and marriage, and children, then what did she want? Did she want to leave it all behind, like Elena had, and like Helen of Troy before her?

But perhaps she simply longed for a path of her own, forged not from the past but anew, shaped by her hands, the hands of a woman, though she had never known what it meant to be a woman before.

Alex turned to her father when a thought occurred to her. "Dad, what book did you find her letter in?"

Malcolm shrugged. "Some cheesy romance novel."

They both smiled.

Epilogue

A MONTH PASSED AND Alex did not enroll in any classes. October brought bitter winds heralding a cold winter and she spent most days curled up in the living room watching TV with Simona while baby Malcolm was at preschool.

Late in the night, Alex heard the wind whistling down the hallway from her spot on the couch, as though the sliding back doors were open. Her father and Simona were out of the house for the weekend and Alex did not know what to do with her time. Without school or work, she had little to occupy her days, though she had started walking dogs around the neighborhood to earn some cash.

The wind whistled in the house again. She got up and walked down the hall. The glass doors were indeed open, letting in the cold air. She didn't remember opening them. Her heart beat a little faster in her chest as she closed the door, making sure to lock it. As she turned away, she noticed the door to the library was ajar, as if the wind had nudged it open.

Alex paused, then walked inside. It was like falling into a dream. The library was as old and musty as she remembered, the velvet curtains draped over the windows and dust coating the rows and rows of books. She hadn't been inside since before the summer. There was a book perched on the armchair her mother used to sit on by the fire. Had her father come in to read one day?

The door shut softly behind her, cloaking her in that peculiar silence, as though the rest of the world were shut out. Alex walked over to the armchair and picked up the book.

It was a small red volume illuminated with gold and bearing no title. She checked the spine and nearly dropped the book. *Helen of Troy.* She opened to the title page. *Helen of Troy,* or *The Face that Launched a Thousand Ships.* Beneath it was a familiar drawing of ships at sea, the waves cresting against the hull. It was the same book she had picked up in the library at the New Academy all those months ago.

Alex could not fathom why it was here, unless her grandparents had bought the same book or her mother had taken a copy from the New Academy back here. But it was too much of a coincidence, and at this point, Alex no longer believed in them.

Then she heard it. That familiar, sweet song, the song of the nightingale. She turned and saw a shadow flit behind the velvet curtains of one of the tall windows, as though there were a bird perched on the windowsill, the same bird that had come to her that fateful night and asked, *Are you listening?*

Was this how her mother had disappeared into thin air all those years ago?

Maybe it didn't matter if her mother had a choice. Perhaps she left for another lover, a face that had long haunted her memory. Perhaps the nightingale came and swept her away, bound by the laws of Fate to die for love. Alex did not know what she wanted, but for the first time, she didn't care. She needed the desert, she needed to see mountains looming on the horizon, she needed to have her own path blazing in front of her like sunlight glittering on the sea.

Alex left the library. The bird was just a messenger, after all, and only she knew where her heart longed to go. She ran upstairs and shoved her keys, wallet, and a few changes of clothes in a backpack.

Before she left the house, Alex realized she was still holding the small red book in her hand. She hesitated for a moment, then went to the kitchen and grabbed a pen. On the title page she jotted down the words she had long since memorized, though perhaps they were nothing more than a pretty turn of phrase.

I must follow the sad nightingale.

Then she left the book on the counter and went to her car. Once she was on the road, Alex could finally breathe again, the engine humming a familiar tune beneath her. Her life stretched out before and behind her, the future hovering like a distant horizon, the past like the road in her rear-view mirror, only showing how far she had come.

She had no idea where she was going, but that didn't matter. The only thing that mattered was that she held her Fate in her own two hands, and her road was merely the pathway of her heart.

As the car flew down the highway, a sea of green hills rolling on either side, the sun flashing hot on the windshield, and the windows down to let the breeze lift her hand in the air like wings caught on a current, Alex was no longer a daughter or a woman or even herself, but one with the wind, poised on the edge of something wonderful and terrifying.

Appendix of Untranslated Ancient Greek

Ἔλθετε, ὦ πότνια. "Come, O Queen."

Πότνιά μου? "My Queen?"

Ἕπευ μοι, πότνια. "Follow me, Queen."

Τί ζητεῖτε, ὦ πότνια? "What do you seek, O Queen?"

Οὐ πότνια εἶ. "You are not the Queen."

Πάντως χαῖρε, ὦ βασιλεῦ! "All hail, O King!"

Χαῖρε, πότνια. "Hello, Queen."

Χαῖρε, ἱέρεια τοῦ Ἀπόλλωνος. "Hello, priestess of Apollo."

Οὐ εἰσέρχεσθε. Ἐκείνη νυστάζει. "You cannot go inside. She is sleeping."

Χαῖρε, ὦ πότνια. "Hello, O Queen."

Ἑλένη καὶ Ἀλέξανδρος! "Helen and Alexandros!"

Φίλη θύγατερ! "Dear daughter!"

Πότνια μήτηρ. "Holy mother!"

Ὦ σεβαστέ βασιλεῦ. Οἱ κακοῦργοι πρός τῷ θεάτρῳ ἐοίκοτες τῷ Ὥρῳ και τῇ νύμφῃ βεβλέπαται. "O holy King. The criminals have been spotted by the theater looking like Horus and his bride."

Ὡς δεξιοί! Σφᾶς ὠφελεῖ τις. Χρή τὴν κόρην εὑρίσκειν. "How clever [of them]! Someone is helping them. We need to find the girl."

Καῖε. Καῖε νότου τὸν πρός τὴν χθόνα. Ὁρῶμεν εἰ σφέτερος θεὸς τότε ὠφελήσοι ἄν. "Burn it. Burn the South Quarter to the ground. We shall see if their god will help them then."

Τί οὐ ἐν τῷ θαλάμῳ του εἶ? "Why are you not in your bedroom?"

Οὐ λεγείς? "Do you not speak?"

Σφᾶς συλλαμβάνεσθε! "Arrest them!"

Ἐκείνη καλός ἄνθος ἐστι! "She is a pretty flower!"

Ἄνδρες! Λύετε ἐκείνην! "Men! Release her!"

Πηνελόπη. Κάλλιστα παρθένος εἶ ἣν ποτέ βέβλεφα. Ἠράσθην σε ἀπό τοῦ πρώτου καιροῦ εἰς σε εἶδον. Ἐρᾷς καί με? "Penélope. You are the most beautiful girl I have ever seen. I fell in love with you the first time I saw you. Do you love me too?"

Acknowledgements

The creation of this story began many years ago and there were times when I thought it would not come to fruition. In fact, its development was paused in order to write and publish *The Sun of God,* and I was not sure I would be able to pick up the threads that I had started weaving. Therefore I must thank those along the way who listened to my ideas of a tale inspired by ancient Mediterranean religion, literature, history, and philosophy and encouraged me not to give up on it.

My first thanks goes to my parents and my sister, whose unfailing support in my creative endeavors is the very wind in my sails as I venture across uncharted waters. Without their love and belief in me, I would not have the courage to write in the first place. A special thank you to my dad, who read the first draft of this story and helped me work out those pesty, initial plot holes, and smooth out any rough edges. Your persistent confidence in my abilities not only to write but to publish my books keeps my head above water at the worst of times and brings my dreams that much closer at the best.

Thank you to my fellow Classicist, Centrista, and friend, Grace DeAngelis, who read the first draft of this novel and also painstakingly edited my composition of an Ancient Greek hymn to Hermes, as well as all instances of Ancient Greek dialogue in the city. Your passion and vast knowledge of the Classical world always inspire me to dig deeper into the past and find new avenues of creativity through dead languages and long-lost cultures. I am indebted to our discussions about my stories, the ancient world, and all that ultimately has not changed with the passing centuries—the important things, at least.

A big thank you to my family, friends, and those around the world who read my previous works, whether it be a book or a blog post. Your support both aided my publishing journey and gave me the strength to keep writing day after day. My favorite part about writing stories, after all, is the connection my books form with their readers, which I deem a sacred relationship at the heart of storytelling. If not for those who listen, stories would never be told, and the world would be a much darker place indeed.

I must also recognize the various texts that helped me write my story. Much of the creation of the city of Helena I owe to the invaluable book *The Library of Alexandria: Centre of Learning in the Ancient World* by Roy MacLeod. My story was also greatly influenced by Charles Boer's translation of the Homeric Hymns, especially the hymn to Earth, to Hermes, to Demeter, and to Dionysus. Thank you to great translators like Mary Barnard, whose translation of Sappho I included and which first drew me to Classics, and Robert D. Lamberton and his translation of the Odyssey, which I also included. I am indebted to Wallis Budge's *The Book of the Dead: the Papyrus Ani in the British Museum* for my inclusion of the spells—both in hieroglyphic form, translated form, and phonetic form—used by Alexandria and her friends in their descent to the Underworld.

A fond thank you to my handy *Hansen and Quinn* textbook which not only helped me learn Ancient Greek years ago but served an amusing role in this story. Similarly, I borrowed my translation of the Homeric Hymn to Hermes from Hugh G. Evelyn-White's translation on the free website, *Perseus,* which was a faithful, invaluable friend to me while writing this book as it has always been. I would also like to mention the poetry of John Keats, namely his *Ode to a Nightingale, Ode to a Grecian Urn,* and *Bards of Passion and of Mirth,* and T.S. Eliot's renowned *Four Quartets,* as crucial thematic influences during the conception of my story, especially the imagery of the nightingale.

Lastly, I must thank the great bard, Homer, and his epic poems, which have inspired storytellers for thousands of years. Without you, Helen would never have sailed to Troy, nor launched a thousand ships to war. Without you, the city of Helena would never have been born, and my story nothing more than dreams from another realm.

About the Author

Zoë Tavares Bennett is a writer based in Los Angeles, California. She is also the author of the YA romance series *My Sister's Best Friend* and the historical novel *The Sun of God*. She has a degree in Classics from Williams College, specializing in Ancient Greek and Latin.

Printed in the USA
CPSIA information can be obtained
at www.ICGtesting.com
CBHW051819181124
17605CB00005B/31